OTHER
PEOPLE'S
MARRIAGES

OTHER
PEOPLE'S
MARRIAGES

ROSIE THOMAS

William Morrow and Company, Inc.   *New York*

Library of Congress Cataloging-in-Publication Data

Thomas, Rosie.
    Other people's marriages / Rosie Thomas.
       p.   cm.
    ISBN 0-688-12962-5
    I. Title.
    PR6070.H655O84   1994
    823'.914—dc20   93-8885
                                   CIP

Printed in the United States of America

First Edition

1   2   3   4   5   6   7   8   9   10

BOOK DESIGN BY PATRICE FODERO

For Charlie and Flora

Acknowledgments

Grateful thanks for their advice and help during the writing of this book are due to Nicholas Browne and Angelica Mitchell, Huw Alban-Davies, Helen Powers, and other friends, Lindsay Thomas, Beatrice Gehr, Susie Orbach, Stephen Amiel and Sally Berry, Tony Lacey, and to the best editor, Susan Watt.

OTHER
PEOPLE'S
MARRIAGES

1

*I*t was the end of October. As London receded and the freeway bisected open country, the flamboyant colors of the trees began to wash over them. Autumn in the city was a decorous affair of fading plane trees and horse chestnuts, but out here the leaves made fires against the brown fields and silvery sky.

"Look at it," Nina said. "There's no elegant restraint out here, is there? That's real countryside. Where I belong now. How does the poem go?"

She knew it perfectly well, but she sifted cautiously through the layers of her recollection anyway. Memory could still play tricks on her, bringing her up against some scene or a view or simply some remembered words that would make her cry. She had cried more than enough for now.

" 'Season of mists and mellow fruitfulness,' " Patrick supplied for her.

"Yes, that's it."

The poem brought to mind completion, or rather the conclusion of some important cycle, the slow but inevitable stilling of the blood and consequent decay.

Nina turned her head and stared out of the rear window as if she hoped to catch a last glimpse of London. There was nothing to be seen except the road, and the traffic, and the unreticent scenery. She had left London and had not yet arrived anywhere else. It was as if the expansive world she had unthinkingly occupied had shrunk until it was contained within Patrick's car. "It's how I feel, rather."

"You are not particularly mellow."

She laughed, then said: "Nor fruitful."

"You have your work, that's fruit. And you're only thirty-five."

By which he meant: even though she was a widow, there was still time for her to meet and marry another man, to mother a brood of children if she should wish to do so. Not much time, but enough. In his kindly way Patrick did not want her to lose sight of this, although he was too tactful to say it out loud. She was grateful for his consideration, but with another part of herself Nina also wished that her loving friends would stop being so careful. She thought that she needed someone to shout at her, *Your husband is dead but you are alive and you must bloody get on with it.*

It was what she was trying to shout at herself. Going to Grafton—coming to Grafton, rather, now that they were on the road and more than halfway there—was part of getting on with it.

Nina reached out one hand and put it on Patrick's leg, above the knee, and felt his solid warmth. He didn't shrink, didn't even move, but Nina quickly lifted her hand and settled it back with the rest of herself, where it belonged. She felt, as she quite often did nowadays, that Richard's death had removed her from the corporeal world just as conclusively as it had removed him. Widows didn't touch. They accepted unspeaking hugs and silent pats on the shoulder and strokings of their cold hands, but they themselves didn't reach out for the reassurances of the flesh.

"Thank you for driving me all this way."

He took his eyes off the road for a second to look at her. Patrick was a careful driver, as his car proclaimed; it was a sensible station-wagon, armored all round with heavy bumpers and crumple zones. Today the rear seats were folded down and the most precious and valuable of Nina's belongings were packed on top of them. The rest of her things were in the moving van traveling somewhere on the same road.

"I wanted to drive you. I want to see you settled in the house."

His eyes returned to the road. A German tour bus was swelling in the rear window, and he moved aside at once to let it pass. Richard would have stamped down hard on the accelerator and sent his frivolous car swirling ahead. Nina peered up at the faces behind the skin of glass. They were all elderly couples, on a good holiday, intent on enjoyment. She pinched down hard on the blister of her own sadness before it could pointlessly inflate.

"Do you want to stop off somewhere for a cup of tea?" Patrick asked.

"No, not unless you do. Let's just get there."

There was a basket in the back of the car packed with a kettle, cups, and tea for themselves and the moving men, the way an article on relocating in a magazine had advised her to do. In the past few days Nina had become a paragon of organization. She had made dozens of lists, adding and crossing off, defining and redefining her intentions. She would not be caught out by the small details, at least. Every box and carton and piece of furniture was labeled with its eventual destination in the new house; she had measured and checked every dimension twice, and she knew the whereabouts of every necessary key and switch and security code.

It was the large details that were more problematic, like whether it was right to be moving at all, or whether she was insane to do it, as most of her friends suspected.

"Are you okay?" Patrick asked.

She smiled sideways at him. "Fine."

The countryside unscrolled alongside them. In an hour, more or less, they would be in Grafton.

The great twin towers of the cathedral were visible first. They stood, with the town drawn around them, amid quiet and fertile fields enclosed by a rim of little gray hills. It was a perfectly English prospect. Winding their way down from the chalk uplands, the pilgrims who had come to Grafton five hundred years before would have seen the same view.

The town had grown some ugly outskirts since Nina's childhood. Coming from the London road, they did not go by the new business district set in its landscaped gardens. Instead, on this eastern side, there was a huge red-brick supermarket, a development of miniature red-brick houses shuffled close together, a pair of gas stations confronting each other across a stream of cars, and a food shop called the Little Chef. The road became a maze of rotaries and traffic lights, and litter whirled up in the wind.

"Drive straight through," Nina said, wanting to apologize for this modern mess. Patrick pointed the car toward the cathedral towers.

Once they had crossed the river by the Old Bridge, they were in the old town where the medieval streets curled in their protective pattern toward the cathedral and the close. It was four o'clock in the afternoon, the traffic was curdled, and there were crowds of shoppers on the pavements, mothers with carriages and school-children and pensioners outside McDonald's but the sight of the place still made Nina happy. The superficial look of it had changed, but its bones were the same as they had been when she was growing up, the same as they had been for hundreds of years, and the bones were beautiful.

The pale limestone of the building was butter-soft in the late-afternoon sun. The curves of the streets, Southgate and Coign and Drovers, were graceful and the proportions of the houses and the lines of their roofs were intimate and pleasing. There was a glimpse of a cobbled square through an archway, and the gray front of a Norman church.

"Where now?" Patrick asked.

"That way."

Nina pointed. There was a narrow entry, just wide enough for the car, where the stone of the old walls was pocked and darkened with the rubbing of countless shoulders.

They passed through the entry and came out into the glory at the heart of Grafton, the cathedral green, with the close to one side behind high walls, and the great west front of the cathedral itself.

Patrick looked up in silence at the wide tiers of golden stone, the carved companies of faceless saints and archangels in their niches, ranked upward and rising between the exuberance of columns and piers, to the vast darkened eye of the west window and the height of the Gothic pinnacles towering above.

"I had forgotten how very grand it is," he murmured at last.

Nina was pleased, possessive.

"I forget, too. Every time, it amazes me. Look, there's my house."

To one side of the green, forming its northern border, was a terrace of fine Georgian houses. There were four wide steps with iron railings leading up to each front door, and the balconies to the tall, first-floor windows were an intricate tracery of wrought-iron leaves. Nina's new house was in the middle of the row, looking directly out over the mulberry tree in the center of the green.

As she got out of Patrick's car, stretching her legs and easing her shoulders after the confinement of the long drive, she stopped for a moment to gaze up at her own blank windows.

"When I was a little girl, I always said that I wanted to live on Dean's Row. My mother used to laugh. 'Why settle for that?' she used to say. 'Why not the Bishop's Palace itself?' The answer was always that I didn't want to marry the bishop—because he had funny teeth."

Patrick came to stand beside her, looking upward in turn.

"And now here you are."

She heard the silent addendum—*Maybe it isn't such a half-arsed scheme to come live down here*—as clearly as if he had enunciated it.

"Have you got the keys?"

Nina took the heavy bunch out of her bag and held it up. "Yale, Chubb, and burglar alarm."

Patrick waited beside his car and let her go alone up the four steps to unlock the door.

She liked the house like this, empty. She could see and admire its ribs and joints. In the living room, the oak floorboards were two handspans broad, smooth and glowing with age. The shutters in the dining room folded into their own recesses in the paneling with seductive precision, and the thin glazing bars divided the glass and the late-afternoon light into eights, sixteenths, tidy fractions. Above her, in the hallway, the curving wrought-ironwork of the stair rails sprang up from each stone step and drew her upward through the center of the house. The bedrooms were square, well-proportioned, each with its iron grate and painted overmantel. There were too many of them, the house was much too big for her, but that didn't really matter. Richard had left her wealthy. The memory of that, the surprising figures in his will, could still catch her off-balance.

The previous owners had created a studio at the top of the house. The slope of the pitched roof, concealed from the green and the cathedral's west pinnacle by a low parapet, was like a sheet of ice. The Gothic pinnacles seemed to float above Nina's head in the breadth of the sky.

It was here that she would work. Her plan-chests and her drawing board and desk would be installed, neat and complete. Along with her boxes of paints and rows of inks and pencils. Nina was an illustrator of children's books. Her work was much admired.

"Nina?"

Patrick's voice came from downstairs.

"I'm coming."

He was standing outside the living room. The door was ajar behind him, to admit a view of the mulberry tree and of the saints and archangels in their stone niches.

"What do you think?"

"It's wonderful. A beautiful house."

She put her arms around him and hugged him. Again she felt the resistance, not rejection as much as containment, that told her he didn't know what to do with her. It wasn't that she expected anything. Patrick was gay, and she had known that for the whole ten years that they had been friends. But his awkwardness emphasized that her bereavement and the sympathy that followed it had set her apart. She was separate, she was to be treated with care, when in reality her grief and her needs made her long to be pulled in, to be loved so roughly that all the memories would vanish. Nina longed for that, bled for it.

"Shall we go down to the kitchen and have some tea?"

Patrick patted her shoulder. "Excellent."

He had unloaded the boxes from the back of his car and stacked them inside the front door.

"You should have waited for me to help you carry all that in."

"Nina, darling, if I can't manhandle a few boxes, who can?"

Patrick dealt in antiques, on his own and rather discriminatingly, from his house in Spitalfields. His specialty was early English oak.

Nina said quickly, "I'm grateful for everything you've done. Not just today, but ever since Richard died."

Patrick had come to her directly, on that first afternoon, after her telephone call from the house in Norfolk.

"It's okay," Patrick said. "You know where I am if you need me."

She did know, but she was also convinced, with a sudden burst of spirit, that she had done the right thing to sell the houses and the cars, to put Richard's modern art collection in store, and come to Grafton. She couldn't remake herself in London except as Richard Cort's widow. Here she was free to make of herself what she would.

"Tea."

The kitchen was in the basement. There were cupboards, painted teal-blue, expanses of brick and slate. French windows looked out on a small paved yard at the back of the house. Nina took the kettle out of the basket, filled it, plugged it in, and set out the cups and saucers. Patrick prowled behind her, opening the doors to the larder and the utility room, inspecting empty cupboards and wine racks, sliding drawers in and out on their smooth runners.

Nina did not care much for the kitchen. Its opulent rusticity was not to her taste. In London she had cooked in a functional space of stainless steel and black granite. But she did not plan to change this place—it would not be the center of the house, as her last kitchen had been. She would cook for herself, as quickly as possible, and that would be all.

She poured out the tea and handed Patrick his cup. For lack of anywhere else to sit, they hoisted themselves up side-by-side on one of the counters. Patrick gave his characteristic short snuffle of amusement.

"Look at all these dinky cutouts and finials. I'm surprised there are no stenciled flowers."

"I could paint some in. You're right, though, Richard wouldn't have liked it, would he?"

In London they had also lived in a Georgian house. But Richard's architect had gutted the interior, made it into a series of huge, light spaces, and they had furnished it sparsely. Richard had also owned a modern apartment, where he kept his ever-growing collection of paintings and sculptures, and where they sometimes gave parties. And then there had been the house near the sea in Norfolk, stone-floored and thick-walled. Those three solid, geometric places had contained their life together, and after his death Nina had been unable to contemplate their emptiness. She had sold them, adding even more money to his startling legacy. Richard had been a lawyer; he had also bought, renovated and resold properties. The mid-eighties had made him rich, although it was not until after he died that Nina realized exactly how rich.

Patrick drank his tea and looked at her. Nina sat with her shoulders hunched forward, her fingers laced around her cup. She looked composed, quite capable of making her own decisions and ordering her life the way she had always done. He admired her, and her strength. He had witnessed other deaths recently, and seen their effects on those left behind. Nina's levelness impressed him.

He asked. "Is that why you've come here?"

"Because a cathedral close, a little place like Grafton, and this house are so much not Richard's kind of thing?"

"Yes."

"Partly. But I also like the feeling that I belong here. A sense of being rooted. That's important, isn't it?"

Patrick, who had grown up in Ilford, let the question pass.

"Don't you know anyone here anymore?"

"Not a soul."

Nina was an only child. She had spent her childhood and youth in Grafton, but she had left to go to art school when she was eighteen. Her parents had moved away less than a year later, and both of them were dead now. Her remaining links with the town had long ago broken. She laughed suddenly.

"I'll be able to re-create myself entirely, with no one looking over my shoulder. Don't you envy me the chance to get rid of all those tiresome labels that people attach to one over the years? 'Nina doesn't like curry, knows nothing about music, always cries at those sentimental French films.' "

He nodded, agreeing with her. " 'Patrick drives like an old lady, is such a coffee snob, will never learn to ski.' "

They were both laughing now, affectionately.

"Don't make yourself too different. All your friends who love you as you are will miss you."

"I won't." Nina was thinking, *If I start again, away from all the places we knew together, I won't feel left behind. Is that a naive expectation?*

Upstairs, there was a heavy double thump on the door knocker. The men had arrived with the van.

* * *

Patrick directed the unloading. The job took less time than he had expected because Nina had brought so little with her. There were a few pieces he remembered from the London house: a Queen Anne chest-on-chest, some Biedermeier that would look well in the plain, square rooms, sofas and chairs, and a French *bateau lit*. Within two hours the van was empty and the men were on their way home again.

After they had gone, Nina and Patrick had a drink in the living room. It was furnished so sparely that their voices echoed faintly. The illuminated cathedral façade swam in the darkness beyond the windows.

"Will you be comfortable enough?" Patrick asked.

"I wanted to bring as little as possible." She was not so sure, now. She remembered how the storage people had come to wrap the pictures and modern pieces in burlap and polyethylene before carrying them away.

"This will be fine for the time being. I can always add more."

Different things, she meant, not the old ones.

"Would you like me to stay? I could take you out to dinner somewhere."

"Thank you, that's nice of you. But it's a long drive back. And I should unpack a bit, I suppose."

Patrick understood that she wanted him to go, to leave her alone to confront whatever it was she intended to confront. He drank a second glass of wine, reluctant to leave her, and then stood up. Nina went downstairs with him and out to the green, where his car was parked. They made arrangements for a weekend, and promised to telephone each other. Then Patrick kissed her on both cheeks, climbed into his car, and drove away.

Nina went back into the house and shut the door. She walked slowly up the stairs to her bedroom and stood at the foot of the bed, her fingertips resting on the high, smooth scroll of polished wood. Richard had bought the French bed for her as a wedding present.

On their wedding night he had held her in his arms, rocked her, and told her to imagine that they were in a real boat adrift on a benign ocean. She had smiled at him, drowsy with happiness and sex, and the sea of contentment had seemed boundless.

Nina wrapped her arms around herself now, digging her nails into the flesh of her shoulders to feel the confirmation of pain.

"Why did you leave me?" she asked the empty air. "I can't bear it without you."

To have come home to Grafton seemed a pointless gesture now. Even if she sold everything she and Richard had owned, shedding all the possessions of their shared life, his absence would still come at her out of the mundane actions of each successive day.

Nina began to cry, noisily, into the silence of her new house.

2

Janice Frost and Marcelle Wickham were the first to notice Nina. They were in the big supermarket; in the distance, as if the perspective lines of the shelves held her vividly spotlit just before the vanishing point, they saw a tall, thin woman in a long black skirt. Her red hair was pinned up in an untidy nest on the top of her head, and her mouth was painted the same color, over-bright in her white face.

"Who is that?" Janice wondered out loud. Janice knew everybody interesting in town, at least by sight.

Marcelle looked. As they watched, the woman moved away with her empty wire basket and disappeared.

Marcelle lifted a giant box of detergent into her cart and squared it up alongside the cereals and bottles of apple juice.

"Haven't a clue. Some visitor, I suppose. Crazy hair."

They worked their way methodically up one side of the aisle and down the other, and then up and down the succeeding aisles, the way they always did, but they didn't catch sight of the red-haired woman again.

Nina paid for her purchases, sandwiching them precisely on the conveyor belt between two metal bars labeled NEXT CUSTOMER PLEASE, all the time disliking the frugal appearance of the single portions of meat and vegetables and fish. She loved cooking, but as a solitary pursuit she could find no pleasure in it.

She had no car in Grafton. She had sold the Alfa Romeo that Richard had bought her, along with his Bentley coupe, in her grief-fueled rejection of their possessions immediately after his death. Now there was a little round-nosed shuttle bus that reminded her of a child's toy took her back into the center of town. She squeezed inside it among the pensioners and young mothers with their folding carriages, and balanced her light load of shopping against her hip. The bus swung out of the parking lot immediately in front of Janice and Marcelle in Janice's Volvo.

The next person to see Nina was Andrew Frost, Janice's husband. Andrew did recognize her.

Nina had been working. She was painting the face of a tiger peering out of the leaves of a jungle, which was to illustrate one of the letters in an animal alphabet. For a long morning she had been able to lose herself behind the creature's striped mask, in the green depths of the foliage. She worked steadily, loading the tip of her tiny brush with points of gold and emerald and jade, but then she looked up and saw blue sky over her head.

It was time to eat lunch, but she could find no enthusiasm for preparing even the simplest meal. Instead she took a bright red jacket off a peg and went out to walk on the green.

Andrew had left his offices to go to an organ recital in the cathedral. He was walking over the grass toward the west front, pleased with the prospect of an hour's music and freedom from meetings and telephones. He saw a red-haired woman in a crimson jacket crossing diagonally in front of him, and knew at once who she was. She had once worn a costume in the same shade of red to play Beatrice.

He quickened his pace to intercept her.

"It's Nina Strange, isn't it?"

Nina stopped. She turned to see a square-set man with thinning fair hair, a man in a suit who carried a raincoat even though the sky was blue.

"You don't remember me," the man said equably.

A thread of recollection snagged in her head.

"Yes, yes I do. Wait a minute . . ."

" 'When I said I would die a bachelor, I did not think I should live till I were married.' "

"Oh God, I *do* remember. It's Andrew, isn't it?"

"Andrew Frost. Benedick to your elegant Beatrice."

"Don't try to remind me of how long ago." Nina held out her hand and shook his. She was laughing and her face was suddenly bright. She remembered the plump teenaged boy who had played opposite her in their respective grammar schools' joint Shakespeare production.

"You were very good. I was dreadful," Andrew said.

"No you weren't. And your calves looked lovely in stockings."

Andrew beamed at her. "I was going to hear some music, but why don't we go across to the Eagle instead? Have you had lunch?"

Nina hesitated.

Small fragments of memory were rapidly coalescing and strengthening in her mind, swimming into focus like the images in a developing Polaroid snapshot. Now she could see the boy inside this grown man, and as she looked harder at him the boy's features grew more pronounced until it seemed that it was the man who was the memory. The sight of the young face brought back to her the long hours of rehearsal in the school hall that smelled of floor polish and musty costumes, that was filled with the miniature and tearful dramas of adolescence, the voices of teachers and friends. It was suddenly disorienting to find herself standing on the green again, almost under the shade of the mulberry tree, but cloaked in the body of a middle-aged woman instead of a schoolgirl.

"I can't, I really shouldn't today. I'm working, I've only come out for a bit of fresh air."

It was three days since she had spoken more than half a dozen words to anyone, and she didn't want the questions to start at the bar in the Eagle. She was afraid that if she was given a chance she would let too many words come pouring out.

"Working? Are you staying in Grafton?" He was standing with one hand in his pocket, the other hitching his raincoat over his shoulder. He was friendly and relaxed, no more than naturally curious.

"I . . . I've come back to live. I bought the house, in Dean's Row."

Andrew pursed his mouth in a soundless whistle. "Did you, now?"

Nina asked quickly, "What about you—did you follow on from Benedick and find your Beatrice?" There was a gold wedding ring on his finger.

"I married Janice Bell, do you remember her?"

Nina shook her head.

"Perhaps she came after your time."

Nina wanted to move on. It was reassuring to have made this small contact, but she needed space now to adjust Andrew Frost in her mind. She pointed to the cathedral entrance.

"Look, you can still get into the recital. Perhaps we can have lunch another day?"

Andrew took a business card out of his wallet and wrote something on the blank side. When he handed it to her she read the inscription—FROST RANSOME, CONSULTING ENGINEERS—with Andrew's name underneath it, followed by a string of letters. Nina pursed her lips and whistled, mimicking his gesture.

"We're having a party, at home, on Thursday evening," Andrew said. "That's the address. It's Halloween," he added, as if some explanation were necessary.

"So it is."

"Ghost costumes are not obligatory. But come, won't you? Janice would love to meet you."

"Thank you. I'm not sure . . . I'll try."

"Who do you know in Grafton these days?" He was looking at her with his head cocked to one side.

"Not a soul."

"Then you must come. No argument." He reached out and shook her hand, concluding a deal. "Thursday."

Nina would have turned the invitation down, but he was already walking away toward the cathedral. She returned home, went back to her desk, and bent over her tiger painting with renewed concentration.

She had not intended to go. She had thought that when Thursday came she would telephone Andrew's office and leave an apology with his secretary. But when the morning and half the afternoon passed and she still had not made the call, she recognized, to her surprise, that her real intention was to go.

Nina finished the painting she was working on. She was pleased with the work she had done so far. The new studio suited her, and she was making better progress than she and the publishers had estimated. She would go to the Frosts' party—there was no reason not to. As if to forestall any second thoughts, she looked up the number of a cab company in the phone book and arranged for a car to pick her up at eight-thirty.

Marcelle Wickham was a professional cook, and she was spending the afternoon at Janice's to help her with the party. The two of them were working comfortably to the background murmur of music on the radio.

Janice admired the rows of tiny golden croustades as they came out of the oven, taking one hot and popped it into her mouth.

"Delicious. You're a doll to do all this, Mar, do you know that?"

"Pass me the piping bag." Marcelle wiped her hands on her apron. The logo of the school where she worked as an instructor was printed on the bib.

"I like doing it. I just like the . . ."—she gestured in the air with her fingers—"the pinching and the peeling, all the textures, mixing them together." Her face relaxed into a smile, elastic, like dough. "I love it, really. I always have, since I was a little girl. And I love seeing the finished thing, and the pleasure it gives."

Janice sighed. "You're lucky."

Marcelle filled the piping bag with eggplant puree and began to squeeze immaculate rosettes into the pastry shells.

"I read somewhere that cooking is one of the three human activities that occupy the exact middle ground between nature and art."

"What are the others?"

"Gardening."

"Ha." Janice looked out her kitchen window. Her large, unkempt garden functioned mainly as a football field for her two boys.

"And sex."

"Ha ha."

They glanced at each other over the baking sheets. There was the wry, unspoken acknowledgment, the kind familiar to long-married women who know each other well, of the humdrum realities of tired husbands, demanding children, and sex that becomes a matter of domestic habit rather than passion. They also silently affirmed that within their own bodies, and notwithstanding any evidence to the contrary, they still felt like girls, springy and full of sap.

"Perhaps I'll concentrate on flower arranging," Janice said with a sigh, and they both laughed.

"So just who is coming tonight?"

"The usual crowd—the Roses, the Cleggs, the Ransomes."

These, along with the Frosts and the Wickhams, were the five families in their set. They ate and relaxed and gossiped in one another's houses, and made weekend arrangements for their children to play together—all of them except for the Roses had young children who, in various permutations, made up pairs or groups for games and sports and went on summer holidays together. There were other couples, other families among their friends, of course, and Janice listed some of their names now, but these five were the inner circle.

"Five points of a glittering star in the Grafton firmament," Darcy Clegg had called them once, half-drunkenly and half-seriously, as he surveyed the couples gathered around his dinner table. They had drunk a toast to themselves with Darcy's good wine.

"That's about fifty altogether, isn't it? No one you don't know, I think," Janice concluded. "Except some woman Andrew was at school with; he bumped into her on the green the other day."

"Oh, well, there's always Jimmy."

Again a little flicker of amused acknowledgment passed between them. All the wives liked Jimmy Rose. He danced with them and flirted at parties. It was his special talent to make each of them feel that, although he paid an obligatory amount of attention to the others, she was the special one, the one who really interested him.

"What are you wearing?"

Janice made a face. "My best black. It's witchy enough. And I've gotten too fat for anything else. Oh, God. Look at the time. The children will be back in half an hour."

The children came home at four o'clock. Vicky Ransome, the wife of Andrew's partner, had offered to do the car pool, even though it was not her day and she was eight and a half months pregnant. Janice's boys ran yelling into the kitchen, with Vicky and Marcelle's children in tow. The Frost boys, eleven and nine, were large, sturdy children with their father's fair hair and square chin. The elder one, Toby, whisked a Halloween mask from inside his school blazer and covered his face with it. He turned on Marcelle's timid seven-year-old with a banshee wail, and the little girl screamed and ran to hide behind her mother.

"Don't be such a baby, Daisy," Marcelle ordered. "It's only Toby. Hello, Vicky."

The boys ran out again, taking Marcelle's son with them. Daisy and Vicky's daughter clung around the mothers, weepily sheltering from the boys. Vicky's second daughter, only four, was asleep in the car.

Vicky wearily leaned against the countertop. "They fought all the way home."

Janice pulled out a stool for her. "You poor thing, here. And there's some tea."

The boys thundered back in again, clamoring for food. Janice dispensed drinks, bread and honey, slices of chocolate cake. The noise and skirmishing temporarily subsided, and the mothers' conversation went on in its practiced way over the children's heads.

"How are you feeling?" Marcelle asked Vicky.

"Like John Hurt in *Alien*, if you really want to know."

"Oh, gross," Toby Frost shouted from across the kitchen table.

Vicky shifted her weight uncomfortably on the stool and with both hands began to massage her stomach. Her hair was clipped back from her face with a barrette and her cheeks were shiny and pink. She reached out for a slice of chocolate cake with one hand and went on rubbing with the other.

"And I can't stop eating. Potato chips, chocolate, instant rice pudding. I'm huge—look at me. It wasn't like this with either of the others."

"Not much longer," Janice consoled her.

"And never again, amen," Vicky prayed.

The relative peace of the tea interval did not last long.

Once the food had been demolished there was a great cry for help with jack-o'-lanterns and ghost costumes. William Frost had already spiked his hair up into green points with luminous gel, and Daisy Wickham, her fears momentarily forgotten, was squirming into a skeleton suit. Andrew had promised to take his own children and the Wickhams' trick-or-treating for an hour before the adults' party.

"I'll leave you to it," Vicky said, leading away her six-year-old, Mary, who screamed in protest at being removed from the fun. "See you later. I'll be wearing my white thing. You'll be able to tell me from Moby Dick by my scarlet face."

After she left, Marcelle frowned and said, "Vicky's not so good this time, is she?"

Janice was preoccupied. "She'll be okay once it's born. Oh, no, look at the *time*. Toby, will you get out of here? Please God that Andrew gets himself home soon."

"Shouldn't bank on it," Marcelle said cheerfully.

Nina chose her clothes with care. She was not sure what Andrew had meant when he said that costumes were not obligatory. Did that mean that only half the guests would be trailing about in white bedsheets?

In the end she opted for an asymmetric column of greenish silk wound about with pointed panels of sea-colored chiffon. The dress had cost a mint, and when she had first worn it Richard remarked that it made her look like a Victorian medium rigged out for a séance.

And as she remembered his words, the exact cadence of his voice came back to her as clearly as if he were standing at her shoulder.

She stood still for a moment and rested her face against the cold glass of her bathroom mirror. Then, when the spasm had passed, she managed to fix all her attention on applying makeup to her eyes. At eight-thirty exactly her car arrived.

The Frosts' house was at the end of a quiet cul-de-sac on the "good" rural side of the town. From what was visible of the dark frame against the glare of lighted windows, Nina registered that the house was large, prewar, with a jumble of gables and tall chimneys. There were jack-o'-lanterns grinning on the gateposts, and a bunch of silver, helium-filled balloons rattling and whipping in the wind. Nina's high heels crunched on the gravel.

When someone opened the door for her, Nina's first impressions were a babel of noise, crashing music, and a horde of overexcited children running up and down the stairs. Something in a red suit, with horns and a tail, whisked in and out of her sight. She went blank for a second, and then focused on the woman who had opened the door. She was dark, with well-defined eyes and a wide mouth, and was dressed in a good black dress that probably hid some excess weight. On her head she wore a wire-brimmed witch's hat with the point tipsily drooping to one side. She looked closely at Nina, then smiled.

"You must be Andrew's friend? Nina, isn't it? Come on in, and welcome."

The door opened hospitably wide. Once she was inside, Nina realized that Andrew's wife had spoken to her in a pleasant, low voice. The noise wasn't nearly as loud as it had at first seemed, and there were only four children visible. Nina understood that it was simply that she had been utterly alone for a week, and was unused to any noise but for her own thoughts.

"I'm Janice," Janice said.

"Nina Cort. Used to be Nina Strange, when Andrew knew me. I'm sorry I haven't come in costume."

Janice waved her glass. "Your dress is beautiful. I only put this hat on at the last minute, and Andrew is defiantly wearing his penguin suit." Her mouth pouted in disparagement, but her eyes revealed her pride in him. "Come on, come with me. I'll get you a drink, and introduce you to everyone."

Nina followed her down the hallway toward the back of the house. The man in the devil suit was sitting at the foot of the stairs now, and he looked up at her as she passed. His eyebrows rose in triangular points.

Andrew Frost kissed her by way of welcome and gave her a glass of champagne. Nina drank it gratefully, quickly, and accepted another.

She was launched into a succession of conversations, but felt as if she was bobbing on a rip tide of unfamiliar faces. The surreal effect was heightened by the fact that some of the faces were ghoulishly made up, swaying above ghost costumes or witches' robes, while others sprouted conventionally from cocktail dresses or naked and pink from the necks of dress shirts constricted by black ties. The man in the devil suit prowled the room, flicking around his arrow-headed tail. A delectably pretty girl of about eighteen threaded through the crowd offering a tray of canapés, and the devil capered behind her, grinning.

Nina loved parties, but Richard had always been there for her, a buoy to which she could hitch herself when she found herself drifting. Now she was cut loose, and the swirl of the current alarmed her.

The room was hot, and confusingly scented with a dozen different perfumes. There was a woman in a long white dress, majestically pregnant, and another, younger, in a shimmering outfit that exposed two thirds of her creamy white breasts. There was a dark man with a beaky profile, two more men who were talking about a golf tournament, a thin woman with a reflective expression who did not smile when Nina was introduced to her.

Nina finished her third glass of champagne. She had been talking very quickly, animatedly, and laughing too readily. She realized that she had been apprehensive of coming alone to this house of strangers. Now her only fear was that she might be going to faint.

She wanted to hold onto someone. She wanted it so badly that her hands balled into fists.

She held up her head and walked slowly through the chattering groups. It was just a party, like a hundred others she had been to, perhaps a little rowdier because all these people seemed to know each other so well.

The kitchen was ahead of her, more brightly lit than the other rooms. There were people gathered in here too, only fewer of them. In the middle of them was Janice, without her hat now, and another woman in an apron. They were laying out more food on a long table.

"Can I help?" Nina asked politely.

"No, but come and talk," Janice answered at once. "Have you met Marcelle? This is Marcelle Wickham."

The woman in the apron held out her hand and Nina shook it. It was small and warm and dry, like a child's.

"Hi. We saw you in the supermarket, Jan and I. Did she tell you?"

"I've hardly had a chance to speak to her. I'm sorry, Nina. I'm just about to tell everyone that the food's ready." Janice pushed her hair off her damp forehead with the back of her hand.

"We wondered who you were," Marcelle explained.

Nina's hands moved again. "Just me."

"Who, exactly?" A man's voice asked behind her.

"Look after her for me, Darcy, will you?" Janice begged, hurrying by. The man inclined his head obediently and passed a high stool to Nina. She sat down in the place that Vicky Ransome had occupied earlier.

"I'm Darcy Clegg," the man said.

He was older than most of the Frosts' other friends, perhaps in his early fifties. He had a well-fleshed, handsome face and gray eyes with heavy lids. He was wearing what looked like a Gaultier dinner jacket, conventionally and expensively cut except for a line of black fringing across the back and over the upper arms and breast, like a cowboy suit. He had a glass and his own bottle of whisky at one elbow.

"That is a spectacular dress," Darcy Clegg drawled.

Nina liked men who noticed clothes and bothered to comment on them.

"How long have you been in Grafton?" he asked.

Sitting upright, in the kitchen light, Nina sensed that the inquisition was about to begin.

She explained, as bloodlessly as she could, who she was and what she was doing. Darcy listened, turning his whisky glass around and around in his fingers, occasionally taking a long gulp. This new woman, with her green eyes and extraordinary hair, was interesting, although perhaps neurotic. There was some strange, strong current emanating from her that he did not understand. Her fingers kept moving, as if she wanted to grab hold of something. Darcy wondered what she would be like in bed. One of those hot-skinned, clawing women who emitted throaty cries. Nothing like Hannah.

"And has your husband come down here with you?" Darcy asked. Nina still wore Richard's rings.

"He died nearly a year ago. Of an asthma attack, at our house in the country. He was there alone."

"I'm very sorry," Darcy murmured. A troubling recollection stirred in him, although he couldn't identify a reason for it, and he made a half-hearted effort to pursue it. Who had told him a similar tragic story? When the connection continued to elude him, Darcy shrugged it away. In many ways he was a lazy man, although he was tenacious in others.

"What about you? Do you live in Grafton?" Nina felt that it was her turn now.

"Outside. About three miles away, toward Pendlebury."

"And are *you* married?"

Darcy turned his gray eyes on her and smiled, acknowledging the question. "Yes. My wife's name is Hannah. In the silver décolleté."

Of course—the luscious blonde with the bare breasts. Nina was beginning to fit the couples together now, pairing the unfamiliar smiling faces two-by-two.

"And the girl handing around the canapés is Cathy, one of my daughters. By my first wife." The smile again, showing his good teeth. Darcy Clegg was attractive, Nina was now fully aware. Politely he filled her glass and they began to talk about how Grafton had changed since Nina's school days.

More guests filtered into the kitchen, following the scent of Marcelle's cooking, and the noise swelled around Nina again.

Gordon Ransome brought his wife a plate of food and a knife and fork wrapped in a napkin. Vicky was sitting in a low chair in a corner of the living room, a side lamp shining on the top of her head. He looked down at her for an instant and saw, where her hair parted, the vulnerable pallor of her scalp. He had not noticed before that it grew in exactly the same way as their daughters', and he felt a spasm of exasperated tenderness. She had collapsed into a chair that was too low for her, and she would need help to struggle to her feet again. The voluminous white folds of her dress emphasized her bulge.

When she looked up he saw also that there were dark circles under her eyes and that her face looked small and sharp-pointed.

Vicky took the plate and hoisted herself awkwardly upright, wincing as she did so. She began to eat, ravenously, even though she knew that after half a dozen mouthfuls the burning would begin under her breastbone. She was made more uncomfortable by Gordon looming impatiently above her.

"We mustn't be too late," she said. Alice had a cough and their sitter was only fifteen.

"I don't want to go yet," Gordon snapped. "We've only just got here." He swung away with his hands in his pockets, feeling immediately ashamed of his bad temper. But he often felt now that his helplessly pregnant wife and his little daughters were like small, soft obstacles that he had to skirt around, day by day, walking softly all the time lest somebody should start to cry. He loved them all, but they took so much from him.

Darcy Clegg came to Vicky with a cushion for her back.

A little later the dancing began in another room, which extended sideways from the main part of the house. It had a wood-block floor and tall windows at one of its gable ends, looking out on a swimming pool covered over for the winter. Andrew had hired a mobile disco, a boy with two turntables, a set of speakers, and some lights that made globs of color revolve softly in the beamed recess of the roof. The young deejay quickly sized up his audience and opted for an opening medley of pounding sixties rock. The innocent exuberance of lights and music and jigging couples was suddenly so powerfully reminiscent of student parties fifteen years earlier that Nina found herself laughing. It also made her want to leap up and dance.

Gordon watched the dancers, too. On top of several glasses of champagne and a malt whisky he had swallowed quickly in the kitchen with Jimmy Rose, he was trying to identify exactly what it was that he wanted. There was Cathy Clegg, in some tiny stretchy tube of a skirt that showed off her thighs and small bottom, or Hannah, with her expanse of soft breast and her habit of biting her cushiony bottom lip with her little white teeth. Darcy's women, of course. Not either of them.

He did want a woman, Gordon recognized, in the hot, impatient way he had done when he was much younger. The realization shocked him a little, but allowing himself to admit it added a second-ary charge to his excitement. He had to be so careful with Vicky now. She slept badly, suffered from cramps and tiredness, and needed his reassurance and sympathy at every turn. He no longer felt that his wife was his equal, as he had thought when they were first married. Somehow, over the intervening years, her happiness had become his responsibility instead of his reward.

He still loved her, but the love was muted and tinged with disappointment.

Gordon went on surveying the room. He liked Stella Rose, Jimmy's wife, whom everyone called Star. He enjoyed dancing with her at the Grafton parties, and talking to her, too. She had a quick, acerbic intelligence that challenged him and a tight-knit, bony body that did the same. To single out Star was also some kind of retort to Jimmy, who was always whispering and cuddling with other men's wives. But he did not feel drawn to Star tonight. She had been drinking hard, as she sometimes did, and he had last seen her in the kitchen, haranguing kindly Marcelle about something, dark patches of smudged mascara under her eyes.

There were others among the wider group, but Gordon did not look at any of them. Instead, deliberately, he let his eyes circle back to the new woman in the look-at-me dress. He had met her briefly at the beginning of the evening, what seemed like many hours ago now. She had been polite but slightly remote. He thought she was aloof, that she probably considered this party dully provincial. Then, a little while later, she had slipped past in a knot of people and her exotic draperies had fluttered against him.

Now, he noticed, she was standing on her own, apart, and apparently laughing to herself. One of the discs of revolving light, a blue one, passed slowly over her face and then over her hair. It turned a rich purple, like a light in a stained-glass window, and faded as soon as he had seen it. Gordon felt a tightening in his throat.

"Would you like to dance?"

Nina, that was her name. It came to him once he had asked her.

"Thank you."

She let him take her hand, quite easily and naturally, and lead her into the throng of people. They began to dance. He saw how she become absorbed by the music, as if relieved to forget herself for a moment. Some of the tautness faded from her face, and left her looking merely pretty instead of stiff and imperious.

The change aroused Gordon's interest and made him wonder

who she was and what her circumstances might be. She was the only stranger in this room full of too-familiar faces and stale allegiances, and her newness made her intriguing. As they danced Gordon was drawn closer to her, and he became intensely aware of her body moving in neat and rhythmic patterns only inches away from his. With this awareness he looked into her face again and saw that Nina was not pretty, but beautiful. Her eyelids were rounded and heavy over her dark eyes, reminding him of a voluptuary in some pre-Raphaelite painting, and her mouth was slightly open, its full contours emphasized by fresh lipstick. Gordon found that his tongue had moved to the side of his mouth.

Nina tilted her head toward him, narrowing the space between them by another fraction. Gordon was thinking that if he were to reach out and touch her thick hair, he would feel the tingle of electric shocks, invisible sparks discharging themselves beneath his fingertips.

"Do the Frosts often give parties?" Nina asked.

He reined in his thoughts, marshaling himself to answer the routine question. He lifted his hand, wanting to touch her, but restrained himself.

"Often. And always just like this."

The flip of his fingers, she saw, acknowledged the evening's combination of sophistication and hearty enthusiasm, champagne and student disco, fancy dress and cocktail frock, that she herself had found so beguiling. Nina had forgotten this man's name, but she suddenly felt an upward beat of pure pleasure to find herself here, dancing, among all these people who knew nothing about her.

Darcy was lounging in the doorway, watching the dancers, with Jimmy beside him. Jimmy had pulled off the red hood of his devil suit and raked his fingers through his hair so that it stood up on top of his head in a crest.

Jimmy murmured to his companion, "Who is *La Belle Dame Sans Merci*? Nobody will introduce me."

Nina and Gordon were on the far side of the room, absorbed in their dancing.

Mick Jagger sang out of the speakers, *Pleased to meet you, hope you guessed my name* . . . and all the couples in their thirties obligingly sang back, *Whhoo hoo* . . . .

"Perhaps she doesn't want to meet the devil," Darcy suavely anwered. "But her name is Nina something, and she has bought the house on Dean's Row where the Collinses used to live. She's a widow, apparently."

"*La belle veuve*, then," Jimmy said. And then he added, with relish, "I smell trouble, oh yes I do."

Nina had arranged for the car to come back for her at twelve-thirty, and she was ready for it when the time came.

Her dancing partner had been reclaimed by his rosy, pregnant wife. The little Irish devil man and the tall woman with the reflective face had made a surprising pair. Andrew and Janice had come to the door together, to see Nina off, and had stood shoulder-to-shoulder, smiling and waving.

In the taxi Nina leaned her head back and closed her eyes.

In her mind's eye the people swam up two by two out of the swirl of the party. She could recall all the faces, not so many of the names. Somebody and somebody, somebody and somebody else. It seemed that everyone was half of a pair. The whole world was populated by handsome, smiling couples, and behind them, behind the secure doors of their houses, were the unseen but equally happy ranks of their children.

Nina's loneliness descended on her again. It was like a gag, tearing the soft tissues of her mouth, stifling her.

"Dean's Row, Miss," the driver called over his shoulder.

Inside her house the silence felt thick enough to touch. Nina poured herself a last drink and took it upstairs to the living room. She stood at the window without turning on the lights behind her. The floodlights that illuminated the cathedral's west façade were doused at midnight, but Nina felt the eternal presence of the saints and archangels in their niches more closely than if they had been visible.

She rolled her tumbler against the side of her face, letting the ice cool her cheek.

To her surprise, she realized that the pressure of her solitude had eased a little, as if the ranks of statues provided the company she needed. Or perhaps it was the party that had done it.

It had been a good evening, and she had met interesting people. They were nothing like her London friends, these Grafton couples, but she was glad just the same.

"And so, good night," Nina said dryly to the saints and archangels.

3

Vicky stooped down, lowering herself from the knees; it was weeks since she had been able to bend from the waist. She held on to the railing with one hand and with the other gathered up the trail of Lego blocks that Alice had left scattered along the landing. The effort made her breathless and she had to wait for a few seconds before making the journey into the bedroom to put the blocks away.

The girls' room was messy, heaped with clothes, a jumble of toys, and Vicky wearily pushed her hair back from her face as she surveyed it. She had no strength left to do anything more than sleepwalk through these last days, and so she turned away and closed the door, feeling guilty as she did so. She was not particularly house-proud, but she was not happy to see the threads of her domestic organization unravel completely because she was too exhausted to hold them together.

Across the landing was the room prepared for the baby, and on her slow way downstairs again she stopped for a moment at its threshold. The cot had done duty for Mary and Alice and the white paint was chipped, but there were new curtains and a new cover on the daybed, and the drawers of the chest were layered with tiny clothes. The bassinette with its little folded white blankets lay ready for Gordon to bring to the hospital so they could carry the baby home in it together.

Vicky thought about how in a few days' time she would be here again with her new child. She would sit in this room, in the silence of the night, to feed it, to watch the play of muscles in its face as it blindly sucked, feeling the steady flow of her milk. Her breasts ached now, and there was a pain low in her back that made her stretch awkwardly to try to ease it.

Downstairs, Alice was sitting on the sofa, watching television. She had her bed blanket with her, and her thumb and one corner of the blanket were poked into her mouth. Alice only went to nursery school in the mornings. Vicky plodded across to her, and the child made room without taking her eyes off the screen.

"Tired Mummy," Alice remarked automatically.

"That's right."

Vicky lowered herself, letting out a gasp of breath, and Alice snuggled up against her. Vicky put an arm around her shoulders, and they settled down to watch together.

The little girl's bare arm was round and smooth, still with a babyish ring in the soft flesh around her wrist. There was Plasticine under her sticky fingernails and a faint smell of damp hay emanated from her hair.

"That man is silly," Alice said, pointing to the television screen.

"Is he?"

Vicky was thinking vaguely of the business of her children growing, the invisible multiplication of their busy cells, the branching of veins and laying down of bone to support more growth, upward and away from Gordon and herself, so that one day their own adulthood would become Mary and Alice's, too. She imagined, under her daughter's fine hair and the armor of her skull, the eye of her brain restlessly moving, photographing the infinitesimal details of her world, storing them up, creating a miraculous index that would help her occupy the enlarging shell of her body.

The small shape resting against her suddenly seemed charged with an almost unbearable perfection.

From the moment after Mary's birth when the midwife had hoisted the baby into Vicky's arms and her womb had contracted with an amazed spasm of love and tenderness, she had always felt an intense physical pleasure in her children's bodies, a pleasure that was almost but not quite erotic. She remembered how when Mary was tiny, six years ago, Gordon used to carry her into their bed in the early morning, and they would lean over her naked, folded limbs and serrated face to feast on this embodiment and extension of their love.

Six years ago, not now. Vicky smiled a little at the contrast.

Gordon's practice was much busier these days, his hours longer, and the mornings were a scramble to dispatch him and the girls to their separate destinations. There was too little time to spare, but she knew that all parents of young children suffered from the same thing. There would be time again, she was sure of it. She shifted her position a little, her thoughts sliding away in another direction, to the pain in her back.

Then she said suddenly, "Alice, will you run into the kitchen and fetch me a towel from the big cupboard?"

Alice ran, unquestioning for once, because of the sharp note in her mother's voice. Vicky's waters had broken.

Gordon drove home from the office. He had telephoned Vicky's mother, who was already on her way to collect the girls, and Marcelle Wickham would pick Mary up from school and stay at home with the two of them until their grandmother arrived. He concentrated on the road and the swirl of the traffic, frowning, trying to channel his attention down a single avenue, toward reaching the house and getting Vicky to the hospital. He had been called out of a meeting; fragments of the discussion and the points he had been intending to make collided in his head.

There was a long line of cars snaking up to the rotary onto the city freeway, but he calculated rapidly that it would be quicker to wait in the line than to turn back and take a less direct route. As the car inched closer to it, his thoughts ran forward to the hours ahead in the obstetrics ward, and then jumped backward to the births of Mary and Alice. He could remember the contractions being reflected in Vicky's face, the way her mouth pinched in at the corners as she struggled to ride them out, her cries and wails, and her final triumph and the emergence of the wet, black head, like a conjuring trick. Each time, he recalled, he had been amazed by the climax, the appearance of a baby. It was as if the months of preparation and anticipation and childbirth classes had been academic for him, or theoretical, with no particular end in view. And then there had been the extraordinary emergence of a third and completely other individual from what had once been only himself and Vicky. Now it was about to happen yet again; there would be a new person, around whom they would rearrange the formulae of

41

their lives. Gordon wished that it would be a boy. He had begun
to feel, lately, that he might end up overpowered by the collusion
of women in his house.

The car had almost reached the rotary. In the middle of
this November afternoon, the fading light drew a greenish halo
around the buildings and bridges, but the autumn trees were still
bright. The burning colors made him think of the new woman,
the one who had come to Andrew's party, the splashes of colored
light roving over her hair. Gordon circled the rotary and saw the
highway's two lanes stretch ahead of him. He accelerated hard
toward home.

Janice had arrived to wait with Vicky; Marcelle had taken Alice
with her on the school run. The two women were sitting on upright
chairs in the kitchen. Vicky's chin was tucked into her chest as she
concentrated on her breathing, but she looked up as soon as she
heard Gordon come in. He saw her relief at the sight of him, the
way her hair fell childishly straight on either side of her cheeks. He
wanted to lift her up, the way he might lift Alice, and at the same
time to shake her back into herself, to remake the Vicky she had
once been out of the Vicky and mother she had become. He took
hold of her hand and smiled at her.

"It's all right, I'm here now." He spoke to her, too, the way he
might have done to the children. "Are you having contractions?"

"Not very big ones yet. But they're coming quite often. The
hospital says to come now."

He could see that it was an effort for her to talk. "Let's go,
then," he said calmly.

"Her bag is in the hall," Janice told him. "Everything's in it.
Here's her coat." They draped it around her shoulders, and helped
her to her feet.

"Don't worry about the girls," Janice told Vicky when they had
shuffled to the car. "Away you go, both of you."

She stood in the driveway and waved them off as if they were
going away on holiday.

It was only a fifteen-minute drive to the hospital, but by the
time they reached it Vicky felt afraid. An orderly and a nurse saw
them arriving and came out with a wheelchair. When she looked up
at their faces, Vicky saw them through a fog of pain and confusion.

* * *

As the days passed Nina began to establish a pattern to live by. She went upstairs to her studio early in the morning to work, and by the middle of the day she had done enough painting to satisfy herself. Then, in the hollow afternoons, she went for long walks. It soothed her to have a routine: she found that by keeping to it she could still some of her restlessness. Sometimes her walks took her through town, and she looked at the new façades of shops and restaurants pasted up onto the old buildings, and the faces of the people as they crisscrossed the liver-colored paving blocks of the pedestrian-only shopping precinct. At other times she headed in the opposite direction, through one of the new developments at the city limits, out through a no-man's-land of half-made rutted tracks that led to windy fields slated for more development, and on into the open country. She walked quickly, with her hands in the pockets of her coat, observing the dips and folds of the mild landscape and the pencil lines of plough furrows and leafless trees. Back at home in the evenings she read, and telephoned her friends in London, assuring Patrick and the others that she was neither lonely nor going mad.

Nor did she spend all of her time alone. She found herself beginning to be included in the circle of women that quietly revolved within the group of smiling couples.

It was Janice Frost who made the first overture. She telephoned Nina one morning and invited her to lunch, and Nina had accepted before she could think of any particular reason to refuse. She walked to the Frosts' this time, and when she reached their neighborhood she looked with interest at the big houses set back in their gardens. She had once had a schoolfriend who lived around here, and it seemed that nothing much had changed since those days. There were perhaps more cars, matronly sedans, parked in the sloping driveways. The streets were quiet and a stillness hung over the roofs and treetops, but it seemed to Nina that she could actually hear the sonorous bass note of prosperity humming away. *If I had stayed in Grafton*, she wondered, *would I have married and come to rest in one of these solid houses?*

She had already turned into the Frosts' driveway when a car braked and stopped on the gravel behind her. Nina turned and saw a BMW driven by Darcy Clegg's wife. The two women reached Janice's front door together.

"Hi," Hannah said breathlessly. "Jan just called me and asked me to come on over for lunch with the two of you. I left Mandy in charge of the shop."

Nina was wondering if she was supposed to know anything about the shop or Mandy when Janice opened the door. She was wearing jeans and a loose shirt, but her eyes were made up, and she looked younger than she had on the night of her party. She kissed Hannah and waved her inside, and drew Nina after her. The kitchen was warm and scented with food, and the table was properly laid for three with linen napkins and wine glasses. Nina had been feeling a prickle of impatience, but it subsided now. She accepted a glass of white wine and leaned against one of Janice's counters. Janice began to chop herbs beside her. There was a view of garden and fruit trees and a soccer goal from the window.

Janice said, "I'm glad you could come. I didn't have a chance to speak to you the other night, it was such a scramble. I realized afterwards how unfriendly I must have seemed."

"No. I remember what it's like, giving a party."

"The Frosts are wildly hospitable. Without them, none of us in Grafton would ever see one another."

Hannah had perched on a stool, her legs crossed. She was wearing suede trousers and a light cashmere sweater, and her pale blond hair was pinned halfway up to show her soft neck. Quite soon she might cross the dividing line between voluptuous and fat, but for now she was luscious, with her pearly skin and plump mouth. Nina thought that she looked milk-fed, sated. Darcy must be attentive in bed. Her own singleness made her feel dry and angular in comparison, with creases in her skin and a sour ache between her shoulder blades from the effort of holding her head up ramrod-straight.

"I like it; I need to have people around. I'm the only one of us who doesn't have a proper job," Janice explained to Nina. "I wanted Marcelle to come to lunch, too, but she's working today. She teaches cooking at the Pond School, you know."

Hannah laughed. "Nina, Janice may not have a job, but she does everything else. She sits on every committee in Grafton, Friends of the Cathedral, PTA, all that. She works for at least three different charities, and if anyone wants something done they invariably ask Mrs. Frost first. Her energy exhausts us all."

Nina smiled, too. She began to see a more rounded version of this hospitable Janice, with her neat dark hair and faintly domineering manner, and she liked what she saw.

"Let's eat while we're talking," Janice said briskly, and moved them to the table.

There was a warm salad with wild mushrooms, and a vegetable pie. Hannah drank steadily and Janice kept their glasses filled. Nina had been intending to work that afternoon, but she drank more wine and ate hungrily out of sheer pleasure at having good food cooked and laid out in front of her. She abandoned the idea of work without regrets. It was pleasant to sit here in the kitchen glow, talking to the women.

It came to Nina suddenly that she had been stiff lately from the effort of containing herself. She could feel the rigidness in her face, in her spine.

Then there was a surprising blurred moment when the wine and the women's unforced friendliness seemed to dissolve her tension, and she felt that she could be who she really was instead of pretending to be otherwise. Hannah said something, although Nina immediately forgot what, something about how the house on Dean's Row must seem big and quiet.

Nina began to cry.

She still cried when she was alone, too often, but she had not broken down in front of other people, strangers, since the first weeks after Richard's death. It was both a shock and a relief to find the tears running down her face.

The two women came around the table to her and stooped down on either side of Nina's chair. Hannah touched her shoulder.

"Is it what I said about your house? I'm so sorry if it is. I didn't think."

Nina took a tissue that Janice held out to her and blew her nose.

"It's all right. It's not you. It just happens, I'll stop in a minute."

They knew, of course, both of them. She had told Darcy Clegg at the party that Richard was dead. It had been absurd of her to imagine that she could come down here and re-create herself as a different person. There was, always and forever, the same old self to live with, with the same dull catalogue of griefs and anxieties. The thought made her mouth twist in resignation. Now she had to explain some part of what she was feeling to these friendly women with their unvoiced curiosity.

Nina took a breath. "My husband died a year ago. I came back to live here because I thought it would be easier than staying in London, where everything reminded me of him. And sometimes it *is* easier. Then I remember all over again that he's gone, and I think for a minute that I can't bear it. But I can, of course. That's all it is. I'm sorry to be so embarrassing when I hardly know you."

"You aren't embarrassing." Hannah was indignant. "I am, if anyone is."

Janice nodded. "And you do know us. You can talk to us, if you want to. Or forget all about it if you'd rather."

The moment was over. Nina was grateful to them, but more grateful still to have regained her own self-control.

"I would rather," she said softly.

The women went back to their places. Janice took another bottle of wine out of the rack behind Nina. More wine glinted into their glasses.

Nina turned to Hannah.

"Tell me about your shop."

It seemed important to go on talking about something else, anything else at all. She was touched by their concern, but she felt too raw to accept it. She wanted to show them that she was not receding, only that she couldn't advance any further toward them.

Hannah was anxious to make amends for her own apparent insensitivity.

"It's a dress shop. La Couture. Darcy bought it for me not long after we were married. He thought I needed something to keep me amused. I surprised him, rather, by making a bit of a success of it."

Janice chipped in, pleased that Nina was coming back to herself.

"You should go in and have a look. It's in Southgate, opposite the bookshop. I don't go because I can't afford it. Can I, Hannah? There isn't a thing in there under ninety quid."

Hannah ignored her.

"It became a success because there's plenty of money in Grafton." She rubbed her thumb and forefinger together. "And people like to dress up and show it off once in a while. At Jan's parties, for instance. Or at least they did. They're not so sure, now that there's this recession. I think they've still got the money, most of them, but they're not convinced they should wave it around for everyone to see."

You and Darcy wouldn't worry, Nina thought. And she also thought of Richard's money, wedged behind her like some invisible wall. She saw that Janice's dark eyebrows had risen a fraction. There was some puritan disapproval of Hannah in them, of Hannah's cheerful vulgarity. Nina wondered how these two women and their partners actually fitted together. Did they really like one another? The friendliness that had warmed her earlier assumed chillier undertones now.

Nina finished her wine and held her hand over her glass when Janice inquiringly lifted the second bottle. They began a laughing exchange of Grafton gossip. All three of them were relieved that they had safely negotiated the moment of Nina's tears.

"I'll give you a lift back," Hannah said when it was time to leave. Janice came out to the car with them and put her hand lightly on Nina's arm.

"You know where we are," she said, without emphasis.

"Yes," Nina answered, liking her again.

Hannah drove fast and carelessly and deposited Nina at the entry to the cathedral green.

"Come and see me in the shop?" she asked suddenly.

"Yes, of course I will."

"I'm sorry I made things so awkward today. Darcy always says I don't think before opening my mouth."

"It's all right," Nina said, meaning it. "I'm not usually so precarious."

Hannah nodded, confident she had been forgiven.

"Come and see us at Wilton," she said, smiling. Then she drove away, revving the engine too hard, leaving Nina on the curb.

Vicky Ransome's baby was delivered by cesarean section six hours after she had been admitted into the hospital. Her obstetrician had been inclined to let her labor on for a while, as he explained to Gordon, because she had already achieved two normal deliveries. But then the monitors had indicated that the baby was becoming distressed, and an examination revealed that it had turned in the birth canal and was now presenting its left shoulder instead of its head. Vicky herself was exhausted and growing panicky.

"I won't try to turn it again. I think we'll just whip her in next door," the doctor said. Gordon was given a mask and a green gown to put on over his business suit, and followed the trolley bearing his wife into the theater. There was a calm flurry of surgical procedures. He watched, aware of his own helpless detachment, even though he was holding Vicky's hand and whispering encouragement to her. He waited, and then, beyond the screen that protected Vicky, he saw the baby lifted out from her sliced belly like a marine creature being wrested from a viscous crimson sea.

"A beautiful little girl," the medical team told him.

"A girl?" Vicky repeated

The baby cried, and after they had handled its tiny body and wrapped it for him, he was given her to hold. They were busy with Vicky now, with the white-and-crimson folds of flesh and fat and muscle, stitching the flopping bag of her body back into place. Gordon felt cold and shivers of nausea fluttered under his breastbone, but he made himself breathe in and exhale steady gulps of medicated air. He bent his stiff neck and looked down into the baby's opaque black eyes.

"I'm sorry," Vicky said later. They had sponged her face and put her into bed in the ward, and the flowery curtains had been closed around them. The baby was with the pediatricians, but they had been assured that everything was quite normal.

"Why sorry?" Gordon felt jerky with tiredness. He had been briefly hungry but his appetite had left him again even though he had eaten nothing. His mouth was slimed with hospital tea, and he could smell his wife's blood thickly in the back of his nose.

"Not to do it properly. Was it horrible? It's just a blur to me."

"No, it wasn't horrible. How could it be? It was beautiful." He lied halfheartedly, wishing that he could command sincerity. He was sure that there must be some formula of words that would reassure her, and would light her face from beneath the skin in the way that it had been lit after the births of the other two babies, but the formula escaped him and he heard himself disappointing her.

"I know you wanted a boy."

They were whispering. The ward lights had been turned off for the night, and Gordon and Vicky were artificially held together in a small circle of light directed downward from over Vicky's head. She was past tiredness now, and looked bright with the skin stretched taut over her cheekbones. He knew that she needed to talk, although the ward sister had warned him that he could only stay to see her settled down. He thought of their bed at home, the silence of the empty house. He had made the necessary telephone calls. The girls were safely with their grandparents.

"I don't mind what it is, so long as it has everything intact and you're safe. You know that." He bent his head and kissed her folded hands.

"She. *She* has everything intact. She's a little girl."

Vicky was becoming querulous now. He knew that she was near tears, and he wanted to leave so that she could close her eyes on the tears and drift away into sleep.

"A beautiful little girl. A little sister," he reassured her.

"Helen. We're going to call her Helen, aren't we?"

It was one of the names they had discussed. Gordon preferred Olivia, and for a boy he had wanted Oliver. But he whispered, "If that's what you would like. Yes, of course."

It was like soothing the children at bedtime so that they could turn inward to sleep, with the day's wrinkles straightened behind them. Vicky and he had lovingly argued the merits of Mary versus Alice when the first one was born, and it was Vicky who had capitulated then.

"Mr. Ransome?"

The white paper turret of a nurse's cap appeared around the curtain. Gordon stood up at once and pressed his mouth against his wife's forehead.

"Sleep now," he said. "I'll come in as soon as I can tomorrow."

He left her, and the leather soles of his shoes squeaking on the linoleum floor faded into the nighttime murmurs of the ward.

* * *

The cathedral was almost empty. Gordon sat at the back of the nave, with his briefcase and a file of papers relating to the cathedral works on the wooden seat beside him. His head was tilted back while he tried to discern the familiar outlines of the Gothic vaulting above him, and at the same time he reflected on the slow weathering and decay of the pale limestone that the Conservation Committee was so worried about. It seemed that the organ notes seeping through the arches and between the huge pillars, then fading and falling away into silence, eloquently expressed the crumbling of the stone in the silences of seven centuries.

When the thirteenth-century stone masons had completed their work on the cathedral, the artists followed, glorifying their creation with the brilliance of gilding and the exuberance of primitive colors. Every wall and screen was painted, pattern on vibrant color, and the paint and gilt lay over the stone like a skin, protecting it from the air's abrasion. Then, over the centuries, the custodians of the cathedral had lived and died and changed like everything else, and the raucous hues of the original decorations were slowly stripped away, replaced by pale classical colors or by nothing at all, leaving the gray-gold limestone naked and exposed to the onslaught of sulphur dioxide.

Gordon had worked with the rest of the Grafton Cathedral Conservation Advisory Committee for more than two years in preparation for this week. Over the next few days the scaffolders would arrive with their poles and planks to erect a membrane around the cathedral. After that the restoration of the sickened stone could begin. He had just come from another committee meeting, at which the cathedral's conservationist dean had announced that the Preservation Trust, with the Prince of Wales as its patron, had raised a further million pounds to enable a second stage of restoration to follow on from the first. The work would take years, but the prospect of it beginning gave Gordon a firm sense of professional achievement. This solid spur stuck up from the sea of his personal confusion like the ridged back of an island.

He stood up now and gathered his belongings. He was not quite sure where he was going. The house was empty and he was disinclined to go back to it. Vicky would be in the hospital for several more days and his daughters were still with his parents-in-law. He had no obligations except for his work and the daily visits to Vicky and the baby. The brief interval of freedom was liberating, but also disconcerting. He found himself moving cautiously, as if probing for invisible barriers. He received the telephone calls, the invitations from the Grafton couples, one by one, and politely refused all of them.

Gordon went out the side door, closing it behind him on the organ music and its echoes. It was not yet dark, but the green was rainy and windswept, an expanse of wet grass and fugitive leaves. He hesitated, with the massed ranks of saints and prophets soaring in their blackened niches behind him. Then he began to walk. He was halfway down the length of Dean's Row when he met the woman. At first she was just a face possessing the kind of unknown familiarity that might have sprung out of a dream. Then she took on a more solid shape. She was wearing a rainproof jacket, boots, and an emerald-green scarf, and her red hair was pulled haphazardly back and tied at the nape. Her face was shiny, as if she had walked a long way in the open air. They were almost past each other, but then they stopped and looked back.

"I'm Gordon Ransome," he reminded her. "We met at the Frosts'. We danced together."

"I remember." Nina had reached the steps to her front door. She climbed one step up, and with the height advantage could look down at him. He was pale, and the rims of his eyes were reddened and sore.

"I heard about the baby. Congratulations."

"Thank you."

Gordon wanted to keep her where she was, to hold her shining face in front of him, and he wondered nervously what to say next. But it was Nina who asked him, "Are you busy? Would you like to come in and have a cup of tea?"

They talked in the kitchen together, making the conventional exchanges about the house and its position and Nina's move to Grafton, and all the time Gordon watched her opening cupboard doors, reaching up to take cups from a shelf, placing the filled teapot on a tray. She was tall, with long bones and faintly awkward limbs. He could imagine her white feet, the spaces between her toes, and the curved chain of her spine, nape to coccyx, as clearly as if they were exposed to his eyes. She was smooth and clean, like her surroundings. The kitchen was very neat, all its surfaces bare and gleaming, and this orderliness contrasted sharply with Vicky's housekeeping. Vicky believed that the children's happiness and creativity counted for more than clean tiles, and so the floors silted up with toys and the walls sprouted drawings and crayoned messages.

"How is Vicky?" Nina asked.

"Not as fit as after the other two. It takes longer to recover from a cesarean, obviously. She might be there for as long as a week. But she'll be fine, and there are no problems with the baby. She's feeding well, doing the right things. Vicky's a natural mother."

"Is she?"

"She always has been, even before we had our own. She has an extraordinary affinity for children. Partly to do with her work—she's a psychotherapist. She works with troubled children. She has only been able to do it part-time recently, of course. But I'm told she's very, very good."

He took the tray from her and followed her up the stairs.

"What will Vicky do now?"

The question startled him at first, but then he realized that Nina meant about her career now that they had Helen to take care of as well.

"She'll be able to work in the mornings I should think. There's a woman who lives locally—her own children are grown up—and she comes in sometimes to take over when Vicky's at work. She's completely trustworthy."

"That's good," Nina answered, conscious of the surface neutrality of the exchange. Her ears strained to hear some barely audible subtext. It was there, but she couldn't decipher it yet.

Next to the hearth there was a basket of kindling and logs. Gordon knelt down and twisted newspaper into a thick wad, then flicked a match to it. He made a pyramid of kindling over the flames in the grate, deftly supplementing it with thicker pieces of wood as the fire crackled and caught. He rested on his heels for a moment, watching its progress, his back to Nina. The yellow light transformed the bare room, softening and warming it.

For Nina it was like being given a present to have the luxury of company, to have Gordon making a fire for her with casual masculine efficiency. Her own efforts usually led to a half-charred mound of wood and nothing more than a wisp of acrid smoke, so that quite often she didn't even bother to try. Nina half-smiled at the blatancy of this stereotyping. She would have liked to imagine that she could light a fire as well as any Boy Scout, but the truth was that she couldn't. She had made many such discoveries since Richard's death.

Gordon turned around. He saw the glimmer of her amusement, and wondered at it. He thought perhaps she was laughing at his fire-lighting technique.

"Don't you have any bigger logs than these?"

"Come and have your tea," Nina said. "I haven't found out where to get logs yet. I don't suppose it's too difficult."

"I can arrange a delivery for you, if that would help."

As he moved, leaving the fire and coming to sit down opposite her, Nina became aware that she was attracted to him.

At the beginning, at the Frosts' party, she had only seen that Gordon was sleek and prosperous-looking, and no more than conventionally handsome. Now the firelight illuminated much more. She sensed the avid curiosity and alertness in him, a raw eagerness for new experience that lifted him out of the ordinary. He also gave off a distinct tang of sexual challenge. Nina scented it and responded. The realization that Gordon attracted her delivered itself fully formed, with all the physical manifestations. A thick heat spread like a slow current pumping through her veins. She shifted in her place, glancing behind her as if her burning skin might mark the cushions where she sat. Gordon's cup rattled in its saucer when she passed it across to him.

"Perhaps," she said. "Yes, that would be kind."

The man wasn't looking at her. She was grateful and also disappointed. There was a confused image of his wife behind him, in the full sail of pregnancy, and the faces of his children like cherubs out of the stained glass in the cathedral. Gordon's head was turned away to the windows.

"You have a wonderful view from here."

The sun had set, and the lights illuminating the west façade had come on while they were watching the fire.

"It makes me and my belongings seem rather poor by comparison."

"I don't think so," he said quietly. And then, "Do you know what's about to happen?"

She put her cup down slowly. Gordon looked at her hands, with the wedding ring and a diamond on her left one. She pushed her fingers through her hair, and he remembered the revolving lights settling on it and changing its color before circling on.

"What is about to happen?"

"A huge conservation program. To restore the exterior first and then, eventually, the interior. Have you noticed how eroded the statues are?"

He beckoned to her and they went and stood at the window. In the floodlights the stone figures shone in their ascending tiers.

"Look at the faces, the hands."

They were worn, chewed down almost to featurelessness. Noses and fingers and in places feet and whole heads had been lost. The stone was blackened and pitted.

"They are very old," Nina said softly, to defend them.

"They're so old and fragile that if we don't do something to preserve them they'll crumble away altogether. Luckily something can be done. Tomorrow the first scaffolding crews arrive. That portion of the façade will be covered"—he gestured with his hand close to her shoulder—"so the work can begin."

"Is that your work?" she asked.

"I'm an engineer, not a conservationist. But my company is part of the restoration team, yes."

Nina gazed at the inscrutable faces.

"How can they be repaired?"

"The damage has been done by sulphate crystals building up on the stone. The rain dissolves the salts and washes them into the tiny cracks, and then the wind and sun dry them and harden them into crusts that split and flake the stone away. The treatment is to apply a coat of lime, like a poultice."

Gordon wanted to talk about this. The prospect of the ancient fabric being regenerated was an affirmation of some greater good, which he was anxious to have acknowledged, and he was also fascinated by the mechanical and chemical techniques used by the conservationists. But he did not want to bore the woman by ploughing unstoppably on about stone and scaffolding.

"That won't bring the faces back, will it?" Nina asked.

He said, "There is a way of rebuilding them."

"How?"

She *was* interested, he could tell by her voice and expression. He felt a charge of pleasure.

"They soak lengths of hessian in baths of lime wash, then they wrap the statues in the hessian. The wash sucks out the dirt—the blackness that you can see—and at the same time feeds natural lime back into the stone."

"Giving it back its strength."

"Exactly. And the missing features—noses or fingers or even whole heads—can be rebuilt with mortar."

Nina looked out at the statues. She saw now, in the floodlighting, that many of them were damaged. She imagined all the battalions of prophets and angels reawakening, intact again, and shining out once their shrouds of limed cloth had fallen away.

"It will be like a little Judgment Day," she said, more to herself than to Gordon.

"Yes. I thought that, too."

"Only that would be to deify the Conservation Committee, wouldn't it?" She smiled sidelong at him.

"No, we're only the instrument of a higher authority, of course," Gordon answered.

They stood in silence for a moment, contemplating the scale of the work that was about to begin. There was perhaps a foot of empty air between them, but it was as if their skins were touching.

"How many statues are there?"

"Three hundred and twelve, from the Madonna and Child to the rank-and-file martyrs in the topmost row."

"I shall enjoy watching the work."

"There won't be a great deal to see. You'll lose your splendid view to an expanse of tarpaulin, I'm afraid."

"I shan't mind that," Nina replied.

Gordon looked at his watch. It took him a moment to register what time it was. He had been in Nina's house much longer than he would have guessed, and it was time he went to the hospital to see Vicky and the baby. He found himself looking at Nina's hair, wondering what would happen if he picked up a strand and wound it between his fingers. He cleared his throat, sounding in his own ears like an over-eager schoolboy.

"If you're interested, I could take you around the cathedral to show you what the long-term conservation plans are."

"Yes. I would like that. Very much."

She was facing him now. They were silhouettes in the uncurtained window, for any invisible passersby on the green to see. Gordon moved away toward the door, saying quickly, "I'll call tomorrow afternoon, at about the same time, and we can go across together."

Nina agreed. She would wait for him, and then they would go to look at the cathedral's Gothic arches and fan vaulting.

When he was gone and she was alone again, she missed him in the spaces of the house.

4

Through the glass partition at the end of his office, Gordon could just see his partner at his desk.

Andrew was working with his head bent over a sheaf of estimates and a calculator. He had been sitting in the same position for perhaps an hour, while Gordon shifted the papers on his own desk into different heaps.

Andrew's calm absorption grated on him; the irritation felt like sandpaper patches caught between the hard plates and the tender lining of his skull. He had plenty of his own work to do. He had spent the first hour of his day out on a site on the other side of the county, and had gone from there to a meeting with the county planners, who were proposing to build a sports complex there. He was supposed to be writing a report to accompany the Frost Ransome tender for the structural-engineering work, but he had not even looked at his notes. He had thought of nothing but the day's slow progress toward four o'clock, and his visit with Nina to the cathedral.

His private line rang. He picked it up, wondering if she could somehow have discovered this number, but it was Vicky.

"Yes. Yes, love, of course I am. Just busy. How are *you*?"

"Stitches are a bit sore, and I'm quite tired. The ward was very noisy last night. Two new arrivals. One woman with twins."

He heard the quiver in her voice. She wanted his sympathy but didn't want to admit to it. This tremulous mixure of vulnerability and stoicism worked again at the sandpaper patches in his head.

"Poor Vicky. And poor woman. How's Helen today?"

"Much more wide awake. I've just fed her, and she's lying here with her eyes open, looking at me."

He felt a jolt of protective love for both of them that went awkwardly but inevitably in tandem with his irritation. "Look after yourselves until I come in this evening."

"Talk to me for five minutes. Tell me some news. It's so boring and lonely in here."

She was about to cry. It was the complicated measure of post-partum hormones, Gordon reasoned for her. Was the rush of anxious sadness the same after a cesarean birth as after a normal one? Of course, it had to be. Perhaps even more intense. He must try to have a word with the ward sister in the evening.

"Gordon?"

He told her about the morning's work, about the site visit and the report waiting to be written, parceling up and delivering the small subjects and avoiding the big one that he felt like a thick layer of felted wool between them.

"Darling, I have to get on with some work now," he said at the end. "I'll see you later."

"Love you," Vicky said in a small voice.

"Love you, too."

He picked up his pen and made himself pitch into the dreary depths of his morning's notes as if they were a cold sea. At the end of twenty minutes he had written an acceptable draft. He looked at his watch and saw that it was three-forty.

In the corridor, as he struggled into his coat in his hurry to leave the building, he met Andrew. Andrew's blue shirt was as crisp as it had been earlier in the day, but the knot of his blue-and-lilac paisley tie was loosened to indicate that he was in full-tilt mode.

"Are you going to the hospital?" Andrew asked mildly. He was interested, properly concerned, without giving out even a breath of criticism of his partner's unscheduled departure in the middle of a busy day.

"Yes. Looking in at the cathedral for something first, actually."

Andrew was less interested in the restoration project than Gordon was.

"Ah. See you in the morning then, about the supermarket drawings?"

"Yes. Yes, I'll be in by half-eight," Gordon called over his shoulder. His car was parked in his reserved slot in the rear of the building. Behind the wheel, on the short drive into town, he felt as if he had made some thrilling and ingenious escape.

He found that he was laughing with pleasure and exhilaration, at his freedom and at the prospect of seeing Nina.

Nina was already in the cathedral. In the last days she had begun to feel comfortable in Grafton, as if she were settled in her own place rather than crouching in hiding, and this new feeling of being at ease had grown with the welcome that the women had extended to her.

But since yesterday afternoon, since watching Gordon light the fire in her living room, her perspective had shifted again. She was excited and fearful, and so she had left the house early and walked the short way over the green, certain that Gordon would find her. She sat at the back of the nave, at the end of the last row of wooden pews, watching the darkening glory of the east window.

Gordon had to cross the green from the opposite side, and so when he passed the west door he made the small detour under the bare ribs of the newly erected scaffolding and in through the inner door, as if to check that the interior was all that it should be before he called her. He saw her at once, sitting with her back to him, with her long limbs folded and seeming more elegant in repose. He was overtaken by gratitude and happiness that she should be here, in the great dim space, quietly waiting for him. He went to her and put his hand on her shoulder. He didn't lift it when she turned her face up to look at him.

"I'm glad to see you," he told her, offering her the truth without any varnish of social nicety.

"And I you."

The quiet solemnity of her response pleased him, too.

When she stood up, her height and the shoes she was wearing put her eyes on a level with his.

"Show me," Nina said.

He said, trying to sound light, "Now you've asked for it."

He took her on a slow tour of the aisles and side-chapels. She listened gravely as he explained the projected works, asking an occasional question but mostly staying quiet while he talked.

"It takes a long time to assess the effects of stone-conservation work," Gordon said. "Perhaps a hundred years, or even more. The

Victorians saw what was happening here and tried to reverse it by painting over the stone with a kind of impervious varnish. It was the favored technique at the time, the best available to them. But the outer coat hardened still further with years of exposure, and underneath it the stone just softened and crumbled away. See this?"

They had passed through a Gothic doorway on the south side of the chancel into a pillared hallway. Ahead of them an exuberant flight of stone steps curved upward under an intricately vaulted ceiling. Nina paused at the bottom step. It was hollowed and worn to a shine, but when the springing geometry of the stairs drew her eyes upward, she also saw the black flakes of stone that were breaking away to reveal the paler crust beneath. The thirteenth-century magnificence had come to look sickly, diseased. Gordon stooped beside her, one hand splayed over the base of a pillar. He rubbed with the tips of his fingers into a stone hollow the size of his fist, then withdrew his hand to show her that it was gritty with dust.

"Can it be put right?" Nina asked.

"We can try. Using the best methods at our disposal, and hoping to be more successful than the Victorians. Some of these pillars will have to be replaced."

Nina tilted her head back, following the jets of stone with her eyes, imagining the scale of the work.

"The rest will be treated in the same way as the exterior, with lime wash colored with stone dust and skimmed milk to match the old stone as closely as possible. The coating protects the stone but lets it breathe at the same time. In a hundred years or so the cathedral's new conservators will know whether we have been successful or not."

Nina liked the absence from his meticulous explanation of both arrogance and the assumption of omnipotence, but she was also warmed by his underlying optimism. It was satisfying to contemplate the endurance of the cathedral, this medieval glory of branching pillars and moldings decorated with ball flowers, solid and cared-for and beloved, at the heart of the other, careless Grafton, with its parking lots and chain stores and shopping precinct. She thought of the perpetual counterpoise that underlay this urban contrast, between spiritual endurance and material desire, and was pleased to find it so neatly summarized around her.

Somewhere out of sight, beyond the curve of the stairs, a door opened and the dim air filled with chattering voices. Around the corner appeared a stream of choirboys dressed in ruffs and white surplices over plum-colored robes. They swept past Nina and Gordon, jostling one another and surreptitiously laughing, and descended into the cathedral. Behind them came the choirmaster and a line of senior choristers, and then a chaplain with a heavy bunch of keys. Gordon nodded to most of the men as they passed and held up his hand in greeting to the priest. It was time for evensong

Nina and Gordon followed behind them, then turned down the length of the nave to the west door again.

"Thank you," Nina said when they reached the door. Inside her head was a rich collage of decorated stone and candlelight and fluttering surplices.

"I hope I didn't bore you?" Gordon asked stiffly. He was suddenly aware that he had done all the talking and that she had barely spoken.

"No." Nina smiled at him. The choir had begun to rehearse a Te Deum. The boys' voices climbed up, and higher, as invincible in their harmony as the soaring steps they had just come scuffling down.

Outside, it was dark. Gordon wondered disconnectedly where he should offer to take her now, trying to calculate how much time was left to him. Could they go to the Eagle? Across to the Dean's Row house again? He couldn't bear the idea of losing sight of her, but he knew he would soon have to go to the hospital, and somewhere within himself find the buoyancy to lift Vicky out of her depression.

Nina was still smiling. The splendor of the cathedral, and the singing, and the startling pleasure she felt in Gordon's company had lapped together with the images of regeneration in the conservation work to produce a high, curling wave of happiness in her.

She knew that since Richard's death she had been walking inside a blank-walled box and had been unable to raise her head to look outside it. Now, astoundingly, there seemed to be a glimpse of another world beyond the confinement of her loneliness. She longed for the luxury of giving and receiving love again, and the intensity of her need blurred her awareness of other realities.

The memory of Vicky Ransome pregnant in her white dress

came back to Nina, and she felt a premonition of guilt. Gordon was another woman's husband, and Nina was familiar enough with pain not to wish to inflict it on anyone else. But then, she thought, through the distorting blur of longing, Vicky had her babies and her husband and their life together, whereas she had no one. She did not want to hurt anyone, only to take some secret share of the happiness that seemed so close, and tangible, and utterly desirable.

Nina closed her eyes for a second. She was dizzy with a sense of multiplying possibilities. She was half-afraid of what Gordon Ransome threatened, of the edge they were balanced upon, but at the same time she was compelled to pitch herself over it. She thought that Gordon was going to reach out and touch her. She stepped away, containing herself for the moment, although she knew she would not be able to do so for much longer. She muttered, "I should get back now. I have some work to finish."

Her immediate need was for solitude. She had no doubt that there would be tomorrow for Gordon and herself, tomorrow and other days. This confidence surprised her, but she did not question it.

Gordon found that he almost ran after her like a boy. He darted out to stand in front of her, cutting off her line of retreat.

"Shall we meet again? Perhaps I could buy you lunch tomorrow?"

No, not lunch, he remembered. He was committed to lunch with Andrew and a pair of retailing entrepreneurs for whom they did a great deal of work.

"Or dinner, rather? Could you manage that? It would have to be a little late, perhaps after the hospital . . ."

He heard her cutting short his own bluster.

"Dinner would be fine. Thank you."

"I'll pick you up at about half past eight." He had to call after her. Her heels clicked musically on the cobbles as she swung away from him. Gordon found that he was smiling when he went to retrieve his car from the malodorous recesses of the multi-level parking garage.

He was early for visiting. Vicky looked up in pleased surprise when he edged around the floral curtain protecting her bed. Helen was in her arms, a white bundle of hospital blanket, and Marcelle Wickham was sitting in the single armchair next to her.

"Hello, darling, is everything all right?" Vicky asked him. He acknowledged silently that it was a matter for concern nowadays if he did anything even a minute off schedule.

"Of course it is. I wanted to see you both, that's all." He kissed her overheated forehead and laid one finger against the baby's cheek. He kissed Marcelle too, noticing her perfume, reminded by it of dancing with her at parties. Then he looked around for somewhere to sit. The curtained space was full of bunches of flowers, fading fast in the heat. The flowers, pushed into inappropriate vases that were mostly too small, looked as uncomfortable as he felt.

"Sit here, Gordon. I'm on my way back to pick up the kids from their nativity play rehearsal." Marcelle stood up.

"No, Marcelle, you don't have to rush away because Gordon's arrived."

"Stay a bit longer. I haven't seen you for weeks." Husband and wife spoke in unison, unwilling to have the buffer removed from between them.

"This baby is gorgeous." Marcelle bent over to admire her once more. "You're so lucky."

Her face was drawn with sadness. Gordon wondered if she wanted another baby herself, and if dour Michael Wickham wouldn't agree to it. He remembered how, at a barbecue one summer afternoon, his tongue loosened by beer, Michael had complained to him. "Bloody kids. They're like vampires aren't they? They take every hour of the day and every ounce of your energy, more from your wife, even, and they still want more. Why do we do it, all of us?"

They had been surrounded by the children of the various families, by the noise of a rounders game and cries of "It's not fair" and "He hurt me." Gordon couldn't remember what he had said in response.

Marcelle had gone. Gordon sat down in the chair and Vicky gave the baby to him. He looked down at the little face, seeing Mary and Alice in the compressed features. The same, each time, but different. He held this tenacious fragment of optimistically combined genes for a moment and then laid her in the crib beside the bed.

"Marcelle brought me a picnic from the school. I was hungry," Vicky explained. There was a white box on the bedside table, and when he looked into it he saw the remnants of some savory pie and two brandy snaps. Vicky had a sweet tooth. He felt he was being criticized for not having thought to bring her anything to eat himself, especially when he knew the hospital food was poor. He took her hand and wound his fingers through hers. Her fingers had swollen up toward the end of the pregnancy, and she had had to take off her rings.

"Are you still feeling blue?"

"Not too bad."

Vicky hoisted herself up against the pillows, making a face at the discomfort as she did so.

"It's only the stitches, really."

Gordon had not seen the wound since he had watched the delivery itself. He imagined the line of stitching now, just above the curling hair where he had liked to kiss her. It would be like a closed mouth, he thought. The scar would fade to a faint white line—the doctors had told them that.

"You'll be better soon."

"I know. It's okay. Have you had a busy day?"

Very clearly, he heard the tonelessness of their questions and the other, unspoken dialogue concerning their separate and irreconcilable needs.

"Not really. I came here straight from the cathedral. The scaffolding is going up."

Vicky was even less interested in the conservation work than Andrew was. "It'll be up forever, I suppose. What a shame it has to be done now."

Now or in a hundred years, Gordon mused. *I might have missed seeing it.* He felt privileged to be part of this regeneration, and the thought of seeing it with Nina made him falter on a dancing beat of pleasure, so that he had to lean sideways, twitching at a parched flower that hung out of a vase, to hide his joy from Vicky.

Visiting time was in full flood. The ward was clicking with

cameras and humming with the noise of older siblings who slid on the polished floor and swung on the high ends of the beds.

"I called the girls this afternoon, after I spoke to you," Vicky said, her eyes on the other mothers' children.

"Is everything all right?"

"Mum says they're both a bit weepy and anxious. Alice wet her bed last night." She hesitated, and then said without looking at him. "I wondered if it might be a good idea for you to bring them back early? They could have the weekend at home with you, and come in to see the baby before we bring her back."

It was a challenge to him, like an unorthodox move in a chess game. Vicky was giving him an opening to show his concern for his children's well-being by removing them from their grandparents and attending to them himself through a winter weekend. Like a drowning man, Gordon glimpsed a series of flickering images from his two days of freedom. He saw Nina in her green scarf, and the squared lights and shadows that divided the ceiling of her cool, bare living room.

"I have a mound of paperwork to do, love. If I clear it while you're in here, I'll have more time once you do get home. And I think it'll be more unsettling for the girls to whisk them back again when they're expecting to stay longer with Marjorie and Alec. They'll think something is wrong."

Vicky pleated the white sheet between her fingers. Her stomach still made a noticeable mound under the covers.

"All right. It was just a thought."

He put his hand over hers. "Mary and Alice are fine. How could they not be, with a mother like you?"

"And a father like you." There were a dozen edges to her words. Gordon felt the stubborn bedrock of his resistance when he smiled back at her.

"We'll be okay, all of us. Just rest and get your strength back."

It was almost the end of visiting hours. He leaned over Vicky and kissed her as he had done when he arrived, and he patted her folded hands, but she would not look at him. Gordon felt the queasy swell of tenderness and rancor, although now spiked with premonitory guilt.

"See you tomorrow."

"Yes. Gordon?"

"What is it?"

"Is everything all right?" The bland formula of a searching question. It delivered her fears up to him, a package she wanted him to unwrap.

"Of course it is. I want you to come home, that's all." Bland and tidy lies, also. Putting aside the parcel.

"Only two or three more days." She leaned back against the pillows, relinquishing him.

On his way out, Gordon found the ward sister in her office. He mentioned Vicky's depression as if she might offer some potion to dispel it.

"Nothing to worry about," she reassured him. "Mums with two or three children already at home often worry if they will be able to cope with the new one, you know. It can seem a daunting prospect, especially after the physical stress of a Caesar."

The sister seemed young for such a position of responsibility. She had a round face and short hair under her cap. Gordon noted her attractiveness automatically, without further speculation.

"Vicky will cope," he said. It was the rampart of maternal competence that she had erected that made him feel excluded, or at best edged out to the margins in their all-female family. The petulant thought eased his guilt a little.

"With the right backup," the sister said. Gordon caught the hint of a rebuke, but now that he was almost free he was ready to ignore it.

"Of course." He smiled at her, then made his way down the corridors with the stream of departing visitors and out to his car.

The quiet house soothed him. Gordon walked through the rooms with a tumbler of whisky in his hand. He didn't want anything to eat, and in any case the spirits tasted much better than food, good and fiery in the back of his throat.

He went upstairs into the children's bedroom and knelt beside Alice's bed to bury his face in her pillow. He smelled the ghost of her in the sheets, in her nightgown which was pushed under the quilt. The absence of their antiphonal breathing, of the hot exhalations of childish dreams, made him long for them to be home again.

But at the same time he savored this brief isolation in his own house. He listened to its sounds, to the boiler firing and the swill of water in the pipes, with a fresh ear.

Gordon stood up again and smoothed Alice's pillow to remove the imprint of his face. He went through into the big bedroom and made a slow circuit of the bed. He had made it this morning, although he could never get the white cover to lie in the right folds, like Vicky did. The bed looked lumpy, disheveled, as if it were concealing something. Gordon picked up an ornate perfume bottle from the dressing table, then put it down again without sniffing it. He rearranged the boxes and photographs on top of it and saw the prints they left against the faint film of dust that covered the dresser. One of the top drawers was open a little. He drew it out further and looked in at the satiny straps, bones, and folds of Vicky's underwear.

Suddenly he turned away and sat down heavily on his own side of the bed. He picked up the bedside telephone and sat with it on his lap while he groped on a lower shelf for the directory. When he found it he flipped impatiently through the pages looking for the name of the couple who had owned the Dean's Row house before Nina. It was the only "Collins" listed and he found it quickly. He dialed the number without waiting to think.

She answered after two rings, saying her name rather than hello. Her voice sounded amused, as if she were smiling into the mouthpiece.

"Nina, it's Gordon. Gordon Ransome."

"Yes."

It was a statement, not a question, and it made him think that she had even been expecting his call.

"I just wanted to talk to you."

It was much easier to say it over the telephone. He suddenly felt that he could confess anything to her and that she would listen with sympathy. "I couldn't wait all the time until tomorrow evening."

He had crossed a divide now. He couldn't go back and pretend merely to be a friendly conservationist. He felt a new pressure within himself, like an inflating balloon, and realized that it was happiness.

"I'm glad you called. I wanted to talk, too. I thought you might be a friend of mine, Patrick, from London."

Gordon was fired with jealousy toward this unknown man.

"Are you disappointed that it isn't?"

Nina laughed then. "No. Not disappointed at all."

Gordon felt this first avowal like a thread between them that stretched through the air from the well-worn territory of his house away into the darkness, to some new terrain that was lying in wait for him to discover.

"What are you doing?" he asked.

"Sitting in my kitchen. Looking at all these doors and cupboards with nothing much in them."

She had not wanted to sit in the upstairs living room; the view, and the ashes of the fire he had lit still lying in the grate, seemed too closely connected with him. She was as eager as a girl, and also fearful of whatever maneuvers tomorrow evening would bring.

Gordon recalled the bareness of her house. "You're traveling light."

"It seemed the easiest way."

He knew that this was an acknowledgment of her reason for coming to Grafton and of all the attendant truths that she would reveal to him in time, in their own shared time. He imagined these truths peeling away like layers of fine tissue, each layer matched by a discarded layer of his own, until they knew each other entirely.

The vision made him confident and he asked. "Would you like me to come over now?"

After a moment's pause she answered, "No. Let's meet tomorrow, as we arranged."

It was illogical, but she felt the need to preserve some propriety in case it became necessary to defend herself against him. She also wanted to give herself the pleasure of anticipation. It seemed a long time since she had looked forward to anything. She tried to imagine Gordon at the other end of the line, in some orderly domestic setting like Janice Frost's, amid children's toys and family-dented furniture.

A black wing of guilt shadowed her. Gordon did have a home with his wife and their three little girls, and it would indeed be full of the accumulated memories of family life. Nina knew that she did not want to disturb any of that. She only wanted to take a small piece of comfort for herself. The black wing hovered for a moment longer, and then flew on.

"Gordon?"

"I'm still here."

"Is everything all right?"

The same question that Vicky had asked, but this time meriting an altogether different answer.

"Yes," he said simply, knowing that it was, and that if it wasn't they would make it so between them.

"Good night, then," Nina whispered.

"Good night. I'll be there tomorrow."

The dinner was not a success. Gordon chose the restaurant because it was some miles away from Grafton and not much frequented by anyone he knew. When they arrived, they found that they were almost the only people in the over-frilled dining room. They sat facing each other across a daunting table, feeling themselves under the scrutiny of the tiptoeing waitresses. The food was pretentious and poor, and soupy music washed over them all the time they were eating.

Gordon was angry at himself for his bad choice, and as embarrassed as an adolescent on a disastrous first date. He dissected the food on his plate, chewing but tasting nothing, while Nina barely touched hers. Gordon was made more uncomfortable by his conviction that Nina and her husband would have been regulars in whichever London restaurants were the fashion of the week, and that she must be judging this provincial fiasco with a cold eye. Gordon did not know London well and was mistrustful of city gloss. He understood himself well enough to know that he was a success in a small town and that he had been satisfied with that—until now, when he contemplated his distance from Nina.

Their talk was stilted. They made openings and waited for each other to respond, but their gambits were not bold enough to overcome the music and the eavesdroppers, and the subjects faltered and dried up one by one. In the end they discussed their work, the cathedral project, Grafton, and the achievements of Gordon's daughters like the strangers they were. Nina was wearing a scarlet

jacket braided and frogged with black silk, and with her pale face
Gordon thought she looked like some androgynous, doomed hussar.
He wanted to hold her, to shield her from enemy cavalry, instead of
sitting over cooling food and talking about his children's education.
Gordon wondered if yesterday's intimacy had been a hallucination.

At last the meal was over. He paid for it without totaling the
bill and they went out into the cold air. He held open the door of
his car for her and she got in, composedly arranging her limbs and
her large hands and feet and then keeping still in the way that he
now recognized, with a helpless wash of admiration, as familiar.

They drove in silence for a little while. Then, because he
thought he had to say something or they would drive all the way
to Grafton without speaking, Gordon ventured, "Sorry. That was
bloody awful."

"It doesn't matter."

She said it coolly, a statement of fact. He realized that she was
telling him the truth. She wasn't judging him or the restaurant or
adopting an air of martyrdom about the disappointing evening, as
Vicky would have done. The meal had not been important; whether
it was magnificent or mediocre, it was simply a preliminary rite
they had to enact together.

"I wanted to take you somewhere special, a place you'd remember," he explained. The intimacy had not disappeared. In this
leathery space, dimly illuminated by the dashboard lights, he felt
its softness between them.

"I will remember."

To his amazement, she reached out and took his hand, lifting it
off the wheel so that he had to drive one-handed, and then she
linked her fingers through his. She held both their hands tight
against her warm thigh. In his happiness and gratitude Gordon
wanted to close his eyes and rest his head in her lap.

"Let's go home," Nina said.

They reached Grafton, and Gordon parked his inconspicuous
car in an inconspicuous corner a short distance from the cathedral.
They walked quickly through the narrow entryway onto the green,
where a street lamp shone on them and made them hurry, not
looking at each other, out into the relative darkness of the green
itself. The cathedral was a black shape hanging perpendicular to

their left. They turned right, down Dean's Row, passing the secure doors and curtained windows of Nina's neighbors. Gordon thought fleetingly of the families behind these domestic defenses. He knew that he was about to leave his own married castle behind him, with its moat and battlements, and that he was doing it gladly.

They reached Nina's front door. She unlocked it and let him into her house.

They stood in the hallway, the door secured behind them. There was a light burning over their heads, a plain glass lantern too bright for their eyes. Gordon watched her unbutton her coat and set her bag down.

Then she turned to him, and he caught her by the elbows and held her against him. She turned her face up and he kissed her. Her mouth opened at once, he tasted her tongue, and suddenly both of them were full of hot confusion, rubbing their faces together and panting a little. He pushed her backward against the wall. His fingers fumbled with the frogging of her jacket until somehow it opened. He found a silky layer underneath it, a confusion of lace and straps, and into his head swam the memory of Vicky's drawer filled with the same female things. Only they were not quite the same, and his surprise and pleasure at the difference shot through him like a hot, burning wire so that he closed his eyes and knotted his fingers in her hair while their mouths sucked greedily together.

The light was very bright. When he opened his eyes again he saw Nina staring into them, the reflections in her black pupils receding to a point beyond his reach. She wriggled sideways and slipped out of his grasp. In the same movement she shrugged off her coat and left it hanging over the banister. The open front of her jacket showed a black slip and some black lace over white skin faintly marked with tea-colored freckles.

"Come upstairs," she said in her clear voice.

She held her hand out to lead him but he followed at once, watching the swing of her hips and the tightening of her calf muscles as she climbed the stairs.

Her bedroom was on the third floor, above the living room. It has the same view of the shrouded cathedral façade. Nina released the shutters from their wooden recesses and folded them across the windows, securing them neatly with the old catches. Gordon waited at the foot of the bed, watching her. She switched on a lamp on a low table and he saw a scrolled wooden headboard and a plain white cover. There were none of the lace-edged pillows or ancestral teddy bears favored by Vicky.

Nina took off her red jacket and put it aside. She stepped out of her skirt and he saw that she was wearing stockings with lace tops and ribbon suspenders. Vicky always wore tights, and he recalled how the mesh paled over the half-moons of her buttocks when she bent down in the closed space of their bedroom.

He stumbled toward Nina, reaching for her, his mouth dry. But she evaded him, smiling a little, and he was left standing while she bent and stretched to pull her short slip over her head by the lacy hem. Then she raised first one foot and then the other on to a chair to unhook her stockings from the ribbon tongues. He watched her peel the nylon skin down the freckled whiteness of her thighs.

Nina watched him watching her, evidently gauging the impact of this half-ironic sketch of a striptease.

She shook out the wisps of stocking and laid them tidily across her folded skirt and slip. Then she stood upright, in her black panties and brassiere, with one arm folded across her chest and the other over her stomach.

"It's a long time since I undressed in front of a man."

A man not her husband, Gordon translated, *a man not connected to her by the daily familiarity of body textures and scents, sweet or stale, in the uncritical and mundane context of marriage.*

"You are lovely," he said, although he had not yet arranged his impressions into an opinion. "Let me look at you."

Wanting to match her, he unbuckled his belt and undid the trousers of his second-best suit, navy-blue with faint pinstripes. Vicky called it his Tory suit because she thought it made him look like the Home Secretary. He hung the trousers over the back of another chair and faced her in his socks and shirt-tails, his erection tenting the white cotton in front of him. Nina unwound her arms and slid against him, quickly, so he only glimpsed her white belly and the blue shadow between the lace cups of her bra. She unbuttoned his shirt and slid her hands inside it, over the muscles of his back and the collar of flesh around his midriff.

"Getting fat," he whispered, his mouth against her hair.

"Just acquiring some solidity."

Her head was bent. She seemed smaller now out of her high heels, more fine-boned. Her shoulders were narrow and marked by bigger freckles, almost blotches. She was looking down, sliding her hand under the elastic waistband of his shorts. Her fingers grasped him. Gordon lifted his hands over her head, like a victorious boxer, to give her the freedom to do what she wanted. He tore open his cuffs and dropped his shirt to the floor. She stretched the elastic ribbing and pulled it down over his hips to expose him. Her mouth was slightly open, her lower lip protruding. It made her look solemn, judicious. She moved her fist up and down so that the head of his penis was shrouded and then revealed again. While they looked at it a tear of moisture bled from its open eye.

It's odd, this slow motion, Gordon thought. He couldn't remember when he had last felt so aroused, but at the same time he was held back from the burning in his balls and the threatened kick at the base of his spine by Nina's dreamy detachment.

"You're making it stand up and touch my chin," he said.

That was better. He saw the fastidious twitch at the corner of her mouth, but at the same time there was a drooping and thickening of her eyelids, as if a little surge of blood had puffed them out. It made him think she liked to hear him speak that way.

Nina held him in her hand, weighing his balls. She put her thumb under his shaft and ran it upward to the tip, feeling the shiver the motion drew out of him.

The man, Gordon, rocked on his feet, spreading his toes on her polished floorboards, leaving faint, moist prints. Richard had never used words like *dick*. His lovemaking had been tender, affectionate rather than headlong. But this man was not Richard, nor was he anything like Richard. That was a good thing.

She knelt down, looking at him for a moment, at the thick mat of hair that tapered upward to the umbilicus, the solid thighs and broad belly. Then, using her fingers to guide it, she took his penis in her mouth. She ran her tongue around the constricted neck, tasting the salt and iron. Gordon cupped his hands around the back of her skull, bracing his legs and arching his back so that she could attend to him.

He let himself think of staying like that, swelling into her mouth until he came against her palate. *But no*, he thought.

"Let me look at you," he said again.

He tilted her head back so that he saw her foggy eyes, then he lifted her up. He unhooked her bra, drew the straps off her shoulders, and put his mouth against the red chafe line, where the color of her freckles changed from tea to rust. Her breasts were small, with bumpy brown nipples, and they pointed downward and outward. He rubbed the nipples in turn between his fingers as she wound her arm around his neck. She drew him backward, in an awkward dance-step, until the side of the bed caught her behind the knees and they fell onto the white cover. Nina bumped her hips up against him, pushing, trying to guide him with her hands, greedy now. Her eyes were closed, turned inward into her head. Her breasts fell aside, no longer elastic, to reveal the tender knobs of her breastbone.

Gordon held himself over her for an instant, enjoying this moment of dominance. He splayed his hands over her belly, then crooked his arm under her hips so that he could lift her. He slipped off her panties and knelt with his knees beneath her buttocks. She had a sparse lick of sandy hair and a surprisingly tight, flat stomach, like a boy's. Her hip bones jutted out prominently to either side. Vicky's belly was rounded and generous like the pillows on her bed, even between her pregnancies.

He bent his head over Nina, kneading her skin with the heels of his hands.

"Not a single stretch mark," he marveled, meaning only to convey his admiration. Vicky's skin between her navel and the points of her hips was marked with two fans of fine, silvery lines.

"Not a single pregnancy, either."

"I'm sorry. That was thoughtless of me."

"It's all right. We were happy as we were."

He didn't want to think of her husband at this minute, or of Nina's past life that he had no knowledge of, nor did he want to remember Vicky and everything else he knew too well. He lowered Nina's hips and slid away, over the side of the bed, to kneel in front of her. He put his tongue to the wet gingery hair, parted the lips, and worked at her until he heard her sigh.

Gordon lifted his head. Her hair was wound across her face like a veil. He moved again to lean over her, big and dark, and she opened her eyes to contemplate his face.

"I want to make love to you now," Gordon said.

"Yes," Nina said.

He pushed her legs wider, excited and made rough by her apparent submission, but she put her hands in the way to stop him.

"Shouldn't you use something?"

"I've got some in my jacket pocket."

After his lunch with Andrew and the retailers he had made an excuse before going back to the office. He had hurried to the pharmacy, making sure he didn't know the girl at the checkout, and had bundled his purchase through with some toothpaste and dental floss. In spite of his forethought, now that the time had come he didn't want to use them.

"But I had a medical a month ago, for insurance. A full blood test. Everything negative."

Her eyes were very close to his. The proximity made her appear cross-eyed, greedy.

"I trust you, then. And I haven't been with anyone since Richard died. I was always faithful to him before that."

He didn't want to hear about this fidelity, a tribute paid to love that was locked and sealed away from him. For answer he moved her hand out of the way and spread her open with his fingers. As he came into her, she asked, "Are you faithful to Vicky?"

He made the first thrust. "Not as of this minute."

She was hot and pleasingly tight around him. His entering her seemed to have released some catch. Her face changed and softened. She wound her legs around him, and when he found his rhythm her fingers raked over his back and worked his buttocks, pulling him into her. They rolled over and over again, their mouths covering each other's eyes and cheeks and throats.

She's good, Gordon thought. She was responsive and he liked that; he liked the whistle of her breath and the way she came up on top of him and worked up and down so that her bumpy little nipples hung over his chest with a sheen of sweat gleaming between them. They fitted together hand-in-glove.

"Turn over," he whispered. "I want to see your backside." He saw the concupiscent thickening of her eyelids again. Perhaps her husband hadn't talked to her in bed. She did as she was told, turning her head to one side with her mouth open so that a little wet patch of saliva formed on the pillow.

He came into her from behind and she stretched out her arms over the coiled sheets, clenching and opening her fists in alternating submission and aggression. Gordon licked her shoulders and rubbed them until the white skin flushed a dull pink, and then they rolled again and she twisted her legs around his waist, trapping him.

"Now you are mine," she said fiercely. She was holding his wrists, too.

"Is that what you want?" he whispered. Her hair had fallen back so that he could see her face. The skin was loosening over her cheekbones and under her eyes. The recognition of her imperfections, and of his own, filled him with sympathy and compassion for them both.

"I do *now*," Nina said.

"I am here now."

Her mouth looked sore. She bit her lower lip and he kissed it where the teeth marks showed for an instant in the chafed skin. He freed his hands and stroked her face as she tilted her hips upward to reach for him. Their carnality seemed interleaved with tenderness, and he knew that she felt it, too, because her face had changed again. It had become clear; he could see directly into it, as if the crosshatched skin had become transparent.

She said, "Oh," seemingly surprised.

He knew that she would come soon, and he worked harder at her. Both of them were panting now. When she did come it was with a series of small yelps that made him think of a nocturnal animal caught in the undergrowth. Her fingers dug into the thick muscles of his back, and her head fell blindly back to offer him the taut white cords of her throat.

Afterward she was breathless. She laughed, as if still surprised, and held herself against him, rocking them both.

After a little while she said, "Do you know what I would like?"

"What would you like?"

She had grown more confident, he noticed, made secure by their success so far and by her own satisfaction. Her eyes were bright and her tongue showed between her teeth.

"I'd like to drink you."

Gordon's breath caught. It had been his first thought when she knelt in front of him, and now the suggestion, offered so coolly, made him stiffen as he had done at the very beginning.

"Do, then."

She knelt between his legs and tucked her hair behind her ears with a prim gesture before lowering her mouth to him.

"Vicky doesn't like it. She says it makes her feel that she's going to choke," he said betraying her.

Nina raised her head for a second. "Braggart." Her coolness struck him with a jolt of lust.

He came quickly, feeling her mouth hard and soft, with a spasm that seemed to wring his heart.

She lay down beside him, her lips still shiny, and he tasted the juice of himself when he kissed her.

"Thank you," he offered, but she moved to stop him. She put her arms around him, motherly now, and rearranged the crumpled quilt around their shoulders.

Nina lay quietly, looking up at the contours of the shuttered windows and the ceiling. The room seemed to have changed its dimensions. It was enlarged, made to seem a light space full of humming air by her unexpected happiness. She wanted to lock her arms more tightly around the man, holding him to her so as to preserve this minute, but she made herself stay still. She would not think of what would happen next, only of what had just happened.

"It seems very simple, doesn't it?"

Gordon had almost drifted off to sleep. He had slept badly the night before, in intermittent snatches disturbed by dreams. For a second he was surprised at where he was, at hearing Nina's voice. He roused himself with an effort.

"Sex? Yes. Or else as complicated as . . . molecular biology. Or astrophysics."

"It starts off simple." She meant just between the two of them, new as they were now, before they had to make further reckonings. Nina wanted to have that acknowledged, to exonerate them for the time being. Now that they had come this far, she knew, there was the potential for damage ahead of them, and the worst of that damage might not be to themselves. *Be careful*, she thought. The possibilities seemed to multiply ahead of her again, but the avenues looked darker now that she had traveled closer toward them. Yet for now the white light of her happiness was too strong, and it dispelled the shadows.

"I know what you mean," he helped her. "But I don't agree. Every time you take someone new to bed, after the first person, it is a process of re-creating yourself through a new pair of eyes, a different set of sensors. Each attempt at re-creation has to refer to all the successes and failures that have gone before."

His hand was resting in the hollow of her waist. He lifted it and settled it higher, over the convex span of her ribs, and she felt the two hand-shaped patches of skin cooling and warming by turn.

"It becomes more complicated with each renewal, just because each of you brings to bed more history. Under the skin and behind the eyes."

He had been thinking of Vicky, and home, and superimposing this woman and her bedroom over the other, noting where the images overlapped and where the differences were, shadowy outlines like an improperly developed color print.

Nina said, "That sounds . . . intensely narcissistic."

Gordon laughed. "I'm sure you're right. But not simple."

He intended it as an oblique tribute, wanting her not to think that he had just fucked her out of blind lust. But he was also wary now, as he lay with her arms around him and her bedcovers heaped over them. He was not sure what expectations she might have. He thought of their separate histories, skipping connections in his head that led him to ask more abruptly than he otherwise would have, "What was your husband like?"

"In bed?"

"I didn't mean in bed, particularly."

"He was very gentle."

Nina turned away a little, stretching out on her back. The happiness was still with her. It wasn't threatening to become dislodged and float away.

"Can you stay? Stay the night, I mean?"

Gordon thought about it. The idea was tempting, and the alternative wasn't. If he got up early enough in the morning, he could drive quietly home to feed the cats and change his shirt and still be in the office by eight-thirty.

"If I may."

He saw that she was pleased. She turned back again, cuddling up to him the way Vicky did. He was more awake now. The images of there and here were not overlapping or blurring together any longer. They stood apart, sharp in their differences. He let himself savor them for now.

"We had a very nice life," Nina said slowly. "We had a lot of friends, we did all kinds of things, but really we were doing them just the two of us, on our own, together." She wanted to tell Gordon what it had been like, but she chose deliberately colorless words. It was an attempt to spare them both.

"Go on," he said, settling her head against his shoulder to encourage her.

"We had a house in London, and a house in Norfolk, not far from the sea. Richard was a weekend painter, and he liked the sky. We used to walk on the beach and bring back driftwood. There was an open fireplace. We were forever arguing about which pieces to burn and which to put on the mantleshelf."

Gordon relaxed. He felt his body weight increasing, sinking downward into a comfortable place. He stroked Nina's hair.

"Go on," he said again.

"When he died, at first I only felt angry. For a long time, it felt like a terribly long time, I was so angry with him for breaking our contract, as if death didn't break any and all agreements."

"What happened?"

"He was in Norfolk, on his own. It was the middle of the week and I was in London because my agent and I were meeting an American publisher. Richard sometimes went up there alone to work. He had a fax and telephone there. He liked the peace. On the morning he died he had been working in the garden. The wheelbarrow was on the path, and there was a rake and a spade beside it. He had a severe asthma attack. A neighbor found him lying between the wheelbarrow and the kitchen door."

Gordon said nothing, just holding her and stroking her hair.

"I should have been there. He shouldn't have been doing anything strenuous without his inhaler. He needn't have died."

When Nina had reached the house with Patrick, he had already been taken away. But she could still see him lying on the path under the crab apple tree, twisted around his defeated lungs. Dry-eyed and with a stiff face, she had made the neighbor describe exactly what she had seen.

"Are you still angry?"

Nina told him, "No. It's a year ago, now."

But he could feel her loneliness. The hunger it generated in her was magnetic, and also faintly repellent. He felt a weight of sympathy coupling with his liking for her, and then a tinge of alarm. The alarm concentrated under his diaphragm like the onset of indigestion.

"Go on talking," he said. Nina settled more comfortably against him. As he listened to her, Gordon was conscious of the planes and angles of her house around them, an unknown place with the potential to become familiar. He felt already that he knew this room, that he would remember its details even if he never saw it again.

Nina told him about Richard and their life before his death. She told him small things, pictures of their ordinary days, and he liked the way she was doing it for him, filling in the domestic background like a painter at a canvas. She described the house in London; he remembered reading about the conversion in an architectural magazine and was impressed. Her descriptions gave him a picture of the civilized life she had shared with her husband. The houses and dinners and parties sounded grand, but oddly formal, making him doubt that her earlier existence had contained much passion. Gordon felt his perceptions of her changing all the time. She had been so passionate here with him. He was sleepy again, and although he struggled against it he dropped into a doze for a few seconds. When he woke up again it was with the momentary impression that he knew Nina very well, better than he knew Vicky.

Nina saw that he was almost asleep. She watched him while she talked, saw the involuntary flickers of his facial muscles, the relaxation of his jaw that left his mouth a little open as his breathing steadied and deepened. At last she switched off the light and in the darkness turned to curl herself against him. In his sleep he put his heavy arm over her hip. She knew that this was how he slept with Vicky.

When Nina woke up in the morning, the feeling of lightness was still with her. It was dark in the room behind the heavy shutters, but she could make out the shape of Gordon's features as he slept. She remembered the night and its happiness and was still secure, even though she knew that now they would have to face the day. She lay still, memorizing the outlines of his mouth. Nina knew now that she had not mistaken the raw eagerness she had glimpsed in Gordon at the beginning. Their avid coupling had lit a fire in her that Richard had never managed to kindle, for all the affection and consideration he had shown her. At last, Nina's stare penetrated his sleep and he stirred and opened his eyes to her. Almost at once he was looking around for his watch.

"Twenty past seven," Nina told him. It was early to her.

He sat up. "Is it? As late as that? I have to go."

"Do you?"

She had imagined that they would have breakfast together. She had even planned how she would lay out a tray and bring it up.

"Yes. I have to be in by eight-thirty." He was thinking of the drive home, a hot shower, and heading right out again for the office. He put his hand out to touch her cheek. "I'm sorry. Perhaps I should have gone home last night."

"I'm glad you didn't." She knew that he was about to get out of bed and leave her. "I'm glad you were here. I felt happy when I woke up. I lay and looked at your face. You made me feel happy." She knew that it was too much to tell him, but she smiled, anyway.

"That's good. I'm just sorry I have to go," he said.

He leaned across to kiss her, and then quickly climbed out of bed. Nina propped herself against the pillows while he retrieved his clothes and dressed. He felt silly in his socks and underclothes, with her watching him, half-smiling. When he was ready to leave he came to the end of the bed, feeling itchy and constricted in his rumpled Tory suit. She sat up and swung her legs out from under the quilt. When she stood up he remembered her the way she had been, and at once he wanted to push her back into the nest of heat and strawy scents they had made. Nina wrapped herself in a striped bathrobe and tied its belt. She came and stood close to him, and he put his arms around her, letting her warmth seep into him.

"Thank you," he said.

There was a movement of her shoulders, not quite a shrug. She didn't want his thanks, but his reassurance.

"I'll call you," Gordon said.

Nina nodded. "Yes."

He kissed her forehead and then let her go. She watched him walk to the door of her bedroom but made no attempt to follow him down the stairs. Gordon went out through the dark house and into the street.

It was only barely light, and Dean's Row was deserted. Across the green he saw the scaffolders' truck arriving with a load of poles and planks. Quickly he turned the corner into the narrow alley. It was a relief to shut himself into the sanctuary of his car.

He drove around the ring road, through the first wave of commuter traffic, passing the turn-off that led to the hospital. He did not think he had been seen by anyone who knew him: he was safe if he could just reach home. He listened to the weather and traffic reports without taking any note of them. Memories and impressions of the night were beginning to sort themselves inside his head. When the traffic summary was replaced by rock music, he realized that he was smiling and drumming his fingers on the wheel.

There was one more danger point to go. When he turned into his road he craned down the length of it, but there was no one about. His neighbors' new Mercedes was parked in their driveway where it could be properly admired, and the upstairs and downstairs curtains were still closed. No one else was likely to have noticed that he had been out all night. Gordon swung into the drive of his own solid Victorian house. Everything was secure. He locked the car again and went quietly around the side of the house, past the conservatory, to let himself in through the back door.

The kitchen was warm and silent. He heard a rattle and a bang beside him when Alice's cat slid in through its flap. The animal came up to rub itself against his legs, purring mechanically. Gordon rubbed his chin with the tips of his fingers. He had fifteen minutes: time for a shave and a shower, perhaps even a cup of coffee. Whistling softly, he put the kettle on.

Gordon was glad to find his home quiet and safe, as if the night had never happened.

But for all his sense of relief and reprieve, he knew already that he could not bear the thought of not taking Nina to bed again.

5

Nina waited the whole day for Gordon Ransome to telephone her. She went up to her studio and sat at her drawing board, mechanically dipping the tip of the fine brush into her paints, but she was only pretending to work.

She felt loose in her joints, and as languid and sleepy as if she had eaten a heavy meal. Sometimes she found herself smiling when she remembered some detail of the night before. She tried to manufacture some sense of irritation at her new, hypnotized state, but all that came was stubborn satisfaction. She began to imagine what certain of her women friends would say if she told them, their various shades of skepticism or envy.

At first she was happy, with an edge of anticipation warmed by certainty, when she looked at the telephone beside her. But then, as the hours crept by, she grew colder and less confident. She thought more often of Vicky, full-blown in her pregnancy, of the new baby, and of her own thoughtless capitulation to a man she hardly knew. The night they had shared seemed to change its significance, losing its warmth and becoming merely sordid and shameful. From longing to hear his voice, she swung to embarrassment at the thought of ever having to see him again.

The telephone rang only once, at five o'clock, and she snatched it up immediately. Betraying herself. But it was Janice Frost.

"Nina? Andrew and I wondered if you'd like to come over and have supper on Sunday. Nothing elaborate, just the Cleggs and the Roses after golf, and probably Gordon Ransome before Vicky comes home on Monday. Not the Wickhams, because they're busy."

Nina said at once, "That sounds nice."

Then she grew flustered at the thought of facing Gordon under the scrutiny of the smiling couples. She lied hastily, "But . . . I had thought of going to London for the weekend, I don't know if I'd be back in time . . ."

"Don't worry," Janice said easily. "It's only a kitchen supper. Just come along by eight if you're back, and if you feel like it. Have a good weekend. 'Bye."

At last, at seven o'clock, Nina could bear the silence no longer. She had made no plans for the weekend, but she ran down to her bedroom, crammed some clothes into a bag, and then telephoned Patrick. It would be better to leave Grafton, to make herself unavailable. That would be the right statement to make. As she walked through the wintry rain to the station, Nina wished, for the first time since leaving London, she had the freedom of a car.

Patrick was waiting for her at home in the Spitalfields house. When she arrived, Nina was relieved to see the familiar paneled rooms, the same as always. Patrick had lit candles in the old black iron sconces, and there was a smell of melted wax and woodsmoke. He looked critically at Nina.

"What happened?" he asked her.

Nina tilted her wine goblet, looking at the pinhead bubbles faintly distorted and rainbowed by Patrick's handblown Venetian glass. Small details from the physical world seemed suddenly to have become very clear to her; there were the tiny stitches in a tapestry cushion beneath her elbow, a faint smear of wood ash on the oak table, the whispered scratch of nylon stocking as her calves rubbed together.

"Happened?"

"Yes. Is it a man?"

There was a different look to her, he had noticed it as soon as she arrived.

Nina laughed. "Clever you."

"Not especially. It's plain to see."

Patrick stood up and put another log on the fire. The half-burned ones were mantled with white ash seamed with glowing scarlet threads. Watching him, and seeing his economical, faintly old-maidish movements as he tidied the stone hearth, Nina thought how much she loved him, and also loved this room, where everything had been chosen for its beauty and placed with care and attention. It drew her back to Richard's world and contrasted with the Grafton houses she had visited, bursting with children and haphazard furniture and color-supplement chintzes. This small piece of superiority distanced her from Gordon, who had occupied her mind throughout the train journey. The recognition of their differences reassured her.

"It's nothing. One night, that's all. He's married, with about a dozen children. But it *was* very nice, just for the one night."

Patrick didn't give any sign of approval. He was wary and tentative in his own relationships, and celibate now. He had shared the months of Nina's grieving for her husband, and he was glad to see her sudden brightness, but the circumstances were not what he would have wished for her.

"Be careful," he said, knowing that he sounded joyless.

She nodded her head to acknowledge the warning, moral and emotional and physical.

"I was. I shall be."

But she felt wonderful, sitting and drinking her wine and watching the fire in Patrick's company. It was good to have given and received love again, however briefly. The shame she had felt had faded away, leaving her with clear eyes to admire the miniature perfections of the ordinary world.

"Nina, what would you like to do? We could go to a late film, if there's anything you'd like to see."

Patrick looked at her.

"I don't want to go out. Unless you do."

He could remember the precise mixture of dreaminess and sharp awareness, although he had not felt it himself for a long time. The contemplation of it made him both envious and sad.

"Are you hungry? Shall I cook something?"

Nina uncrossed her legs, stood up, went to Patrick, and put her arms around him. There was a tiny hole at the shoulder seam of his vicuña sweater, and the fairish hair at the neat, shaved line beside his ear glittered with silver. When they hugged each other she felt him stand there solidly, no longer involuntarily recoiling from her grief. She patted his shoulder gently, like a mother, and released him.

"Let's cook something together. It's ages since I made a proper meal."

She was hungry, she realized.

Nina followed Patrick into his spartan kitchen. She opened his refrigerator and looked in at the neat single portions of food. She had not been expected, of course.

They were both lonely. The various modes and varieties of loneliness confronted her like the meat and vegetables on the white racks. She remembered the Grafton couples with their big warm kitchens and pine tables and easy hospitality, and the façades of smiles.

Her first judgment of them had been a simplification. It had been born out of envy and the over-awareness of her own solitude. Last night with Gordon Ransome she had glimpsed confusion behind the smooth faces, and now she felt a beat of gratitude for the happiness of her own marriage.

She held the refrigerator door open wider.

"What shall we make?" she asked Patrick.

At seven-thirty, after a day of meetings and a distant site visit, and after he had been to the hospital and come home at last, Gordon dialed Nina's number. There was no answer, not even the bland invitation of an answering machine. He held the receiver for a long time, listening to the hollow ringing tone.

He tried again and again through the slow weekend until the digits were imprinted in his head like a mantra.

For Nina it was a London weekend like many others she had known. Its form was both familiar and already consigned to history. She went with Patrick to the theater to see a play by a new feminist writer, and to Bloom's for dinner with Patrick's friends. On Sunday morning they went to Brick Lane Market to rummage for treasures among the faded bric-a-brac, and then to Hampstead for a lengthy lunch with more old friends, who only noted with pleasure that Nina looked well, almost herself again.

At the lunch there was an architect, recently divorced, whom she had not met before, although he claimed to have known Richard. After they ate they all went out to walk on the Heath among the Sunday crowds of dog-exercisers and kite-flyers and children on tricycles. The architect walked beside Nina, and after a little while he asked her if she would like to have dinner with him one evening.

Nina's hands were in her coat pockets. She rubbed the residue of crumbs and fluff between her fingers, and looked ahead at the silhouettes of walkers against the greenish sky on the crest of Parliament Hill. This afternoon was perfectly familiar to her, like the wider axis that contained it, and she had felt herself growing impatient with it as the hours passed. She was thinking about Grafton and wanted to hurry back there.

She smiled at the architect.

"I can't, but thank you. I don't live in London. I moved to the country and I have to go back this evening."

"Next time you're in town then, perhaps," the man said, observing the conventions.

It was getting dark, with the sudden sinking gloom of a December afternoon. The party broke up when one couple with their children turned at an angle across the Heath toward their own house.

"I should get back to Grafton," Nina said to Patrick. She calculated that if she caught the six o'clock train she could be at the Frosts' house by not long after eight. She did not let herself reckon beyond that. Patrick heard the note of urgency in her voice.

"I'll drive you to Paddington," he offered.

At the station, Nina hugged him again. He made a surprised face to indicate that he was unused to such an abundance of affection.

"Next time, will you come down to stay with me?" she asked. Her face was bright. She had discovered something, some seam of happiness, and she wanted to share it with him or to have him admire it. "There are nice people. I'd like you to meet them."

He accepted that she was being generous. "Of course I'll come."

"Good. I'll give a party, perhaps." There had been lots of parties before Richard died.

"Be careful, won't you?" Patrick repeated.

"Certainly," she laughed, and again he found himself envying her abandonment to whatever would come. He stood on the platform and waved as the train pulled away, and then drove slowly back to Spitalfields through the Sunday blackness of the city.

All the way back to Grafton, Nina willed the train to go faster, like a schoolgirl longing for the hour of a crucial party.

Jimmy Rose held up the television remote control, aiming it at the screen as if he wanted to shoot and kill. He made the circuit of the channels and discovered what he already knew, that there was nothing he wanted to watch. He depressed the volume control and watched Harry Secombe's face, silently mouthing, swell to fill the screen.

Star was upstairs somewhere. The Roses lived in a small modern house and without the noise from the television Jimmy could hear the creaks that she made crossing the bedroom floor to open a cupboard, and then the metallic rasp as she set up the ironing board.

Jimmy stretched his legs in front of him and drank the remains of a beer from the can. It was dark outside, but he had not yet drawn the curtains across the big window that looked into Star's garden. He could see himself fishily reflected in the black glass.

Usually Jimmy enjoyed Sundays. He made it a rule not to do any work, nor even to think about work if that was feasible, and to concentrate on pleasing himself. It was a matter of satisfaction to him that he and Star had long ago come to a comfortable agreement about this. Star liked to garden on Sundays, or to sit quietly and read, whereas Jimmy was not at all interested in the garden, and he read only occasional thrillers or sports biographies. Jimmy's preference was to stay late in bed, to go off to play squash or golf with one or more of the Grafton men, and afterward to drink with them in the bar or the clubhouse. Sometimes Star and the other wives would join them for the drinking part, although he preferred it when they did not. Sunday evenings, if they were not entertaining or invited out anywhere, were a pleasantly hazy slide toward bedtime and the jolt of Monday morning.

This Sunday, however, had not been one of the best. Darcy Clegg was Jimmy's usual golf partner, but today Darcy had proposed a swap. Darcy himself had partnered a regular golfer named Francis Kelly, and Jimmy had ended up with Michael Wickham. Michael had hardly spoken to Jimmy or anyone else all through the round and seemed to take a grim satisfaction in playing extremely badly. He had hooked most of his drives into the rough halfway along the fairway, and putted as if he was using a yard broom.

Through Jimmy's efforts they had managed to hold level as far as the short fifteenth hole, but they lost that one and the next three in succession. By the time they reached the clubhouse bar, Jimmy was in as bad a mood as Michael himself. He did not like to lose at any game, and he particularly disliked losing to Darcy.

The bar was crowded with golfers, most of them men, although not many of the members had braved the wintry fairways beforehand. It was a popular Sunday drinking place for the prosperous and established Grafton set, who considered the Eagle on the cathedral green to cater only to tourists and the other city pubs to be spoiled by kids and electronic games and loud music. Francis and Jimmy edged through the knots of convivial drinkers, with Michael, frowning, in their wake.

"A man could die of thirst," Jimmy said, eyeing the press at the bar.

The other three had had to shoulder their way forward, but Darcy did not. A way opened into the groups in front of him as heads turned and hands reached out in greeting. Satisfaction was perceptible, as if the drinkers were now reassured that they were in the right and proper place because Darcy had arrived.

"Darcy Clegg, the man himself."

"You haven't been out there this morning, Darcy? It's much more comfortable in here with a glass in your hand, I can tell you."

Darcy nodded his big head, smiling a faint but amiable smile and bestowing a word here and there. He reached the bar and held up a finger to the sweating barman.

"Morning, Mr. Clegg. What'll it be?"

"Four pints, Gerry, and whatever you're having."

Darcy didn't ask his companions what they were drinking, nor did anyone question his right to buy the first round. He handled the barroom exchange adroitly, as he did everything else, but his expression indicated that he was part of this only insofar as he wanted to be, and also somewhat above it.

The bar was unusually crowded, and once their drinks were served they had to perch on stools around one of the low tables in the main body of the room because there was no space up at the bar.

"What's up, Michael?" Jimmy had taken a pull, and tiny wings of froth were left at the corners of his mouth. He added, "Apart from your golf, that is."

Michael shrugged. "Nothing's up. Sorry to lose you the game."

He turned his glass on the table. He was a dark, lean man with crisp hair now turning gray. He had doctorly hands, faintly reddened and with prominent wristbones. He was never forthcoming, but his moroseness this morning was beginning to affect them all.

Jimmy felt almost physically pained that this precious and pleasant Sunday time should be spoiled. Darcy's big frame looked uncomfortable on the small stool, and he was already glancing over Francis Kelly's shoulder to the noisy crowd at the bar. In a minute, Jimmy knew, he would get up and go join them. Jimmy's response to all of this, for which he disliked himself, was to talk too much, clowning for the benefit of the three other men. He told a story about events at a recent conference he had organized, but he spoke too hurriedly and with too much false comic emphasis. Darcy looked at him with his eyebrows slightly lifted, and only Francis laughed.

When Jimmy saw Hannah Clegg in the doorway he was relieved. Normally he would not have been pleased to have this Sunday session disrupted, although under most other circumstances he liked Hannah as well as admiring her looks. But today she was welcome. Now, at least, Darcy would not stroll away in search of better company.

Hannah saw them and came across to their table, trailing appreciative glances. She was wearing a sleeveless suede jerkin over a cream sweater, and cream knitted trousers that showed the vee between her thighs. She kissed all four of them in turn, Darcy last.

"I thought I'd catch you all in here," she said gaily. "Just a small gin and tonic for me, Darcy. I'm on my way to pick up Freddie from the Harvey's."

"Is he all right now?" Michael asked, looking up from his beer.

"Yes, thanks Michael, he's fine. A lot of fuss about nothing, as it turned out."

Freddie was the Cleggs' six-year-old. Hannah explained to Francis and Jimmy that the little boy had developed a startlingly high temperature a few days before, when Darcy was away on business, and their GP had been slow to arrive. In a panic Hannah had telephoned Michael, who was at least a doctor, although his field was orthopedic surgery, not pediatrics. Michael had driven around to the Cleggs' mansion to examine the little boy and reassure Hannah.

Jimmy and Francis listened to this recital without much interest. Hannah was inclined to talk at length about her children. Now she put her hand out and touched Michael's shoulder. Her fingers, with elongated, pale-pink nails, rested there lightly for a moment.

"Thank you," she said again.

Michael's body skewed sideways as he tried unobtrusively to lean away from her, but still his manner lost some of its stiffness.

"It was nothing. I said so at the time. I was glad to do what I could, which was not much."

"Just the same, thank you."

Hannah's soft face was pink, and her full lower lip jutted out to reveal the darker pink tissue within. Michael looked at her head-on, unnoticed by the others, and then dropped his gaze back to his drink. Hannah settled comfortably at the table. She told Jimmy that they would be meeting later at the Frosts', and that Nina Cort would be there, and then she turned away to talk to Michael.

Jimmy bought another round and concentrated on drinking steadily, hoping to recapture some of the sense of Sunday camaraderie that stayed with him like a blessing all through the following week. He loved the way the men were friendly and informal at these times, but yet were held together by unwritten rules. It offended him when someone failed to obey the rules, as Michael had done this morning.

Hannah showed no signs of leaving. She accepted Jimmy's offer of a second gin and tonic, and when the drinks had been consumed Darcy looked at his watch and announced that they had to go. Hannah made no protest, and five minutes after they had left Michael followed suit. Finally Francis also drifted away.

Jimmy went to the bar and drank a quick whisky, wondering if he should join another group, but the day was already spoiled. He went home and found the house empty. Star had told him she was going out somewhere, although he had forgotten exactly where. He made himself a sandwich and fell asleep in front of the television, and then woke up when Star came back. He had a headache.

He heard her coming downstairs now, and then clicking across the woodblock floor of the hall.

"Why are you sitting with the curtains open?" she asked when she saw him.

"Why not? Nobody can see in."

Star went across and closed them. She was wearing a shirt cut like a man's, but made of peacock-blue silk, and a pair of tight trousers in some stretchy material that showed the lines of her good legs. She didn't usually take so much trouble with her appearance for a Sunday supper at the Frosts'.

"You look nice," Jimmy said lazily. He held out a hand. "Come over here."

She came and stood in front of him for a moment. Jimmy reached up and put his hands on her hips, kneading the flesh over her long bones, and then sliding his palms inward over the slight protuberance of her stomach so that the smooth silk slithered under his fingers.

"I like this shirt. Is tonight something special?"

He was looking forward to it, he realized, after the fiasco of the day. He liked well-upholstered Janice and her dark eyes just as much as he liked Hannah Clegg, and his ears had sharpened at the news that Nina Cort was also coming, although he had not betrayed his interest to Hannah.

"Special? No, I don't think so. Aren't you going to change?"

He stood up. Star was two inches taller than he, and when he was in his socks the difference seemed greater than that. He had always liked it, ever since they had first met, this feeling of being overreached by her. He pressed his face forward now, and his mouth found her neck, warm inside the collar of her shirt.

"Mmm. You smell lovely."

"Aren't you going to change?" Star repeated.

Jimmy sighed. His mood had completely altered. He felt light-hearted and optimistic now.

"If I must." He made his eyebrows into beguiling peaks and looked at her. "Won't you come up?"

"It's a quarter to eight." She had turned away and bent down to straighten the sofa cushions behind him.

Jimmy sighed again, more theatrically. "A quarter of an hour used to be plenty," he cajoled.

She seemed not to hear what he was saying. Jimmy hesitated, and then shrugged and went whistling upstairs in his good humor to change out of his golf clothes.

Nina was the last to arrive at the Frosts'. As she paid off her taxi at the gate she saw Gordon's car parked a little farther along the road. She rang the doorbell, remembering the night of Halloween, and Andrew came to open the door. Instead of a suit he was wearing a patterned sweater that proclaimed Sunday.

The Frosts' other guests were sitting in the room where they had danced at the party. Now she saw Darcy Clegg's handsome, heavy face, and Hannah with her hair pinned up in a sleek chignon, and Star in a bright blue shirt. To her left, a dark shape in an armchair, was Gordon. Nina could not look directly at him.

Of the three women, only Star greeted her with friendly attention. Janice distractedly offered her her cheek, and Hannah waved her ringed fingers from the other side of the room. There was a cool edge to the atmosphere, Nina thought, or perhaps she was just beginning to see these people more clearly.

She found her way to a place on the sofa beside Darcy. Andrew put a glass into her hand and she cupped her hands around it. There were soft cushions behind her, and when she tasted the wine there were complicated flavors on her tongue. The physical world took on sharp significance again.

"You've just come back from London?" Darcy asked. He too was wearing the sweater-and-corduroys Sunday uniform, but his slacks were Italian and his sweater was cashmere.

"Yes. I went up to stay with an old friend of Richard's and mine, to see a play and have lunch with some people."

She offered this simple account to Gordon, without looking in his direction, and she knew that he was listening to her.

Darcy had read the reviews of the play in the Sunday papers, and they began to talk about what Nina had thought of it. The conversations elsewhere in the room started up again, although

Nina did not hear Gordon speak. Someone was describing a disastrous round of golf and generating a good deal of brittle laughter. It was Jimmy Rose, of course. Each of Nina's senses, not just her hearing, seemed abnormally sharpened. She could hear the unspoken words underlying the bantering talk. Jimmy had been upset and disappointed to lose the game. The sudden clarity of her perceptions made her feel strong and lively.

Darcy was watching her from beneath the shield of his thick eyelids. There was a faint red flush over her cheekbones and her fingers fluttered up and down the stem of her glass.

And then, without warning, the recollection that had stirred in him when they were first introduced delivered itself to him, almost complete. Somebody had described the circumstances of Richard Cort's death, and then had made an allegation that did not particularly interest him at the time. But he remembered it now, with a sharpening of curiosity. A woman had told him the story, a woman he knew quite well. It had been at a party in London a few months before.

The theater conversation continued while Darcy idly speculated.

"Did you see the Arthur Miller?" he asked, and Nina offered her response, still with the faint color in her face. Across the room Jimmy Rose was grinning at them, although neither Darcy nor Nina paid him any attention.

The elder Frost boy, Toby, came in. His hair was shaved close at the nape of his neck and a long hank at the front fell forward over his eyes. He was wearing a loose top with a hood and enormous shoes.

"Hi, all."

With this generalized greeting he seated himself on the edge of the low table that occupied the middle of the room. With one hand he swept back the lock of hair, which immediately fell forward again. Nina noticed with interest that he was perfectly at ease, and thought that at the same age both she and Toby's father would have been paralyzed with shyness at the unlikely prospect of being asked to confront a roomful of their parents' friends.

I'm getting old, she thought, amused.

"Have you done your homework, Toby?" Andrew demanded.

"Yeah. Dad, it's okay," the boy answered, raking at his hair again.

"I hear you played well yesterday," Darcy offered.

"Not too badly."

They began to talk about a school soccer match. Nina had nothing to contribute, and in any case she did not know how to talk to eleven-year-old boys. Under the cover of momentary invisibility, she let herself glance across at Gordon. His eyes met hers.

She was shaken at once by a sense of intense familiarity.

Her knowledge of his shape and all the lines of his face was so intimate and tender that it seemed shocking to contemplate it in the midst of this neutral gathering of friends.

She felt that she knew this man so well that it was as if Richard were here, sitting in an armchair in Andrew Frost's den. The room would certainly be called the den. Nina's mouth curved and she saw her smile answered in Gordon's eyes. They looked at each other with amazed pleasure for another two seconds, and then Nina turned her head away.

It was inconceivable that the conversation around them had not stopped, that everyone else in the room had not fallen into silence as they took stock of what must be blindingly obvious. But they were all still talking; no one had even glanced at them. Nina's heart was knocking irregularly and her mouth seemed full of sand.

She took a long gulp of wine and at once felt drunk, her head and limbs seeming to drift an alarming distance apart.

Janice leaned forward with her hand on her son's shoulder.

"Is Will ready for bed? And if you've finished your work, Toby, you could think of an early night as well."

"Oh, *Mum*."

"Do as your mother says," Andrew told him.

There was no real protest in the boy's voice, nor reprimand in Andrew's. With her sharpened perceptions Nina understood that they were playing the roles of parents and child in the ordinary loving Frost family for the benefit of the rest of them. Hannah Clegg was nodding and smiling. *Façades*, Nina thought, and remembered the handsome, happy couples as she had first seen them. The sense that she was beginning to look beyond the obvious came sharply back to her. Her eyes met Gordon's again, guiltily, greedily.

"I'll just go up to check on Will, and then we can eat," Janice was saying. The boy gave his hair a last shake and wished them all a languid good night.

A moment later came the general move. Darcy escorted Nina, the fingers of one hand just touching the small of her back. She felt and heard Gordon following behind her.

Janice was now standing behind the kitchen counter in her apron. "I told you it was just a family supper," she apologized to Nina. "If we eat in the dining room it all seems rather formal and serious, like entertaining clients."

Andrew passed behind her and patted her bottom. "I prefer the dining room, myself."

"Stay home in the morning to do the extra clearing-up, then," she answered coolly. "Nina doesn't mind. Do you, Nina?"

"Of course not."

"Sit where you like, everyone. *Not* next to your partners, please."

Nina found herself placed between Darcy and Jimmy Rose. Gordon was on Jimmy's other side, out of her sight. The table was elaborately laid with linen napkins, heavy silver, cutlery and thickets of polished glasses, which contradicted Janice's insistence that this was a casual evening. Evidently perfectly at home, Darcy walked behind the chairs pouring white Alsace into a glass at each place.

"Toast," Hannah declared loudly when everyone's glass had been filled. With her luxuriant hair pinned up she looked different, and older, as if her eyes and mouth were brightly drawn upward by tiny, taut threads.

"To friendship."

"To loving friendship."

Surprisingly, it was Star who had amended the toast. From her place opposite she nodded her grave head at Nina. There was a moment's silence around the table until Jimmy satirically echoed his wife.

"To loving friendship."

They all drank, except for Janice, who was busy behind her kitchen counter.

She brought an oval dish to the table. Resting in a bed of green salad leaves was a terrine of vegetables in which tiny juliennes of carrot and zucchini and flowers of broccoli floated in a clear golden jelly amid a rain of green peppercorns. Nina knew how long such things took to concoct, and wondered again about the protestations of simplicity. This was competitive cooking.

"Oh, Janice, look at this. It's so *pretty*," Hannah said.

Janice pursed her lips. "Have you ever seen Marcelle's version? This is a pale imitation; hers just *glows* with goodness." She added, for Nina's benefit, "Marcelle is a wonderful cook."

"I remember from your Halloween party," Nina murmured. Then she heard Gordon's quiet voice, which seemed to set currents stirring in the air between them.

"Michael is a lucky man."

"Is he, would you say?" Jimmy Rose smirked.

Janice took her place at the end of the table opposite Andrew. She was pleased by the reaction to her terrine. Raising her glass, she said, "I want to drink the toast, too. To loving friendship, Star. That's what it's all for, isn't it? All the hard work and the risks and the planning and the worrying, all the difficult things each of us does, to make the lives we have and to keep hold of them . . . It's so that we can enjoy the pleasure of evenings like this, with our friends around us. Good friends, loving friends. We're missing Vicky, of course, but she'll be home tomorrow, and at the same time we're welcoming Nina." She looked earnestly around the table. "This is what counts, isn't it? All of us, being here together for food and wine and talk?"

Janice's cheeks were flushed.

"Of course it is, darling," Andrew murmured.

"Eloquently put, Janice," Darcy said, and she gave him a defiantly grateful smile.

"Well, I don't care. You know I'm not particularly clever, and you may think I'm sentimental. But I love you all, and this is my favorite way to spend a Sunday evening." She drained her glass with a flourish.

Hannah clapped her hands. "Hear hear," she called. "May there be many more evenings just like this one."

"Darling, of course there will be. Exactly like this," Darcy said softly. "Why shouldn't there be?"

Nina listened more than she talked.

It occurred to her that the edge of uneasiness lay within the partnerships themselves, and not among the couples. The couples clung together in their group to affirm themselves and their partnerships.

The voices rose around her and wove themselves in and out of the clink of cutlery and glasses. She chose to pick out one voice at a time and follow it through the twists of the conversation like a colored thread through fabric. She heard Star, and the way that she spun her words so fluently and punctured Jimmy's nonsensical chatter, and then she heard Darcy, who pronounced things and knew that his lazy drawl would be listened to, and Hannah's cries and giggles, and Janice's gossip that grew less coherent as the wine influenced her, and Jimmy distracting her by grinningly stroking her bare forearm. Andrew directed the conversation from the head of the table, and through it all she strained to hear Gordon's low, unemphatic comments, although he spoke almost as little as she did herself.

Nina tried to yoke the couples together in her mind, making Hannah's trills counterpoint Darcy's bass, setting Star's sarcastic wit against Jimmy's sly Irish loquacity and Andrew's faint pomposity against Janice's tipsy skittishness. But now they resisted her efforts to pair them, and so to eavesdrop on them as couples. They split away into individuals, then coalesced again into a group of friends, a group whose homogeneity, in the end, surprised her.

Andrew filled another set of the good glasses, this time with second-growth Bordeaux. Janice brought beef Wellington to the table and covered the plates with overlapping circles of rosy meat rimmed with golden pastry. There were immaculate vegetables in white-and-gold dishes, and Janice was praised again for the excellence of her dinner.

"You're not a very great talker," Jimmy said to Nina as they ate their beef.

The conversation had just turned from skiing to cars. Hannah was resting her chin in her hands as she sighed. "I love my little 325. It's *soooo* sexy."

"I don't know much about cars," Nina answered neutrally.

"But aren't you interested in what they tell you about their owners?'

She thought, *I can't remember Gordon's.* She had spent more than an hour sitting in it, but she had no idea what variety it was. *Something gray and solid. Not like him at all. That's a stupid game.*

"What would you guess Darcy drives?" Jimmy pursued.

"Let me think . . . . I know—a red Porsche."

"Wrong," he scoffed. "That's what *I* would choose if I could afford it. No, Darcy has a Maserati. Obviously. And a Range Rover, of course, for the mud and when he mixes with the County. Which are usually one and the same thing."

"Quite true," Darcy said equably from her other side. "Jimmy is only jealous, of course."

Nina found herself laughing. Jimmy Rose was amusing, in his sharp way.

"Who would not be jealous of the man who possesses Wilton Manor and a Maserati *and* Hannah?"

"I thought I might buy myself a car," Nina heard herself saying.

"Haven't you got one? No heavenly chariot?" Jimmy's eyebrows peaked.

Quickly she said, "I used to have an Alfa Romeo Spyder, but I sold it."

"Beautiful machines," Andrew declared.

"Sexy machines," Jimmy added.

"You must buy another glamorous car because you are a glamorous person," Hannah told her with slightly drunken assertiveness, and Nina found herself smiling across the table at Star. Even though Star had talked and laughed almost as much as the others, her voice was cool, and Nina had the impression that she had held herself a little aloof from the party. Perhaps it was her intention to act as an antidote to Jimmy, who had made more noise than anyone else.

"Then you will have to advise me, Hannah," Nina said.

Andrew had cleared away the dinner plates and now there were individual chocolate soufflés with cocoa-brown crusts puffed high above the white rims of their dishes. There was another chorus of admiration.

"The person to ask is Gordon." Hannah waved her spoon at

him. "Gordon knows the most; he's an engine expert even more than Andrew is, even though he's staying pretty buttoned up to-night. What's the matter, Gordon? Post-partum depression?"

Janice stood up, not very steadily. "Coffee for everyone? Andrew, what else have we got for people to drink?"

He sighed. "She'll have a headache all day tomorrow, you know."

"So long as she doesn't have one tonight," Jimmy said, winking.

Nina slipped out of her chair. Jimmy hopped to his feet and drew it back for her with a flourish. Janice waved a hand.

"Use my bathroom, Nina. First on the left up the stairs. The downstairs one is probably full of sweatshirts and rugby shorts. The boys never pick up a thing."

It was a relief to escape the hot room and the smoke from Darcy's cigar. The hall was cool and dark. Nina went slowly up the stairs, peering in the dimness at the gilt-framed pictures on the walls. She opened a door and saw the Frosts' bedroom, with a light on in the bathroom beyond it. There was a thick carpet here, sculpted into patterns, and a long wall of mirrored cupboards. Janice's negligee was laid out across one corner of the plump bed. Nina tiptoed like an intruder. On a tallboy there was a silver-framed photograph of a slimmer Janice in her wedding dress, one hand holding back a billow of net veiling. Nina picked it up, and the breath of her curiosity fogged the polished silver. She replaced the picture hastily and went on into the bathroom.

She sat down without locking the door.

Gordon had left the table. He could think of nothing but finding Nina, and securing a few seconds of her for himself, away from the intolerable, repetitive babble of the dinner party.

He opened the bathroom and saw her. She looked up at him, shocked, like a scared little girl with her tights twisted around her knees and her ankles crossed.

"What are you doing here?"

He was touched by her anger and shame. "I wanted to see you."

She finished, then dried herself and straightened her clothes with neat womanly movements that he loved.

"They'll notice we're both missing."

"No they won't. They'll think I'm downstairs with the rugby shorts."

They moved together, and after they had kissed he held her face between his hands and examined it intently.

"I called you. I called you all weekend."

"I ran away," she told him simply.

"Don't run away again."

"There's nowhere to go."

"I'd find you anyway."

He was pushing against her and Nina put her arm up to one of the mirrors to support herself. As he turned his head Gordon saw the reflection of her, and the way the loose sleeve of her blouse fell back to reveal the bluish-white, egg-shaped hollow of her armpit. He was swept by a wave of tenderness that contradicted and intensified his need for her.

"Nina, Nina. Can I see you again? When can I see you?"

"Yes. I don't know when."

"Yes is enough for now." He kissed her again, wanting to fuse himself to her, but she slipped away from him.

"We must go back downstairs. You first."

He loved her carefulness and self-control. "I wish we didn't have to. It's a particularly silly evening." He wanted to apologize for its deficiencies.

"No, it isn't," she contradicted him. "It's warm and friendly, like Janice said. You must go now, or they'll guess what's happening."

He kissed her again, his mouth scraping hers. Then he went off, and Nina was left staring in the mirror into her own anxious eyes.

Jimmy and Janice were the only ones left in the kitchen. Jimmy cleared the table and Janice haphazardly loaded plates into the dishwasher. He brought a stacked tray around to her and put it to one side while she bent over the wire racks.

"God, Janice, look at you. You know you've got a great ass on you."

Jimmy said it half-jokingly, as he always did, but there was enough wistful sincerity in his voice to make Janice straighten up at once and face him. Her face was damp and flushed and wisps of dark hair stuck to her cheeks. Her hostess manner of the early evening had all evaporated.

"Great's the word. Half of it would be plenty. Don't be an idiot, Jimmy."

He had reached out and with the tips of his fingers lifted one of the strands of hair. She was alarmed and almost eager. Jimmy twisted the coil of hair, his face flat.

"Yes, an *eejit*, that's what I am." Gently he withdrew his hand.

They contemplated each other for a minute more, their eyes on a level. Then Janice frowned, groping for something through her sudden tiredness and the effects of the wine.

"Are you and Star all right?"

His smile came back as quickly as it had vanished, with all the associated repertoire of eyebrow contortions.

"As right as rain. As right as ever. Shall I carry through the coffee tray for you, madam?"

When Nina came back to the den she found that someone had put on some slow music, and Janice and Jimmy and Hannah and Andrew were dancing in the space in front of the fire. Hannah rested her head on Andrew's shoulder. Gordon and Star were sitting a little apart, talking intently together. Nina sat down beside Darcy.

"Would you care to dance?"

She felt the full weight of his disconcerting charm. He was very handsome, although pads of flesh almost obliterated the strong bones of his face. Even after all the alcohol his eyes remained sharp under the puffy lids.

She smiled. "I think I would rather just sit."

Nina was tired now. She wanted to go back to the peace of her own house, but at the same time she did not wish to be away from Gordon.

"Let's sit, then," Darcy said. After a moment in which they watched the two couples slowly gyrating he leaned closer to her, so intimately as to close off the rest of the room. Nina smelled cigars and cologne, and the whisky on his breath.

"Tell me," he invited, "what do you think of our provincial little world?"

"What do I think of Grafton? I grew up here, remember."

"Yes, I remember that. I meant, do you ever regret exchanging everything in London just for this?"

He nodded at the dancers.

Nina realized that he was trying to set the two of them apart, at a sophisticated, metropolitan distance from the others, even Hannah. He wanted her to conspire gently with him in noticing the ways that Janice's furniture and food and even their mutual friends fell short of their London counterparts.

Nina felt a dislike of Darcy flare up inside her, in defense of Gordon and the evening's warmth. She tried to resist the impulse, but her eyes slid across the room to where Gordon was still sitting with Star. Star's head was bent and she was shading her eyes with her fingers. She looked as if she was trying not to cry.

"I don't regret the exchange at all," Nina answered sharply, trying to focus all her attention on Darcy. "I'm very happy to be here. Besides, the advantages of living in Grafton far outweigh the disadvantages. The way I've been made to feel welcome, for instance. I probably wouldn't have enountered anything like it if I had made the move in the opposite direction."

Some of her dislike was for herself. She had noticed the details of the Frosts' hospitality that would have told her immediately, had it been the first time she met them, that these were not London people. She had probably noted them with an eye just as sharp as Darcy Clegg's. But that still did not mean she wanted to collude with him.

Darcy's intentions seemed to change at once, with alcoholic unpredictability.

"*I* miss it," he said. "More than I am usually prepared to admit. More than most people would guess, given everything I have here."

"I wouldn't have guessed," Nina said. Her dislike of him melted away again.

Darcy suddenly added, "But we provincials have to find our challenges and diversions where we can."

She had no idea what he meant. He lifted his hands, with his fingers bunched, as if he were holding strings. She had the impression suddenly that he was the puppet master of the group, and the others, tired and more or less drunk as they were now at the end of the evening, were the puppets who danced for him. Her skin prickled down the length of her spine. At the same moment she became aware that Jimmy Rose was watching the two of them over Janice's lolling head.

Across in their corner, Star said softly to Gordon, "It isn't just tonight. It's every night. I think to myself that I don't mind, that I don't care what he does, but I do. I care for myself, for being humiliated in front of my friends. I'm sorry, Gordon. I've drunk too much. Not for the first time, eh?"

Gordon was vividly aware that Nina had looked at them, then looked away again. What was Darcy whispering to her about?

Star reached her hand out, and reluctantly he took it.

"If he makes you unhappy, why don't you leave him?" he asked her.

Star raised her head.

"Will *you* have me if I do?"

It was a joke, and not a joke.

"Star, how could I?"

"You couldn't, of course. But you know it's you I'd have, if I could." She smiled at him then, a lopsided smile of self-mockery.

The record ended and Hannah stepped back from Andrew, making an elaborate curtsy of thanks. He put his arm around her waist and steered her back toward Darcy.

Nina saw that Star was on her feet now, apparently quite composed. It was clear that the evening was winding down.

The three women left with Janice to find their coats, and Gordon and Andrew were conferring in hushed voices about some business they needed to attend to in the morning. Jimmy and Darcy found themselves standing together by the front door.

"Well then," Jimmy said softly. "It's *La belle veuve*, is it?"

"What do you mean?" It pleased Darcy to appear not to catch his meaning.

"She likes you."

"Does she?" He accepted Jimmy's tribute without betraying any interest in it, although he experienced a flicker of satisfaction strengthened by his certainty that he felt no reciprocal liking for Nina Cort. Such aloof, contained women had never attracted him.

Jimmy laughed, and, having sown the idea, was subtle enough to leave it to germinate alone.

"What was the matter with Mike Wickham today, do you think?"

Darcy shrugged. "How would I know? Time of the month, probably."

Jimmy laughed again. "Just the same, I'd prefer not to be landed with him next week."

Darcy draped his heavy arm around Jimmy's shoulder and patted it reassuringly. "Back to the usual setup on Sunday, then. That way we can be sure of winning."

The women came down the stairs in a group. Jimmy allowed himself a moment's luxurious contemplation of their separate possibilities, abundant Hannah and tawny, mysterious Nina, juicy, unobtainable Janice, and Star, his own.

He called cheerfully to Nina, "We'll give you a ride home, since we're the nearest to you."

"Thank you. Star kindly offered already," Nina said.

All of them had reached the door in a flurry of thanks and good nights. Nina was caught up with the Roses and swept out, away from Gordon, and she was only aware that he was watching her go and wanted to hold her back. The evening was finally over.

When everyone had gone Janice leaned against the banisters. "Did I drink a lot?"

Her eyes looked smudged, as if they were melting into the frail surrounding skin, and the rosy pencil line with which she had outlined her lips at the beginning of the evening had faded and turned brown. When she had been drinking and came to the end of an evening's high, Janice's confidence sometimes collapsed, leaving her confused and vulnerable, and vividly reminding Andrew of the much more tentative girl he had married.

"You did," he told her. She followed him back into the kitchen.

"Not badly too much?"

"No. You were just enjoying yourself. It was a good evening."

Andrew opened the window and a draft of cold air that tasted of earth and rain penetrated the smoke and perfume hanging in the room. He looked inside the dishwasher and began to rearrange the dirty plates properly. Behind him Janice asked, "We do give good evenings, don't we?"

Andrew straightened up. The beef Wellington dish was covered with a layer of congealed fat, and the butcher's string made a greasy curl on the countertop. He wanted to set the kitchen straight and then to spend a few minutes in the dark and silence of the garden before bed. But Janice stumbled toward him, needing reassurance, and he gave it to her.

"Of course we do. Thanks to you. You do all the arranging and the shopping and the cooking. All I do is open the wine." It was an old joke between them, a joke that had worn thin and shiny with time.

"No, you do such a lot more than that." She reached out and caught his hand. "You're a very good husband." She groped for the words, mistily now. "You're very good to me. We all love you. *I* love you."

Andrew stood still, hugging her, feeling her weight in his arms. Her hair smelled of the cooking she had done, the afternoon spent chopping and sautéeing. Without knowing that he was doing it, he leaned slightly away from her toward the washing still to be done. The understanding between them on these evenings was that Janice prepared and he cleaned up.

"I love you, too." The formal exchange. It was not an untruth, not exactly, rather a truth that had changed its coloring. Andrew shut off the thought. He did not want to pursue it now.

"Jimmy was very lively tonight," Janice began. She wanted to make amends in case her flirtatiousness had disturbed him.

"Jimmy is just Jimmy."

"I know," she sighed. Andrew heard a whisper of regret in her admission, but he let this second thought follow the first into limbo.

"I'll help you finish here," Janice said after a moment. "It won't take a minute." She had regained some of her briskness.

They worked side by side, stepping around each other in the familiar space. Janice imagined the pattern of their footsteps on the tiled floor, like the intricate movements of some domestic dance. The unaccustomed whimsy of the idea made her smile. Sometimes Andrew's footsteps would diverge, leaping to work and away from them all, while hers would lay down more regular loops, to school and to other houses. But still, the center of the pattern was printed here, on the kitchen tiles. It was a comforting notion.

The kitchen was tidy enough to satisfy them both. Andrew wiped the top of the units with a cloth, sweeping the crumbs and remnants carefully into the cup of his hand. He had always been neater around the house than she.

"I'm going to bed," Janice said, giving a little yawn like a cat's.

"I'll be with you in a minute. Five minutes' fresh air, and then I'll lock up."

It had been raining, but now the sky was partially clear. There was a ribbon of thick cloud overhead, marked by a paler rim, and beyond it in the west a few stars were visible.

Andrew made a slow circuit of the garden. It was too dark to see much and he took each step carefully, testing his familiarity with the ground against the confusion of darkness. He ducked his head under the branches of a cherry tree that overhung the path, and then found a bench set back between the bare twigs of the dogwoods. He sat down, feeling the damp, grainy wood under his fingers. The small noises of the garden were magnified, much more important than the low note of distant traffic on the throughway.

Andrew let his head fall back against the seat back. His eyes closed and the damp air sealed them like a compress. He had also drunk a good deal. The voices of the evening sounded briefly within his skull, and then he dismissed them. The silence was sweet.

When he opened his eyes again he looked with dark-adjusted eyes at the irregular bulk of the house and the loose composition of trees that framed it. One corner of the trellis that supported a wisteria against one wall had come loose, he remembered. He would have to fix it on Saturday.

With the domestic certainty of the plan came an unexpected happiness that suddenly lifted and ballooned inside him. There was this house and its gardens, and the solid, inarticulate love he felt for his sons, and there was Janice. He remembered her blurred glance at him this evening when she had brought up Jimmy's behavior, her need for love and reassurance, and the kitchen smell in her hair.

He still felt the happiness, taut as a drum beneath his ribcage. As he got up and walked back toward the house he was thinking that it was not an exciting life, but round, sufficient. It was what he had. Upstairs in the silence of the house Janice was already asleep. Andrew undressed and got into bed beside her, warming himself against the generous curve of her back.

6

Forty boisterous children seethed under the magnificent fan-vaulted roof of the cathedral's chapter house, leaping on and off the ancient stone seats that lined the walls, unawed by their surroundings. It was the first full rehearsal for the annual Grafton nativity play.

Marcelle Wickham sat on a folding chair with a list and a clip-board, and a wicker hamper beside her. Daisy Wickham had been chosen to be in the angels' choir. It was an honor but a double-edged one, because with the invitation had come a suggestion that Daisy's mother might like to help with the costumes. Marcelle had sighed, and then for Daisy's sake said that she would be glad to do it. Now, with just three weeks before the first performance, sixteen of the children were still uncostumed, including the ox and the ass.

Marcelle looked up from her list to see Nina standing beside her.

Nina was wearing her bright red jacket and her hair frizzed out over her shoulders, reminding Marcelle of her first glimpse of her in the supermarket. She shone like a beacon now against the austere stone backdrop of the chapter house.

"Thanks for coming," Marcelle said gratefully.

The director was calling his cast to order. Marcelle and Nina lowered their voices.

"The ones I've finished are in here." Marcelle lifted the lid of her hamper.

Nina unfolded an angel's robe. The fabric was the cheapest plain white cotton, but the garment was beautifully cut, with a yoke and falling folds of sleeve.

"No tinsel halos?" she asked with a smile.

"No tinsel halos. To Daisy's great disappointment."

"So what would you like me to do?"

She had heard Marcelle talking about the cathedral play, and about the sewing that remained to be done, and had diffidently offered to help her. In the last weeks Nina had felt the cathedral beckoning her, so that her steps continually returned to it. The creamy stone of the great pillars and arches and the pieced-together miracle of the medieval glass thrilled her as they had always done, but now she was as much affected by its place at the heart of Grafton. The towers and pinnacles seemed to gather the streets inward, anchoring and interpreting them, and connecting the lives beyond them.

Once she would have dismissed the idea as fanciful, but now she was convinced that the cathedral and its works were the secular as well as spiritual heart of Grafton. The business district and the shopping area and the closes and avenues of new houses were only peripheral, the bright green leaves, whereas the cathedral was the roots. More than the roots—the black earth itself. Nina had never experienced any religious sentiments, and she did not know if what she was feeling now was religious, but she loved the sense of continuity, the daily services that were performed whether the people came or not, the rhythms of the chapter and the close beyond her windows.

Marcelle said, apologetically, "It's the animals, really. The ox and the ass and the lambs. I know it's pushy, asking a professional artist like you, but I thought perhaps some painted masks . . ."

Nina cut her short. "I can do masks, if you like. Or more representational heads, if you would rather. Not fiberglass or anything too ambitious. But papier-mâché needn't be as tacky as it sounds."

"Could you?"

"Easily."

"I *think* masks. The children are quite small, especially the lambs. Those are the two, at the front."

A pair of six-year-olds, one with a head of tight brassy curls, squirmed at the front of the group of children.

The angel choir had shuffled to its feet, Daisy Wickham among them. They were joined by the twelve choir boys from the cathedral school, whose musical director raised his hand.

The children began to sing the Coventry Carol.

Nina's eyes and throat were stung by its sweetness. Her parents had brought her to the cathedral every Christmas to see the nativity play and to hear the carols, and now she was swept back to childhood and the memories of hard wooden seats and the faint smell of cough drops and fir boughs.

Daisy Wickham peered sideways to make sure her mother was watching, then made an embarrassed face at her.

From the four rows of children Nina picked out another face she knew, or thought she recognized. He was in the choir, a boy of about nine. He had a cap of fair hair cut in a square fringe above his eyebrows, and a round, sweet, rather stolid face.

"That must be a little Frost, surely, the one at the front on the left?"

"Yes. It's William, the youngest."

He was like his brother, but his features were still girlish and pretty. Nina watched the little boy as the carol ended, and reflected on the slow changes that would transmute him into a glowering adolescent and then, at last, into a version of Andrew Frost.

For the first time in many months she wished for a child of her own, to see her growing and unfolding in the way William Frost would do.

The rehearsal ended at eight. By the time it was over, Marcelle and Nina had divided the remaining cutting and sewing between them, and Nina had promised to bring roughs of her masks to the next rehearsal.

"I'm so grateful," Marcelle said. She was, in truth, because she was sure that whatever Nina undertook would be done well.

They said their good nights and separated. Nina walked away across the green, thinking of Vicky at home with her husband and her new baby, and of the choir of angels, other women's children rehearsing carols.

Marcelle drove across town with Daisy in the back seat. She was a good driver and she felt comfortable, in this brief interlude, within the insulated box of her car. She liked the soft greenish glow of the instrument panel and the slow burr of the heater, and the way the lights outside licked over her face and then receded behind her. She would have been happy if home had been much further away, if she could have driven on, suspended like this, with the traffic blinking past on the opposite side of the road.

When she reached the house, Marcelle noted that a light was on behind the drawn curtains in Michael's upstairs study. The tranquillity induced by the night drive was slipping away from her. Her mouth tightened, she felt it, and felt the vertical lines marking her cheeks.

"Here we are, home again," she said brightly to Daisy. Michael's car was in the garage. She left hers on the sloping drive and carried Daisy's music case up to the front door as the tired child shuffled behind her.

The house was quiet except for the distant sound of the television. Marcelle let her bag and Daisy's case drop to the hall floor.

The air still seemed heavy and stale with the taint of Sunday's unresolved quarrel.

It had been a terrible argument, the more frightening because it had swelled out of almost nothing, an ordinary weekend disagreement about whether Michael devoted enough time to his children. He had come into the kitchen dressed for golf.

Marcelle had demanded, "Are you going out again? What about Jon and Daisy, don't you think they might like to see their father on a Sunday? They don't see you all week, do they?"

"Yes, I am going out. I'm going to play golf. I work hard and I need time away from there"—he meant the concrete slabs and glass of the hospital—"and from here as well." Michael had made a gesture with his hand as if to push back the walls of their house.

The resolute coldness in him had scared her, then made her angry. She stared back at him over the chopping board, the kitchen table, the basket of ironing waiting to be folded.

"I work hard, too, Michael. What about me?"

His anger had answered hers, and then exceeded it.

"Everything here is about you. Your standards, your ideals. You want to be the perfect mother with the perfect family, you want your job, you want your house just so. It's all to do with what *you* want. You want it, you have it. But don't expect me to conform to the design."

"It isn't a design. I do it out of love for you all."

Marcelle had begun to shout. Her fear was intensifying, but it became fear of herself, because she never shouted, never made scenes.

"It doesn't come across as love."

"I can't help that, Michael. Perhaps you can't accept what you can't give."

"It's always me, isn't it? What I can't or won't do. I support you all, don't I? You have your children, your hobbies, your sewing and cooking. It doesn't seem to me that you have a bad bargain."

"Cooking isn't a hobby, it's my job. I make my contribution as best I can, with two children to care for as well."

The argument had grown, sloughing and bouncing between the two of them and gathering momentum until it became an avalanche of unleashed resentment. Reason and consideration had seemed to stand up like sticks in its path, only to be snapped and swept away.

"Perhaps the truth is that you don't love me anymore," Marcelle said.

"Perhaps," Michael answered coldly.

With no more ground to consume, the avalanche had run out of impetus. Hot-mouthed, they looked at each other across a bleak landscape of murrain.

Marcelle had become aware of the heavy silence spreading through the house. She knew that the children were crouching upstairs in their bedrooms, listening to their parents' ranting voices. She had felt pinched with shame for herself and for them.

A moment later, Jonathan had appeared pale-faced at the head of the stairs.

"Don't argue," he had shouted. "Stop arguing."

"Adults argue," Michael had told him sharply. "That's something you'll learn." And then he had gone out, his golf bag slung over his shoulder.

Jonathan's homework books were spread on the kitchen table now, but he was in the next room watching television. Michael had picked him up from a late evening at school. The boy glanced up at his mother and sister.

"Hello, Ma, hello, Daze."

"Hello, Jon. Had a good day? Where's Daddy?"

Marcelle asked the question although she knew the answer already.

Jonathan shrugged. His eyes had returned to the television screen. "Upstairs, working."

Marcelle ran Daisy's bath and saw her into it. Then she went along the landing to Michael's study and opened the door. He was sitting at his desk, surrounded by papers and files and medical journals. He had been staring at a research paper, but he had taken in none of the information it contained. Instead, since Marcelle had come in he had been listening to the sounds of the house. There had been a quickening of the air, and the joists and timbers had seemed to creak under the pressure of her presence. He heard her feet on the stairs, and the sound of water running, and the children following her directions. This was all so familiar to him that he had to concentrate to extract the idea of his wife, separate in herself, from the fug of domesticity. He was frowning when she opened the door.

"Had a good day?" he asked, taking off his reading glasses and rubbing the bridge of his nose.

Marcelle saw the frown.

"Yes, quite good. Nina's going to help me with the costumes for the play."

"That's nice."

"I'll just see Daisy into bed, then I'll make some supper."

"Fine. I'll be down before too long."

Marcelle hesitated, running her fingers around the smooth circumference of the doorknob. She was reassured to see him, here in his place, because she was half-afraid that an evening would come when he would not return home. But her relief was immediately soured by her resentment of him, and the two sensations made a sickly brew inside her. Struggling with herself, she went over and stood beside his chair. When she looked down she could see the patch of thin hair on his crown, and the fine network of thread veins on the nearest cheek.

In a distant voice she offered, "If what happened on Sunday was my fault, I'm sorry for it."

It was the first time it had been mentioned since Michael's return on Sunday afternoon.

After a moment, he said. "I'm sorry, too."

He didn't make any move to touch her, even to take her hand, the way he once would have done. Marcelle waited, looking down at the work on his desk. It was a report on the orthopedic rehabilitation of geriatric patients after hip-replacement operations.

"Will you come down and have a drink?" she asked, wanting to find a warmer voice than the small, cold one that came out of her.

"I won't be too long," he repeated.

She left him to his work, and went to see the children into bed.

Gradually the baby's mouth went slack and the drowsy sucking stopped completely. Her head fell back as the baby's gums released her breast. Vicky held her still for a minute, looking at the tiny dark crescents of her eyelashes and the whitish pad of tissue on her upper lip, rimmed with milk. This baby was like Mary and Alice had been, but she was also different, more beautiful and more precious, because she would be the last one. There was no doubt about that. Gordon would never agree to a third try for a boy.

Vicky rocked the baby in her arms, softly humming. She had already forgotten the painful labor and her stitches and the depression that had assailed her in the hospital. She had come home and her life had closed around her again. The little girls were pleased with their new sister, and Gordon was being assiduous in his efforts to help. Helen slept, and fed, and slept again. The house enclosed them all like a warm cocoon.

When she was quite sure that the baby was asleep, Vicky lifted her up and walked softly into the next room. She wrapped her in her white blanket and laid her down in the basinette.

It was the middle of the morning, the time that always seemed to Vicky to be the brightest and safest part of the whole day. It was an optimistic interim of radio music and kettles and vacuum cleaners, before the day tipped over into the more ambivalent stretches of the afternoon. When she was at work, at the clinic, she liked to see her children at this innocent time.

There was no need to think about work yet, she reflected. The remaining weeks of her maternity leave stretched ahead of her.

Vicky went into the kitchen and leaned against the sink, looking out into the wintry garden. There was an inverted pyramid of baby clothes hanging on the rotary clothesline. It was a day of thin, bright sunshine, and the shafts of light struck horizontally through the windows. Dust motes swirled like light particles in the solid-seeming bars of brightness. She felt dreamy, almost dazed by the colorless sunlight falling on her face.

When the telephone on the wall beside her rang she lifted it absently and murmured, "Hello?"

There was the momentary, weightless silence that signaled Gordon on his car telephone.

"Darling? Is that you? You sound funny. Are you all right?"

"Yes. I'm fine. Helen has just gone to sleep. Isn't it a lovely day?"

"What? Yes, beautiful. I just wanted to make sure you were all right. I'm going to be on site for most of the rest of the day, and it'll be difficult to reach me."

"Don't worry. We're perfect here, Helen and me."

"I'll ring you later, then. You'll call Janice or someone if you need anything?"

"Of course I will. I don't need anything. Thanks, anyway. Gordon?"

"Yes?"

"I love you." She cradled the receiver against her shoulder, still looking out at the garden and at the clothes gently rotating on the line.

"Love you, too. I won't be late," Gordon said.

Vicky hung up. Moving slowly, luxuriating in the the light, she filled the kettle and admired the diamond flashes in the water as it splashed in the sink.

Gordon drove back the way he had just come, this time with Nina beside him. The interior of the car seemed full of her scent, and the ends of her hair and the soft points of wool that stood up from her clothes gave off a crackle of static electricity. He wanted to touch her, rubbing her to discharge the sparks, and then to press his mouth against her and drink her in.

"Where are we going?"

He was watching the road, but still he was pricklingly aware of the pull of the muscles around her mouth, the sheen of her skin, the bloom of tiny hairs revealed by the oblique sunlight. It was no less than miraculous that he had pulled off this expedition with her, at the cost of nothing more than a small lie to Vicky and a penetrating look from Andrew as he had prised himself out of the office.

"You know where we're going," he answered. "To buy you a car."

Teasingly, Nina had repeated Hannah's suggestion to him, and he had responded to it in full seriousness. She had been touched.

"Yes, I know that, and it's very kind of you to take me."

"*Kind?*"

"Certainly. But where are we going to buy me a car?"

"To a Mercedes dealership I know. Near Bristol."

"Ah. Do I definitely need a Mercedes? Wouldn't it be more sensible to settle for something utilitarian and Japanese?"

"There is a Nissan place right opposite the Merc showroom, if you need to make a comparison. But it was you who mentioned a Mercedes in the first place."

"I know. I've always rather liked the idea."

His hand left the wheel and reached for hers. Their hands locked together, but they looked ahead, at the road signs that loomed and then whirled past, rather than to venture a glance at each other.

"A Mercedes is a sensible car. Solid, reliable, impeccably engineered."

Nina laughed at his earnestness. "If you say so."

"And sexy. If you choose the right model."

"Sexier than . . ." Nina pursed her lips, "Hannah's BMW, say?"

"Much." He did look at her then, and she was surprised and then caught undefended by the heat in him. Their linked hands rested against her thigh. Nina heard the rasp of her own breathing.

"Just as you are sexier than Hannah herself."

"I don't think so."

"Oh, but you are. Hannah is obvious, whereas you're subtle. Hannah is a hot day at the beach and you, you are . . . a forest path in the moonlight. A matter of shadows and suggestions, and sudden clear patches of pure silver."

This poetic flight from a man so unpoetical touched her again.

She felt a kindling of affection that was separate from the welter of her other hot and confused sensations.

Nina looked ahead of her again. A sign swept toward them, BRISTOL, 20 M. Gordon disengaged his hand from hers while he overtook a Volvo the same color as Janice's. Lightheartedly, but also out of a secret kind of retrospective jealousy, she asked him. "Which of the other wives do you like, if not Hannah?"

Gordon shrugged. "I don't know. Star, perhaps."

Nina remembered the impression of her weeping at the Frosts' on Sunday evening.

"Is she unhappy?"

"Who knows? No more unhappy than anyone else would be, I imagine, being married to Jimmy Rose."

It was a deliberate deflection, and Nina silently accepted it.

The Mercedes showroom was a sleek affair of plate-glass windows and shining bodywork, by the side of a busy road amid a network of more busy roads. There was indeed a Nissan dealership directly opposite it, a much brasher-looking place with a border of flags snapping on tall white poles.

Nina and Gordon stepped out of Gordon's car into a bright world of steel-blue glass reflections and long, polished hoods and cold sunlight shooting darts off mirrors and chrome. Even the specks of mica underfoot twinkled up at them. They walked shyly to the doors of the showroom, half-dazzled by the light and pleased to find themselves as a couple in this adventure, as if they had suddenly emerged into a surprise holiday.

Once they were inside a salesman in a blue suit came briskly to meet them.

"Good morning sir, madam. Can I help you at all?" He had a mouth over-full of teeth, all of them bared in a smile.

"Madam is looking for a car," Gordon said. Nina was seized by an urge to giggle and to dig him in the ribs with her elbow. Controlling herself, she said seriously, pointing to the nearest blur of shining metal. "Something like this one, perhaps."

"Ah, yes. The 190E. That particular car is two years old, but covered by our full warranty, of course.

"What else is there?"

"What are you looking for, exactly?"

Nina blinked and said "I'm not sure." Then, seeing the man's smile patronizingly widen, she improvised, "A sedan, not too big. It doesn't have to be new."

Gordon, her lifeline, had wandered away. She saw him, among the curves and planes of metal, appraising the machines. She followed him toward the back of the showroom, the salesman beside her.

Gordon stopped alongside a red car. It was the color of audacious lipstick, and it had a black convertible top and wheels with silver spokes and the look of being inappropriately corralled here among the humbler models.

"What about this?" Gordon murmured.

"*This* one?" Nina touched its long nose. Her fingertip left a tiny smudge on the sheen of scarlet.

The salesman was there at once.

"The 500SL. Power top, thirty-two valve engine, the top of the line. A very nice car. This one is just a year old, twelve thousand miles, one gentleman owner, fully serviced by us since new, of course."

"It is very pretty," Nina said.

"Top speed of a hundred-fifty-five miles per hour, not that that's much use to us here of course, but dead handy on the Continent. The car's capable of more, naturally, but the governor cuts in at that point. Zero to sixty in six point five seconds, so you won't be finding many of the boy racers in XR3's outrunning you at the lights."

"Very impressive."

Behind the salesman's shoulder, Gordon silently mouthed at her, "*Very sexy.*"

Nina kept her face straight.

"Would you like to test-drive it?"

The car gleamed at her in all its bright red glory. She could see her face reflected in the voluptuous curve of the door panel, her hair reddened to a blaze. This wasn't at all the sober sedan she had envisaged.

"Why not?"

There was at once a clicking of fingers and opening of tall doors behind her. The salesman sprang into the black leather seat and switched on the engine. A soft purr, with a threatening, throaty undertone, rose like bubbles through champagne. Smiling like truant children, Gordon and Nina followed the car outside. The salesman climbed out and held the driver's door open for Nina.

"But there are only two seats," she said.

Gordon bowed. "I'll wait. Enjoy the drive."

Nina slid into the car and braced her hands experimentally on the wheel. She looked down the cowling to the gunsight of the three-pointed star at its end, and gently touched her foot to the accelerator.

"Left around the building, and then right into the main road," the salesman said encouragingly. As she eased the Mercedes away, Nina distinctly heard Gordon's wolf whistle.

At first she was nervous, and then she was exhilarated. The purr modulated to a noise like tearing silk and the car shot forward. She swung the wheel too hard and had to jerk it back again, and they sailed out into the stream of traffic.

"Power steering," the salesman reminded her.

It was very fast. The road opened up and the bunch of dull cars in their wake suddenly dwindled to dots in her mirror. She braced her arms and felt the car respond to the lightest touch on the wheel. The glossy hood in front of her shimmered like a stretched satin ribbon, and the gray road temptingly unwound ahead.

The salesman had been reciting the selling points, but now he had gone quiet. Nina glanced at his face, and then at the speedometer. She was doing a hundred and five miles an hour. She lifted her foot, and the scenery caught up with her again.

"Quite a virile motor," the man said, "I can see you like that."

"I do, rather," Nina said, surprised by herself.

But she knew that she had been entirely seduced. The more she drove the car, the more she wanted to drive it. The speedometer crept up again, and her head fell back, and she wanted to turn on the radio and sing and drive straight on forever into the winter sun.

"We could make a turn just ahead," the salesman ventured.

Reluctantly, she did as she was told.

When they swooped back to the showroom and Nina saw Gordon innocently lounging with hands in his pockets beside his own unremarkable family sedan, she muttered a mock curse under her breath. It cost her a pang to climb out of the black leather seat and abandon her bright-red seducer, even temporarily.

Gordon strolled over to them.

"How was it?"

The salesman fanned himself with his clipboard.

"I like it," Nina said demurely.

"Shall we go across there and have a look?" Gordon nodded at the busy flags over the lines of Nissans.

Nina turned her back on them and stretched her fingers out again to the red shine. There was nothing so vulgar as a price ticket anywhere in sight.

"How much is it?"

The man consulted a list on his clipboard. "Sixty-two, nine-fifty, this particular car."

She was opening her mouth, amazingly, to say *I'll take it*, when she felt Gordon's hand descend very firmly on her arm.

"We'll just take a walk, then, and think about it."

Then they were outside again in the cold sunshine. A stronger wind had begun to blow, and there was a fringe of cloud off to the east.

"I loved it. It isn't at all what I intended to buy, but now I can't bear to think of settling for anything less."

Her cheeks were hot. Gordon's arm and shoulder felt very warm on one side and the chill on the other sliced into her. She realized that her blood was racing, and that she was excited, for the car and for the bright day and for Gordon himself. He lowered his head and kissed her, open-mouthed. His hand slid inside her coat.

"Can you afford it?"

She thought of the money that Richard had left her, dead weights of it invisibly stored up in banks and securities, and of Richard himself, as she had never seen him, lying on the path under the branches of the trees. He was gone and would never come back.

"Yes. I can pay cash."

His eyes widened a fraction, and the palm of his hand grazed her nipple under the layers of clothes.

Speed and money and sex, Nina thought giddily. The old cliché. But it was no less exciting for that.

"Then let me do the deal for you," Gordon whispered.

They went back to the showroom together, and he began to negotiate.

From the salesman's face Nina knew that he was jealous of them both. He was jealous of her for her car and her money, and of Gordon for his possession of her. The atmosphere in the mock-plush little side office was as tense as a drawn wire.

"I can't go any lower than that. That's shaved our profit right down to a couple of points," the man complained.

"Then we'll go along to Forshaw's and see what they can offer us," Gordon said simply. Nina was awed.

After half an hour, she had her red car for exactly fifty-nine thousand pounds, and the salesman was wiping his forehead with a folded handkerchief.

"I'll come in with a bank check the day after tomorrow," Nina said with a smile.

They shook hands at last.

Outside again, Nina put her arm through Gordon's.

"You were terrible. The poor little man."

"Poor nothing. He doesn't sell many of those in a week."

"My beautiful new car. Thank you."

On the front lot, faced by lines of Nissans, they kissed again. Nina shivered with his arms around her.

"Get in," Gordon said, and held the door for her. They drove away, in silence now, aware of their own breathing and the fog of each other's breath in the cold air. When they reached the freeway Nina slyly put her hand out, reaching for him, the images of smooth red wings and the glitter of chrome still in her mind.

"It's a long way home," she whispered.

He knew that she had been turned on by the car, by the whole secret, frivolous expedition they had made together, and that seemed to him delightful and also erotic.

"I can't wait that long," Gordon said roughly.

Ahead of them was a sign for a rest area, and among the little blue-and-white symbols offering themselves innocently was one that showed a bed. It had a head and foot and a neatly turned down white sheet.

Nina heard the tick-tick of the directional, and they swung left in a line of drivers leaving the freeway. The Travelodge at the far side of the enclave was deserted at this time of day, its double row of windows masked by net curtains. There were no other cars in the motel's parking area.

"Wait here for me," Gordon said.

After he had gone through a door at the end of the block marked RECEPTION, Nina felt suddenly conspicuous sitting alone in his car. She sank a little lower into her seat, drawing the collar of her coat up around her neck, then dismissed her fears as absurd and sat upright again. A moment later Gordon came back and took his place behind the wheel once more. Then he opened his hand to show her a key with a plastic number tag. They both stared at it.

"Do you want to do this?" he asked her. "In a motel room, with me?"

She looked out at the windswept tarmac and the tossing branches of trees that had been planted to break the noise of the road.

Gordon said, "The other night was happenstance. We can dismiss that, if you like. You were lonely, I stepped out of line, Vicky was in the hospital."

The second time, she supplied for him, *is different*. It was a matter of volition, and if the act was repeated they would have to make the necessary reckonings afterward. Her own husband was dead; suddenly the knowledge came back to her with full force, battering her with its finality, as brutally as it had done in the first terrible days after her loss. The pain made Nina catch her breath and narrow her eyes to contain the stab of tears. She had not felt such hurt for months, and its return made her shrink from the possibility of inflicting the same pain on Vicky.

Gordon's direct language and appetite had excited her as no one had ever done before, but he was another woman's husband. Nina knew the weight of her own loneliness and remembered how Gordon had lightened it, but she knew equally well that he would not and could not entirely dissolve it for her, because he belonged elsewhere.

With her powers of reasoning distorted by pain and anger, Nina struggled to balance the equation of need and guilt. As she stared unseeing through the windshield, she was forced to acknowledge that she did want Gordon again. The grip of pain began to loosen. As it faded, leaving her weak and witless, she knew that she did not have the strength of will to deny him, or herself. This mundane place, the breeze-block outline of the motel, and the key in his hand, were invested with significance because of their association with him. She did not understand how this had happened, only that it had, and now she could not escape whatever was to follow.

She took the key from his hand, the metal and plastic jingling together.

"I do want to," she told him.

He kissed her, forcing her back against the headrest, and his mouth grazed her skin. They left the car and walked unsteadily toward the motel room.

It was a small rectangular box with a hollowed bed flanked by cheap drawers faced in brown plastic veneer. A bathroom walled into one corner revealed pink tiles and a floral curtain.

Gordon tossed the key onto the bedcover.

"I'm sorry. This is horrible."

He was thinking of the pale, dignified spaces of her house on Dean's Row. He remembered her bedroom as clearly as if he were looking at a photograph of it. But he had wanted this second time, if it was to happen, to be in a neutral place neither hers nor his.

"It isn't horrible or beautiful. It's nowhere," Nina said gently.

He was grateful to her for reading of his needs. But now they faced each other in the perfunctory approximation of a bedroom, a place that was occupied without affection by hurried businessmen and travelers and illicit lovers like themselves, he saw their condition more clearly, when it was stripped of its romantic glow. He saw a middle-aged man, made weary of his good wife by the repetition of too many days. He had brought Nina here—and in this clear light he knew that she was not the wild girl he had conjured up the other night, but a sad widow, also no longer young, with fine lines in her face—to commit an act of adultery.

A memory of the cathedral on the night of their meeting came back to him. He had been intent on her, but he also remembered the organ music and the singing of the choir at practice. He was not a conventionally religious man, and he had married Vicky in a registry office, but he had a confused sense now of a simple and faithful life, established and approved by a higher authority, that might have been lived along lines that were parallel to but infinitely distant from the tangle and heat and disillusion of his real existence.

"What is it?" Nina asked him.

He tried to say *Nothing* but at the same time he half-turned away from her and looked through the net curtains to where his car was parked between oblique white lines.

"Guilt. And fear, and a belated desire not to hurt anyone."

She came close to him and put her arms around his waist, under the shelter of his jacket, and held him as if he were a child, or an old friend.

"Yes," Nina said. "I know."

Because of the simplicity of her response, and also because he saw her face so clearly and close up, with the marks of time and grief in it, he felt his doubts gather together and lift and swing away from him again. He was left with pure conviction.

"I love you," he said. "I loved you the other night at Andrew's. In that bathroom."

He also wanted her more insistently than he had ever wanted Vicky or any of the women he had ever known.

She put her hand up to his mouth to stop him, but he caught it and held it.

"I love you," he repeated. "I don't know how this has happened. I didn't ask for it, but it's here now, and I don't want it to go away. I don't want you to go away. Never, never."

He was whispering to her, his lips against her face. All the perspectives had changed. The room had become a sanctuary, benign and familiar and precious for that, and the horizons beyond it had vanished as if a thick, kindly mist had descended over it.

"You don't love me. You can't love me because you don't know me," Nina told him. Richard had known her, after all their years together.

"I do know you. What more do I need to learn?"

He undid her clothes and peeled them off her tea-freckled shoulders. He kissed her skin and tasted its warm saltiness and pushed her back until they lay in the bed's hollow and looked into the reflections in each other's eyes.

"Take off your clothes, too," she ordered him.

He clawed at the buttons and buckles, discarding his business uniform. Her knuckles clashed against his while their hands worked. Then, when he knelt above her, she looked up at him and her lips and eyelids thickened with concupiscence. He remembered how she had looked the first time, in her unornamented bedroom.

Nina's hand descended on him, and she watched the effect through half-closed eyes. A moment later they were tangled together, mouths and hands and limbs. Her narrow hips insinuated themselves beneath him, snakily lifting, not offering herself but commanding him. She was different from Vicky, who waited to be led. Vicky was not submissive, not exactly, but there was an understanding that she preferred to bestow rather than to demand. There was a moment's pure confusion as the woman beneath him receded and then merged with the familiar images of his wife, and then split away again to resume her own identity, utterly strange to him.

The marriage of strangeness with intimacy was like a chemical entering his bloodstream, sending such a narcotic kick through his body that he was afraid he would come now, too soon, like a boy.

"Tell me what you think. What you feel," she demanded when he entered her. And then, "Oh, I *want* you."

"You've got me. Nina, Nina. I think you're extraordinary, unmatchable. I feel like making love to you forever."

He wanted to bury himself, to shoot himself into a milky galaxy of stars inside her. He wanted to become timeless and fathomless, as if he had died and turned into a star, as his mother had long ago promised he would.

Instead, their coupling was quick and feverish, and its carnality startled them both. There was no time, as they had felt there was the first night. They longed to reclaim each other after the separation. There were the Frosts' dinner party and London and the days in between to be obliterated, and the car showroom and the salesman and the motel itself. They went at each other blindly, as if it was the last thing they would ever do.

Afterward, lying with Nina's hair spread over his eyes and her weight on top of him, Gordon imagined the noise they had made penetrating the walls into the mirror-image boxes to either side of them, and into the ones beyond those, and he prayed fervently that they were all empty.

When his breathing became even again he stroked her hair away and peered downward, trying to see her face. She was looking up at the woodchip-papered ceiling. He was at once intensely jealous of whatever it was that took her attention away from him.

"I meant it, you know."

"Meant?"

"I love you."

"Hush."

Her face, the skin over the bone, and all the rest of her body, had now become irrelevant, although he loved them, too, with a kind of detached affection. He was much more vividly aware of the internal spark, the invisible imp, that animated her. He wanted to catch hold of it, and wondered at his own possessiveness.

"Tell me more about Richard."

"I was just thinking about him. How did you know?"

"A guess. Not a particularly inspired one."

She leaned over him, her small bumpy breasts falling against his chest.

"I'm sorry. I didn't mean to withdraw from you. I think of him often. It's very odd when someone who is still quite young and apparently fit dies suddenly. One minute the person is there, filling your life, and then, in a day, in an hour, he's completely gone and will never come back. For a long time I felt so angry with him for abandoning me."

"Yes. What do you feel now?"

"I don't know. Grateful, usually. For what we had, you know."

He digested that for a moment.

"What do you want from me?" He heard himself asking, like a petulant boy, for reassurance, compliments, approval.

Nina propped her head on one elbow, looking down at him. She seemed amused, and he was momentarily irritated by her.

"I mean, I'm just a simple bloody engineer. I'm not rich or smart or clever. I don't know the right restaurants in London. I can't even fix the right restaurant here. I'm married. I've got three kids, too much work to do . . ."

She cut him short. "I don't want anything from you."

Then she indicated the room. He looked at the cheap furniture, the wall-mounted mirror, the round tin tray bearing a kettle and a sugarbowl filled with teabags and packets of coffee and milk powder.

"Just this," she said. And with a touch of coquetry, she ran the flat of her hand up his flank, over the thickening flesh at his waist to rest on his chest. Under her hand, it seemed to Gordon that she had it in her power to make the drab place beautiful, and to invest him with more significance than he could ever truly possess. He felt a surge of undiluted happiness.

"Are you afraid of it? Of me?" Nina demanded.

"No, not a bit. I can't believe my luck, that's all."

"Or I mine," she told him softly.

He saw that she was cold and he drew the covers around her shoulders. She settled herself comfortably against him and they lay in silence for a minute.

"I won't try to take you away from Vicky."

It was hard enough, with this present intimacy salving her loneliness, to accept that she must relinquish him in an hour, as she knew she would have to. Her imagination had been spiraling ahead, through the permutations of future encounters, to the vanishing point, when Gordon might somehow come to be with her. She had to offer the promise to stem her guilt at even allowing herself the thought.

"I know that. Thank you."

He felt a separate, invincible tenderness now for his wife and daughters. It was important that they should not be hurt, whatever happened.

Gordon felt lighthearted. He kissed the top of Nina's head. "Come and get into the bath with me," he said.

They went into the windowless pink cell and ran the water. Nina emptied the contents of all the complimentary sachets into it so that bubbles mounted to engulf the taps, and steam obliterated the mirrors. They lay down in the foam, folding their limbs to accommodate themselves, and the sickly-scented water slopped over the edge of the bath and made a puddle on the tiles.

They talked through the steam, exchanging simple details about their lives. It seemed suddenly important that they should know if the other had sisters or not, had traveled and how far, could speak French if not German, had read Updike, disliked Margaret Thatcher.

When the water was cold, Gordon said, "I must go back now."

They dried each other gently, like children, and disentangled their clothes.

When they were ready to leave they stood in the doorway, looking back at the bed and the tea tray and the surfaces of plastic veneer. Then Gordon closed the door affectionately, as if he were sealing a portion of their history into the room.

They drove quietly back to Grafton. The weather was changing; the sky was clouded and a bruised light looked as if it might be the herald of snow.

7

*I*t was a cold December, and the fields and hills beyond the city had been stilled and drained of colors by night after night of hard frost. A Christmas tree was put up on the cathedral green, exactly as Nina remembered from her childhood. Looking out at it from her windows, she thought that even the strings of colored bulbs twisted through its branches were the same.

Darcy and Hannah Clegg sent out elaborate printed invitations to their Christmas Eve party. It was to be their fifth consecutive one, and it had long been established as the social centerpiece of the couples' year.

Nina had put the Cleggs' invitation on the mantelpiece in her living room, where Gordon now picked it out from among all the other Christmas cards there. He had called to see her after a visit to the cathedral, whose whole west façade was now masked with scaffolding and protective sheeting.

"Are you going to this?"

"Yes, I am. Why not, after all?"

They were edgy with each other today, although she had run downstairs at the sound of his knock and when the door was closed they had fallen back against it in a rush of mutual eagerness.

"I can only stay for a few minutes," he had whispered, his fingers already busy with the buttons of her shirt.

Afterward they had pulled their clothes together again and stood uneasily in the living room in front of the cold afternoon hearth. Gordon had refused her offer of tea, explaining that Andrew was waiting for him back at the office.

Nina was galled by what she interpreted as a suggestion that she stay away from the party. It would be the first time that Gordon would have to face her with Vicky beside him.

"I didn't mean that you shouldn't come," he said at once, taking her hands. "I want to see you, every possible time, wherever it is. I'm only afraid that I won't be able to hide how much I do want it."

"You'll be able to. It will be like at the Frosts'. Easier than that, because Vicky will be there."

"It won't be easy."

His answer was so simple, so heartfelt, that Nina saw that she was being unreasonable. It was no more than the unpalatable truth that she would be jealous of Vicky, and it was also true that she would have to learn to swallow her jealousy, because there was nothing else to be done.

"I'm sorry," she said at once.

They held on to each other as if the tenderness between them could keep everything else at bay. Their separate identities miraculously melted together, and they were convinced that they understood each other entirely. So it was that they swung in one moment from distance to delight.

To Gordon, the spare Georgian house across from the cathedral was both a sanctuary and a snare. When he was away from it he thought of it constantly, yet when he came into it he moved cautiously, always reckoning up the time he could spare in minutes, and replaying in his head the evasions he had made in order to reach it.

Today Andrew had been clearly impatient when he had announced that he had to make another visit to the cathedral. Had he only imagined that it was the dawn of suspicion? There had been several half-explained absences lately. Yet Gordon could not bear to think of staying away from Dean's Row. Nina filled his head and all his thoughts. He believed that he now knew how a compulsive gambler or an addict felt, and at the same time was repelled by the connection he drew between Nina and such things.

He asked her, with his mouth moving against her forehead, "When can we meet again?"

He felt the small movement of her shoulders, a gesture of impotence rather than carelessness.

"When you next can spare an hour."

That was how it had been since the day of buying Nina's car. They had met four or five times, always hurriedly, always with a sense that the rest of the world was lying in wait for them.

The minutes added up for Gordon now. He could almost hear them ticking, like a bomb. It was a long time: it was hardly time to draw a breath.

"I'm sorry," he offered in his turn. "That's just how it is. I'd spend every hour with you if I could."

Nina nodded and then raised her head. He could see the tiny whorls and knots of color in her irises, and the black pupils fractionally dilating. He imagined the pull of the ciliary muscles on the tiny lens in her eyes, and the twin inverted images of himself laid on the retina, only to be righted again by the brain's efforts. That was the brain's power, he thought, to make logic out of what it saw clearly to be the wrong way up.

"I'm going to drive to Bristol tomorrow. I want to give the car a proper trial," Nina said. Since she had taken delivery of the red Mercedes, it had spent almost all its time in the garage of the cobbled mews behind Dean's Row.

She added, "I need to buy some materials for Marcelle's nativity costumes."

"I'll come with you," Gordon said, obliterating all the next day's obligations in one grandiose stroke. Her pleasure immediately rewarded him.

"Will you?"

"Somehow," he promised, already ambushed by his own anxiety.

Marcelle was driving to work at the Pond School. She was currently teaching one of the college's best money-makers, a twelve-week intensive course designed to bring novices up to a standard suitable for finding work as ski-chalet cooks. Her current set included Cathy Clegg, one of Darcy's nineteen-year-old twins, a perfect example of the Pond's introductory cooking student. Cathy's only real interest in food was in how much or how little of it she could consume before a millimeter of surplus flesh appeared on her miniskirted hips.

As she drove, Marcelle was reflecting on the lack of enthusiasm in her class, and in another compartment of her mind she was running through the afternoon's demonstration. She would be showing the students how to make *ciabatta* bread, and enlarging on some techniques associated with dough-preparation before the next morning's practical session.

Her attention was fully engaged and she drove the familiar route automatically, almost unseeingly.

Marcelle had taken a roundabout way via the ring road instead of facing the morning's traffic through the middle of the town. By this route she would cross a branch of the main railway line that ran out to the west of Grafton. If one could hear the fading echo of mainline expresses heard from the cathedral green, it was supposed to mean that rain was coming.

The branch line was not much used, but today, as she looked ahead over the flat crowns of the hawthorn hedges, Marcelle saw the red-and-white arms of the crossing barrier begin to descend. When she rounded a bend and could see the crossing itself, the gates were already down and the red warning lights were flashing. Marcelle muttered "damn" and stopped.

On her own side of the line hers was the only waiting car. At first, because she was busy with her own thoughts, she registered only that there was another vehicle drawing up on the other side.

Then, after two or three seconds, some recollection of shine and redness made her look again.

Immediately she recognized Nina's new Mercedes. The flashiness of the car had given rise to some wry remarks among the Grafton wives. Marcelle saw now that it was Nina at the wheel, and that there was a passenger with her.

The train was approaching. She could hear its rumble, and out of the corner of her eye she saw a blur of movement as the dark shape rolled around a bend toward the crossing.

At that moment Marcelle realized that Nina and her passenger were laughing, and that there was a shiver of intimacy between them that couldn't be accounted for by their expressions or postures. She was only certain that it was there, and that the couple had not seen her, and that the man was Gordon Ransome.

A second later the locomotive hid them from her sight. It was a heavy diesel pulling a line of clanking freight cars. Marcelle counted them as they went by, sixteen in all, and then the swaying brown box of the crew's caboose at the end. In the minute it took the train to pass, she collected her thoughts and began to compose the simple explanations that would account for Gordon and Nina laughing together, alone in her car on a weekday morning, enjoying a closeness that seemed to exclude the rest of the world.

The caboose swept by, clearing her view like a curtain being drawn back.

Marcelle saw Nina's hands still braced on the wheel, two small white patches. She also saw that the two heads were slowly drawing apart, and she knew for certain, as surely as she knew who the two people were, that they had kissed while they were waiting for the train to pass by.

The red lights stopped flashing. In a moment the gates would automatically swing upward once again. But while the two cars waited, still separated by the rails and the red-and-white bars, Gordon and Nina saw Marcelle watching them.

In her turn, Marcelle saw how their faces turned into stiff ovals pocked with the dark holes of shock.

The train had disappeared. The gates silently lifted, describing an arc until the twin arms pointed upward and the way was clear.

Both drivers eased their cars into gear and crept toward each other over the wooden ramp. Marcelle lifted her hand in a wave and Gordon and Nina both smiled back at her. Even as they passed each other Marcelle saw what it took for them to overlay their expressions of alarm with conventional smiles of greeting.

Then the Mercedes was gone, dwindling in her rearview mirror and vanishing around the bend in the road.

Marcelle drove on toward the Pond School, trying to straighten out in her mind the implications of what she had just seen. Two miles further on, while she was still thinking of Vicky with Helen strapped to her front in a baby sling, she caught a glimpse of Gordon's gray Peugeot. He had left it in a corner of a roadside-restaurant car lot.

"Did she see you?" Nina gasped. "Did she recognize you?"

"Of course she did."

Pale-faced, Gordon stared ahead at the road and tried to work out the significance of what had happened.

"She couldn't have seen us kiss. The train was in the way," Nina said.

"I think she must have seen enough."

How, he wondered, *could we have imagined that we were invisible and impregnable just because we're so happy to be together?*

They were both shaking. Their instinct was to pull off the road and find comfort and reassurance in touching each other, but to do so where they could be seen would be to compound their absurd mistake. Gordon was asking himself, even now, *Where can we go in future? Where will we be safe?*

"There could be a perfectly ordinary explanation. Your car could have broken down. I was giving you a lift. I just passed by. Gordon?"

She was looking for his reassurance, and he tried to give it.

"Yes. Maybe."

"What shall we do, then?"

He couldn't think of anything in particular. It seemed inevitable now that someone would eventually have seen them, and he was amazed by his carelessness. "Nothing. I don't believe there's anything we can do except brazen it out, if we have to, with the breakdown story."

"Do you think Marcelle will say anything to Vicky?"

He thought about it. "No, I don't suppose so. Not directly. Perhaps she'll try to warn her in some more oblique way. I don't know—what do women say to each other in these circumstances?"

"I've never been in these circumstances before."

The edginess came back again, and they veered from complicity to opposition.

They drove for a little way in silence. Gordon was trying to work out what would happen if he told Nina that it had to end before anything else happened. But it was only a distant speculation. He knew that they had already come too far to imagine retracing their steps.

They came to a crossroads and a sign indicating that they were only a few miles from the highway. Nina lifted her hands from the wheel for an instant.

"What do you want to do? Shall we go on?"

He answered at once. "Yes. Let's get as far away from here as we can. Just for a few hours."

His certainty won her back, and her spirits lifted. Their story would be believed; there was no reason why it shouldn't be. It had been a warning. They would be more careful in the future.

She put her foot down and the car shot forward.

In the demonstration kitchen, Marcelle went through the motions of mixing and kneading her bread dough while a dozen students lounged on the benches in front of her, yawning and whispering and taking notes. Cathy Clegg sat at the front, with her long legs in thick black tights negligently propped up on the dais. She twined a mutinous strand of streaky blond hair through her fingers and gazed out of the window.

Marcelle had given the lesson often enough to be able to do it on autopilot. As she worked and talked, a segment of her mind slid over the morning's conundrum, and then beyond it to musings about all of the Grafton couples.

What she had seen made her feel fragile. She had not confessed, even to Janice, that she was afraid her own marriage was faltering: her communications on the subject were, even with her closest friend, always on the level of wry jokes, jokes that turned on the helplessness and childishness of their men. They never had to do with their own loneliness or disappointment, and even so Janice sometimes shrank back from this comic half-truthtelling to reaffirm her own contentment.

"But they aren't so bad, the two of them, are they, Mar? They could be much worse, after all." And Janice would wrinkle her nose in the pretty way she had and smooth the loose folds of her skirt over her hips.

Their men could be drunks or womanizers, Marcelle supplied for her. Or violent or cruel or criminal—but those were the traits of men in other places, weren't they? Husbands on television programs or in newspaper articles. They had nothing to do with the steady couples and the security of Grafton, with its golf club and good schools and the golden cathedral at its heart.

Marcelle had assumed it was only her own marriage that was dying away into silence, and that it must be doing so through some fault of her own. If she could be better in some way, she reasoned, then Michael would warm to her again. In the meantime she would not admit that she was afraid, even to Janice. She didn't want to betray too much, to admit that there was so much darkness beneath the smooth, shining surface of their lives.

This morning's glimpse of Gordon with Nina had not troubled her just for Vicky's sake, although that did concern her also. It was more as if in the moment at the crossing some stretched-taut piece of insulating fabric had been pierced, and now the pinprick was tearing apart into a gaping hole. Through the hole came a cold and threatening draft of suspicion that blew all around her. It was not just her own life that was in difficulties. The placid and normal world she struggled to maintain had become as precarious as so many props in a conjuring trick. What was the reality in Grafton, Marcelle wondered, and what was the illusion?

The oven buzzer interrupted her thoughts.

"Mrs. Wickham? The bread?" a student helpfully reminded her.

"Thank you, Emma."

There had been a time when Marcelle had found it definitely uplifting to cook good food for lovers and friends, although for some reason it had never seemed quite acceptable to admit as much. The young were less worried about such things now. But in the last years—for how long had she felt it?—cooking had become a matter of work to her, of repetitive family duty.

Art and nature, Marcelle thought, remembering one of her oblique conversations with Janice. *Gardening and cooking and sex. Where had all the subtle and diverse pleasures gone?*

It was four o'clock. She could hear the clatter of other students in the corridor outside.

"That's all for today," she told her class.

She went quickly to the staff room to collect her coat, avoiding the tea-drinking gaggle of other teachers, and emerged from the front door. Immediately she caught sight of Cathy ahead of her; she must have skipped out without doing her share of the cleaning up. Cathy ran down the steps toward a young man who had just clambered out of an illegally parked Golf. Loud music issued from the wound-down window.

Cathy shouted, "Barney!"

Marcelle paused at the top of the steps, wrapping her arms around her chest to keep out the cold. Her breath made clouds in front of her.

Barney Clegg greeted his sister with a double feint to her head, and then a bear hug.

"Hey, I'm home, are you pleased? Good day's cooking?"

"Great. The cooking was okay. Here, have some bread, you're always hungry."

He took the chunk she produced for him and gnawed enthusiastically at it.

"This is great. Did you make it?"

"Don't be a dope. Marcelle did. She'd be thrilled if I had. Wouldn't you, Marcelle?"

She had come quietly down the steps behind Cathy. The two Cleggs turned their smiles on her. They both had long upper lips, and very white, perfectly even teeth that proclaimed expensive orthodontics. Marcelle could see their resemblance to their mother, whom she had never met.

"You could, Cathy, you know, if you felt like it." She knew she sounded like a schoolmistress, not the bestower of culinary inspiration to last a lifetime. The realization depressed her. "Hello, Barney. Are you home for Christmas?"

Darcy's eldest child was away studying at agricultural college.

"Yup. Come to liven the old place up a bit." He grinned engagingly at her, displaying his father's charm and what would turn into the same creases at the corners of his eyes. Barney was over six feet tall, broad-shouldered and blond-haired, with a healthy aura that suggested much time in the fresh air. In his sweats and American baseball jacket with white leather sleeves he seemed huge, towering over Marcelle like some benevolent if not very intelligent giant.

"So, how're you, Marcelle? Apart from having to teach Cathy, that is? And the family?"

Cathy swiped at him with her black leather rucksack. *They're like healthy animal cubs*, Marcelle thought, *playing outside the nest*. She smiled up at Barney.

"Very well, thank you. But I must go pick them up from Janice's or they'll be wondering where I am. Have a happy holiday, won't you?"

As Marcelle crossed the road to the parking lot, the two Cleggs piled into the Golf and slammed the doors, calling their good-byes to her. The car accelerated away in a diminishing blast of noise and music.

It was Janice's day for the school run. When Marcelle reached the Frosts' house, the winter daylight had all but gone and the streetlights made the sky look thick and black. Janice's car was already in the driveway. The children were all in the kitchen, and so was Vicky Ransome with her baby and the two little girls.

Marcelle took the mug of tea that Janice handed her and gave her children the attention they needed. Jonathan had scored a goal in a soccer game, and Daisy was anxious about the evening's singing rehearsal.

"Well done, Jon. There's plenty of time, Daisy. We'll have supper and then go to the cathedral. Look, William isn't worried, is he?"

William didn't take his eyes from the television screen.

Marcelle sat down at the table with her mug of tea, facing Vicky.

Vicky's open blouse showed the strong stalk of her neck, and her head nodded tenderly over the contented baby. While she watched Vicky, Marcelle became sure that she could not possibly say anything about what she had seen. But her anxiety about what it meant, together with the responsibility for keeping silent, pressed heavily on her. She wondered if there were other secrets, secrets that she could not guess at, inhabiting the room and separating the three of them.

"How are you?" she heard herself asking Vicky.

Vicky looked up. Her wings of hair swung back to expose her cheeks and the collar of flesh, not yet dissolved, that pregnancy had laid down around her jawline.

"It's tiring, with three of them. Alice wakes up often at night, always when this one has just gone off. I spend a lot of time creaking across the landing from one bedroom to the other, hurrying to stifle the cries. And then sitting in the baby's room, feeding her, imagining we're the only people in the world who are awake.

There's that particular silence in the small hours that seems un-breakable."

"I remember."

"But Gordon is being very good. Better by far than he was with the other two."

Marcelle could well imagine that Gordon would come home and guiltily try to compensate for what he was doing elsewhere. She felt hot shivers of indignation directed at him, and at Nina.

"That's good," she said pointlessly, seeing the red car again and the two bewitched profiles sliding apart from each other.

Later the same evening, Vicky was watching television. She was sitting in her usual chair with her feet curled up beneath her and her hands wrapped round a mug of hot milk. It was only the reminder that the milk must not be spilt that kept her from dozing off. She was tired, but there was no point in going to bed before Helen had woken for her last feed. The baby lay in her basket on the sofa. Vicky drank some of her milk, and the skin that had formed on the surface of it caught on her top lip. The act of rubbing it away reminded her strongly of being a little girl, sitting in her dressing gown, ready for bed, while her mother listened to *The Archers*. The comforting childhood feeling of being secure and in the right place pervaded the present too, spilling around her and enclosing the children and Gordon in its warmth.

In the kitchen Gordon was tidying up after dinner, a Marks & Spencer curried chicken dish he was not particularly fond of. There was a milk-rimmed saucepan filled with tepid water on the draining board, and Vicky had stood a bunch of dirty cutlery to soak in it. Yellow-crusted eggshells and toast fragments left from the children's supper spilled out of a bent tinfoil dish on the worktop, and there was a high-water mark of tea leaves and whitish scum clinging to the sides of the sink. Next to the tinfoil dish was the clear polycarbonate sterilizing drum for Helen's bottles.

As he worked, Gordon thought deliberately about Nina. He set himself the test of recalling the shape of her hands and finger-nails, the way her hair grew back from her forehead, the exact timber of her voice. The details came to him without effort, but invested with an importance that was separate from the jumble of everything else that made up his life. He knew that he was in love with her.

When he was satisfied with the kitchen, he went through to the living room to find Vicky. When she saw him she pushed out her jaw in a yawn that turned into a lazy smile, and stretched her arms with the fingers bent inward at the knuckles in a way that made him think of a cat.

"Vicky?"

He was exhausted with the weight of having to keep the truth from her, and by the opposing need to tell her, to blurt out what was happening and to share the bewilderment of it with her.

"Mmm?"

I've fallen in love with Nina. I want to live with her. I don't know how not to be with her all the time. How can I explain that to you?

"Did you see Marcelle today?"

She saw us at the crossing. I know what she saw, and therefore what she knows.

"Yes. She came to pick the kids up from Janice's while I was over there this afternoon. Why?"

Marcelle had said nothing, then. Not yet.

"No reason, really. It seems a while since we've seen the Wickhams. I passed her in the car this morning, which made me think of it."

The room seemed to shiver around him, with all its accumulated weight of familiarity, curtains and covers chosen, books collected, photographs and mementos and worn patches accumulated through years of being together. It shivered with the precarious balance between truth and deception.

Vicky sighed. "We should have an evening, I know. But to be honest I don't think I've got the energy to do it. Perhaps we could have some people in over Christmas?"

He put his hand on her shoulder. There was a pad of flesh there, and he felt the dent where the broad strap of her nursing bra bit into it. He knew her so well; he saw her set in her separate place like a fly in amber or a fish held fast in the winter ice, and himself beside her, but apart. The two of them no longer flowed together, they didn't blur and coalesce and give off energy by their combination, as they once had done.

"You don't have to bother about anything like that. We'll only do it if you want to."

Vicky stretched herself again, luxuriating in his concern for her.

"All right. Only if we both feel like it. Is that Helen waking up? Have a look for me."

He leaned over the basket. The baby's eyes were open, very deep and dark in her tiny red face, and they looked straight up into his.

"Yes, she's awake. Do you want her?"

Vicky undid her front buttons in answer to him. He saw the armory of her underclothes, and then the veined blue-whiteness of the over-full breast when she released it. The loose flesh of her belly swelled up in another curve below it. There was a tissue pad in her bra cup that gave off a stale-milk smell. He thought of Nina's spare, freckled body and its touching knobs of bone.

Gordon lifted the baby carefully out of the basket. Her heavy head wobbled against him and he cupped it in his hand, noticing how the silky skin wrinkled over the hard, fragile skull. As he held her with her tiny face against his cheek, he felt a rising pain inside him that made him want to cry out. He breathed in the scent from the downy head and the pain grew so acute that he didn't know how to contain it.

Then Vicky held her empty arms out for the baby, and he handed his daughter over to her.

Just before the dress rehearsal for the nativity play, Marcelle and Nina met at the Wickhams' house. The two women had not seen each other since that morning at the crossing. Nina brought with her the animal masks she had made in her studio over the last few days. She had taken a lot of trouble with them, as if doing so would somehow atone for everything else.

In Marcelle's dining room Nina took the masks one by one out of their wrappings and laid them out for her approval. They were very light and simple, stylized suggestions of animal faces rather than attempts at realism, but Marcelle could see at once how effective they would look.

"They are so good," she said, picking up one of the lambs to examine it more closely. She held it up to her face, and looked at

Nina through the oval, slanting eye holes. Then she lowered the mask again, and the two women's eyes met straight-on.

"Are you sure they're what you wanted?"

"Yes. Really, they're perfect. I could never have made anything half so good."

Marcelle wrapped them up carefully and set them aside. There were play costumes all around the room, arranged on hangers hooked to the picture rail, everything labeled and pressed ready for the dress rehearsal.

There was a moment's silence.

Marcelle wondered what she should say, whether there was some word of caution or advice or admonition for Vicky's sake that she might offer. Nothing came into her head, and she saw Nina twisting her wedding ring around and around her finger. The ring looked too loose for her. She felt sad, and sorry for Nina as well as Vicky.

Nina also waited. She didn't know Marcelle well enough, but she wished she could confide in her. Could she plead with her now? (*Don't judge us too harshly. Don't assume it's only a bald and commonplace act of adultery.*)

But how else could she explain what it was to Vicky's friend? By emphasizing her own need, or Gordon's, or the happiness they generated for each other when they were together?

There was nothing, she realized, she could say to excuse herself or Gordon. The weight of dislike and mistrust coming from Marcelle was no more than she could have expected.

Neither of them spoke, and the silence lengthened into awkwardness. It was Marcelle who broke it at last.

"Thank you for helping me out. It must have taken hours of your time."

Now they couldn't mention what they both knew, because the moment for it had slipped past. Marcelle felt angry with herself, and at the two of them for putting her in this difficult position.

"It didn't take that long," Nina lied. "I'm glad there was something useful I could do."

Marcelle wouldn't tell anyone. Nina was finally sure of that. *We must be careful from now on*, she thought, experiencing a surprising surge of relief and gratitude that made her almost light-headed.

Michael Wickham looked into the dining room. It was after eight, but he was dressed as if he had only just come in from the hospital. Nina had the impression that he was irritated by the sight of them hovering with their masks and by the clutter of costumes, but he made the offer of a drink politely enough.

"Yes, do stay and have a drink," Marcelle echoed. "A drink, at least. I feel that I ought to be offering you dinner, after all you've done."

"*Is* there any dinner?" Michael dryly interrupted.

"Yes. In half an hour."

Gordon had promised Nina that he would telephone in the evening. Vicky would be out of the house for two hours after the children were asleep. She said quickly, "I can't even stay for a drink, but thank you anyway. If there's anything else last-minute I can do . . ."

Marcelle did not suggest anything else. Nina said good night to the Wickhams and drove back to Dean's Row.

"Did Marcelle say anything?' Gordon asked when he called.

"No."

It was one of their flat, melancholy telephone conversations. Sometimes they could forget the distance and talk as if they were touching each other, but tonight everything they said seemed to convey less than they meant. They both wondered what they were doing, begging questions, making these banal offerings of words into thin, humming space.

"When can I see you again?" Nina asked. She twisted the spiral cord of the telephone around her little finger.

"I don't know. I'm not sure, it's not a good week. And Andrew made some crack this evening about my disappearing acts."

Nina wondered why he should have to account for himself to Andrew, but she only said, "Does that make it difficult? I'm sorry."

"There's no reason for you to be sorry." With an effort, wanting to change the tone of the talk, he said, "I love you."

"I know," Nina answered soberly.

It was plain that the mood would not change, and neither could offer the other any comfort. Gordon tried to imagine how it would be if he left the house and the children and drove straight to her.

"I'll call you soon," he promised.

"Yes. Please call."

She hung up, wanting to sever the connection herself.

The night of the nativity play came.

Nina had imagined that she wouldn't go, but when it was time she found herself drawn across the cathedral green to join the people who gathered together in convivial groups at the west door. After all, she told herself, she couldn't hide in her house forever.

The chapter house was packed. Nina slipped quietly around the octagonal wall, looking for an empty place on one of the benches. She nodded to the handful of familiar faces in the crowd as she passed by. At length she found a single seat removed from anyone she knew, and sat down with her hands folded in her lap.

Marcelle and Michael sat near the front, with Jonathan fidgeting in between them. Marcelle felt a flutter of nerves for Daisy's sake. Star Rose sat on the other side of Marcelle. Her face was calm as she gazed intently upward at the geometrical tracery of the windows. Jimmy Rose was a Catholic. He very rarely chose to accompany his wife to the great barn, as he called the cathedral.

The Frosts and Toby, nagged into a dark blazer for the occasion, sat two rows behind them. By tradition they would join the Wickhams later for a drink. Andrew always jovially referred to this occasion as "the Christmas kickoff." Janice knew and greeted almost everybody in the audience.

Nina saw the Cleggs come in. Hannah was wearing an ankle-length dark mink, her blond hair in striking contrast to the smooth fur. Hannah held little Laura's hand and Darcy guided Freddie. The two small children were dressed in double-breasted dark-blue coats with velvet collars. Behind their father came Cathy and Lucy, attracting their due of covertly or openly admiring glances. Following the twins was a big, blond young man Nina had never seen before. When he turned sideways to ease between the benches she saw his profile and recognized the family resemblance.

She had been looking at the Clegg boy, and then her glance traveled away, drawn along a valley between the row of heads. With the shock that was now becoming familiar, she saw Gordon. His two little girls were sitting between him and Vicky. Vicky was on the end of a row, with a white bundle in her arms. Her hair had been cut into a neat, shiny bob. All four of them were looking straight ahead, a model family quietly waiting for the play to begin.

There was a movement to Nina's right, at the great double doors of the chapter house. Then there was an organ chord and the cathedral choristers came slowly forward, two-by-two, in their blue cassocks and snow-white surplices.

They were singing, and the chapter house fell silent.

O come, *all ye faithful*, the choir sang.

William Frost sang a solo verse. His voice was perfect, rounded and strong and pure, and it rose as effortlessly as a hawk riding an air thermal. Under the square-cut fringe of fair hair the boy's mouth made an innocent secondary oval within the choirboy oval of his face.

O come ye, O come ye to Bethlehem.

Through the doors of the chapter house came two children dressed as Joseph and Mary, the latter in the blue robe Nina had last seen hanging from the picture rail in Marcelle's dining room. Mary, awed and solemn-faced, was leaning on a third child who paced between them. This boy was wearing a plain gray leotard with a dark cross etched on the back from shoulder to hip, and his face was covered by Nina's donkey mask.

Nina and Star Rose and the Grafton couples and their children sat with all the other people under the great fan vaults of the chapter house roof and watched the unfolding of the nativity play.

The shepherds in their rough coats and the kings in their magnificent robes came to offer their gifts to the Christ child, the lessons from the Gospels were read, and the carefully memorized lines were clearly spoken. The Holy Family and the white-robed angels and the animals in their masks gathered around the crib. Daisy Wickham and the school's choir and William and the other choristers sang their carols, and the children's solemn faces reflected the renewed wonder of the Christmas message.

The play was both simple and grand.

Nina was moved, and she felt the collective emotion around her, all the rows of heads with their hidden thoughts made momentarily clear. She felt that she was gathered in with the rest, and made safe, as she had not been in the cathedral since she was a young girl.

Just before the end, Helen began to cry. Vicky tried to quiet her, and through the valley of seats Nina saw Gordon's face as he inclined his head toward his wife. He looked different, like someone else, like any one of these other husbands and fathers, not like the man who was her lover.

Vicky slipped out with Helen in her arms. She drew a soft wake of smiles after her as the double doors opened to let her out. Her cheeks were pink, and she held her head up.

For the last carol, the audience stood up to sing with the choirs. The familiar words and music drew Nina backward into herself as a child, standing between her parents in the same place to sing the same carol. And as if she was contemplating it with the imperfect, simplified judgment of a child, it seemed sad that there was no continuity beyond her, that she had no child of her own to bring in her turn.

When the play was over Nina sat still among the flurry of departure until almost everyone else had filed away. Gordon went by, not seeing her, with Andrew and Janice. The Cleggs waved as they passed, and the tall boy who must be Darcy's son nodded as if he believed he should know her. When she was sure that everyone must have gone far enough ahead, she followed them through the double doors and down the steps into the nave. She looked upward, to the compound shafts of the pillars and the Gothic arches that sprang from them. It was here that Gordon's tour of the restoration work had begun.

She did not want to leave by the west door, because she was sure that the Grafton couples would be gathering on the green beside the Christmas tree, ready to begin their season's celebrations. If anyone looked for her, they would assume that she had slipped out by the north side.

Nina sat down in the shadows of the nave. The organist was playing a Handel voluntary. She could see the shaft of light behind the curtain up in the loft. She wondered if she should pray, but she could not think of how to expiate herself.

At last, after a long time, one of the vergers came to stand beside her. He was a very tall young man in a black cassock that was too short for him.

"I'm afraid that the cathedral is closing now."

There was no one left in the aisles or in the rows of wooden seats.

Nina smiled. "I'm going home," she told him.

8

On Christmas Eve, Wilton Manor was lit up like a cruise ship at anchor in a sea of parked cars.

Michael and Marcelle Wickham walked the short distance to the house in silence, but as soon as they opened the door they found their smiles and went into the party together.

Marcelle glimpsed Jimmy's crest of sandy hair, and the Clegg twins, one in ankle-length and the other in thigh-high black Lycra, and Gordon Ransome's narrow, handsome head politely inclined as he listened to something Hannah was whispering to him. Hannah was wearing a tight sheath of gold that barely contained her.

Marcelle took a glass of champagne from the tray someone held out, and drank half of it. Now that she had escaped her own house, she was eager for company and conversation. She heard music, and raised voices, and a chorus of greetings. Her spirits lifted in response.

"Marcelle, Michael. At last."

Darcy's cowboy-fringed arm descended around her shoulders.

"Merry Christmas, Darcy."

"Have you got a drink? Hey, that's only half a drink. Let me fill it up for you."

More champagne foamed into her glass. She was aware that Michael had moved away from her side. She could see Janice now, and the Kellys, and a dozen other familiar faces in the hallway under the Christmas tree and among the crowd of people in the drawing room. She let herself be carried forward to meet them, to the kisses and the greetings and the gossip, her fingers curled firmly around her glass.

Gordon watched her go. Then, involuntarily, he searched out

Nina. She looked pale, thinner than usual, in a simple black dress that revealed the bony wings beneath her throat. Their eyes met and then moved apart.

The manor house was polished and scented; elaborately decorated with great silvered garlands of pine and holly, and warmed with log fires in all the wide grates. Hannah and her stepchildren had overseen the preparations because Darcy was unusually preoccupied with his work. The little Clegg children were asleep upstairs, but Darcy's three grown-up children were a noticeable presence at this year's party.

Lucy and Cathy and Barney had invited a contingent of their own friends, and these younger people with their different haircuts and casual clothes wove a contrasting thread through the fabric of the party. They asked the disc jockey behind his turntables in the conservatory to play unfamiliar music in place of the sixties and seventies hits, and they danced, waving their arms, in loose groups.

The Grafton couples, whose own visiting mothers and fathers were mostly at home watching over their grandchildren, were suddenly aware that another generation was crowding up behind them.

Michael and Darcy stood shoulder-to-shoulder in their dinner jackets, watching the young. Michael had refused champagne and was drinking whisky from a tumbler. He said to Darcy, over the rim of his glass, "Did you ever believe you would grow old? We children of the sixties always knew we had it, whatever it was, the big secret. We always thought we'd hold on to it, too. It makes it doubly hard to accept that it's already gone, spent, inherited by this lot."

He tilted his glass toward them. He was not quite sober, and the whisky slopped a little.

Darcy shrugged, preoccupied. He was giving Michael Wickham's rambling talk only a fraction of his attention. He had been able to forget his anxiety for a moment, but then it came skittering back like a black spider emerging from a web.

Michael glanced at him, noticing that Darcy was not as eager as usual to play the role of expansive host. He looked tired, and his tanned face had a grayish tinge to it. He wondered if he might be ill.

"Darcy, you're an example to us all. Nobody could ever accuse you of leftover hippie idealism. And look what you have to show for growing up so eagerly—Wilton Manor, several cars, wives, and children. A place at the very epicenter of Grafton society."

Darcy did not rise to the bait. He turned away from the dancers. "Let's get another drink. You've spilled most of that one."

Jimmy Rose was less affected by the specter of his own middle age. He had no children to catch him up, and his wife knew better than to follow him around at parties. He felt entirely free to admire Lucy Clegg's exposed thighs and the twists of colored cloth she had wound in her hair, and to melt into the noise in the conservatory in pursuit of her.

The Clegg twins drew him into the dance, one on either side of him. They smiled and waved their fingers and undulated their slim hips in time to the music. None of the hulking boys in the vicinity seemed inclined to lay claim to either of them. Jimmy slid his arm around Lucy's waist and danced for a moment with his cheek pressed against hers. She smelled very young, and fresh, like a bluebell stalk.

When she wriggled out of his grasp again he grinned at her in rueful acknowledgment and lifted a full glass of champagne from a passing tray as a consolation. Jimmy had been drinking steadily, but the only effect that alcohol ever had on him was to increase his capacity for mischief.

A little later he looked across the dance floor and saw Marcelle. She was standing on her own, her head and arms seeming to hang a little awkwardly. He left the twins and their friends and skirted around the edge of the floor until he reached her.

"Dance with me?" he asked.

"Yes. I will." She held out her hands, rather stiffly, and he guided her. He knew that they made an odd contrast, a pair of waltzers among loose-limbed youngsters. He drew her closer to him. She was wearing a full-skirted dress made of blue-green taffeta that rustled around his legs. Marcelle's head drooped a little, and then rested on his shoulder. Her perfume was heavy and musky, quite unlike Lucy's; the scent was intensified to the point of sickliness by the dry heat of her skin.

"You don't want to dance."

"Not really," she admitted.

"Let's sit it out, then."

He took her hand and drew her behind him. Jimmy knew Darcy's house as well as he knew his own. He opened the door to a small room under the angle of the stairway. It was half-cloakroom, half-gunroom, furnished with hung-up coats and mackintoshes, dismantled fishing rods in green canvas cases, creaking wicker chairs, and too-pristine sporting prints introduced by Hannah. It was otherwise empty, as Jimmy had known it would be.

Marcelle sank down into one of the chairs, letting her head fall back with a long sigh.

"Too much champagne," she said, swallowing a laugh and a hiccup together.

Jimmy sat beside her. He turned her wrist in his fingers to expose her underarm where the skin puckered in tiny folds towards her armpit. He put his mouth to the blue vein in the crook of her elbow.

"Tell me all," he commanded, rubbing his mouth in the hollow.

"Nothing to tell."

He lifted his head a little and circled her with his arm.

"Yes, there is, I can see there is."

Now he bent forward so that his mouth reached the top part of her breast left exposed by the taffeta bodice.

Marcelle knew that there were minute crepe-paper folds between her breasts. She was afraid that in the heat the dusting of powder she had applied there might have turned into gray, wormy threads. Suddenly she felt shy, inexperienced, and full of anxiety about her body's imperfections, like an awkward adolescent.

"Jimmy, don't."

"Ah, why ever not? Isn't it nice?"

It felt good to him. At this moment Jimmy loved Marcelle, and he loved Hannah and Janice as well. All the women with their different shapes and textures and scents appealed to him like so many dishes on an endless table, and the fact that he couldn't have all of them did nothing to diminish his appetite.

"Yes," Marcelle said sadly. "It is nice. Only not now."

Jimmy grinned at her. "When? When Mike's at the hospital?"

"You know I didn't mean that."

This was how Jimmy was, all the wives knew it. Marcelle always parried his advances, very gently and with a touch of regret. She didn't know what the others did, not exactly, not even Janice, although they joked together out of Star's earshot about there always being Jimmy to fall back on.

"What a shame. Well then, talk to me instead. Tell Jimmy all your troubles."

The combined effect of his attention and sympathy and the champagne made Marcelle's eyes suddenly fill with unwelcome tears.

"Oh, it's nothing. Just domestic bickering."

"Is that all?"

He stroked her wrist with the tip of his finger, little soothing strokes. She watched the movement, hypnotized by it, wishing that she hadn't drunk so much. Alcohol always loosened her tongue. She hesitated, trying to think of something light to say, then she opened her mouth and the words came spilling out anyhow, although she wanted to keep them in to preserve the marriage myth.

"No, that's not all. It's much more than that. And less, in a way. Michael just seems to have . . . gone away somewhere. I don't mean actually away, although, God knows, he's in the house with us less and less of the time; the hospital and patients and committees seem to consume him. It's as if he's retreated into himself, closed a door on me, and I find myself at one minute angry with him for rejecting me, and bitter and resentful, and at the next what must seem, I don't know, cloyingly *there*, with all my claims and expectations, wifely, needing to be loved. Like an obligation."

Marcelle took a breath.

"I don't know when we stopped being partners and became antagonists. The two of us, drawn up on either side of some battle line. Looking back, I don't know when it happened, only that it *has* happened. We quarrel and the arguments are never resolved, and then there are silences, and times when we preserve this terrible politeness, and then we argue all over again."

Now she was crying. Tears spouted out of her eyes and she felt them making hot runnels down her face. There would be tracks in the foundation she had applied to give herself some color.

Jimmy murmured, "Poor thing, poor old Mar. Here you are."

He produced a big, clean, white handkerchief. Marcelle sniffed into it, then bit her lips to stop herself from crying any more.

"This evening, for instance. We were late, it made me anxious, and then my anxiety made us both irritable, so we quarrelled."

"You hate being late, you hate apparent failures. Nobody notices them except you, but then you're a perfectionist."

"Am I? I don't believe I am. Do you and Star make each other happy?"

"Oh. Star and I have evolved our own system. After so many years, long-married couples do, don't they?"

Marcelle thought of Star's aloof dignity, at all the parties where Jimmy flirted and murmured and kissed. She had seen her tonight, with a diamanté star-clip holding her hair back behind one ear, dancing with Andrew Frost while Jimmy skimmed between the Clegg twins. The Roses would have had to have a system.

"Michael and I loved each other; I thought that was our arrangement, but it seems not to be. I don't believe he loves me any longer."

Jimmy was still stroking her arm. "I'm sure it's not as bad as that. Do you think he's got someone else?"

Marcelle shook her head. "No. He seems too cold for that, too frosted up inside."

"Have *you* got someone else?"

"Of course not."

They were quiet for a minute. She cast around for some way of diminishing in his eyes what had seemed, only a moment earlier, to be an important confession.

"It's probably just restless *ennui* before we settle down to a comfortable twilight together."

"Perhaps," Jimmy said. He shrugged, a little comic contrivance of bafflement. Then he rolled her hand into a fist for her and, placed it back in her lap.

Partly to reinforce her statement, partly to shift the focus from herself, and just a little because she wanted to reward him for this moment of intimacy, Marcelle smiled faintly and said, "It isn't just Michael and me who are having our problems."

"Hmm?"

Jimmy's face sharpened a little, but his eyes held hers.

"Perhaps we're all going through it in our different ways." It was a comfort to identify herself with the group. She wanted to share what she knew. "I saw Gordon the other day. With Nina. They were together in her car."

As soon as she said it she regretted it, but it was out and so she shrugged. She smiled at him again, a smile of complicity now.

"Together?"

"Oh, yes. I don't know exactly how I knew, but I did, as soon as I saw them. It was unmistakeable. I felt it here." Her fist, still clenched, pointed at the pit of her stomach. "They were horrified to see me."

Jimmy grinned. "I imagine they would have been."

He looked pleased, smiling his narrow-eyed smile. The look made Marcelle feel slightly disgusted, and this distaste surprised her.

"How interesting," he mused, more to himself than her. "How interesting it all is. Don't you think so?"

"I don't know. I suppose so, if you can detach yourself sufficiently not to feel concern." It was as if Nina and Gordon and Vicky had shrunk into tiny organisms that divided and recombined in some petri dish under Jimmy Rose's observation. "You won't say anything, Jimmy, will you?" she asked.

He touched her hand once again.

"You know me," he assured her.

Marcelle nodded reluctantly. "I suppose we should go back and join in, should we?"

He leaned forward and kissed her, on the mouth, but only very lightly, dismissively.

"I think we must. Only you should go and fix your makeup first."

Outside the gunroom, they went their separate ways.

Jimmy strolled into the noisy thick of the party, his hands in his pockets, smiling and joking his way through the various groups. At the buffet in the dining room he helped himself to a plateful of the excellent food that Hannah's caterers had prepared. He made himself comfortable in the niche of a padded window seat half-hidden by a curtain, and watched the procession in front of him as he ate.

He saw Nina in her black dress, and observed the way that her face fell into sad lines when she thought nobody was looking at her. He watched Gordon solicitously steering Vicky to a comfortable chair, bringing her a plate of food and cutlery and a napkin, and then looking up over his wife's bent head toward Nina, who was standing with her back turned to him. Jimmy read the brief contraction of Gordon's dark features as an expression of powerful longing.

From his vantage point he also saw Andrew, flushed with champagne, and Janice following him with Marcelle, her face now freshly powdered. Hannah was commanding them to come and eat, laughing a great deal and wobbling slightly on her stiletto heels. Behind them came his own wife, her arm in Michael Wickham's. They were the same height. Jimmy tried to imagine what he would want now if he were seeing Star for the first time. He thought that her androgynous, mysterious air would still interest him.

There was no sign of Darcy, the person he really wanted to see. Jimmy left his dirty plate on the window seat and slipped away in search of him.

He found him in the drawing room, leaning, his arms outstretched, on the mantelpiece, smoking and observing his guests.

"Howdy, pardner," Jimmy drawled, flicking at the fringes on Darcy's Gaultier jacket.

Darcy said nothing. It was silently recognized between them that they needed each other as a focus for aggression, but tonight Darcy could not even summon up the energy to spar with the little man. Jimmy ranged himself beside him, looking out into the room. Darcy felt, as he sometimes did, that the disparity in their sizes made them both look a little absurd.

"There are demons abroad tonight," Jimmy announced.

"That was Halloween, surely. The last time we all gathered together."

"Ah, yes, it was indeed. The first time we saw our Belle Dame. And now you've lost her."

Darcy turned his head now. "Lost her to whom?" His voice was soft.

The currents between them shifted like dry sand.

"To Gordon Ransome, I hear."

The tick-tick of mutual reckoning was almost audible. At first

Jimmy was pleased with the effect of his news; he liked to overturn Darcy's easy assumption of sexual preeminence.

"How do you know?"

Jimmy shrugged. He hazarded, "Ask any of the women. The women always know these things."

To Jimmy's surprise, Darcy began to laugh. It was a big, genuine laugh that betrayed none of the disappointment or pique that he had expected.

"Gordon Ransome? Is that so? Good for Gordon, then. It was bound to be somebody, I suppose."

"Not you?"

Darcy was still laughing. "I'm not going to live out your fantasies for you, James, you should know that by now. Has Vicky heard about it?"

"I wouldn't have thought so. Not yet. No doubt she will."

Jimmy was irritated. It seemed now that he had traded his information for nothing. Darcy patted him on the shoulder.

"Happy Christmas," he said triumphantly.

Jimmy couldn't gauge quite why Darcy was so pleased with himself. He looked at his watch, trying to conceal his annoyance.

"Thanks. The same to you. And thanks for the party. I have to go."

"So early?"

"I'm going to midnight mass."

"Of course you are. Forgive me. I'd forgotten that. Pray for all us sinners, Jim, won't you?"

Jimmy left him. He went out into the cold, clear night and found his small car in the lines of bigger, glossier models. Star would get a lift home with the Frosts.

Vicky sat feeding Helen in the armchair in the corner of the Cleggs' big bedroom. It gave her an unreal, dislocated, but still pleasant feeling to be suddenly translated from the brightness of the party to the silence upstairs, and to the familiar small intimacies of ministering to Helen.

She had laid a towel on Hannah's quilted bedcover and changed the baby's diaper, gently swabbing the inward-turning folds of skin with her concentration pleasingly blurred by champagne. Then she undid her dress and sat down in the armchair. After a minute's hungry attack Helen's sucking gradually moderated into a sleepy rhythm. Vicky began to hum to her, long, low notes that did not connect into any recognizable tune but were soothing to both of them.

Darcy found her sitting there with the coils and loops of her party hairdo beginning to collapse softly around her rosy face.

"Do you mind if I come in?" he asked.

Vicky smiled, caught out in her humming. "Of course not. It's your bedroom."

Instead of opening a drawer, as she would have expected, in search of a stud or a fresh handkerchief, he came directly to her and stooped down, turning back the corner of Helen's white blanket with one finger so that he could see the baby's face.

"She is beautiful," he said.

The floor of the bedroom vibrated under his feet with the bass notes of the music pounding below. There was the distant sound of shouting, and then the crack of breaking glass.

"Is that your conservatory?" Vicky whispered.

"I don't care about the conservatory."

As he stroked the small head, Darcy felt a sudden calm. He forgot about the party and Hannah and Jimmy, and about the business and all the colored balls of his concerns that were about to fall out of their juggled sequence.

He found that he hardly dared to breathe in case he upset the physical balance of light and air and warmth that held the three of them suspended here. Very gently, flexing his heavy fingers, he stroked again, once and then twice. He heard the contented sound that the baby made, a soft half-sigh, as her jaws slackened and released her mother's nipple. Darcy withdrew his hand and Vicky laid her in the hollow of her lap.

"Halftime," Vicky explained. Her lightness, her matter-of-fact acceptance of the fact that he was watching, filled him with amazement and pleasure.

While Darcy looked on, mesmerized, Vicky drew the white elastic cup of her bra over the breast and clipped the silvery hooks into the corresponding eyelets. Then, with a deft movement, she released the other side.

He saw the rounded, drooping, heavy weight, and the net of blue distended veins around the nipple, and the brown shiny nipple itself. It seemed to Darcy, in his trance state, that she was offering it to him.

Darcy leaned forward over the baby in her lap and put his lips over the nipple.

He heard Vicky gasp, the tiny but sharp intake of breath making the exact opposite of the baby's satisfied exhalation. At once his mouth filled with the thick, sweet, secret taste of milk.

The effect of it was extraordinary.

It took him all the way back to the jealous possessiveness he had felt when he watched his mother feeding his next-youngest brother, and way beyond that, back past the boundaries of memory, to his own connection to his mother and his need for her. Even as Darcy recognized all this with one part of his adult, analytical mind, still the rest of him was overwhelmed by the physical shock of his longing for Vicky Ransome once his mouth had connected with her breast.

He became aware that her hand had come to rest at the back of his head, neither drawing him closer nor pushing him away, but simply holding him, just as he had cupped the baby's head a moment before.

If it had not been for the baby between them he could not have done anything but push her backwards, covering her, pinning her underneath him on the wide space of the bed.

As it was he painfully drew his head back and saw a little whitish dribble of milk trickle down the lower curve of the exposed breast and threaten to drip on to her unfastened evening dress. He put out one finger to stop it, and then licked the fingertip. The taste in his mouth was an echo of his longing. He wanted to submerge himself in Vicky, to submerge himself and simultaneously to obliterate everything else, as he had never wanted anything else before.

"Darcy? *Darcy?*"

He made himself look up into her face. There was no hostility in it, only the aftermath of surprise and—was this possible?—the faintest ember of a response to him.

They held still for a moment, staring at each other.

Darcy had come straight from Jimmy Rose to look for Vicky.

He had come in concern and sympathy, which was commendable enough, but he knew that there had also been a baser intention, to assess and then, perhaps, to make use of her vulnerability. He had always found Vicky attractive, and in the last months of her pregnancy and since the birth, he had found her even more so. The peak of his interest in his two wives had also coincided with the birth of his own children. There was a secretive, intent side to a woman absorbed in a baby that he had always found intensely arousing.

Yet now, as Vicky lifted Helen once again and pinched the nipple—*his* nipple—expertly between fingers and thumb for the baby to latch on, Darcy recognized a counterpoint to his expendable desire.

Vicky was watching him, not her baby. She had round brown eyes, he saw, with bronze flecks at the outer rim of the iris. It came to him that he wanted to smother himself inside her.

"My God," Darcy said aloud.

He would not let anything harm her. He would not let her gauche husband and the skinny widow hurt her, nor anyone else in Grafton, either. He would protect her and defend her.

Vicky put her fingers over his mouth.

"Shh."

It was to make him contain his promises even before any could be formulated.

He was still kneeling in front of her, between the end of the quilted bed and the padded and frilled armchair Hannah liked to curl up in with her copies of *The World of Interiors*. The noise from downstairs swelled up to them again. In his enthrallment, Darcy had forgotten that there were more than a hundred people drinking and dancing in his house.

"Darcy?"

It was Hannah not Vicky who called his name. She had come in behind them, unawares.

Darcy turned around to look at her. She was flushed, a breadth of crimson skin showing above her gold dress, and two red patches burning through the creamy makeup on her cheeks. She strode forward into the room, her hips swinging in the tight swathe of satin.

"I've been looking everywhere for you. One of Barney's friends was fooling round with a chair, pretending to dance with it or something stupid, and managed to fall through the French windows and cut his hand open. Didn't you hear the noise?"

"Yes, I did. Is he hurt? Is Mike Wickham still here? Or David Poynter? How many other medicos have we got on the bloody premises?"

"Bloody's about right. Mike's seeing to him. You'd better come down. What's the matter with everyone this evening?"

Hannah faced them, the red spots in her face burning. Darcy stood up, stiff from kneeling and suddenly conscious of his age in front of these younger women.

He remembered Jimmy's words. "Demons are abroad," he murmured.

"What?"

Hannah was angry. Her face reminded him of Laura's in the midst of one of her fits of temper. Darcy looked down and saw that there was a white stain of milk on the satin lapel of his coat.

"Don't worry, I'll sort everything out downstairs," he said, and left them.

Hannah looked coldly at Vicky.

"Have you got everything you need?"

Vicky blushed. She felt caught by Darcy and by her own surprised and guilty pleasure in what had just happened. She was further trapped by her semi-nakedness, by the weight of the baby, by the splendor of Hannah's bedroom.

"Yes, thanks. I'll just finish feeding her, and then I must take Gordon home." And then she offered, because she felt that she must say something even if it was not the truth, "You know, Darcy was just keeping me company."

Hannah shrugged. "It's quite all right. I know what Darcy likes. He is my husband, after all."

Nina had been dancing with Andrew when a boy with one of Hannah's curlicued metal garden chairs in his arms had tripped and crashed forward through the glass doors. For a long moment he had lain quite still with the chair on top of him, under a ragged blanket of glass, while the music thumped on over his head.

Nina was the first to reach him. The glass crunched under her thin shoes as she lifted the chair away.

"Christ," the boy said, blinking.

More people pushed beside Nina. There was a confused babble of orders and instructions. The boy raised his arm to look at it and a broad, bright fountain of blood sprayed from his wrist.

"*Christ*," he repeated.

Nina knelt over him. She put her hand down to balance herself and felt a sharp stab in the heel of it.

"Keep still," she ordered. "Keep your arm up like that."

Andrew fumbled beside her with a big white handkerchief in his hands. Nina snatched it and tied it around the boy's arm, knotting it over the shirtsleeve that was already soaked in blood. *Tight*, she told herself. *Is that an artery?* The boy's face had turned paper-white. *How long before I must loosen the tourniquet?*

"Where's Michael?" Andrew was shouting. "Get Mike, will someone?"

Nina heard herself saying to the boy, "It's all right, you're all right."

There was more shoving and issuing of orders in the crowd of people surrounding them, and then Michael Wickham emerged. He had stripped off his jacket and rolled up the sleeves of his dress shirt. Hannah hovered in a nimbus of gold behind him.

"Let's see."

Michael pressed his thumb over the cut and undid the handkerchief. Nina saw the blood ooze and felt her head swim. Michael glanced briefly at her.

"It's all right," he echoed her own words. "He'll live."

Someone helped Nina to her feet.

"Well done. Give them some room now. Oh, God, you're covered in blood, too. Look at your dress."

Nina recognized Darcy's big blond son.

"It's all right. It doesn't matter." But she spread her hands out in front of her in helpless disgust. They were smeared scarlet like a murderer's. The large young man took hold of one of them regardless.

He ordered. "Come on. Let me look after you now. Tom will be okay with Mike."

She let him lead her away. A path lined with sympathetic faces opened for them through the onlookers.

In the huge kitchen he made her sit down, and then filled a bowl with warm water and brought it to her. He sponged her hands and Nina saw the brown clouds of blood shadow the water when he rinsed the cloth.

"You've cut yourself, too."

"Only a scratch."

He took a Band-Aid box out of a drawer, found one of the right size, then applied it for her. Nina noticed that his large hands were clean but rough and split at the fingertips, as though he did heavy work with them.

"I'm Barney Clegg," he said.

"I know. I'm Nina Cort."

They shook hands, Nina's undamaged left held in his right.

"I don't know what we can do about your dress."

There were dark, sticky patches on the top and the skirt. Barney dabbed at one fold in the skirt with his sponge.

"Don't worry. Please, don't. You've done more than enough." Now that the drama had subsided Nina felt a bubble of laughter rising inside her. "It's just that I can't stand the sight of blood."

Barney began to laugh, too. "Neither can I, never have been able to. A guy at college put a rake through his foot and I was the one who passed out."

"We've both been heroically brave tonight, then."

They continued to laugh. The party had taken over the kitchen once again; there were caterers clearing up at the sinks and guests passing through in search of one another and the music had started booming again in the conservatory. Then Nina saw Gordon watching them across what seemed like an acre of quarry-tiled floor.

Her laughter faded. She wanted him to come to her and take Barney Clegg's place, but she knew that he wouldn't. He would look and then look away, and afterward he would ignore her as he had done all evening in case anyone else saw them and drew an incriminating connection between them.

Michael Wickham led the pale-faced Tom into the kitchen and made him sit down next to Nina. His shirtsleeve had been cut away, and his arm was bandaged from wrist to elbow and supported in a makeshift sling made from someone's silk evening scarf.

"Are you all right, my son?" Barney asked in mock Cockney.

"Yeah. Sorry, all." To Nina he said, "Sorry about the mess."

Gordon had turned away, as she had known he would. Nina smiled at the boy. "Don't worry. I'm glad it's not as serious as it looked."

Michael said, "Still, he needs someone to drive him to the emergency room to get that arm stitched up. I'm damned if it's going to be me."

Barney sighed. "I guess that's my job. I'm just about sober enough to do it." He patted Nina on the shoulder. "See you again, I hope. Come on, Thomas. Let's go and join the festivities in the casualty ward."

When they had gone, Michael rolled down his sleeves again and fished for his cufflinks in his trousers pocket. Without thinking, Nina held out her hand for the gold links, and when he gave them to her she threaded them through the double cuffs for him as she had always done for Richard.

"Well done," he commended her.

"Well done, doctor," she returned.

Michael sighed. "It's one of the hazards of the job; it never quite lets one get away from it."

She saw that when he was not frowning he had a good, plain, likeable face.

"Join me for one last drink?" he asked her. "Before we all head home for Christmas? A proper drink, not bloody champagne."

"I will. Thank you." She knew that Gordon was nowhere to be seen.

When Gordon crossed the hall, Marcelle stepped out and put her hand on his arm. He stopped at once. They saw Darcy hurrying down the stairs but he brushed by them, unseeing, heading for the kitchen.

"I feel like the Ancient Mariner." Marcelle's mouth made a sad, acknowledging twist. "Can we talk for a minute?"

He looked down at her fingers, at the red-painted fingernails against his black sleeve. She had capable, domestic hands and the red polish looked slightly incongruous on them. Gordon's head was full of Nina's pale, imploring face. He answered vaguely, but with a cold sense of impending catastrophe.

"Talk? Yes, of course."

"In here."

Marcelle opened the door to the little gunroom. There were the two creaky wicker chairs that she and Jimmy had occupied, and Jimmy's empty glass on the floor where he had left it.

"Parties, all these parties. All of us getting together and talking and drinking and being good fun. At all costs, good fun." She was very tired now.

"Marcelle? What do you want to say?"

She nodded, feeling that her skull was too heavy for her spine. Was it only this evening, how many hours ago, that Jimmy had kissed her in here and she had worried about the creases in the skin between her breasts?

"I know it isn't any of my business," she began, and then faltered. "Gordon, I'm sorry. That's what malicious gossips always say, isn't it?"

"I wouldn't know." His mouth made a grim line. "Do you listen to gossip?"

She felt rebuked, but also that the rebuke was justified. "All right. I'll just tell you how it is. You know what I saw the other day, and you should also know that until this evening I hadn't mentioned it to anyone, not to Michael or anyone else."

He said stiffly, "Thank you. You were right, of course: it isn't any of your business."

Marcelle felt a prickle of anger.

"Even though Vicky is my friend?"

"It would be an act of friendship, wouldn't it, not to pass on speculative whispers about a brief glimpse of two people? A glimpse that might easily have been mistaken or misinterpreted?"

"But I don't think I was mistaken, was I?"

When Gordon said nothing, she rushed at her admission, wanting to get it over with so that she could escape.

"This isn't coming out the way I meant it to, not that I know how I meant it. We know each other well enough, don't we? I wanted you to know that I meant to keep my mouth shut, but I didn't, stupidly, and I'm very sorry. I told Jimmy Rose about it."

Gordon said in disbelief, "You told *Jimmy*?"

His fuddled mind filled up with images of Jimmy's cunning, foxlike head bent close to a circle of other heads, and then the heads turning to more circles of listening heads, and mouths whispering, all of them Jimmy's mouth, on and on, in widening ripples into infinity.

"I'm very sorry. It was a thoughtless and damaging thing to do."

"Yes."

He could think of nothing else to say other than to acknowledge the truth.

Marcelle's hand reached out toward him, as if to offer meaningless comfort, but he made no move and she let it fall to her side. Then she turned sharply and ran out the door.

Gordon watched the door close behind her. He stood and stared at it, feeling a leaden pity—for Vicky and Nina, for himself, even for Jimmy and Marcelle—that he knew would shortly flower into pain.

The party was coming to an end, and Darcy had stationed himself near the front door to say good night to his guests.

Gordon and Vicky came downstairs together, Gordon carrying the baby basket. Darcy kissed Vicky on the cheek and she leaned against him for an instant, looking up at him, her fingers closing on his arm, while Gordon stood stiffly beside her. The Wickhams followed the Ransomes out into the cold darkness, with the Frosts and Star not far behind them. They called out, wishing each other a merry Christmas, separating into the usual pairs for the drive home into Christmas day.

Marcelle stared ahead, watching the way their car's headlights sliced at angles over the flat-topped hedges. She wanted to build a bridge to Michael now, before they reached home.

"Was the boy all right?"

"Yes, more or less. He was quite lucky." Michael glanced at her. "Did you enjoy the party? I didn't see much of you."

He was aware of all the evenings of their years together meshing behind them. He thought of all the parties they had been to after the one at which they had first met, the clothes and places and friendships that had been discarded, temporary attractions to other people flaring and fading, leaving just the two of them. The weight of so much history bore down on him.

Marcelle thought of Jimmy with his head bent to kiss her lined skin, and Gordon's rebuke, and his cold face. She also remembered the furtive delight that she had glimpsed in the red Mercedes.

"Yes," she lied. "Yes, I did."

Michael took one hand off the wheel to touch her arm.

"Let's try to have a happy Christmas, shall we?"

"Of course," Marcelle answered.

Vicky rested her head against the cool glass of the passenger-side window. She was smiling. There had been a guilelessness in Darcy's advance, a childish directness that she found appealing. She was also pleased that he had so plainly wanted her; after what seemed like years of feeling huge and milky and bovine, it was good to be reminded that she was still alive and interesting. She could feel the stirred-up blood singing inside her.

Vicky had no idea what would happen next, or if anything would happen at all, but she contemplated whatever it would be with sleepy equanimity.

Gordon negotiated the familiar twists of the country road with frozen concentration. He could see the lights of another car, proba-bly the Frosts', winding ahead of him. He thought Vicky must have dropped into a doze and he tried to drive smoothly in order not to wake her or the baby. He needed this time to think.

He was certain that he would have to tell Vicky the truth, before she heard someone else whispering the story.

He would have to tell her as gently and as honestly as he could manage, although he could not imagine what words he would use. Nor did he have any idea of what might happen once Vicky did know. But even now, in the midst of his dread, he knew that he couldn't bear to give Nina up, even though that was what he cer-tainly had to do.

His whole head was alive with images of Nina in her black dress, with her head held up, and her long hands painted with blood. It had been hard enough not to run to her then, to have to leave her to Barney Clegg.

How could he tell Vicky what he barely understood and clung to with all the selfish and vivid need that had woken up in him?

And when could he tell her? He must warn Nina first, somehow, and that would be a second betrayal. A wild impulse to leave Vicky at home and then to turn around and drive straight to Dean's Row fueled him for a second and then died down.

There was nothing to be done today.

There would be the family Christmas with his children and their grandparents, and he would have to live through it with the knowledge of what was waiting for them all. The next day, or the day after that, he would somehow find a way to tell the truth before Jimmy Rose did it for him.

Then, at the end of it all, he would be left without Nina. As he considered this Gordon felt, as dispassionately as if he were registering it in a third person, the first sharp twist of pain.

Darcy sat down on the edge of the bed and took off his shoes. Hannah was already in bed, lying curled up with her back to him.

"What's the matter?" he asked her. "It was a good party. Good enough, anyway." When she said nothing, he undid his tie and shirt and then took off his trousers, dropping each item onto Vicky's chair. He could still see the print of her body in its cushions.

"Does this have to do with Vicky Ransome?" he asked. Hannah muttered something he could not hear. He told her irritably, "Don't sulk, darling, it doesn't suit you."

Darcy padded naked into the bathroom and looked at himself in the mirror. There was a thick roll of flesh around his midriff and the hair on his chest was gray, but the muscles of his belly remained satisfyingly taut. He was not, he told himself, in bad shape for his age.

By the time he slid into bed beside her, Hannah still had not moved. Darcy eased across and pressed himself up against her bulky warmth. He loved the generosity of flesh; it was Jimmy Rose's mistake to imagine that he could have been drawn to Nina's dry bones.

"Hannah?"

He reached an arm over her shoulder and found her breasts. Their looseness connected him to Vicky again, and he felt himself harden.

"Stop it, Darcy. The kids will be awake in three hours."

"Let the nanny see to them. Or the twins."

"It's *Christmas*."

"All the more reason to spread a little cheer."

Her only response was to push his hand away and self-protectively hunch her shoulders. Darcy was too sleepy to make more than a token protest; he knew that this was Hannah's revenge for his interlude with Vicky, and he also knew that by tomorrow it would be forgotten.

When he reached up to turn out the light he was smiling. He had remembered his earlier feeling that he loved Vicky Ransome. He wanted to fuck her, that was true; he still did. But there was no need for love to be a factor in *that* equation.

Jimmy came out of the church. He shook hands with the priest and nodded a greeting to some of the other worshippers, although he knew none of them well.

The Catholic church was a modern brick building on a quiet road. Jimmy walked a little way away from it, down the street, to get away from the people and their cars. It was a cold, clear night. The streetlights spread a murky orange canopy overhead, but he could see through it to the sharp brilliance of the stars. When he was alone he stopped and heard the tinny echo of his own footsteps.

He tilted his head back to look at the stars.

It was Christmas morning, and Jimmy felt at peace.

9

The door of the Dean's Row house was opened by a man Gordon had never seen before. His pale clothes looked incongruous in the metallic winter light and his feet were bare. It was the afternoon of Boxing Day.

"Is Nina here?"

Patrick said, "Yes, she is." He knew at once that this was the man Nina had talked about. Reluctantly he opened the door a little wider. "Come in. She's upstairs."

Nina and Patrick had been watching a film, the Branagh *Henry V*. They had spent many afternoons like this together, immersed in a movie, barricaded by sofa cushions. There was a box of Belgian chocolates on the floor, and a comfortable litter of empty coffee cups and wine glasses. The king's dirty, weary army limped across the television screen in one corner.

"I much prefer the Olivier version," Patrick had sighed just before the knock at the door. "Such romantic Plantagenet splendor."

"You would," Nina had laughed at him through a mouthful of chocolate. "Don't you think mud and dead horses are more realistic?"

"And is realism a real benefit?"

Now Gordon stood in the doorway. Nina was startled, still warm with laughter, sitting in her corner of the sofa with her knees drawn up against the cushions. Looking in, Gordon saw the evidence of an indulgent, adult afternoon of a kind that he had almost forgotten. His own house today was a dense, humid mass of children and grandparents and festive detritus. Nina's bare, elegant drawing room and even the unknown languid man formed a tableau that entirely excluded him.

"I'm sorry, I'm disturbing you."

Nina jumped to her feet. She was wearing leggings and a loose cashmere tunic that he remembered seeing before. It had felt soft enough to melt under his hands.

"No, you're not. Of course you're not."

He clearly saw the pleasure and anticipation in her face, and wished that he had come to tell her something different.

"Only I thought, today . . ." She gestured with the long fingers he wanted to hold. She meant that it was Boxing Day, a time of new dollhouses and noisy parlor games and family attachments.

"I said I had a headache and needed some fresh air. The truth, as it happens."

For a moment he had forgotten the pale-colored man behind him, but Nina had not.

"Gordon, this is Patrick Forbes, an old friend of mine. Patrick, this is Gordon Ransome."

They shook hands, conscious of immediate mutual dislike. Now that they were facing each other, Gordon saw that Patrick had to be gay. He was always uncomfortable with homosexuals, and in his turn Patrick's defensiveness of Nina made him prickly.

Gordon was also disconcerted to realize that he had never considered that Nina might not be alone, even on the day after Christmas. They hadn't discussed their holiday plans. Patrick's presence among the cushions and wine glasses conjured up a world of friends and diversions and allegiances in which he played no part. He felt a desolate, paradoxical jealousy.

He said, with his eyes fixed on hers, "I hoped we might be able to talk for a few minutes."

Patrick's eyebrows lifted. "I'll go and make some tea, shall I?"

Nina smiled at him. "Could you?"

Gordon felt as if he had blundered into a game whose unwritten rules were too subtle for him to comprehend. But as soon as Patrick had gone, Nina came to him, put her hands on his arms, and reached up to kiss him. He held her longingly and despite himself.

"He knows about us, doesn't he?" Gordon asked.

"I had to talk to somebody. I couldn't keep so much so secret. Do you mind very much?"

She was bright-faced with happiness. He considered, briefly, whether he might not after all be able to conceal the real reason for his visit. Then they could sit down together, comfortable among the scattered television listings and hollowed cushions. He hesitated, but her face was already changing, the happiness fading out of it.

"What is it?" she asked.

He noticed that in the time he had been in the room the light outside had faded from midwinter afternoon to premature dusk. In a moment the streetlamps would come on at the edges of the green. When he didn't answer at once, she repeated, "What is it? Tell me."

He sat down on the edge of the warm sofa. He remembered lighting the fire for her on that first afternoon, when they had admired the cathedral's west façade before it had been shrouded by scaffolding. Not many weeks ago. He could count them exactly by the number of times they had managed to see each other. In retrospect they seemed very few, especially for the difficulty of what he was having to do now.

"Marcelle told Jimmy Rose that she saw us together."

Nina looked at him. The firelight polished her cheeks and the golden shields of her earrings.

"Well. That *is* a pity."

He waited, but she had nothing else to say. Her passivity irritated him, but then he remembered that she was an outsider and did not understand the shorthand of the Grafton couples.

"If Jimmy knows, it means that everyone knows. Jimmy has never been one for keeping gossip to himself."

"Vicky?"

"Vicky will know soon enough, obviously. Someone will tell her."

Nina fell silent again.

She raised her eyes to meet Gordon's. In his head the features of the two women blurred.

She said, very quietly, "I see. What does this mean?"

"It means that I must tell her the truth before somebody else gives her some distorted version of it. And it also means that I can't go on seeing you. I'm sorry. I wish I didn't have to be so clumsy. I feel as if I have broken something irreplaceable."

Nina sat still. Her eyes slid away from his toward the fire. When she spoke, it was in the same quiet voice.

"Don't worry. Nothing's broken."

Whatever it was that Gordon had been afraid of, tears or protests or blame, did not come. Her face was immobile, and her silence meant that he had to talk, continue to offer her some other currency now that the old one had become invalid.

"This is very painful, Nina. You made me happy. Guilty, but happy as well. I went through all our tapes, you know, in the racks at home, and dug out all the old rock numbers and fed them into the deck in the car. I used to drive along, going to work or some bloody site meeting, with the volume turned up, music blasting out. Singing along, grinning and drumming my fingers on the wheel. I felt like a boy.

He spread his hands out, offering her this, at least. "A middle-aged engineer, burdened with debt and children and responsibilities. I couldn't believe that it was happening."

Still Nina said nothing.

"I loved you. I love you now."

She looked at him at last.

"And so what happens to it, this *love?*"

He considered the question, knowing that he owed her as much.

To feel love had been seductive and intriguing and flattering, and it had given him an animation he had not felt for years. This woman, whom he had believed he understood, had accepted and reciprocated his love, and all of this had taken place within a frame of secrecy that had been part of its delight. Gordon had enjoyed having a secret, after all the years of an interior life as clean and plain and colorless as the external world. The possession of it had added an extra erotic charge to everything he and Nina did together. But once the secrecy was gone, he did not see how the rest could remain. Whatever gloss he longed to give it, the affair was now public property.

"I love you still," he said helplessly.

That was the truth. Greedy and possessive as he knew it was, he wanted to keep her. Even now it would have been easy, delightful, to reach out, to undo buttons and expose her white, tea-freckled skin.

Gordon touched the tip of his tongue to his dry lips.

"But I'm married and therefore responsible to people other than myself. I thought you understood that, Nina?"

"Understood that wives must be protected at all costs?"

Her eyes were as flat as the discs of her earrings.

"Wives. And children." Gordon said.

As he uttered the words, he gained another surprising insight. This loss of love and Nina hurt him and would continue to hurt him, but he also wanted to be saved. Salvation was in sight now, and this glimpse of it filled him with relief.

"What about me?" Nina asked. Her voice was dry, toneless.

He shook his head slowly from side to side, accepting the darts of pain inside his skull as his due. He was eager for the pain of losing her to begin. It was the penance he had to undergo.

"I don't want to hurt you. I want to hold you and make it better for you, but I can't. I can't bear the thought of hurting you."

"But clearly you can."

It was fully dark outside. The streetlamps made an ugly, amber haze in the drifted snow-shapes of condensation in the corners of the windowpanes.

In the silence that followed, Nina went to the nearest of the tall windows and unfolded the shutters from their paneled niches, carefully fitting the old iron catch with its curled tail into the slot to secure them. She did the same with the other two windows, moving carefully behind the Christmas tree to reach them. Nina's tree was hung with silver trinkets and illuminated with pure white light. Gordon made an automatic comparison with Vicky's, which was loaded with crayoned ornaments made by the girls and lit with multicolored lanterns.

Nina finished the task of closing out the darkness, then came back to her place.

"Thank you for coming to tell me first," she said. "Before Vicky."

He had never seen this coldness, this composure, in her before. She had always been warm and eager, generous with herself in a way that had been enticingly at odds with her physical slightness. He wanted to defend Vicky, who had done nothing, but he restrained himself.

"I'm truly sorry," was all he could think of to say.

"Yes. As I said, however, nothing is broken," Nina repeated.

How strong she is, Gordon thought. *Much stronger than I am.* He had not known her properly, after all.

Her strength unbalanced him and revealed his own weakness.

Now that the business was concluded, he felt a terrible urge to throw himself at her, to hide his face and cry in her arms, to have her comfort him, the way Vicky soothed Alice with inarticulate murmurings after the child had a bad dream. Nina's smell and the texture of her skin and hair returned sharply to his imagination. He propped his elbow on his knee and rested his head in his hand. But she did not reach out to soothe or console him; instead she looked at her watch, and the loose cuff of her tunic fell back to expose her thin wrist and the freckles on her arm.

She said, in her cool, unemphatic voice, "I wonder where Patrick is with the tea."

Gordon lifted his head again. "I don't want any tea."

"No. Yours will be waiting for you at home, of course."

The glimpse of her bitterness stirred him. She was not unaffected, after all, and he felt himself melting. He made a tiny move toward her, but she held up her hands, fending him off.

The conversation was over. She would not look at him now.

There was nothing for him to do but stand and pick up his coat, which he had draped over a chair when Patrick led him into the room.

He blurted foolishly, "Will I . . . will we see each other again?"

Nina sat on the cushions, not moving, one side of her face still gilded by the firelight.

"At the Frosts', or the Cleggs', of course."

"Don't be hard."

"Don't you be soft, then."

"I'm sorry," he attempted for the last time.

"Yes," Nina said.

Gordon nodded. It was clear that there was no more to be said. He went downstairs and let himself out. His Peugeot was parked beyond the archway that led onto the green. He drove out of the city in the opposite direction from home, and stopped in a field gateway off a lane that led in the direction of Wilton. In the distance he could just make out the lights of Darcy's house on its little hill.

He sat for a long time, with the car heater making a small burr of warmth around him. The hedge trees loomed in the darkness, and no other car passed. Once, he reached out to the tongue of the cassette tape protruding from the player, but he stopped before pushing it in. He thought about all the households between here and the city, imagining the rooms, the decorations that had been put up for the holiday, and the complicated arrangements of families gathered for Christmas. He felt omniscient, elevated by his sadness, as if he could look into the houses and interpret their secrets.

Then, with a sudden affection colored by relief, he thought about his own fireside. Now it only remained for him to make his confession to Vicky, and then he would be safe.

He began to feel stiff and cold, even with the heater running, so he restarted the engine, turned the car around, and headed home.

In the empty room Nina leaned forward and picked up a shred of gold wrapping paper from the rug. She folded it and buffed it with her fingernail to make it shine, then twisted it around her ring finger to make a wedding band, as she had done as a child in games of make-believe.

My husband will be handsome and rich, and we'll have eight children, four of each.

My *husband will buy us a big house in London and another by the sea, and we'll have eight children as well.*

With Richard's rings, the paper one made a gaudy triplet.

She asked him, *Why aren't you here? Why did you leave me when I needed you? We had our houses and our happiness.*

No children. I'm sorry for that, my love.

And then you had to go and die, and leave me here.

Nina stared at the blank wooden shutters. A month earlier, even a week earlier, she would have cried and battered herself against the wall of her own grief. Nothing had changed, only herself, but this time she did not cry.

Now that he had stumbled away, with his needs and his confusion, Nina knew that she had only tried to make a shadow husband out of Gordon Ransome. She had imagined he would dispel her loneliness. Her judgment had been hardly more developed than that of the little girl playing weddings.

She had been too harsh with Gordon. In the end his strength had turned out to be an illusion, and his loyalty was all for himself and his wife and his children, not for her at all.

She took off the paper ring and screwed it into a ball before throwing it in the fire. The only strength that was valuable to her was her own, and for the protection of friendship there was always Patrick.

She found him sitting in the kitchen, a room whose faux-rustic cupboards and tiles she disliked. The tea-tray was immaculately laid and waiting on the table beside him. He was smoking a brightly colored Balkan Sobranie.

"I heard him leaving," Patrick said.

"The final exit."

He raised his eyebrows at her, squinting through the smoke, making his Noël Coward face. Nina burst out laughing.

"Funny?" Patrick inquired.

"Not really. No, not at all."

"Tell me, then." He lifted the teapot, poured, and passed her the cup.

"It's just how you would have predicted. You warned me at the beginning, didn't you?"

He made a dismissive gesture.

"One of the wives, half of one of the couples, happened to see us together. She told someone else, one of the husbands, who will in turn tell all the others. And so Gordon's wife will get to hear of it. And so it has to end, so that he can confess all and ask for forgiveness."

"How can you bear it?" Patrick asked. "This little provincial world of couples all pecking away at one another, at one another's secrets?"

Nina took a sip of her tea. "It isn't quite like that. This isn't a metropolitan world, there isn't the same luxurious privacy that cities give. But there is a feeling of us all being here together. Of having committed ourselves to the same life. It was just a mistake to have had an affair."

She was thinking of the different faces of the Grafton couples and the ways that their friendships and allegiances seemed to knit them together, and remembering her reluctance to join Darcy Clegg in his mild mockery of them.

Patrick was watching her face.

"So it's all over."

"Oh, yes."

There was a moment's silence. "He was wearing those shoes. The kind that look like pork pies left out in the rain."

"Don't laugh at him, Patrick. I liked him very much."

"And now he's made you sad."

"Yes."

Patrick put his arms around her. She rested her forehead against his shoulder.

"Why don't you come back to London? Instead of staying out here in this suburban ghetto."

Nina shook her head. "I like it here," she said. She was thinking of the statues in their cathedral niches, their faces reemerging from the lime bandages. Images of regeneration.

Patrick let her go. "Well, I suppose that's that, then. Do you want to watch the end of the film?"

"Why not? We could have a glass of champagne at the same time. It *is* Christmas."

"That's my girl."

They finished their tea, then drank champagne in front of the television. Later there was another knock at the door, and Nina went downstairs to answer it. A car was parked out front, two of its wheels on the pavement, and Barney Clegg and his friend with the bandaged hand were standing on the steps. Barney held up two bottles; Tom was bearing an ivory-flowered plant wrapped in green tissue paper in the crook of his good arm. They were both beaming at her.

"You did live, then," Nina said to Tom.

"I did. We've just called to say thank you. And to give you this. Whatever it is."

"It's a Christmas rose," Barney Clegg protested. "*Helleborus niger*. For your garden. I suppose you've got a garden back there?"

She accepted the offering. Its fragile cup-shaped flowers were tinged with green, with a central boss of golden anthers. "How beautiful. My garden isn't worthy of it. Would you like to come in and have a drink? Provided you don't bleed on anything?"

The boys trampled in, looking huge in her hallway.

"Eleven stitches," Tom said proudly, holding out his arm.

"After eleven hours sitting in the emergency room, or thereabouts," Barney cheerfully complained.

They followed Nina upstairs, filling the house with noise.

"We've just been round to Mike Wickham's, to thank him as well."

"And how were they?"

The boys snorted with laughter. "Pretty dire. Howling kids everywhere."

"Just like Barney's place, in fact."

Nina opened the living room door for them.

"Well, there are no kids here, howling or otherwise. Just Patrick and me."

Patrick uncoiled himself from the sofa and rose while Nina made the introductions. "This is Barney and his friend Tom. They've come to thank me for doing not very much when Tom cut his arm on Christmas Eve."

After the handshakes, Barney offered his bottles of wine.

"I don't know what these are, are they drinkable? I lifted them from Dad's cellar."

Patrick examined the labels.

"Better than drinkable. Two rather good Pomerols."

"Shall we open them? Let them breathe and all that?"

More glasses were brought, logs were put on the fire, and the humming television was switched off. The boys made themselves comfortable. Patrick and Nina refilled glasses and passed plates, and learned among other things that Barney was a student of landscape design and horticulture at an agricultural college and Tom was at the nearby Poly. They had been friends since their not-very-distant school days. They had been vaguely planning to move on to Grafton's one disco later in the evening, but Barney complained that it was full of kids. "Lucy and Cathy's crowd." Soon it became clear that Barney and Tom were staying to dinner.

When Patrick and Nina found themselves alone for a moment

in the kitchen. Patrick said, "I thought you said you knew no one in Grafton except middle-aged married couples."

"Surprise, surprise."

It was a convivial supper. Patrick was never openly camp, but the wine melted his reserve and made him funny and loquacious. It was clear that he liked the company of the two boys, and Nina was pleased to see that he was enjoying himself. Patrick seemed too often to be an observer nowadays. For her part, Nina was amused by Barney and Tom's good humor and their enthusiasm for everything from her food to Patrick's wry jokes. Whenever she remembered Gordon and experienced the twist of angry sadness that accompanied the thought of him, she made herself concentrate instead on the friendly faces around her kitchen table.

The Christmas rose stood stripped of its paper on the draining board. There were crumbs of earth around the lip of the clay pot and more mud rimming its bottom. Nina was brushing some of it away with her fingertips when Barney came with a neat pile of dirty plates and stood beside her at the sink.

"I lifted it from the nursery bed especially for you," he told her. He was a head taller than Nina, and she had to look up at him.

"Did you lift one for Mike Wickham, too?"

"No, of course not."

They both looked at the ivory petals and their faint suffusion of green. Nina was disconcerted to find that that she was blushing. Behind them, she heard Tom explaining to Patrick the rules of some complicated word game that he had suddenly decided they all had to play.

"Shall I put it in the garden for you?" Barney asked her. "It's too hot for it to be happy in here."

Nina turned on the outside light and led Barney out to her tiny back courtyard. It was a dismal prospect of bare earth drifted over with dead leaves and windblown litter.

"I did say that my garden wasn't worthy of it."

Barney unlocked the door and carried the plant outside. Nina watched him find a sheltered corner and tenderly heap up dead leaves around the pot to protect it from the frost. He rubbed his large hands on his jeans and ducked back inside.

"I'll come back in the daylight to plant it properly for you. I could tidy up the rest and plant some other stuff as well, if you like."

He waited.

Nina said gently, "That's very kind of you. But I don't think you should waste your time on my neglected garden."

Richard had always been the gardener. He had loved his garden in Norfolk, the garden where he had died.

Barney shrugged. "That's okay. It's my job, or it will be if I ever get qualified."

Tom called to them. "Are we going to play this game, then?"

They had had a good deal to drink, Nina realized, but she took another bottle of wine from the rack, opened it, and sat down at the table again.

The game was a rambling, open-ended affair of inventing words and then supplying meanings for them. Patrick was the best at devising words and definitions; he had always been good at crosswords and riddles and charades, but Barney came in a surprisingly sharp second. Nina was hopeless, her wits were too scattered, but it was a pleasure to see Patrick enjoying himself so much.

After midnight the boys decided that they did, after all, have to make a late-night-raid on the disco. They tried to persuade Nina and Patrick to join them, but without success.

Finally, with promises to come back another day, they roared off into the night.

Patrick leaned against the teal-blue cupboards and drank the last of his glass of wine.

"Do you think I'm a silly old queen?" he asked. "Enjoying the company of a pair of nice straight boys like them?"

"No more than I'm a silly old woman," Nina answered. She was smiling, but Patrick was not deceived.

"Are you thinking about Gordon?"

"Yes." And about Richard, too, only she wouldn't burden him with that.

"Then don't," Patrick said to her.

Vicky's parents went home the morning after Boxing Day. Gordon carried their tartan suitcases out to the front of the house and stowed them side-by-side in the trunk of Alec's Vauxhall.

Vicky came out and stood beside him in the driveway, and Alice and Mary waved, and Alec revved the engine too fiercely before letting out the clutch, as he always did. The Vauxhall bucked forward, narrowly missing the rose bushes bordering the front lawn, and then achieved the correct momentum to pass between the gateposts and swing left into the roadway.

The children shouted gamely "Good-bye Granny, good-bye Grandad," and Gordon and Vicky raised their arms in salute, frozen for an instant in a happy-family tableau.

When the Vauxhall had finally passed out of sight, they all went back into the house. Vicky lifted the baby to her shoulder and massaged her back through the thickness of the shawl.

Gordon looked carefully around him, as if he were seeing the interior of his home for the first time. There was a hard, yellowish light that revealed the chipped paint of the skirting boards and the sticky handprints on the walls, and now that he and Vicky were alone together again the rooms seemed drowned in a sullen, implacable silence.

They all went into the untidy kitchen, and while Vicky put the baby into her basket Gordon covertly watched her face. The skin seemed puffy and unhealthily smooth, as if water had seeped underneath it. It occurred to him that she was suffering, too.

He had decided that he would talk to her in the evening, when the children were asleep. It was the anticipation of what was to come that gave the house and all its surroundings this queasily unfamiliar aspect, and for the hundredth time he toyed with the idea of saying nothing, of trusting to luck and the hope that Vicky would never hear about what had happened. But ever since Christmas Eve he had been imagining the invisible snake of gossip slithering among the Grafton couples, and he knew that he would have to make his confession.

Vicky was listlessly piling toys into a wicker hamper. Someone had spilled sugar on the kitchen floor, and her slippers made a gritty protest as she moved.

Gordon said, "I thought I might take them all out for a walk down to the river. I could put Helen in the carriage. You could go to sleep for an hour, if you like."

She straightened up, and he saw her brief flicker of surprise replaced by disbelief.

"You look tired," he offered. "Go on, have an hour's rest."

Vicky dropped another toy into the basket, looking away from him again. "Thanks. I might, if you don't mind."

After he had searched for and found the necessary pairs of mittens and boots, helped Mary and Alice into their coats and wound scarves around their necks, and once Helen was zipped into her padded bag and strapped into her carriage, Gordon's patience was almost exhausted. Vicky had gone upstairs without a backward glance.

"Off we go," he encouraged his daughters.

They set off down the road. All the neighbors' front doors were tightly closed and their windows were screened by the scrawny arms of winter trees. Alice wanted to stop at every corner, but he made her hurry on with promises of the park beside the river.

"Mummy always lets me say hello to the spotted dog," she complained.

"Don't you want to get to the swings?" he cajoled.

When they reached the park after their slow journey, they stood in a line and peered through the railings at the river. It was swollen and brown, carrying crests of dirty foam on its back. The wind was very cold. Helen's tiny nose had turned red, although the rest of her was almost invisible in her swaddling.

"Sometimes we throw sticks," Mary told him.

"Shall we swing today?" Gordon asked her, recognizing that this numbing outing must be a regular part of Vicky's routine. He left the baby parked against the railings.

Mary ran to a swing and hoisted herself on to the seat.

"Push me," she called to him.

Alice ran to one side, to a yellow plastic cockerel mounted on a heavy spring.

"How high can you go?" Gordon asked Mary, giving her small duffle-coated back a tentative push.

"Much higher. Push harder," Mary shouted, sticking her legs straight out in front of her. "That's better. Like *that*."

To Gordon she seemed terribly fragile, a small cargo of precious humanity rushing backward and forward through the hostile air. Her hair streamed out from under her knitted hat and she shouted with excitement, defying his adult anxiety.

A second later he saw the red blur of Alice's coat out of the corner of his eye. She had abandoned her cockerel and was rushing toward them.

He shouted, "Look out," but he was frozen in mid-push, his hands stretched vertically in front of him. Alice zigzagged in front of the swing and the heel of Mary's boot caught her on the temple before the seat soared on upward over her head.

Alice collapsed on the tarmac under the descending arc of her sister's swing. Gordon caught the chains and held them, arresting Mary at the high point and almost wrenching his arms out of their sockets. He stopped the swing and scooped Mary out of it before rushing over to where Alice was lying in a heap.

"She just ran in front," he heard Mary babbling.

He bent over Alice and saw her face contract and her lips draw back from her teeth. There were three full seconds of silence before the first howl found its way out of her. He was almost crying with relief himself as he snatched her up and held her. Her screams grew louder, and she went rigid.

There was a blue-and-white graze on her temple, and as he looked at it tiny scarlet beads sprang out between the shreds of skin. The herringbone print of Mary's sole was clearly visible.

"Mummy puts cold water," Mary said, pointing to the drinking fountain. Gordon carried the screaming child over to the metal cup and soaked his handkerchief in icy water. The side of Alice's head was already turning red and beginning to swell. Gordon pressed the cold compress onto it and soothed her, listening to the panicky jumps of his own heart.

"It isn't too bad, darling. It will hurt for a bit and then it will go away. It's just a bump. Just an old bump. Something that happens at the swings."

After a while the child's screaming subsided and then stopped, fading away into hiccuping sobs.

"Good girl," he whispered to her, rocking her in his arms. "Brave girl."

"She's stupid," Mary said at his elbow, needing to state her own case now that the panic was over. "She just ran in front, it wasn't my fault."

"It wasn't anyone's fault, it just happened."

Gordon extended his other arm to hold Mary, too. He hugged his daughters close to his chest, daunted by their vulnerability and by the scale of the work involved in keeping them safe, helping them to grow. He felt weighed down by the responsibility of parenthood, but at the same time a different, narrow perspective opened up to him, a reluctant admiration for Vicky and satisfaction in their partnership. They had created these three small individuals, at least. After this evening, he thought, he hoped that everything would be set right again.

The lump on the side of Alice's head had grown to the size of a small, shiny egg, but the graze had stopped bleeding and he could see that no serious damage had been done. Gordon stood up, setting the two little girls side-by-side on the tarmac.

"We had better go home," he told them. "Helen will be waking up soon and will need to be fed."

In the evening, after the children had been put to bed, Vicky made dinner, a random assemblage of leftovers that seemed even more halfhearted than her recent efforts in the kitchen.

"I'll do a big shop tomorrow, when everything is open again," she said before Gordon could complain. Her brief nap in the afternoon only seemed to have increased her tiredness. She moved heavily between the table and the fridge.

"It doesn't matter," Gordon said. He felt clumsy and guilty. He opened a bottle of wine and made himself a cold turkey sandwich. When they were both sitting down he began.

"Can we talk about something?"

"I'm very tired," Vicky answered.

"It's important."

She waited in silence, holding her wine glass in her hands. The puffiness of the skin around her eyes had narrowed the sockets, giving her a Chinese look.

Gordon put down his sandwich. Staring at the plate in front of him, he said. "There isn't any gentle way to tell you this. I wish there were. I have been having an affair with Nina. It's over now."

Behind him the refrigerator gave its familiar shudder as the motor started into life.

Vicky looked as if he had hit her. Gordon made a move to touch her, but she pushed him away with a stiff, panicky gesture.

"Nina?" she repeated.

"I'm so sorry about it. I wanted to tell you."

After a moment Vicky sank down, her shoulders sagging against the back of the kitchen chair.

"I knew there was something. Oh, God, I knew there was something."

She shaded her eyes with her hand. "How long has it been going on?"

"It started when you were in the hospital."

"When I was in the hospital? When I was in the *hospital* having our baby?" She shook her head from side to side as if she couldn't quite make sense of the words.

This is terrible, Gordon thought. He had tried to imagine how it would be, over and over, but he had never envisaged this sick, shocked look of Vicky's.

"When did it end?" she asked.

"I went to tell her yesterday afternoon."

"Why yesterday afternoon?"

He paused, and then said, "Marcelle Wickham saw the two of us together a few days ago. She told Jimmy about it on Christmas Eve."

"But why did you end it?"

"Because I wanted to," he lied. "And because I wanted you to hear about it from me, not from Janice or Star or somebody else."

Vicky nodded her head now, his words seeming to come clear to her at last.

"Christmas Eve?" she repeated. "You ended it because you had to."

"No, that's not true."

She let her hand drop away from her eyes. They stared at each other as if in the last minutes they had become different people. Gordon felt himself beginning to shake.

"So, what was she like in bed, your Nina? Was the sex wonderful?"

"No," he lied again.

Vicky was still staring. Then, with shocking suddenness, her face began to melt. Her mouth spilled wide open, showing her teeth and her tongue, and her eyes narrowed to slits. She started to cry, the tears running down her face. Her shocked composure followed by this collapse reminded Gordon of Alice's stunned silence and then her screams of pain and outrage in the park. He reached out now and managed to take Vicky's hand.

"I'm very sorry," he said humbly. "It was a terrible thing to do."

Vicky was sobbing aloud, thick uncontrolled sobs that went *ahahah* in her throat.

"What can I say?" Gordon muttered wretchedly.

Vicky tore her hand away from his. She made a grand sweep with her arm and knocked her glass to the floor, and the red wine splashed onto the cupboards and over a drawing of Mary's that was pinned to them. The broken glass glinted on the tiles, and Vicky got to her feet, staggering as if she were drunk, and ploughed through it to the sink. With another sweep of her arm she cleared the draining board of cups and plates, sending a wave of china crashing around her.

"Don't say anything," she shouted at him. "Don't. I don't want to hear it."

She reached out, her fingers clawing for something else to smash. Gordon jumped to his feet and ran through the sea of broken china to catch her wrists.

"Stop it," he ordered her.

Vicky jerked one hand free. She swung it back and delivered an open-handed blow to the side of his face. His jaw snapped upward, catching his tongue between his teeth and making his eyes water with humiliating pain. He stepped away from her, angry now, his shoes crunching in the shards of china.

With a last wild swing Vicky knocked the bottle sterilizer off the countertop. As it hit the floor the top came off, sending up a plume of liquid, and dancing bottles crashed over Gordon's feet. For a moment he thought she was laughing as she whirled away from him and out of the kitchen, slamming the door so that the still-unbroken plates on the shelves rattled perilously.

Gordon stood still, breathing hard and tasting the blood on his tongue. He put his fingers up to his stinging cheek, and then wiped the blood from his tongue on the back of his hand. The refrigerator motor cut out and the machine shrugged comfortably into silence again.

Slowly, Gordon stooped down and picked up the first pieces of broken plates. He set to work slowly and methodically, mopping and then sweeping up the debris and wrapping it in newspaper before putting it in the outside trash can. He came in again and locked the back door carefully behind him, then filled a bucket with soapy water and washed the wine stains and sterilizing fluid off the walls and cupboard doors. His cleaning-up went beyond the immediate damage; he swept up a mixture of crumbs and spilled sugar from under the table and the accumulation of household dust from the corners of the room.

After half an hour his anger and guilt had subsided.

He went out of the kitchen, intending to look for Vicky, and then saw that the front door was open. Cold air was funneling down the hallway. There was a bulky pile, a jumble heap in the driveway beyond the front step.

As he stood there, slow-witted, Vicky came down the stairs. In one arm she was carrying a tangle of his belongings; he made out the jacket of his Tory suit, and his squash racket. The other hand was dragging the largest of their suitcases. It bumped down the stairs in her wake.

Vicky threw his things onto the pile outside and pushed the suitcase after them. She was panting with exertion and wiped her mouth with her hand.

"Go on," she shouted at him. "Go on, we don't want you. Get out of here. Go to her if that's what you want."

Her face was burning. He had never seen her so angry. Only half-comprehending what was happening, Gordon ran outside to see what she had done with his things.

The front door slammed behind him.

He turned around again and heard her sliding the bolts and the rattle of the chain as she secured it. Then there was the faint, bland *beep* that signaled the switching on of the burglar alarm.

It was a bitterly cold night, and he was in his shirtsleeves.

Over his head, in the room that looked out over the driveway, one of the girls had woken up. He heard her, Mary or Alice, whichever it was, beginning to cry.

10

The chalet rented by three of the Grafton families for their February skiing holiday was in the upper, quieter part of Méribel, near Rond Point and the ski school. It was a modern building, but its exterior was pleasantly sided with wood and it had a first-floor balcony in rustic Alpine style. Inside, most of the walls and ceilings were lined with tongue-and-groove pine boarding.

Darcy lay on the bed in the best bedroom in the chalet, the only one with its own adjoining bathroom. His hands were folded behind his head and he was staring up at the wooden ceiling. The window opposite him was partly masked with snow, and outside snow was still falling in thick, aimless flakes.

"This is just like living inside some damned great sauna. It even smells the same. I keep wondering why I'm not sweating," Darcy remarked.

Hannah was unpacking, taking her silk shirts out of wreaths of tissue paper and hanging them in the tiny wardrobe.

"Don't start complaining already," she said sharply, without turning to look at him.

Darcy did not answer. Hannah was not usually tart, but recently she had become increasingly so. He continued to stare up at the ceiling, counting the knots in the wood, irritated, on the margin of his consciousness, at being unable to arrange them into a satisfactory pattern.

He was thinking about money, about the shifting and massaging and redeployment of figures, and making flurried computations in his head. Darcy's business was money. In all the years he had worked in the city, looking after money for other people and earning it for himself, he had dealt in it with confidence, certain of his own expertise. Then, when he had semi-retired to Wilton with Hannah, he had retained responsibility for half a dozen of his previous clients. He managed their assets from his office in the manor house, making the journey to London as often as was necessary.

But in the last few months it had begun to seem to Darcy that money was not at all the abstract, docile commodity he had once imagined. It had started to assume characteristics he did not understand, slyness and capriciousness, like an irresistible but unreliable woman he was obliged to court and propitiate.

As he lay on his bed in the chalet, Darcy's heart began to thump uncomfortably. He closed his eyes, forcing himself to breathe evenly, to suppress the anxiety heaving inside him. There was a telephone in the chalet, but no fax machine. He was glad of that; he needed the respite. He was away, legitimately away, on holiday. There was nothing to be done now.

When he looked again, Hannah was still unpacking clothes. She placed the last folded pile into a drawer and then zipped up the empty suitcase with a vicious jerk. The door opened and Freddie appeared, already dressed in his brand-new ski suit. Laura had been left at home with the au pair because Hannah thought she was too young to learn to ski, but this was Freddie's initiation and he was bubbling over with excitement.

"Can we go out in the snow now? Jon and William are having a *snowball* fight, and I want to as well Mummy, can we?"

Hannah turned to Darcy.

"Why don't you take him outside?"

It had been a long drive from the airport up to Méribel. Outside it was almost dark.

"For Christ's sake, not now," Darcy said. "There's plenty of time for that tomorrow. I'm going downstairs for a drink."

He rolled sideways off the bed, feeling weighty and sluggish, as if his body was too heavy for him.

"Thanks," Hannah called after him.

The chalet telephone was in the first-floor living room, sitting on an orange linen table mat on top of a pine cabinet. In Darcy's mind the personification of money as a tantalizing woman had become entangled with thoughts of Vicky. He glanced at the phone, but he knew that he couldn't call her now. Perhaps there would be a chance later in the week, when everyone was out on the slopes.

Michael Wickham was the only person in the room. He was drinking whisky and reading a Sunday newspaper that he had brought with him from England. Darcy had not bought any liquor on the journey, because he couldn't be bothered to stand in a line in a duty-free shop in order to get a few pounds off a bottle of Scotch, but he was pleased to see Michael with his large bottle of Johnny Walker uncapped at his elbow.

Michael glanced up, then pointed out an empty glass to Darcy.

Darcy poured himself a measure, drank it at a gulp, and then refilled the glass.

"Thanks." He stood at the window, gazing through a patch of condensation at the falling snow. "Should be a good week, when this stops."

Michael folded his newspaper. "Yeah. For those of us who can ski."

Darcy had momentarily forgotten that Michael had not yet progressed beyond shaky beginner's runs.

"Hannah will keep you company."

Hannah and Michael were both beginners; it was one of the reasons why the Cleggs had agreed to accompany the Frosts and Wickhams this year. Darcy himself was an excellent skier.

Michael smiled rarely, but when he did his face lit up. The illumination came now, surprising Darcy.

"There *is* that to look forward to," Michael agreed. "What's your room like?"

"Like the sauna in a municipal sports center."

"Lucky. Ours is like a locker outside the sauna in a municipal sports center."

The two men laughed.

In the next room the chalet girl was banging the cutlery as she laid the table for the children's supper. The Grafton couples had already annoyed her by asking for the children's meal to be served early, before their own. The back door of the chalet blew open to admit a blast of cold air and a swirl of snow, together with the Frost boys and Jonathan Wickham, who had been pushing snowballs down one another's backs. The boys fell into the room, a tangle of arms and legs and red faces.

"Close the bloody door," Michael shouted at them.

Hannah came downstairs, dressed in black velvet jeans and suede ankle boots, with Freddie trailing sulkily behind her.

"Why couldn't I play in the snow with the others?" he was demanding.

"Any chance of a drink?" Hannah sighed, not looking at Darcy. Michael got up and poured her one.

"Happy holiday," she thanked him, firmly clinking her glass against his.

Later in the evening, after the children had dispersed to their bunk beds and the dinner had been eaten, they gathered in the living room with their drinks. It was still snowing. They felt cozy and at the same time adventurous, as if there were some unacknowledged risk in being isolated together.

No one said as much, but they all knew that what had happened to Vicky and Gordon and Nina had unexpectedly shaken up the pieces of their tidy, established pattern. It had caused them to look differently at one another, speculatively, as if after so long they knew one another much less well than they had imagined.

After Christmas Gordon had bleakly camped out in his office, and then had moved into the modern hotel on the outskirts of town. Then, some time later, they heard that he was home again. Evidently Vicky had taken her husband back.

In the weeks since Christmas no one had seen very much of the Ransomes, either together or separately. Andrew told Janice that Gordon was working very hard. "And a good thing, too," he had muttered in conclusion. Janice told the other women what she had also heard from Andrew, that Nina had gone back to London for a while, but none of them had anything else to report.

Each of the women, in turn, had taken care to let Vicky know that she was there for her, if there was any need. Vicky had thanked them all, but in the end she hadn't talked much to any of them.

But still, the awareness of a break in the old pattern had accompanied the Frosts and the Wickhams and the Cleggs to Méribel.

Hannah stretched out in front of the fire. She had left her hair loose and a thick, shiny cascade of it partly covered her face and hid the hand propping up her head. Her jeans accentuated the hollow of her waist and the rounded swell of her hips. Andrew and Michael were both looking at her, and Hannah knew it. There was a triumphant curve to her lips that went with all her other curves, still just confined on the right side of the line between voluptuous and fat.

Darcy was the only one who seemed unaware of the effect Hannah was having. He had been drinking steadily since before dinner, and now his attention was fixed on the window where the snowflakes were briefly visible in the last instant before they melted against the glass.

"Well," Janice said softly, breaking a momentary silence. "Are we all glad to be here?"

"Of course we're glad," Michael murmured. Away from the hospital and his beeper and the considerations of tomorrow's patient list, he was cheerful, almost lighthearted. The wine at dinner and the whisky had relaxed him.

Andrew sleepily laced his hands over the small mound that his stomach made under his sweater.

"*I* need a holiday," he said.

It had been a difficult couple of months for him. The recession was affecting business, and until recently Gordon hadn't been pulling his weight. Andrew told himself with satisfied conviction that he deserved a break if anyone did.

Marcelle said nothing. She was wearing jeans and a sweatshirt, an ordinary, workaday translation of Hannah's velvet and cashmere, and she knew that she looked old and faded. It had seemed a bigger struggle than usual, this year, to find everyone's ski things, to wash them and pack them, and to close up the house and to arrange a week's replacement at work, and she had not found time to buy anything new for herself. She was worried that there were no other girls in the party to keep Daisy company. She was irritated that the dinner cooked by the sulky chalet girl had been less good than anything any of her students could have produced, with the possible exception of Cathy Clegg. She felt tired, and anxious, and sad, and she would have liked to tell Michael so, to have him comfort and reassure her. But she knew that she could not tell him, indeed that she would have to pretend to be cheerful, that she was enjoying herself, so as not to increase either his irritation with her or her own sense of disappointment in him. Since their last big argument they had existed in a state of guarded politeness.

"Mar?" Janice was looking at her, her smooth forehead wrinkled with concern.

"Oh, yes." Marcelle summoned a smile, only just able to remember what the question had been. "So long as the skiing's good." She had been an avid skier from childhood, and was probably the strongest in the group, better even than Darcy. Until this year, perhaps even this month, the promise of a week in the snow would have raised her spirits from any depths. That it failed to do so now only increased her fear and sadness.

"So, what shall we do with the rest of this evening?" Hannah asked. "It's late, but it's still just too early for bed."

She shook her hair back from her face, revealing her white throat. Behind her head a log collapsed in the hearth, sending up a tiny shower of sparks.

There was another small silence.

In the quiet room, hemmed in together by the snow while their children slept, they were reminded of Nina and Gordon. Even Marcelle in her isolation sensed the possibility of something new and dangerous happening; even unimaginative Andrew felt it.

"Play a game?" he suggested, not meaning quite that, but wanting to deflect this moment and steer the evening back to normality. There had been a time, when they had all felt that they knew everything there was to know about one another and needed new diversions, that all the Grafton couples had been enthusiastic about after-dinner games.

"For Christ's sake, no, not some fucking game." Darcy looked away from the window at last. The strength of his objection made the others realize that he was drunker than they were. But the tradition of deference to Darcy meant that no one tried to argue in favor of starting up a game.

Hannah looked at him, her smile disappearing for a second.

Then she stood up, lazily stretching her arms and flexing her fingers. She had taken off her suede boots, and her toenails were painted with the same bronze varnish as her long fingernails.

"I know." She went across to the cassette player. There was a neat stack of tapes beside it and she flipped through them until she found one that suited her. Michael and Andrew watched her as she bent down to fit the tape into the player. Janice lay back in her place with her head resting on one arm, smiling a little and waiting to see what would happen. "I think we should dance," Hannah said.

The tape she had chosen was Tina Turner's *Private Dancer*, which was no longer particularly new and was more or less familiar to all of them. She began to hum, low down in her throat, while she searched for a particular point in the tape. Then, when she found it, she stretched her arms wide and threw back her head and began to dance.

They had seen Hannah dance before, all of them, dozens of times, but not quite like this. Her eyes were half-closed but she was still smiling, moving her hips rhythmically to the music, slow gyrations that seemed to ripple up the length of her spine and down her arms to her fingertips. She was absorbed in herself but sang as she danced, *I'm your private dancer, a dancer for money, I'll do what you want me to do . . . .*

Nobody else moved.

As a performance it was overdone, veering close to parody, and there was a moment when someone might have laughed, and then the laughter would have spread and Hannah's solo would have lost its power to transfix them. But there wasn't a sound except for the music and Hannah's singing, and there was a crackle of tension in the room.

Janice lifted her head from her arm and watched, her mouth slightly open. Andrew was fully awake, and Michael rubbed a bead of moisture away from his top lip. Each of them thought, in their different ways, of the change that Gordon and Nina had brought about. The unraveling of the old pattern and the possibility of further unraveling was threatening, but now also, somehow, made fascinating by Hannah's erotic dance.

Only Darcy had turned his attention back to the window and the snow drifting beyond the glass.

Hannah held out her hands to Andrew, insisting that he dance with her. He groped his way to his feet as if hypnotized, and at once Hannah's arms snaked around him. Her head rested on his shoulder and her eyes closed.

"All of you, dance," she said.

Michael's limbs had connected themselves again, and he leaned across to Janice.

"Will you?"

He had wanted to dance with Hannah; he was amazed to discover how much he had wanted to dance with her now that she had chosen Andrew.

Janice's silky robe swished as she uncrossed her legs and stood up. She half-stumbled, because she had drunk plenty of the wine at dinner, but Michael caught her hand. Her loose sleeves fell back, baring her pretty, rounded arms to the elbows as she made a mock-subservient offer of herself to him.

Michael took hold of her. As they began to dance she came closer, and he let his hands slide down over the soft stuff covering her back. She felt much bigger than Marcelle; there were pads of flesh on her shoulders and over her hips. Confusingly, behind his eyelids her ampleness became identified with the image of Hannah dancing.

Darcy saw Marcelle sitting awkwardly in her place past the swaying bodies of the other couples. Her head was raised, but something in the stiffness of her posture betrayed her unhappiness. He got up and edged past the dancers, feeling, as he had earlier, that his own body had grown too bulky to maneuver properly.

"Marcelle?"

"You don't have to be kind, Darcy."

The expression in her eyes made him suddenly angry with Hannah for provoking all this. It was Hannah's way of demonstrating her displeasure with him, of course, and she did not bother to think beyond that.

"It isn't kindness," he said roughly.

When he took them in his, Marcelle's surprisingly small, cold hands reminded him of a little boy's, of Barney's years ago when he had come in from playing in a wintry garden. She felt brittle, too, as they moved together, unfamiliarly light and dry, quite unlike Hannah or Vicky, and tall, so that her eyes were almost level with his.

They danced awkwardly together, and to smooth over this clumsiness, to turn the moment against Hannah, Darcy pressed his cheek against Marcelle's, and then found the corner of her mouth with his own. He heard the small catch of breath in her throat, and opened his mouth to kiss her. As he did so he noticed that with Hannah's limbs wound around him Andrew had begun to look like a rabbit caught in the headlights of a car, and that Janice and Michael were dancing with their eyes shut, heads close together, seemingly unaware of anyone else.

He brought his attention back to the business at hand, that of kissing Marcelle. Her physical type did not attract him, but there was an interesting novelty in exploring the contours of her lips and face. He moved his own face, rubbing himself against her a little, but Marcelle neither responded nor moved away from him. He had the feeling that her eyes were open and that she was looking somewhere beyond him.

Another track began, slower than the last, and the three couples swayed and circled. The fire had burned down to a red glow, and the light in the room had grown dimmer.

Darcy wondered if they were all going to continue with this, if the embraces would get closer, if they would slip away, each pair in turn. The scenes played themselves in his head while he went on slowly circling with Marcelle Wickham and nuzzling her motionless face. He tried to work out what he would do, who would make the first move. The bizarreness of these imaginings, together with the possibility that they might become reality, made him wonder if all the ordinary old conventions of marriage and friendship were about to change, to move in new and uncontrolled directions, as his business life was doing. His heart began its uncomfortable thumping again, and he felt a small, needling pain in his chest.

Somewhere else in the chalet, from somewhere over their heads, someone began to scream.

Darcy thought for an instant that the sound might have to do with the sensations within him, but all the couples froze and then broke apart. They were blinking, momentarily bewildered, and embarrassed as if searchlights had suddenly been turned on them. The screaming stopped, broken off short by a different cry, and then there was a long second's silence followed by a loud thump. They heard the sound of a child's bare feet running overhead.

"Who is it?" Marcelle cried out.

Janice was already on her way to the door, with Michael behind her. The others heard panicky feet thudding down the stairs. A moment later William Frost appeared in the doorway, and Janice swooped to catch him. His round face was flushed and wet with tears and his round eyes stared, only half-seeing, at the semicircle of adults.

"A dream," he sobbed. "Terrible dream."

Janice put her arms around him and smoothed his blond hair.

"It's all right," she murmured, "I'm here. Only a dream, a nasty old dream."

They made way for her to lead him to the sofa, Janice sat down and hugged William. Andrew leaned over them.

"It'll go away, Will. You're awake now. He's been having these dreams," he explained to the others.

Hannah pushed her hair back from her face, gathering it up with one hand into a bunch at the nape of her neck. Michael looked at the ellipse of white skin that was momentarily exposed, and then made himself bend down to look at William Frost instead.

"Poor old chap," he said pleasantly. He felt the child's forehead and then ran his fingers lightly under his jaw. "Nothing to worry about, I'm sure. Some hot milk, perhaps?"

"I'll do it," Hannah said. In the changed atmosphere, with her hair pulled back, she looked almost matronly. Marcelle sat down again in her old place, and Darcy went back to the table where the whisky bottle was waiting. Someone turned off the music and the room became bright and ordinary again, as it had been earlier in the evening.

Janice sat on the edge of the bed, took off her slippers, and slid under the covers. She reached up to turn off the light, then curled herself beside Andrew.

"Are you asleep?" she asked. She had waited up a little longer, to make sure that William had settled down again.

"Not quite. Is Will all right?"

"I think so."

Out of habit Janice listened for the ticking of their bedside clock, as she always did in the intervals of their nighttime conversations, then remembered that they were not in their own bedroom. The evening had left her with a knot of anxiety that she knew would keep her awake.

"What were you doing with Hannah?"

Andrew sighed. "What was Hannah doing with me, you mean?"

"Is there a difference?"

"Of course there is. She was trying to make some point for Darcy's benefit, I suppose. Whatever it was, do we have to analyze it now?"

"You didn't look as if you minded."

"I didn't. That was then and now is now, and here we are in bed, my love, and it's time to go to sleep."

He settled the hard French pillow under his head, offering a little more of himself to her as he did so, but it was as a comforting gesture, without any suggestion of sex.

Janice mumbled to him, with her face pressed against the warmth of his shoulder, "Do you mind that I don't look like Hannah?"

"What? Of course not. What do you think I want? Anyway, in a couple of years Hannah will look like you."

She waited, in the absence of the clock's ticking, for Andrew to realize what he had said, and when he did not she became angry.

Then she understood that he was sliding into sleep, and she knew that it would be easier not to have an argument than to wake him up and insist on one. She suddenly found herself smiling out of affection for his clumsiness, and relief that the evening had ended harmlessly.

Marcelle lay on her back and looked up into the darkness. Michael was breathing evenly beside her. She was not certain that he was asleep, but when she had put out her hand to touch his side he had made no response. That was the pattern now. If one of them was awake, the other was asleep, or seemed to be.

She turned away from him, onto her side, and began to think about the evening. It was Hannah who had set it off, but Marcelle knew that she had only been the trigger. Since the day she had seen Gordon and Nina together at the train crossing, she had known that the possibility of collapse, of the destruction of all their tidy lives, lay quietly just beneath the surface of these featureless days. Dissatisfaction and the desire for change, for the sharpness of some new feeling, whether pleasure or pain, was like a virus that had come to Grafton with Nina Cort. The virus, Marcelle knew, would spread, whichever direction it took.

She put her hand up to where Darcy's mouth and cheek had rubbed against hers. She could still taste the whisky from his tongue.

She closed her eyes, willing sleep to come.

If it had been Jimmy, Marcelle thought. *If it had been Jimmy, tonight, what would I have done then?*

She wasn't certain, but she thought that she might have clung to him, and begged him to rescue her.

Hannah put on the oyster-gray silk robe that matched her pink-and-gray lace-and-silk nightgown, and loosened her hair from the bunch she had tied at the nape of her neck. Standing in front of the small square of mirror fixed to one wall, she examined her reflection. She gave it her full attention, knowing that by doing so she was avoiding thinking of less pleasant things. She spread her hair over her shoulders, admiring the way it rippled over the sheen of the silk.

Not bad, Hannah thought. *Not bad for thirty-four, after having had two children. Better than Vicky Ransome, anyway.*

She had seen the way Andrew and Michael had looked at her. It had given her a wonderful surge of power, to switch on the magnetism and see that it still worked. The pleasure of their admiration stayed with her, energizing her. She lifted her chin and met her own eyes in the mirror. There had been a time, when she and Darcy had met and fallen in love and he had left his first wife for her, when Darcy had looked at her like that every time she came near him.

But still, it was not all bad. Whatever Darcy thought, whatever he thought he wanted, she was still objectively desirable.

Darcy came out of the bathroom and walked across to the bed without looking at her. He took off his robe and lay down in his pyjamas, easing himself into the unfamiliar bed. Watching him as he turned on to his side and his body slackened under the sheets, Hannah realized that he looked heavy and old. She felt a quick and surprising beat of sympathy, as she might have done for her father, or for Freddie if he were unhappy or ill.

She turned out the lights and got into bed beside her husband. Carefully, she fitted herself against the loose curve of his back. Then she edged her arms over and under him. Hannah waited, acknowledging to herself and waiting for Darcy's acknowledgment that the evening had excited her. Darcy didn't pull away, but he didn't respond, either.

Hannah whispered against the meaty slab of his shoulder. "Come on, come to Mummy."

She knew him well. Darcy turned over then, as she had been sure he would. He didn't say anything, but he put his hands under her nightdress and spread them over her breasts.

Hannah pulled him closer, needing to exact another tribute from the evening. Without saying anything more, they went through the customary agenda of their lovemaking.

Afterward, when they lay side-by-side again, Darcy said to the empty space over his head, "I didn't very much like what you did this evening."

Hannah made a small sound in her throat, not quite a laugh. "Were you jealous?"

"No, not at all. The opposite. I didn't like the way what you did affected Marcelle, and Janice."

"I'm sure they understood. Women do understand these things, don't they? They have to."

"What's that supposed to mean?"

Hannah felt the sudden tension in him. It made his arm and leg quiver, tiny shivers that were transmitted to her own warm limbs.

She felt the charge of power again, but this time the power that her knowledge gave her. She chose her words with pleasurable care.

"It means what I said. Women have to understand what their husbands do. Their little lapses, their small betrayals, and the lies that don't quite cover them up. They have to look on, don't they, and pretend not to see, not to mind? It's kind of you to feel for Janice and Marcelle. But why doesn't your sympathy extend to me? Or is it all used up on poor, poor Vicky?"

"On Vicky?"

"Yes, on Vicky. All alone in that house with her lovely, innocent baby girls, without her wicked, unfaithful husband."

"Hannah . . ."

"Don't *Hannah* me with all your pretend bewilderment. I know you're fucking Vicky. What else would you be doing, all those mornings your car is trying to hide itself in her driveway? Advising her on her investments? Why did you think *you* could get away with it, in a place the size of Grafton, when Gordon and his widow woman couldn't?

"Linda Todd, a customer of mine, lives opposite the Ransomes. She couldn't wait to tell me how many times she's seen you there. I drove past myself, just to check. Including the day you said you were going to Bristol."

Darcy said calmly. "There's no reason why I shouldn't call on Vicky. She does need advice, as it happens. That doesn't mean I'm sleeping with her."

Hannah drew away from him so that she could no longer feel the quivers under his skin. She said, softly and finally, "But you *are*, Darcy, aren't you?"

"What can I say to convince you otherwise, when you seem to have made up your mind?"

"Nothing at all, darling. We were talking about what women are obliged to understand. I'm not going to worry about Janice and Marcelle just because their husbands can't take their eyes off my backside."

Hannah turned over with her back to him. She was surprised to find that she was sleepy, that her body felt pleasantly warm and heavy. She had told Darcy what she knew, and there was nothing else she wanted to say. He didn't speak again, and after a few minutes Hannah drifted into sleep.

Darcy lay awake for much longer. He was thinking about Vicky.

Apart from a handful of trivial lapses that were easy enough to discount, Darcy had been faithful to Hannah ever since their marriage. Until a month earlier.

After Vicky had locked Gordon out of the house, she had remained alone with the children for a night and half a day. And then, emerging from a daze of distress and needing to talk, she had telephoned Hannah at Wilton. Only on that day Hannah had gone to her shop to get ready for her after-Christmas sale, and it was Darcy who answered the telephone.

"I'll come over," he said at once.

In the Ransomes' house he found a litter of toys and childrens' detritus underfoot, a half-eaten meal on the kitchen table, a broken-down central heating boiler, and Vicky in her dressing gown with Helen in her arms.

Darcy called up his own central-heating repairman. He found the whisky bottle, then made tea and toast for Vicky and fed the older children. He never performed any domestic tasks at home, because that would have disturbed the natural order of things, but the fetid, baby-redolent muddle of Vicky's house drew him in, enclosing him and making him feel temporarily safe, as if he were a baby, too. It was as different here from Wilton, with its poised flower arrangements and chintz cushions and bowls of potpourri, as milky, disheveled Vicky herself was different from Hannah.

Darcy felt comfortable pottering to and fro with plates and cups, and his sexual attraction to Vicky gave the sense of comfort an added edge. He forgot the unrelenting anxiety of his business, and the pressure on him to generate more money to service the voracious material appetites of Wilton and its inhabitants. He was filled with happy energy and whistled softly as he worked.

Vicky watched Darcy moving around her house.

"It seems that I can't even manage on my own for a day," she said sadly.

"Yes, you can," Darcy told her.

Neither of them mentioned Christmas Eve in Hannah's bedroom. But when it was time to feed the baby he saw the tender and businesslike way with which Vicky settled herself to the task, and it tightened some string inside him and pulled at his heart. He reached out and with the tips of his fingers he brushed her cheek. She blushed but kept her eyes fixed on the baby in her arms. Darcy left her with the name and telephone number of his London solicitor, and promised to come back the next day.

It was not very long before all the couples in the Grafton circle knew that Vicky had turned Gordon out. The wives visited or telephoned her, offering their different versions of support and advice, but it was Darcy she looked forward to seeing. She knew that he came without Hannah's knowledge, and his secret presence in the house seemed to change its quality for her—the light in the rooms became sharper and brighter, and the weight of her anxiety dropped away, leaving her feeling calm and decisive. When she told him this, Darcy laughed and said that Hannah would say the opposite about him at Wilton. But still, Vicky could see that he was pleased.

Gordon telephoned constantly, from his office and then from the hotel, but Vicky told him she didn't want to see him until she had had more time to think. As the days passed her anger turned into weary disappointment, but she held firm, telling him that she did not want him to come back yet. She surprised herself with the strength of her own resolution.

One morning after Gordon had been away for two weeks, Darcy came to visit Vicky, leaving his Range Rover parked to one side of the house, where it was hidden from the road by a screen of evergreens. It was a clear, bright day, and as she went to let him in Vicky saw in the changed angles of the shadows the first intimation of spring.

Darcy sat at her kitchen table while she made coffee for him. The older girls were at school and Helen was asleep in her cot. There was a thick, expectant silence in the house. Vicky turned to the table with his cup in her hand, and when she had put it down she hesitated beside him.

"I'm very grateful," she told him. She meant for the solace of his company, as well as for the practical advice he had given her.

Darcy reached out and took her hand and she looked down gravely at him. He remembered in that instant that he had imagined himself in love with her, as well as wanting to take her to bed. He stood up, and she did not move when he held her by the shoulders and kissed her. She smelled of baby scents, innocent soap and milk.

"Come upstairs with me," Darcy said.

The double bed was unmade, with lacy pillows tumbled on the floor and the quilt still rucked in the contours of her solitary sleep. Standing beside the bed, Darcy unbuttoned her loose shirt and rediscovered her distended breasts, the curves of her belly marked by her pregnancy. She made a move to cover herself with her hands, but he pushed them aside and knelt to follow the silvery lines with his eyes and the tips of his fingers.

"Vicky." He said her name to himself, confirming their being together, here and now.

Her hands rested on his head, and she stroked his hair absently, almost maternally.

"Take your clothes off, too," she said. "Then I won't feel so exposed. I'm ashamed of the way I look these days. I wish I were thin and tight-skinned, like Nina. I wish I had long legs like knitting needles, and no tits. That must be what Gordon wants."

"It isn't what *I* want. I want you. Look at you." He weighed her breasts in his hands, and saw that a colorless bead of liquid had appeared on one brown nipple.

"Take your clothes off, then," Vicky said again. "Before Helen wakes up."

He loved this brisk practicality in her. Hannah liked the transactions of sex to be swathed in ribbons and tulle of romance, even after seven years of marriage.

Vicky helped him undress, arranging his clothes tidily to one side as he discarded them. She looked at him and thought that for a handsome man he had a surprisingly ugly body. His chest and shoulders were covered with thick gray hair and the muscles of his stomach must recently have given way, because when he was not holding it in his belly coyly protruded as if it were not quite part of him. His small, thick penis looked like some hairless, burrowing rodent. When he took her in his arms the gray pelt crinkled minutely against her skin.

They lay down together in her bed, and while one part of her mind was occupied with the attentions that Darcy required, the rest of it seemed free to wonder if this act was revenge against Gordon or something she had wanted for herself.

It was startling to discover that Darcy was not as adept a lover as her husband.

He came quite quickly, very noisily, and the detached part of her remained untouched and unaroused, dreamily watching this scene as if it were nothing to do with her. She wondered what it could be that Hannah liked, and it came to her in a moment of pure perception that Hannah liked herself—it was her own vanity that gave her her habitual glow, and Darcy functioned as a suitably impressive mirror to reflect her. The certainty of this insight lessened Vicky's guilt a little.

"You didn't do that out of gratitude, did you?" Darcy asked afterward. They had been lying with their arms around each other, separately contemplating the room and his presence in it.

"No. I did it because I wanted to."

That was the truth. For the two weeks that Darcy had been visiting her she had known that it would happen, and she had been waiting for it, neither putting it off nor willing it to come.

"Will you let it happen again?"

"Yes," Vicky said, because she knew that she would.

And so Darcy had called on her the next morning, and the one after that. On the third morning, after they had made love, she found herself examining his blunt, handsome face on the pillow in Gordon's place. There were creases and pouches in it that she could not remember noticing before.

"You look tired."

"I'm not sleeping well these days."

"Are you worried about something? About business?"

He was startled by her percipience; Hannah never asked him about his work. But Darcy didn't want to talk to Vicky about the rising tide of his professional problems. Darcy's business was looking after other men's money, business that was beginning to spin away and loop and whirl around him with sickening unpredictability, and he came to her to free himself for a few hours from the delicate web of deception and debt that he had become obliged to weave around himself. In Vicky's house, under her placid maternal eyes and in the company of her three tiny girls, Darcy found that he could shrink away from his full-blown, ambiguous adult self, and become almost an infant again.

He parried her question now. "There are some investments I have made on behalf of other people that haven't performed as I hoped they would." That was only the tip of it, of course. He could not think, now, about the obligations that had followed on from it.

Her clear eyes looked into his. "Is it serious?"

"No," Darcy lied.

"Do you want to talk to me about it? Would it help?"

"It wouldn't be very interesting." With the tip of his forefinger he touched the hollow of her throat. "And it isn't very important, because it can easily be put right."

"That's good." Vicky smiled, and it touched him to see her relief. He kissed her, and burrowed deeper into the warmth and safety of the bed.

It was another two weeks before Vicky answered one of Gordon's telephone calls and heard him say, "Won't you let me come home? I miss the girls. I miss you."

It was the middle of the morning, the safe, domestic time that she had always liked and that had lately come to belong to Darcy's visits, or to the possibility of his visit. She looked at her kitchen, looking at the cups and plates in their glass-fronted cupboards and listening to the industrious thrum of the washing machine and the dishwasher.

This is the life Gordon and I made, she thought. The once-clear picture was now confusingly cross-hatched with images of Nina and Darcy.

The few hours that she had spent with Darcy had been stolen, and retaliatory, but they had also woken her up out of some stale, isolated maternal trance. She felt grateful to Darcy, and under his spell like some narcissistic girl newly and shallowly in love, but she also felt strong. She was suddenly sure that she was much, much stronger than Gordon.

Vicky looked down at her hand, with her engagement and

wedding rings, and extended her fingers to her own pleased contemplation, as if she had just had a manicure.

"Yes," she said. "All right. I'd like you to come back home."

She had told Darcy the same day. "I said he could come back."

"Is that what you want?"

After a moment she had answered, "Yes. I was angry with him, but I'm not any longer." She touched his hand gently. "Doing what you and I have done has made me less . . . less censorious of Gordon. Do you mind that?"

"How could I? What about you and me? May I still see you?"

"Like Gordon seeing Nina, do you mean?"

"Yes, I suppose I do mean like that."

He had heard the smile in her voice before he met her eyes and saw it. "I don't know. I'm not sure. But you know where I am, and I know where you are. Isn't that enough for the time being?"

"I suppose it will have to be," he had answered.

Darcy felt a moment of terrible, suffocating panic. He was losing his place of safety. For a blind instant he thought, *If I lose Vicky, everything else will go, too.*

Then, mercifully, his instinct for self-preservation instinct revived. Vicky did not affect the other areas of his life. With a little effort, and some overdue good luck, he could still pull it back together again.

The dull thumping of his heart behind his breastbone subsided a little. He had imagined, at Christmas, that he was in love with Vicky Ransome. But in truth, he made himself acknowledge then, it had only been sex. Sex, and a little comfort.

Later, in Méribel, Darcy carried the telephone to the window, dialed her number, and stood looking across the balcony to the sunny slopes while he listened to it ring.

"Hello?" he said quietly when she picked up.

"Hello."

He did not need to identify himself, that was an acknowledgment of their intimacy, but there was an infinitesimal pause before Vicky said, "Darcy? Is that you? Is something wrong?"

"Why do you think there's something wrong, because I've called you?"

"You're on holiday with Hannah and Freddie, that's all . . . I didn't expect to hear from you."

He looked out at the skiers, colored matchstick people zigzagging in the sunshine. Everyone was out in the snow except for him.

"I just wanted to talk."

"Oh. Well, do you know what's happened? I'm going back to work part-time. I had a call yesterday from the director of therapy at the center, and they need someone to take on a limited caseload, just two or three days a week, and I talked it over with Gordon last night and we agreed that I should do it. I'm just starting to look for someone to come in and look after Helen . . ."

Darcy listened to her plans, leaning against the window glass with the telephone crooked under his chin. There was snow on the balcony floor and a white rim in the rustic cutouts and on the curved rail of the wooden balustrade. The light danced and sparkled, hurting his eyes.

"That's good, I'm glad," he heard himself say. He felt dirty and creased in the sunshine, full of weariness that seemed to spread all through him, and weak as a child in comparison with Vicky's procreative strength.

"Why *did* you call?" she asked him at last.

It was too much of an effort even to dissemble.

"I talked to Hannah last night. Or rather, she talked to me. Someone called Linda Todd, who lives opposite to you, has been monitoring my movements. Does that sound likely?"

"Yes. Shit. Yes, it does. What exactly did Hannah say?"

"Not much. It was more what she did. A bit of a dance, not quite a striptease, for the benefit of Michael and Andrew, and a warning shot for me at the same time. It stirred up the passions a bit."

"I can imagine."

Vicky knew how it would have been. Hannah dancing, lit up with pleasure at herself. She had been friends with Hannah for a long time, and she wondered now if she liked her at all. She said quietly, so quietly that he had to think for a moment before he was sure that he had heard her correctly, "I think you and I have come to the end of the road, Darcy."

There was the throb of panic again. He took a breath, then another, concentrating on dispelling it.

He was proud of his self-control when he finally answered her, "You may be right. This particular road, perhaps." He still wished that he could contradict her and imagined how his voice would sound if he did so, rising in protest like a frustrated child's.

A moment later they had said good-bye, and he replaced the receiver in its cradle.

Darcy slid open the glass door and stepped out onto the balcony. The cold air caught in his throat. He leaned on the balcony rail and looked across at the nearest slope. Suddenly he saw Hannah, in her silvery ski suit with its fur-lined hood, and Michael Wickham in navy-blue that looked black at this distance. Their ski instructor made a series of fluid turns, and Hannah and Michael obediently followed him.

Hannah had improved, Darcy noticed.

She lifted her arms in triumph and waved her poles after she completed the last turn. Michael punched the air in front of him in laughing acknowledgment of their achievement.

Darcy's fingers spread themselves on the cold, splintery wood. The structure felt flimsy; the chalet must recently have been given a cheap external facelift to convert it from concrete-brutalist to Alpine-picturesque.

It was only a matter of appearances, Darcy suddenly thought, smiling a little, although his lips cracked painfully in the freezing air. His manipulation of other men's money, the increasingly feverish juggling of zeroes across accounts and countries, was likewise a matter of appearances. With luck, he could keep the raw and unlovely truth from exposure. There was no need to panic. He would do it, whatever was necessary, to keep himself one step ahead of a fraud investigation.

Michael and Hannah were plodding away together, their skis over their shoulders. Darcy needed a drink, and he turned away from the view without glancing back.

11

Since Christmastime work on the west façade of the cathedral had been going on behind the contractors' screens of scaffolding and tarpaulins.

One afternoon in February, Nina stood at a corner of the green, where a gap in the coverings offered a narrow view of one column of saints and archangels. The stone figures in their niches were enveloped in dust or swathed in dingy protective coverings, and workmen passed in front of them with plaster-coated tools and buckets. Watching them, Nina could not imagine how the details of folded hands and serene stone faces would ever recover from this desecration.

The wind was cold. At length, wrapping her arms around herself, Nina turned away from the cathedral and slowly began to cross the green. She would have liked to go on in through the west door, to look at the great columns and arches of the interior, but she did not. Ever since Christmas she had avoided the cathedral, because it was associated with Gordon. Lately she had simply preferred to keep away from the places that were most closely connected with him in her mind, because she missed him and it was easier to spare herself this much.

When she reached the opposite, sheltered side of the green, she saw a woman sitting on one of the benches bordering it. The woman was wearing a flamboyant long mackintosh made of some light, banana-colored material. She was watching Nina coming toward her, and eating a sandwich. Nina recognized Star Rose.

"Hello," Star said in her cool voice. "I heard on the bush telegraph that you'd left and gone back to London."

Nina hesitated. Of all the Grafton people she had seen only

Janice and Hannah since Christmas, and those meetings had been accidental. The women had not been unfriendly, but just as it had been easier for Nina to avoid the places that were connected in her mind with Gordon, so it had also been her choice not to meet his friends and Vicky's.

"I did go back for a time. But I'm here again now. This is where I live."

She had spent almost three weeks staying in the Spitalfields house with Patrick, but it had become increasingly hard to ignore the truth that she had left London for Grafton to escape the memories of one man, and had then fled back to London for the same reason but a different man. Patrick had not tried to hide his concern.

"You can't flit to and fro forever, you know, running away from yourself and imagining you can leave your losses behind you like last year's coat."

"I know that," Nina said humbly. "I'll go back to Grafton to confront myself, shall I, and wear that old coat until better weather comes?"

He took her hand. "You know that you can stay here as long as you like," he said.

But in the end Nina had come home. In any case she had work to do, and needed her studio.

Star crumpled the sandwich paper. "I'd offer to share it with you, but that was it. We could go and have a cup of coffee in the cloister, if you like. I am as free as air, it being the midterm break."

Surprised, and pleased by the suggestion, Nina said, "Yes. All right. Let's do that."

Star stood up, brushing the sandwich crumbs from her raincoat. A pair of pigeons swooped down on them. The two women began to walk slowly toward the cathedral.

"Where do you teach?" Nina asked. She had met Star a number of times, but it had always been at dinners or at parties.

"Williamford. Modern languages."

Williamford was the big coed comprehensive that had been created, after Nina's time, by a merger of her girls' grammar with the boys' school where Andrew Frost had gone.

"I went to Dean's School."

"Did you? Oh yes, I remember. Andrew said something about

it. We still use the same buildings, you know. Very inconvenient they are, too."

The red-brick classrooms with tall Victorian windows that let in thin coils of fog in the winter, and concentrated the sun's heat in the short summer. Nina remembered the old-fashioned desks and blackboards and the sharp fins of the green-painted radiators.

"I should think it's very different now."

"Should you? You'd probably find it's much the same. Who used to teach you French?"

"Mr. Jenkins. Gawaine Jenkins, that was his name."

"He retired last year. I took over from him as head of the department."

It was as if Star had tied a tiny, invisible knot, fixing Nina within Grafton again, in a mesh of people and the rubbed, familiar places of her childhood. She had not thought of Mr. Jenkins for more than fifteen years, but now she heard his thin, correct voice reading from Molière and saw the reddened wings of his nose and the ancient corduroy jacket he wore every day to face the ordeals of his classroom.

"Just hearing his name makes me feel seventeen again."

Star hunched her angular shoulders inside the yellow raincoat.

"I feel seventeen most of the time. If some group of kids runs in the corridor at school I start running, too, then I have to rein myself in and make myself shout at them."

Nina laughed. "You don't sound like Mr. Jenkins. The children must like you."

"Most of them do," Star answered in her cool way.

They had crossed to the side of the cathedral and came through an archway into the cloister. One side of it had been glassed in to make a combined bookshop and tea-room for visitors. Nina and Star passed by the stands of books on cathedral history and architecture, and the displays of tea-towels and leather bookmarks with their pictures of the west façade, and came to a long, glass-fronted counter displaying dishes of salads and quiche and whole-wheat scones, and a row of refectory tables with bench seats. Most of the places were occupied by pairs and trios of women, eating salad and talking.

Star surveyed them. "We could have gone to the Eagle and had a drink with the menfolk of Grafton."

"This is fine," Nina said quickly.

She bought two cups of coffee in thick earthenware mugs and carried them over to an empty table. Star sat down, swinging her coat out behind her. She lit a cigarette and stared out at the yew tree in the middle of the cloister garth. Nina covertly examined her face. Star had high cheekbones and a wide mouth, and she wore her hair pushed back behind her ears and no makeup, which emphasized her bones and the clarity of her skin. She was not in any way beautiful, but her height and her faintly inimical manner made her interesting.

After a moment Star looked back at Nina. She picked up her coffee mug and tilted it toward her in a toast.

"Welcome back," she said. "I'm glad you haven't abandoned us."

Nina was surprised and pleased. Unguardedly she asked, "What has everyone been saying?"

Star's eyebrows lifted. "Everyone? I've no idea what *everyone* has been saying. I haven't read any reports about your affair in the national press, or even in *The Grafton Advertiser*. If that's what you're asking about, of course."

Nina felt her cheeks redden. She was irritated by the quick bite of sarcasm, but she also had to admit that she had probably deserved it.

"Not everyone in that sense. I meant the people whose lives I've made such a disastrous intrusion into."

Star smiled at that. "Yes. I thought that was probably what you meant. *Was* it disastrous?"

"In the sense that it caused pain, yes, it was."

"Ah." Star spooned brown sugar crystals into her coffee and then stirred meditatively. There was a silence, and then she said quietly, "I've always thought that if I were going to have an affair with anyone else's husband it would have been with Gordon."

Nina thought that this conversation was moving too quickly for her, or that she had somehow missed some crucial, intervening pieces of it.

She said uncertainly, "I didn't know that. I have this impression of . . . history, shared history, stretching back behind you all. Do you remember when you changed that toast at Janice's dinner party? When you said not just to friendship, but to *loving* friendship? I was impressed by that and by all of you so handsome and happy, and by the way that you seemed to affirm one another."

Star shrugged, using what appeared now to be a characteristic gesture.

"I'm such a romantic when I have a few glasses of wine inside me. There isn't any history stretching behind Gordon and me. Unfortunately. How could you have known anything?"

Then Nina remembered that on that same evening, while she had been talking to Darcy Clegg, she had also covertly been watching Star and Gordon murmuring quietly together in a corner. She had thought at the time that perhaps Star was crying.

Star put out her cigarette and immediately lit another. It was after two o'clock and people were beginning to filter away back to their offices and shops. A girl in green overalls was loading cups and plates onto a tray.

"What was he like?" Star asked.

Nina looked up, and their eyes met. It would have been easy to be affronted or disconcerted by the question, but this directness in Star and the simplicity of her manner appealed to Nina. Nina did not hesitate, and answered with the same simplicity. She was filled with a need to talk about Gordon to Star.

"I suppose the word to describe him would be wholehearted. He gave himself with great enthusiam, and I found that very touching as well as erotic. He was also very straightforward. Not unimaginative, but not particularly poetic either." After a moment she added, very softly, "I suppose it was the best sex I have ever had."

It was an unexpected solace to talk about him, after two months of trying to suppress even passing thoughts. She realized that she could easily go on, might suddenly spill out every detail across the refectory table. She added, "It wasn't only that, not just the sex, although that was important. I was lonely and full of grief, and Gordon made me feel that I could come alive again. He made me feel greedy, too, and I swallowed my guilt and only tasted the happiness. He was so alive himself. He was eager, and I couldn't resist his eagerness."

Nina wanted to be fair, as if at this late stage she owed it to Vicky. "I didn't try very hard to resist."

Star nodded. She said sadly, "Yes. I thought that was how he might be."

They looked at each other again.

And then, unmistakeably, Nina felt a thin, piercing shiver of some different awareness that had nothing to do with Gordon, but had to do with her and Star.

For as long as it lasted, she became acutely conscious of the contours of her own hand resting against the grain of the table, the curl of smoke in the air over Star's head, the insistent rattle of silver and crockery behind them.

Star put out her hand and touched the tips of her fingers to Nina's hand.

"I'm sorry that it was painful."

"It was. It is, but I deserved it. I should have known better," Nina answered.

"One never does know better." Star lifted her hand again. "It's like really being seventeen forever."

The tea-room, the table and cups and everything else, slowly resumed their normal density. Nina said, "I regret it most for Vicky's sake."

"Do you? Do you think Vicky is blameless?"

Star didn't wait for Nina's answer. "Shall we take a walk?" she asked.

Nina had planned to spend the afternoon working, but even as she started to refuse, she changed her mind. Since coming back to Grafton she had resumed her solitary country walks, but now she discovered that she minded solitude more. Sometimes, as she followed the paths and lanes that wound around Grafton, she felt almost disabled by it.

Nina wanted their talk to continue; she wanted to see where it would lead. An intimacy had sprung up between them so quickly that it made her aware of how much she needed a woman friend. She suspected that Star needed a friend also.

They went out onto the green again, and walked away in the opposite direction from Dean's Row. Star strode quickly, with her head up and her hands in her pockets.

Their route took them along Southgate, the best street in Grafton. It was still lined with the bow-fronted façades of eighteenth-century shops, Hannah Clegg's La Couture among them. There were no cars in Southgate. Shiny, black-painted posts closed off either end of the street, and the city council in its civic pride had hung flower baskets from the arms of the Victorian lampposts. The baskets had been planted for the winter with universal pansies and variegated ivies, and the trailing leaves were browned by the wind and lack of water.

Nina and Star walked down the middle of the cobbled street. There was a prosperous, provincial solidity in Grafton that sometimes reassured Nina, and at other times did not.

Star started laughing.

"What's funny?" Nina asked.

"The tidiness of it all. Tidy lives. That's what you were thinking, wasn't it?"

They came out onto Bridge Street, where traffic flattened the polystyrene litter blown outside McDonald's.

"Something like that."

"Grafton is tidy. Socially and emotionally tidy. Pain and passion are mostly kept out of sight, especially by people like us. It's easy to sneer at it, but I rather like it. It's dignified."

"Why should you think I'd sneer at it? I came back to live here, so I must like it, too."

She was thinking about the handsome couples who had at first seemed so smilingly enviable and secure in their comfortable houses, and the contradictions that wove around them now. At the same time an image of the stone figures of the west façade, blackened and pitted by the centuries but still enduring, came into her head.

"Not you. I didn't mean you," Star said.

They were walking toward the river. Ahead of them, as they rounded a curve in the street, they could see the old bridge and a pewter-colored expanse of water. On the far bank were the playing fields and dim red-brick blocks of Dean's School.

219

"What did you mean when you asked me if I thought Vicky was blameless?"

Star flicked a glance at her, a look that was speculative and amused and faintly malicious.

"Just that."

"Oh. So, do I think that Vicky is to blame because I blithely started an affair with her husband while she was in the hospital delivering their third baby by an emergency cesarean?"

Nina saw the tiny contraction of the muscles around Star's mouth that gave away her hurt, and wondered for how long she had loved Gordon. No wonder Star liked Grafton for its bloodless dignity. She possessed exactly the same quality herself. Star was good at suppressing her own pain and passion.

Nina said, more sharply than she had intended, "No, I don't think Vicky is to blame."

"That's not what I'm talking about."

Nina followed the thread of Star's insinuation.

"I see," she said at last, unwillingly. And afterward, "Who is he, then?"

Star nodded, as if Nina were a slow pupil who had at last grasped something.

"Darcy."

They had reached the point where the road ran parallel with the river. Iron railings separated the road from the path beside the water under the naked branches of willow trees. The river was swollen; little crusts of yellowish foam eddied in the current and caught in the twiggy debris beside the bank.

"How do you know?" Nina asked automatically.

"I know because I've heard. Small towns don't keep secrets for long. As you discovered."

"Yes. I did, didn't I?"

They had crossed the bridge, and as if they were acknowledging that they had left Grafton behind, they stopped to stand shoulder-to-shoulder, looking back at it. The cathedral's twin towers rose over the step-like rooftops somber against the graphite sky.

"Does Hannah know?"

"Oh. I should think so. I'm sure she's reeling in his line. Hannah may never have read a book in her life, and she may also think Wittgenstein's a ski resort, but she's not a fool. She has Darcy exactly where she wants him, whatever the old poseur may imagine to the contrary."

"And Gordon?"

"I don't think Gordon knows."

To assimilate this information Nina leaned against the limestone pillar that marked the end of the bridge. She saw Star's expression, the mixture of amusement and malice and cleverness in it, and then Nina began to laugh too.

"It's funny," she explained.

"You're right. It's so funny that it hurts."

They leaned against the limestone pillar, oblivious to the passing traffic, until they could stop laughing. And then they turned their backs to Grafton and walked on, newly comfortable with each other.

"I don't know why I've marched us out here," Star remarked. "Force of habit, I suppose."

They had come to the school gates. They were locked, but there was an old man in overalls just beyond them, dispiritedly brushing long-dead leaves from the drive.

"Hello, Ted," Star called out.

"Afternoon, Mrs. Rose. Can't you keep away from the bloody place, then?"

Nina stood with her fists locked on the railings, like a convict, gazing into the grounds. The line of trees that had marked the far boundary was now gone; she supposed that they must have been elms. There was a new housing development on the slope beyond, where there had once been farmland. Threads and snippets of unimportant memories swam and merged in her head.

"Mrs. Cort's an old girl of the school, Ted. Can we slip inside so she can have a look around?"

This was so much what Nina wanted, without even having expressed it to herself, that she looked at Star in surprise.

"Can't let you in the building, Mrs. Rose, it'd be more than my job's worth. But I'll open these gates for you, if your friend just wants a stroll round."

Star and Nina walked up the driveway to the Victorian building. At the nearest window Nina leaned on the sill, shading her eyes to look in at the rows of desks. As soon as she saw the shape of the room, she immediately became the fomenting schoolgirl she had once been, full of dreams and illusions, unwillingly hunched over her work. The exercise books they used had had stiff gray covers and Nina had drawn all over them, obsessively creating derivative op-art designs and then filling in the divisions and subdivisions with her black pen, as if she could reduce the confusions of adolescence to mosaic patterns.

"It's all different, furniture, colors, everything, but it's still exactly the same. This was the geography room."

It had smelled of hot dust from the radiators, and chalk, like all the other classrooms, but also of the sticky, oiled canvas of the big old-fashioned maps that hung on the walls. The room had had a soporific hum that made it difficult to stay awake in there on warm afternoons.

All these shreds of recollection knitted together. Their coalescence was painful because the life that had contained them was gone, but the revival of so many tiny memories made Nina feel suddenly that she had her place here in Grafton more securely than anywhere else she had ever lived, even with Richard. She knew that her instinct to return had been the right one, even to this mutating city of parking lots and micro-industries and modern couples.

"My theory is that the essence of a place never changes," Star said. "Because it has to do with all the layers of time and experience variously contained within it, not the color of the walls or the style of the furnishings."

"I don't know if your theory would stand close analysis. But I know exactly what you mean. It's rather comforting, isn't it?"

They began to walk slowly around the outside of the building, stopping to look in through the tall windows.

Now Nina could recall the shiny tiles of the corridors and the muted green of the cloakrooms and the beams and arches and echoes of voices as vividly as if she had left them behind only yesterday. She felt that she was linked to Star by their separate travels through the same classrooms. As they reached their starting point again, she put her arm through Star's and they began to walk in step.

"Enough?" Star asked.

"Yes. I liked seeing the place again. Thanks."

"It wasn't difficult to arrange."

Ted let them out into the road again and locked the gates behind them. Nina and Star turned back toward the bridge once more. The sky was already darkening, leaving a faint outline of phosphorescent green around the roofs and chimneys and the cathedral towers.

Nina looked ahead of her, measuring the familiarity of what she saw, the unfamiliar comfort of Star's arm linked through hers, and noticing how the thin, cold wind made her eyes smart. It came to her in that moment that she was content, not happy but content, as she had not been since the day of Richard's death.

As if Star could sense the drift of Nina's thoughts, she turned toward her and abruptly asked, "Were you and your husband happy?"

"Yes, we were very happy."

"Tell me what it was like."

Nina suddenly felt such a plaintive, bewildered need in Star Rose that she wanted to stop and hold her, to comfort her. She held her arm closer, as if that would do.

"What can I tell you? It was a marriage. A friendship, a contract, good and bad like any other."

They were on the bridge now, midway between two pairs of memorial lamps.

Star nodded, staring away over the parapet at the water.

"None of us can look into other people's marriages, can we? There is only our own, and the continual mystery of the rest."

"Yes," Nina said, knowing that that was the truth. They walked on quietly together.

When they reached her house, Nina asked Star if she would like to come in, but Star shook her head.

"I have to go. But can I see you again?"

"Of course."

"I'll call you, then."

Star stepped forward, and they put their arms around each other and hugged. Then Star turned away and recrossed the green, walking briskly so that her long yellow coat flared out behind her.

* * *

As soon as it stopped snowing in Méribel, the families zipped up their padded suits and clomped out into the white world to ski.

The children all went to ski school, while the Frosts with Darcy and Marcelle set out every morning to conquer new and more distant peaks and steeper gullies. They came back each evening with pale circles imprinted by their sunglasses across their reddened faces, to sit around the dinner table and talk about how high and how far they had been, and how much farther and higher they planned to venture the next day.

On previous holidays the families had taken in various permutations, there had never been such determined concentration on skiing. There had been longer lunches, and more hours spent sitting in the blade-bright sun. But this year, after the first evening, they were wary of one another, although Andrew and Janice cheerfully acted as if nothing were different. Marcelle was quiet except when she was with her children, and Darcy was constantly irritable. To gloss over the feeling of discord, the four of them skied longer hours and talked about it all evening.

By unspoken agreement the children were allowed to stay up later, and the extra exercise meant earlier nights for the adults. The threatening intimacy of the snowy chalet was dispelled.

Michael and Hannah were left out of this determined nucleus because they could not ski so well. They took lessons every day with a private teacher, a lean-hipped French boy called Thierry who smoked Marlboro cigarettes on the chairlifts and wore his mirrored sunglasses even inside the mountainside restaurants.

Michael found that he looked forward to the moment every morning when Hannah would appear in her silvery suit, when they would wait outside together for Thierry to ski down to them in a flurry of exhibitionist turns. Hannah was good-humored and courageous all through their lessons, and while Thierry flirted routinely with her, it was to Michael she turned to share their small triumphs and the comedy of their failures. He was flattered, and pleased, and felt himself thawing out in her warmth. Even his joints seemed to loosen—his stiff knees flexed and, to his surprise, his turns became fluid and confident.

The two of them met up with the children for lunch, and Michael liked the easy way Hannah dealt with them all. She let them order French fries and Cokes, found their missing belongings for them, and marshalled them efficiently for the afternoon without making a fuss, as Marcelle would have done.

"You know, I've even enjoyed having lunch every day with the bloody kids?" Michael said to her when they set off on the Friday afternoon. They were standing in line for a chairlift, with Thierry a little behind them because he had lingered to talk to a dishy-looking girl. Hannah's face was framed in the silvery fur of her hood. She smiled, pausing in the act of rubbing some kind of cream into her lips. He could smell its fragrance.

"Why not? They're fun, aren't they? And think of all the brownie points we've earned."

She tipped her forefinger with a tiny extra peak of cream and then reached out and dabbed it on Michael's mouth. He was encumbered by his ski poles, whereas Hannah had looped hers neatly over her forearm. She rubbed the cream in for him, following the lines of his mouth. Her face within its rim of fur was serious, concentrating. He had seen her perform the same little service for Freddie.

Michael wanted to kiss her, but he transferred one ski pole to the other hand instead and in an awkward gesture put his arm around her. The skiers shuffled forward as the chairs scooped them away from the front of the line. Hannah put her sun-cream away in a pocket and zipped it securely. She slid forward, holding her poles ready for the lift, and he reluctantly took back his arm to let her move freely.

Michael had not admitted as much, but he did not enjoy these lift rides. The empty space seemed to yawn nauseatingly under his encumbered feet, and he was always relieved at the end when the chair sailed over the safety net and the bar lifted to allow him to slither forward and stand upright.

This was a three-seater chair, but as the columns formed in the throat of the installation Michael saw that there were two trios ahead of them and no one on Hannah's other side. He was thinking *Good, we'll be on our own*, and then the little gates opened to admit them. They slid forward shoulder-to-shoulder, readying themselves and looking back at the chair as it circled toward them.

Then there was some laughter and scuffling behind them, and someone crashed through the third gate just as it was closing. A skier slithered hastily forward to the third position, almost falling as the chair swept behind them and caught all three of them off-balance.

"Careful," Hannah warned, her voice sounding sharp. There was more laughter behind them and some jeering in French.

All three of them collapsed awkwardly into the chair, and as it swept swiftly upward Michael had to struggle to reach up and pull down the safety bar. He managed to sit upright and place his own skis on the footrests and saw that Hannah had worked herself into the right position, too.

The chair sailed up over the snow-covered tops of some conifers and then a rocky gully. There was a pylon on the other side of the gully and the chair juddered as the cable passed over the rollers. They were swinging uncomfortably, and when he craned forward to see past Hannah Michael suddenly realized that the third skier was rocking the chair because she was trying to rotate her legs from the side to the front. She had fallen into the seat awkwardly, with her upper body twisted and her legs hanging out sideways. He caught a glimpse of a very young scared face. She was a girl of perhaps fourteen, in a red-and-black ski suit.

"Sit still," Hannah cried as the thin dark legs flailed wildly.

The girl's skis looked very long and heavy swinging over the treetops.

"For God's sake," Michael heard himself call out.

"She's slipping," Hannah screamed. The chair lurched wildly.

It seemed that the girl was being dragged under the safety bar by some cruel, invisible hand. Her mittened fists caught at the armrest and at Hannah's leg.

"*Je vais tomber,*" she cried. Her legs flailed again; Michael saw how the skis made arcs against the white slope.

They were over open ground now, spiked with marker poles. It was a steep, an expert run.

Hannah threw herself sideways to try to catch the girl. Her ski poles fell, the chair bounced on the cable, and confused voices shouted in French. There was a scream when the girl lost her precarious hold and Hannah clumsily fought to catch her wrist.

Then there was a terrible instant when the girl was sliding downward, a blur of red and black and skis like scything blades, and after that a jolt that set their chair violently oscillating. Michael's head jerked backward and his teeth snapped on his tongue; for an instant he was blinded by the pain.

When he could see and hear again there was more screaming. He saw that the girl had indeed fallen, but that the hood of her suit had caught on the end of the opposite footrest.

Now she was suspended by the neck over the windy void. Her head lolled forward and her slack body rotated a little to the side and then back again. The lift had stopped.

Hannah had edged along the seat and was leaning down to her, her own body almost beneath the safety bar. Michael was swept by a suffocating wave of vertigo. His mouth was full of blood. His hand shot out involuntarily and clamped on Hannah's arm. The ground sixty feet beneath them seemed to swing dizzily up into his face.

"Don't," he choked. "You'll fall. *Sit up.*"

"I've got to help her."

Hannah knocked his hand away. Through his confusion and fear, Michael felt a kind of admiration for her bravery. He looked up in order not to have to see the drop beneath him. In the chairs ahead were three white faces gazing back down at them. In the chair immediately behind there were three boys, the girl's companions. They were motionless, transfixed with fear. A long way back, still over the gully, Michael could see Thierry's red instructor's suit.

Hannah lowered her head as close as she could to the girl's.

"They'll come quickly," Michael heard her say. "Can you hear me? They'll come soon, I know they will."

The red-and-black bundle stirred. The skis swung lazily, first one and then the other, up and down.

"Don't look down," Hannah ordered. "Look at me."

Michael was amazed that the girl was still alive. He had been imagining the cervical vertebrae, the functional purity of the bluish-white bone stripped of skin and muscle tissue as he might have exposed it on the operating table; he was sure that her neck was broken. But she had slid rather than fallen, he remembered.

A group of skiers had collected on the run below them, and their upturned faces were like discolored blotches on the snow. Two orange-jacketed *pisteurs*, part of the resort's safety patrol, appeared in the center of the huddle. One of them held a walkie-talkie to his mouth. Hannah looked back over her shoulder at Michael.

"How will they reach her?" she whispered.

"I don't know."

Vertigo made him afraid that he would vomit or faint.

"What can we do?"

"Keep still. Nothing else."

It was very quiet now. A little earlier the air had been full of shouts.

Hannah turned away from Michael again. She was talking to the girl in a low, steady voice. He couldn't catch all the words.

". . . can't speak French . . . all right . . . get your skis off . . ."

Amazingly, the girl responded. Her head lifted. They could see her face, gray-white, and black eyes sunken in bluish sockets. Her lips moved, but they couldn't hear what she said. Her eyes darted to one side, and they knew she was looking in terror to see what was holding her suspended.

Hannah went on talking in her low, soothing voice. She told the girl that she couldn't fall, that she was securely held, that all she needed to do was wait until the rescuers came. The girl's eyes fixed on Hannah's face and didn't move from it.

A long time passed. Michael knew that it was a long time because he began to feel cold, and then the cold seeped into his bones. The group on the piste below swelled into a crowd. There was a flurry of coming and going but none of it seemed to relate to the three of them suspended in terrible isolation high above the snow. Michael tried to work out how long it would take for a helicopter to reach them, but he had no idea where rescue helicopters came from. He couldn't think why they didn't winch the chair slowly along to the next pylon, about fifteen yards ahead. Then he saw a man in a *pisteur*'s jacket climbing like a monkey up the ladder at the side of the pylon.

The girl began to swing her legs. The chair picked up the movement at once and began to swing, too. Michael realized that she was trying to kick off her skis and nausea gripped at him again.

"*Non, non, attend,*" he heard Hannah murmur urgently.

The *pisteur* had reached the cable. He was wearing a webbing harness, and now they saw him attach the harness to the cable and launch himself forward. He was winching himself slowly down toward them.

"He's coming, you'll be all right now," Hannah's incantation continued. The girl was too numb and terrified even to turn her head.

With a sliding rattle down the length of the cable, the man reached them. He had a brown face ridged like a walnut. At the sound of his French voice the girl detached her eyes from Hannah's at last and slowly turned her head.

Michael could not figure out how the girl could be freed and brought down to safety. There was a bag of tools suspended from the man's waist, but no second harness, and his own could not have accommodated two people. Then he saw something that made the ground begin to spin again.

The group of rescue workers below had been cutting free the big, orange, plastic-coated mattresses that padded the base of every pylon along the run. They had heaped them into a pile directly below the chair.

Hannah saw it at the same time, and her head swiveled so that her eyes met Michael's. He reached for her hand and imprisoned it under his arm as if it were Hannah the mattresses were waiting for.

The rescuer was calling out in rapid French to the people below. A stretcher on ski runners was standing by. Then the man reached forward and down to the girl. He caught one of her legs and with a deft twist freed the boot from the binding. One ski and then the other dropped downward to the snow.

Michael closed his eyes against his dizziness, and in that brief instant the man had cut the girl free.

He heard Hannah gasp, and looked, and saw a blur of red and black falling through the air; the girl hit the heap of mattresses. They saw her roll, and her arms came up to cradle her head before she lay still again. She was immediately surrounded by the rescuers.

Michael pulled at Hannah's arm; he knew his grip must be

hurting her, but he could not release it. Very slowly she sat upright, and he held her as best he could.

The rescuer hauled himself up the cable in his harness and dropped into the empty place in the chair. He muttered in French, and when he saw they didn't understand him he shrugged and looked away.

They didn't speak. They sat in the frozen silence of shock, watching the activity below them. At last the stretcher was brought across and made ready.

Then Michael said, "She must be all right. If it was bad they'd be waiting for a helicopter to come for her."

Hannah was visibly shuddering now. "It was such a fall. She's only a young girl."

"The mattresses broke the fall for her. Did you see her roll and cover her head? That's a good sign. It means she was conscious. And her legs and back are probably all right."

He heard himself offering wisdom and good sense after the event. During the crisis he had been hopeless, while Hannah had bravely done everything she could. He was filled with admiration for her.

"I think she is good." The Frenchman stabbed downward with his finger.

The loaded stretcher was finally sped away. Michael and Hannah were both still shaking with cold and shock when the chairlift jolted again and their seat began to move forward.

At the top they stood to one side and watched the three boys who had been with the girl ski shakily away toward where she had fallen. While Michael and Hannah were waiting for Thierry to retrieve Hannah's poles, Michael put his hands on her shoulders and looked into her face. "You were wonderful. Amazing," he said.

Hannah smiled, her face white and her lips blue. "I couldn't remember a single word of French. Nothing. I thought she was going to be killed."

Michael drew her closer to him, rubbing her arms in an effort to warm her.

"All I could think of was that we were going to be killed along with her. And I'm supposed to be the doctor."

"I know you don't like heights."

He was amazed again. He didn't think he had given any sign, but somehow she had seen it, and understood it, and excused him. He felt safe and protected, like Freddie, and filled with love for her.

Thierry skied away from the chair and stopped beside them without any flashy display of skill. He had even removed his sunglasses.

"That was bad, I tink. I have seen never that happen before. How is my A-nnah? And Michael? Perhaps we have a drink now in the bar and after go home for today?"

"I think a drink would be a good idea," Hannah said.

In the chalet they were the heroes of the evening. The news of the accident had already traveled around the bars and après-ski rooms, and the children and adults alike were entranced to come home to discover that Michael and Hannah had been so closely involved.

"Tell us all the details," the Frost boys demanded. "Was there any blood?"

"For God's sake," Michael protested, but Hannah only laughed. She had bathed and changed, and either the color had really come back into her face or else she had skillfully applied some.

"None at all. I couldn't have handled that. Remember Barney's friend on Christmas Eve?"

Michael telephoned the Sécurité des Pistes and managed to establish that the girl was in the hospital in Moustiers, not badly hurt. He made a plan with Hannah to visit her the next day.

This good news was taken as reason for a celebration. Andrew went out and bought bottles of champagne, and even the chalet girl was smiling when she served dinner. Michael drank two glasses of whisky and two more of champagne and, as he had intended, became rapidly and pleasantly drunk. He embroidered Hannah's role and his own as a comic pantomime of bravery contrasted with abject terror. Everyone laughed, egging him on as he sprawled at the foot of the table. It pleased him to be the failure in the story, and to make Hannah even more the heroine. He looked at her, shaking her head at the opposite end of the table, and knew that nothing could be more pleasurable or desirable than to undress her, and hold her, and have her for himself.

He saw that Darcy was proud of Hannah, and that his own wife, his Marcelle, was looking at him for once without disapproval or anxiety. Michael sat up a little straighter and focused his eyes on the golden nimbus of a candle flame, and on Hannah's bright hair beyond it.

It was a good evening. The tensions of the first night seemed to have been forgotten, and Andrew and Janice laughed and nodded their relief and approval. The couples sat up later than usual, basking in the unexpected glow of shared happiness.

There was only a moment, when everyone was on the way to bed, when Michael wandered into the kitchen and found Hannah looking for mineral water in the fridge.

He went to her and put his arms around her waist as she stood with her back to him, feeling the breadth of her hips and the roundness of her backside against him.

"I'm a bit drunk," he told her, his mouth against her neck.

"I know." She eased herself away, but smiling and indulgent. He lifted her hand and turned it to kiss the pulse point inside her wrist.

"There," he said tenderly. "That's all."

He stumbled out to the door and upstairs to his bedroom. Marcelle was in bed, but the light was still on. Watching him undress she said, "You were nice tonight."

"I *am* nice."

"I know that."

He groped his way across to her and half-fell onto the bed. Then he reached up and switched off the light before turning to her. He tried, but the buttons of her nightdress defeated him.

"Take that thing off."

He heard the whisper of the sheets and flowered cotton against his wife's skin before she pressed herself into his arms.

He made love to her, feeling her familiar hollows and ridges. And for the whole time he was guiltily and delightedly aware of contemplating a magical photographic negative of Hannah's silvery curves above and beneath and all around him.

12

*B*rushing the earth off his large hands on the legs of his jeans, Barney Clegg stood back to admire his work.

"There. What do you think?"

Nina stood in the doorway to survey her tiny backyard. The early March sunshine felt warm on the top of her head, and Barney's opulent clumps of daffodils and grape hyacinths added to the brightness.

"I think it's the best instant garden I have ever seen."

He had arrived in a van loaded with sacks of compost and pots and tubs of plants, and in the course of the morning had dug over and fed her patch of starved earth and filled it with splashy green shrubs and spring bulbs in full flower.

"I feel fraudulent, that's all."

Barney raised his eyebrows at her. "Why's that?"

"I haven't sprinkled the seed or hoed or watered."

"Well, neither have I, exactly."

"Where did all the plants come from?"

He grinned. "Don't ask. But it looks good, doesn't it?"

"It does. I shall come and sit out here and admire it all summer long."

"And think of me."

Nina laughed. "Of course. I'm very grateful, Barney. I'm not quite sure why you've gone to all this trouble."

She was not sure, but she was glad to have her garden so deftly transformed. Nor would she have denied to herself that it had been a pleasure to sit on a kitchen stool pretending to be busy, and covertly watching him humming and digging outside in the sunshine.

"I promised I'd do it for you."

"I didn't really expect you to keep such a rash promise."

"Actually, I always keep my promises."

They were standing by the French doors into the kitchen. Barney was leaning on a spade with his shirtsleeves rolled up.

"Now I've offended you."

"Not seriously. You could make amends with a cup of tea."

"Wouldn't you rather have a drink?" It was the middle of the afternoon, and the idea of a drink seemed appealingly decadent.

"Yes, I would rather, now you mention it."

Barney followed her into the kitchen. He stood at the sink, washing his hands while Nina foraged in cupboards. She put bread and cheese and fruit on the table, and poured two glasses of wine. The afternoon had mysteriously become an impromptu celebration.

"You'll have to teach me what all these plants are, you realize. I only know the Christmas rose."

"Easy. There's *Choisya ternata*, *Fatsia japonica*, *Hedera* Goldheart and Ravensholst . . ."

"Stop. I'm lost already. My husband was the gardener."

He hesitated. "I'm sorry."

"Don't be. It's all right."

It was, she thought. More than eighteen months had passed since Richard's death. Now she was drinking wine in the middle of the afternoon in her house on Dean's Row with an amiable blond giant of a boy, and she had been pierced by a sudden arrow of happiness.

Barney was thinking that when Nina smiled she reminded him of a picture. Cathy had had a print of it pinned on her bedroom wall. Botticelli, was it?

"Go on," Nina told him. "Have something to eat."

He began with a fist-sized chunk of bread and cheese.

"You'll have to water out there a lot to start with, you know. Even if the weather's wet. The beds won't catch much rain, being overhung by the walls."

"What do I use? A watering can?"

Barney laughed. "If you've got all day. Or I could come back and rig up a hose and a sprinkler for you."

"I can't ask you to do anything more."

"I'd like to do it. And we Cleggs always do what we like."

Barney had reached across and refilled Nina's glass. She could see his father in him now, only Barney was so likeable.

"Do you? All right," she agreed, knowing that it had not taken much to persuade her and resolving that she wouldn't worry about it. "If you can. Come back and rig up some water for me."

"I'll come on Wednesday, then."

He finished his piece of bread and began on another.

"Wednesday?"

"There's a lot of college that's worth bunking on Wednesdays."

"Am I supposed to agree to you missing college in order to come and fiddle with hoses for me?"

He put his head on one side and examined her face. In the strong spring light Nina knew that the fine lines around her eyes and the furrows at the corners of her mouth would be clearly visible, and at the same time she could see the boy's ruddy open-air skin and the unclouded whites of his eyes.

"You needn't agree to anything, Nina. I know that practical experience beats any amount of classroom theory. I've never been much good on paper."

Belatedly, Nina understood that there was a whole subtext to this talk of hoses and practical experience, that the boy was flirting with her, and that she was not at all displeased by the discovery. She began to laugh, and Barney laughed with her.

At last Nina took a deep breath. 'Yes. Well. You're old enough to know your own mind. But you've finished your wine and had enough to eat, and now I should think about going back to work."

"I'll see you on Wednesday," he said as she opened the front door for him. "I'll bring along everything to finish the job."

"I'm sure you will," she said lightly.

She glanced across the green; in the spring sunshine, the world looked bright and clean. The statues would surely reemerge from their lime poultices as crisp as newly budded leaves.

"Where are you going?" Cathy asked her sister.

Lucy was examining her face in the magnifying mirror that extended on a bracket from the wall of their shared bathroom. She had been plucking her eyebrows, and now she turned her head from side to side with a sharply critical expression.

"Just out, okay?"

"I'm sorry, I just asked."

"You're in my light, actually."

"You're always going *just out*. Who is it?"

"Shut up, Cathy, will you? And move so that I can see what I'm doing."

"You look divine, darling. But that's my shirt."

Lucy snapped on the top to her lipstick. She gave her reflection a last narrow-eyed appraisal. Then she turned her back on the glass and faced her sister. The mirrored walls doubled and redoubled their twin likenesses, but the effect was too familiar for them even to notice it.

"You don't mind, Cath, do you? And can I take the car?"

Cathy sighed. "I hope it isn't who I think it is."

Lucy crammed her Chanel purse into her handbag. "Don't say anything. Just don't. I've got to go now."

Cathy followed her out and they met Barney coming up the stairs. He was whistling, but he stopped and took his hands out of his pockets when he saw Lucy.

"Hey. You look real."

"Don't try to be hip, Barn. You're too old."

Lucy framed a kiss in the air. On her way out she looked into the kitchen. Hannah was standing in front of the stove in her dressing gown, heating up bedtime milk for Freddie, a fretful Laura balanced on one hip. Hannah had a cold and so did the two children. Hannah's eyes were puffy and her nose was red.

"See you," Lucy called to her.

Hannah yanked the milk pan off the heat.

"Your father telephoned."

"Is he okay?" Lucy asked.

"Mm. I think. He won't be back for a few days, he said. He's still got some things to sort out."

Darcy had gone to London and then, saying he had some business to do, had told Hannah he was off to Germany. He had never been away from Wilton for so long before.

At least Vicky Ransome was at home, where she should be. Hannah had just seen her in town, at a distance. Hannah tilted the pan now, looking at the flat moon of milk without seeing it, but Lucy was too rushed to notice her anxiety.

"Bye, Hannah. Don't worry if I'm late."

Lucy ran to the car she shared with Cathy. She backed it out hastily and made a turn that sent a spray of gravel pattering over the grass beyond the driveway. Hannah, carrying Laura and the hot milk, saw her taillights through the glass of the front door. They looked like a pair of red eyes in the darkness.

Jimmy Rose was waiting in his car.

They had arranged to meet in a quiet lane between Grafton and Wilton. It was the same field gateway where Gordon had sat on Boxing Day after paying his last visit to Nina, and Jimmy could also see the distant lights of Darcy's house on its little hill. After a few moments he was able to distinguish the lights of a car. The glow brightened and switched direction with the sharp bends in the lane, and he knew that she was driving much too fast.

The dazzle of lights approached, separated abruptly into twin beams, and raked over his face as she swung into the gateway beside him. In the darkness the door of her car opened and slammed shut, and he saw the pale blur of her face and hands as she ran to the passenger door of his own car. A second later she was inside, in the warmth beside him.

They kissed without speaking, her fingers splayed on the back of his neck while she pulled him closer to her.

"You were driving too fast," he said at last, when he raised his head.

Lucy's smile showed her white teeth and the soft glint of her tongue in the dim light.

"I always drive too fast."

"You're a silly girl. I don't want you to smash yourself up."

She answered him by winding her arm around his neck again, searching for his mouth with her tongue, an eager girl. Jimmy's hand found her knee, then her long thigh in some thick, dark stocking material, and the stretchy hem of her tiny skirt.

"Ah, God, Lucy, I've missed you. A week's too long."

"It isn't my fault that we haven't seen each other for a week."

Her voice was soft, teasing, but Jimmy had sharp enough ears to hear the complaint in it.

"Of course it isn't. If I could do anything more I would, you know that. Only the truth is that you shouldn't be wasting your time with an old married man like me."

He felt the muscles of her smooth cheek move against his. Her hand touched his leg and then insinuated itself between his inner thigh and his groin. Jimmy winced pleasurably and shifted his position a little.

"It isn't a waste of time," Lucy whispered.

Jimmy knew that. It wasn't difficult to respond to Lucy Clegg, but she took her own pleasure in him in turn as eagerly and straight-forwardly as anyone he had ever known. He shifted his hand from under her jacket to the front of her blouse, sliding his fingers inside it to find warm silky skin. His mouth searched for hers again.

But Lucy sat up abruptly and flicked her hair back from her face.

"Where are we going tonight?" she asked.

"Ah, to heaven and back, I hope."

"Where are we going first? I want to *go* somewhere, Jimmy, not just to sit in the car. I've got all dressed up for you."

There was a distinctly plaintive note now. Jimmy sighed inaudibly.

"I can see. You look, and smell, fantastic."

In fact he did not much mind what Lucy wore, so long as it came off easily. But she rewarded him for the compliment by sliding closer again, warming his face with her breath.

"I want to go somewhere with you, for once, the two of us. As if you were really mine."

For once? Jimmy thought. He had only been seeing Lucy Clegg for two months, but perhaps that brief interval felt like a much longer time to a nineteen-year-old.

"I *am* yours," he soothed. "Look, here I am. It's these precious hours that count, not all the ordinary ones in between." He was thinking rapidly as he spoke. "Come on, I'll take you for a drink."

There was a pub about ten miles on the other side of Wilton that should be safe enough, and there would still be time afterwards. Star would be back from the Williamford parent-teacher evening by then, but that couldn't be helped. He would think of something. It was Darcy finding out that he really wanted to avoid; things were much more comfortable now that he was away.

Jimmy switched on the ignition, and Lucy's triumphant smile was illuminated for him in the glow from the dashboard. She put her hand back on his thigh, her fingers just grazing him, so that his dwindling erection immediately recharged itself.

Star came home and found the house dark, although Jimmy had not mentioned that he was going out. She went into the kitchen and made herself a cheese sandwich and a cup of tea, listening to the tap dripping into the sink without bothering to turn it off or to switch on the radio to drown it out. She carried her supper into the dining toom and sat down at the table with a pile of exercise books that were waiting to be marked.

Star picked up her red pen, but the silence of the house pressed over her. She could feel it like a weight on her head and hands.

When she looked at the walls, she saw that the striped wallpaper was beginning to peel at the seams, and there was a film of dust on the shallow skirting. The vertical blinds over the windows were of a design she no longer liked; everywhere her eyes turned there seemed to be evidence of neglect. Jimmy and she lived in this house, but it was a long time since they had done anything to improve or cherish it. Star tried to make herself the excuse that they lacked the money; it was true that they had her income, but Jimmy's conference-organizing business had almost collapsed recently. He had never been as successful as the other Grafton men, but they had always been able to make wry jokes about that to each other. Now there were no jokes, but she knew quite well that there was enough money to look after the house if either of them had cared sufficiently about it.

The truth was, Star thought now, that it was good enough to enclose what existed within it.

She twisted the top off her pen and drew the pile of books closer. It was five minutes to midnight, and she was on the second to last book, when she heard Jimmy's car pull into the space in front of the house.

"Hello there," he called out as the front door rattled shut behind him. "Shall I lock up?"

Star waited until he looked in at her, his sandy face coming around the door with his pointy eyebrows raised.

"Unless you're planning to go out again," she said.

"At this time of night?"

"How should I know?"

"Oh, dear God, what's the matter now? How was the school evening?"

Star gazed down at the work in front of her. She wondered if somewhere in some defiant corner of herself she loved Jimmy still, or if she hated him, or if she was simply tired and ashamed of them both, or ultimately indifferent. She wondered who he had been with, and if she knew her, or whether she was some mysterious and therefore incalculably alluring stranger.

"It was exactly the same as usual. Where have you been?"

"I went over to the golf club for a quick drink. Do you want a nightcap?"

He had opened the sideboard and found a bottle of Johnny Walker.

"No, thank you. Who was there?"

"Where? Oh, nobody much."

"Have you eaten?"

"Yes, I had something at the bar."

Looking at her, at her angular face, Jimmy thought *She knows*, but the realization did not dismay him particularly. She only knew in the way that wives always knew, with a mixture of suspicion and intuition, and anyway she would shy away from wanting to find out the real truth. He wondered how he would feel if she was unfaithful to him, and decided as he always did that he would not care for it at all.

He leaned down to her, intending to kiss the top of her head, to make an offering of affection.

"You look tired."

Star jerked away from him, out of his reach, letting her anger show.

"It's late," she said coldly.

Her arm struck against his as she stood up, making him spill some of his drink. Jimmy felt his anger rise, fueled by the whisky.

He wondered if Lucy's scent clung to him. After their drinks, in the confined space of the car, she had wound her long legs around him in the usual gymnastic enthusiasm of their lovemaking. Now he was home and the little bloom of guilt that he had felt when he came in was burned off by a jet of resentment. He did not want to come in and see Star's face stiff with accusation; there was a way a man's home should be, and Star did not make it so. He hated her when she did this. She could have made things easy and pleasant for both of them, but there was some rigid determination in her that would not tolerate the comfortable course of things.

His free hand came up now, grasping her shoulder. His finger and thumb pinched her flesh. "What's the matter with you? I've only been out for a couple of drinks."

Star looked at his face. His eyes were red and there was a flush across his cheekbones that made the fair hairs above the shaving line stand out, but he was a long way from being drunk. A sequence of images passed, dreamlike, through her head. They were violent images in which she struck out and Jimmy hit back at her, blow for blow. Star shrank a little. She was bigger, but he was stronger, she knew that. The scenes in her mind were not all imaginary. Some of them were simply remembered.

Carefully, almost gently, she removed his hand from her shoulder and walked past him without saying anything.

Upstairs in their bedroom Star took off her clothes very deliberately. In bed she turned on her side and waited.

Jimmy came up after a few minutes. She heard him in the bathroom, and then he came in and undressed. There was the clink of loose change as he emptied his pockets on to the dressing table. As she lay there, Star remembered other evenings that had followed this pattern. She thought, *If he tries to touch me, wanting to show what he can do, then he hasn't been with anyone else. If he doesn't try, then I'll know that he has.*

There was a draft of cold air on her skin as he lifted the covers. Jimmy lay down, turning his back as he composed himself for sleep.

* * *

The next day Star telephoned Nina. She felt like some laboratory animal that had explored all the avenues leading out of a cage and found them all blind but the one she could not remember encountering before. As she listened to the ringing, she imagined Nina in her studio, although she had never seen it. It would be tidy and full of white light.

"Nina, this is Star. I'd like to talk. I thought I'd forgotten how to, and then I half-remembered on our walk. Which I very much enjoyed."

There was a brief silence, then Nina's warm response.

"So did I. I'm glad you called. Come and see me. Are you busy this evening? I could make us some supper."

"Thank you, I'd like that."

Star was surprised by the house. Nina showed her around, right up to the studio at the top. There were pale walls, very few pieces of furniture, most of them antiques that looked impressive even given Star's limited knowledge of such things. She liked the feeling of space and air, the sense that fine things had been confidently acquired and then placed exactly where they belonged. There was nothing makeshift or mass-produced; it was a spare, metropolitan look that made the tastes and styles of Grafton, even Wilton Manor, seem labored and hopelessly provincial.

They came back to the living room on the first floor. Nina poured wine and gave Star hers in a thin glass with a knobbed stem.

"Are you rich?" Star asked her. "You must be, to have a house like this, with these things in it. That's an impertinent question, isn't it? You see, I have forgotten how to talk."

"My husband was rich. I didn't really know, until he died."

Star felt something that it took her a moment to recognize as envy.

Nina was free, she possessed the luxury of wealth and independence. It would be easy for Nina to go where she wanted, to make herself into whatever she wished. It was no wonder, she thought, that Gordon had been attracted to her. Gordon was as defined by the limits of Grafton as she was.

"I know what you're thinking," Nina said.

"I rather hope you don't. I'm not proud of it."

"I found it harder rather than easier to have so much, and still to be alone. To have it because I didn't have him. In the beginning, just after he died, I wished that my external circumstances matched the way that I felt inside. I sold the houses in London and the country, the cars, put all of his art collection in storage. I wanted to dispense with what he had left me, as brutally as I could, because he had left *me* so brutally.

"I came here because he had never been here; it was my past, not ours. And I was so jealous of you all, when I first arrived. All you couples."

"Ah. All of us couples. But you're right, that's what I *was* thinking, without thinking about it carefully enough. Are you still very sad?"

Nina rested her head against the high back of her chair. It was her instinct to deflect the question, but Star herself made her want to answer it.

"Sometimes. At other times not. And sometimes when the grief does fade I feel guilty, as if I ought to keep it fresh. Then occasionally I feel really happy, as if I've never noticed what it was like to be happy before. Gordon made me feel like that. And so did you, when we had our walk the other day. And Barney Clegg, who came to do my garden for me."

"Barney *Clegg*?"

"Why not?" Nina protested, but they were both laughing. It seemed that they had passed over some interim stage of acquaintanceship, and had become allies.

"And you?" Nina asked.

Star gave her shrug.

"You said that you wanted to talk," Nina prompted. "You haven't forgotten how. It happens like this, like we're doing now. Was it about Gordon?"

"No, not about Gordon."

"About Jimmy, then?"

Star examined the rim of her glass, then tapped it very lightly with her fingernail. It gave a tiny, clear ring.

"Are you still envious of us all? Now that you've seen us more closely?"

Nina said, "Now that I know about Vicky and Darcy, do you mean, as well as what happened between me and Gordon?"

She did not try to speculate beyond that, not out loud, but she had the sense that the couples were held in some precarious suspension, as if another breath of passion might upset the order and send them all toppling, like a line of dominoes.

She added, very softly, "It was you who said that none of us can look in on other people's marriages. I don't know what Vicky and Gordon are like, or Darcy and Hannah, or you and Jimmy. I can only see the surface. It seemed smooth and shiny when I first came here."

Star lifted her hands and chopped a box shape in the air.

"Did you ever feel that there was nowhere to go?"

"Yes, I did. But there always is. There is somewhere to go, if you look hard enough for it."

Star drank her wine, admiring the glass again, and the carved wooden arms of her chair, and the pretty room that contained them.

"Could we be friends, do you think?" she asked at length.

Nina nodded her head. "Yes. I think perhaps we could."

On Wednesday Barney came as he had promised, with two lengths of differently gauged piping, an armful of garden hose, and a toolbag. He whistled as he carried the load through the kitchen into the garden.

"Have this fixed for you in a second lady," he called out. "Nice place you got here."

Nina watched him roll up the sleeves of his overalls and set to work. He quickly became engrossed in the job. Nina put her red jacket on and looked out to where he was laying plastic piping under the sill of the door.

"I'm going out for half an hour, Barney, to buy us some food for lunch."

He sat back on his heels, rubbing a grease mark on his cheek.

"I was hoping you might let me take you out for lunch. Just to the pub, or somewhere. You wouldn't mind?"

"I would like to. But I need to do some shopping anyway. I'll be back soon."

Nina pulled the front door shut behind her, but lingered for a moment on the top step. It was a pleasure to feel the spring sun on her face, and the warmth trapped in the black paint of the iron handrail under her fingers.

Gordon saw her before she saw him. His first thought was that she had changed, and then he realized that she looked different because the lines in her face had somehow altered.

"You look beautiful," he said when he reached her. "You look happy."

"Do I?" She was startled by his sudden materialization in front of her now, when she had almost stopped wishing for him.

"I wanted to see you."

"Did you? Why now, after all these weeks?"

"You had every right to be angry," he said humbly. "You still have. Nothing has changed, I can't offer you anything, any more than I could at Christmas. I just wanted to see you, to see . . ."

"To see how I am surviving without you? Well enough, thank you. Did you think I wouldn't?"

Even as she spoke, she was disappointed with herself for making a pointless charade of anger that she no longer felt.

"Please, Nina, couldn't we go inside and talk?"

"No. Barney Clegg is here, doing some work in the garden for me."

"Barney *Clegg*?"

He said it in exactly the same tone of disbelief as Star had.

Nina smiled, and he noticed the difference in her face again. Nina said, "Let's walk instead."

She took his arm, folding her own comfortably within it, and they crossed the cathedral green.

Inside, there were scaffolding towers around the pillars on the left side of the nave. They were screened with polyethylene sheeting, but the screens didn't block out the clamor of high-speed drilling and workmen calling to one another. There was a group of Japanese listening intently to a guide in the middle of the central aisle.

Gordon and Nina passed on the opposite side. They walked slowly over stone tablets with their worn inscriptions and the brass memorials to armored knights and mitered bishops.

"Do you remember when we first came? When I showed you around?"

245

"I remember."

They passed behind the choir stalls and the high altar to the Lady Chapel in the apse. The glass in the windows here had been destroyed and then pieced together, after the Reformation, in a fractured pattern of crimson and cobalt. They stood side-by-side, looking up at the brilliance of the mosaic.

Nina felt the fragility and the importance of the threads that briefly held them here, tenuously woven together in their shared and separate places, all the Grafton couples and their families, and herself in her own place, and the filaments that stretched beyond them into infinity.

She was convinced for a moment that they were in a pattern that had its own brightnesses and darknesses, a pattern that was not always legible or comprehensible but was nevertheless there, and the notion comforted her. She thought of Vicky and Darcy, and whatever it happened to be that they needed from each other, and how Gordon did not or would not know about it, and of Star and Jimmy, and all the other precarious links of marriage and desire and disappointment surrounding all of them.

The frailty of the connections saddened her, and she felt the loss of Richard as a blank within her, but at the same time she felt her own strength, and she knew that she would survive.

Gordon turned to her.

"Are you ready to go on?" he asked.

"Yes. I'm ready."

They moved on, down the opposite side of the nave, so that they made a complete circuit of the cathedral under the great vaults of the roof.

Outside, the light seemed even brighter. Gordon walked her back across the green to the steps of her house.

"Is the restoration work going well?"

"Slowly, always slower than anyone expects, but yes. Behind those screens a logical, expensive miracle is happening. It's a perfectly explicable miracle, but still it's wonderful to watch it."

He was suddenly animated, full of pleasure in the work. She loved him for his enthusiasm.

"Are you all right?" he asked her.

"Yes, I am." Nina released his arm. "I hope you will be, too."

They didn't touch each other again. Gordon smiled at her, nodded, and then turned to walk away.

In the enclosed green space of the garden, Barney had almost finished his work. A coil of hose was lying beside the new tap.

"Can I help you carry in the shopping?"

"I didn't get to it in the end, so never mind."

"Look at this."

He turned on the tap and water splashed over the paving stones. Nina clapped her hands and Barney bowed to her in his overalls. For an encore he coupled the length of hose and from a spray nozzle at the other end a jet of water arched upward, catching the light to make a brief rainbow. Droplets spattered on the leaves and released the scent of wet earth from the ground beneath.

"Barney, thank you."

"My pleasure entirely. Now, shall we go across to the Eagle to celebrate?"

"I should be buying lunch for you."

He came closer to her, and his shadow fell over her face. He was very large, and young. But he leaned down and kissed her on the mouth, so that Nina thought, *Whatever next?*

"Barney . . ."

"You didn't mind that, did you?"

"No. No, it was nice. Surprising, but nice."

"There can be other lunches, then, can't there? If you want there to be?"

Why not, Nina thought. *Why not, after all?*

13

Vicky was giving Mary and Alice breakfast. She was dressed for work, in a cream blouse and a pleated skirt, and moved carefully to avoid splashes of milk. Helen was strapped in her bouncing chair with a string of colored plastic balls suspended in front of her. Gordon came downstairs in his shirtsleeves, collecting the mail from where it lay scattered on the hall floor.

Vicky put his breakfast in front of him while he slit open envelopes and frowned and placed the bills in a pile beside his plate. The radio was tuned to the *Today* program, because that was the one Gordon preferred. The two girls chattered through the election news. The kettle boiled, and Vicky caught it before the whistling started. She spooned tea into the pot from a blue tin caddy.

Gordon looked up at her as she put the teapot on the table. She saw anxiety contract to a dark pinpoint in his eyes, but Vicky only smiled and turned to spread honey on Alice's toast.

She felt a surge of satisfaction, after the months of confusion that had followed Helen's birth, in looking at the domestic order that cocooned them all now. Gordon was back in his place at the table and Nina's name was no longer mentioned between them. Even Mary had stopped asking, in fearful moments, if Daddy would have to go away again. Vicky had heard him reassuring her once. "No, darling, I'm not going away anywhere anymore."

She had not tried to meet his eyes then because she had felt no need for it, any more than she did now.

Vicky was not sure how she had done it, when she had imagined that she was weak and defenseless, but by some instinct she had won a victory in the campaign between them.

As soon as she had shut Gordon out of the house, and the fearful hours immediately afterward had passed, she felt strength coming back to her. She had cooked for the children and put them to sleep and wakened them again with a kind of robotic determination that was centered in herself and not around her dependence on anyone else.

It had made her feel stronger still to take Darcy in, and then to discover that it was her motherliness he craved, the very part of herself that had seemed so undesirable to Gordon.

Darcy had sat where Gordon was sitting now, and she had made tea for him, too, and listened to his talk and then calmly taken him into herself. She did not trouble herself with feelings of guilt about the affair, as she would once have done. What had happened was over, the way she believed Gordon's love affair was also over. Instead she looked back with interest, even curiosity, as if all of it had happened to someone else.

Vicky understood that she had taken pleasure in going to bed with Darcy because it had been a retaliation, an unexpected tribute, and a comfort in her solitude. She had felt greedy, and the greediness had reassured her that she was still alive—better than alive, an attractive woman as well as a mother. But the truth was that Darcy's attentions had sharpened her appreciation of Gordon. She had no wish to be Darcy's mother; in fact the exposure of his secret infantile interior had been surprising and faintly repulsive.

The end of their affair had come as a relief.

Vicky knew all through the weeks that Gordon was away that she would eventually let him come back. She counted off his begging telephone calls like beads on a rosary, and finally, almost languidly, she deemed that he had paid enough.

When he came home, and fell with wary gratitude into the old pattern of their life, Vicky made another discovery. Although all the transactions between them indicated that Gordon looked after her, the underlying reality was the opposite. It was she who did the caring. Mothering again.

Perhaps, she thought, Gordon had discovered this, too. Now he knew that he could not survive without her and his children, whereas they could survive without him, and Vicky thought that it must be this awareness that made the pinpricks of anxiety show in her husband's eyes.

But she was not complacent, not anymore. She did not know

for sure, and it was equally possible that Nina had rejected him; or that he had decided it was simply more comfortable to live with the wife he knew than with the lover he did not. It was here that Vicky's reasoning began to blur, and she allowed herself to shrug off the speculation. He was home, and she did not think he would stray again.

All she did know for certain was that the balance of power had subtly shifted between them. She felt calm and strong. If Gordon heard about Darcy from Linda across the road, or Hannah, or Jimmy Rose, or anyone else, she would deal with it. Vicky knew that she would survive. She felt secure, content with what she had.

Vicky looked at the oven clock. It was half past eight. Marcelle would be here in five minutes; it was Marcelle's day for the school run and she was never, ever late. Gordon looked at the clock, too, and put his breakfast aside to wipe the toast and honey from the girls' round faces and find their school things.

Marcelle's shadow appeared at the front door, and Mary ran down the hall, chanting "It's time, it's time."

The women briefly smiled at each other on the doorstep. Marcelle would drop five children off today before driving on to the Pond School. The map of her day was already laid out in her head like some endurance course that she had to negotiate before she could subside into sleep again.

Vicky stood on the step and waved until the car was out of sight, as she always did, then turned back into the house.

In the kitchen, Gordon had lifted Helen out of her seat and was holding her up to the window to see the cats in the garden. Her small fists waved in the air to show her pleasure.

"Marcelle looks tired," Vicky said.

"Marcelle will never rest while there is something within her reach that falls short of perfection. She must be exhausting to live with."

"Not like me, then."

"No, not like you," he agreed.

"Have we got time for another cup of tea?"

Gordon looked at his watch. The middle-aged woman who came in to look after Helen on Vicky's working mornings had not yet arrived; when she came they would leave together.

"I should think so."

Vicky poured it out, and they stood at the sunny end of the kitchen and drank it tepid, aware of the silent reestablishment of normality between them, like a long-awaited truce.

Later he drove her to her therapy center and watched her walk briskly away from him with her leather bag full of case notes swinging at her side. She was still wearing her hair in the short bob that she had had cut just after Helen's birth. He remembered that he had come home one evening from Nina and found her looking quite different, and he had stared helplessly at her as if she and not Nina were the stranger. As Vicky walked in, he saw a younger man on the street glancing after her, following her with his eyes. Gordon was overcome with admiration for his wife, for her grace and strength and good humor.

He turned the Peugeot around and headed toward the office. The windows of many of the buildings were plastered with election posters. Most of them were blue, because Grafton was at the center of a safe constituency, but the Conservative candidate was a new man, an unknown, and both Labour and the Liberal Democrats were fielding strong candidates. Gordon had voted Conservative all his life, but he was beginning to be afraid that some tide had finally turned against them, and that the new government would be Labour.

At lunch only the day before Andrew had complained, "If they get in this time there will be no end to this recession. I can't see how the building industry can ever hope to recover."

Andrew was on the committee that had selected the new Conservative candidate, a lawyer from London. Inevitably, the Frosts were holding an election-night party.

"Let's damn well pray there's something to celebrate," he had said to Gordon when he delivered the invitation.

Gordon's mind was elsewhere as he negotiated the traffic in the town center. He was thinking that the time he had spent away from home, sleeping in his office and then the hotel, pleading with Vicky while longing for Nina, had faded until it had taken on almost the remembered quality of a vivid dream. When he met her yesterday outside her house, he had still felt as if he were in a dream.

He had longed to touch her when they stood next to each other looking up at the stained glass. It made no difference that he could not, and that they both knew he would not; the longing was no less intense. The reality that had replaced the dream was home, and Vicky, and his daughters, but he still loved Nina.

He knew that he was probably an object of pity among their friends: poor Gordon, whose wife had thrown him out and who had eventually been allowed to creep back home again once he had come back to his senses. He didn't really mind that. He knew he had failed some test of bravery or initiative, that he had turned back instead of running forward to Nina and whatever would come after, so pity was no less than he deserved.

The loss of her, and the recognition that he was a man who would stay put rather than leaping into space, that was the worst he would have to live with.

Gordon reached the highway, driving the route he took every day without seeing a meter of it. But as he turned toward the business district he recognized a car coming the other way. It was driven by Michael Wickham, who raised his hand in a negligent wave.

Michael drove on toward Pendlebury. He and a group of surgeons were to spend the day attending a fund-management conference, but the first session that was relevant to his own specialty did not start until midday. He went out early, knowing that one of the routes he could choose would take him close to Wilton. He had hardly seen Hannah since Méribel, and now, as he rounded a corner and caught a glimpse of her house, he knew that he had intended all along to call on her.

His car rolled slowly up the gravel drive under trees fuzzed with the first green of spring. The Range Rover and Hannah's BMW were parked to one side of the house, but Darcy's Maserati was missing. Michael was prepared to encounter Darcy. He would have drunk a cup of coffee with him, and they would have talked desultorily about the election prospects and health-service funding before he drove on to his conference. But he was pleased to discover that there would be no need for that after all. Nor was there any sign of the cars belonging to Darcy's grown-up children, or the au pair girl's Fiat.

He got out of his car and walked swiftly around the side of the house. There were banks of daffodils in the narrow beds all along the wall, and a bird was singing somewhere in the trees on the other side of the path. Michael skirted the conservatory, where the pane of glass smashed by the boy on Christmas Eve had long ago been replaced, and crossed a paved yard at the back of the house. Michael tapped on the glass of the back door, and then when there was no response he opened the door and called out, "Hannah?"

There was no answer, but he thought he could hear a radio playing somewhere in the depths of the house. He called her name again. A black-and-white marble-tiled corridor in front of him led through the conservatory to the kitchen.

A second later a startled-looking Hannah appeared at the opposite end of the kitchen. "Hannah, it's me," he said.

"Michael? Oh God, you frightened me."

"I'm sorry, I did knock and call out. I was just passing by."

"No you weren't. Nobody just passes by this place."

"I wanted to see you, then. Not at a party or at dinner in someone's house or in town, but just to see you."

"I wish you'd called first. I've got a filthy cold and I look a mess."

The thought that she might want to look her best for him delighted Michael. He saw that her eyes were puffy and reddened, and her nose and lips were flaky and swollen. Her face was devoid of makeup and her loose hair needed washing. Two or three darkened strands clung to her neck, inside the collar of her housecoat. There were stains down the front of the silky fabric, and she held it closed with fingers that revealed chipped nail polish. She was barefoot, and her toenails looked equally neglected. Michael found this slatternly spectacle entirely beguiling.

Hannah suddenly smiled at him, forgetting her fright.

"Come on in properly, now that you're here."

He followed her into the kitchen. The room was messy, but Hannah appeared not to notice it. Marcelle would have launched into embarrassed apologies. Hannah simply went to the coffee pot that was keeping warm on the stove and poured out a cup, which she handed him.

"It's funny to see you dressed like that," she said.

He was wearing a suit. It surprised him to realize that Hannah only saw him on holidays, or in the evening or weekends.

"I'm on my way to a conference."

She made a face, pulling down the corners of her lips, mocking his self-importance.

"Where's Darcy?"

She had removed her hand from the front of her housecoat, which gaped a little where there was a button missing. Michael imagined the texture and taste of the warm, unwashed skin underneath. This private, unkempt revelation was far more enticing than any of the public versions of Hannah in her shiny golden party dresses or her silvery, furred ski suit. Hannah shook her head, pushing her hair back from her face in irritation. He tried to concentrate on what she was saying.

"London again, or so he said. Working, anyway. Dealing or fixing or whatever it is."

"Don't you know?"

"Who knows anything with Darcy? He isn't exactly easy to predict, because he always does what he wants and he never wants the same thing for two days at a time. He makes me angry."

"All husbands make their wives angry. It's axiomatic."

He had said it flippantly, but then he saw bleakness behind the chapped planes of her face. Without any premeditation he reached across the corner of the table, resting his forehead against hers for an instant, and then kissed her. After a moment she tilted her chin and kissed him back. Automatically, awkwardly because of the table separating them, he lifted his hand and slipped it inside her housecoat, where the missing button left a place to admit him.

"*Well*, Doctor Wickham." Hannah's voice was amused now. She caught his fingers and held them away from her.

"Mister, actually."

"Oh. Sorry."

The legs of his chair scraped on the tiled floor when he stood up. He went to her and lifted her to her feet. She smelled of Vick's, and tasted of coffee and very faintly of toothpaste. After a moment Hannah lifted her arms and locked them around his neck, but she was neither actively encouraging nor discouraging.

"I've wanted to do this ever since Méribel. No, that's not true.

Since long before." At the corner of his mouth he felt the sly curve of Hannah's smile. "What are you wearing underneath this thing?" he asked.

"Nothing."

"I want to take it off you."

Her hand held it closed against him. She laughed fully now, a deep sound in her throat.

"You can't just sneak in here like a burglar and expect me to let you do that."

"Why not? Wouldn't it be nice?"

"What about Marcelle?"

Michael tilted his head. He could see her bare neck now, and her hair pushed back behind her ear, and the crisscross stitching of the quilted fabric covering her shoulder.

"What can I tell you about Marcelle?"

As he spoke he saw his wife, first of all her face with its neat, brown, birdlike features, and then Marcelle in her kitchen at home with her cooking utensils professionally laid out in front of her, her quick hands moving and her head bent in concentration on what she was doing. He tried to shuffle the images to find a more pleasing one, but he could only conjure up Marcelle hurrying children into the car, or jabbing the iron over the empty limbs of a shirt, or holding Daisy on her lap and looking accusingly at him over the child's head. He knew that there were happy recollections buried under these sharper images, but he couldn't reanimate them. Always he could see her face with her mouth compressed in its thin line of disapproval of him, and he couldn't recollect now exactly when this mask had come to disguise the girl he had married.

"She's my friend," Hannah said mechanically.

"Yes. And I don't know if she's mine anymore."

Michael looked down at her, and she unwound her arms from his neck.

"Is friendship what you want?"

"I think it's what everyone wants, isn't it, once the beginning is over? Companionship and continuity. A shared history and the understanding that comes with it."

Hannah hitched her robe more closely around her. She sat down again and wrapped her hands with their flawed nails around her cup of coffee. He immediately regretted the change of mood and wished that they could go back again to when she had put her arms around him. He felt awkward, hovering over her in his dark suit, and so he reluctantly moved back and sat down facing her in his own chair.

"It isn't what I want," Hannah declared. "Anyway, Darcy and I don't have all that much shared history. His stretches right back through Barney and Lucy and Cathy, to the first wife, and the first business, and the businesses after that, and includes all the old friends and the old places that I know nothing and care less about, not to mention the women who came before, during, and after the first wife and then after her and before me."

"But you have Laura and Freddie and this place together now."

"*I* have them. It's not really a joint enterprise. They're my children and I run the house. Darcy just pays the bills."

Michael was amused by the casual dismissiveness of a rich man's wife. "And so what do you want?" he asked.

Hannah looked at him. "I want to be loved, of course. Loved madly, passionately, addictively, to the exclusion of all others."

She said this grandly, with a red-tipped flourish of her hand, but Michael saw that she meant it.

"And doesn't Darcy love you?"

"Oh, *Michael*. What do you think?"

"I think he does."

"Wrong. Darcy loves himself, getting the best of a deal, making money, drink, food, and cigars, in that order." She counted off on her fingers. "The children, me, our life here, are just home comforts to him. I'm not sure where Vicky Ransome fits in. A non-home comfort, perhaps?"

Michael stared at her. "Vicky?" he said.

"Didn't you know?"

"No, I had no idea." Vicky Ransome had always seemed a quiet, faintly bovine presence to him. He was amazed and embarrassed by his innocence, and troubled by the sense that there were countless secrets and nuances in the world around him that he had never even dreamed of while plodding to the hospital and home again everyday.

"After that boy sliced his arm open on Christmas Eve, I found him with her up in our bedroom. Then, after she pitched Gordon out, he was there all the time. He's got a real thing about women with babies, it's what turns him on. Mothers. Breasts, mothers' milk. He wants to be mothered. He'd like me to be his mother, only I get tired of it."

Hannah gave the faintest shrug, tolerant and dismissive at the same time, and she seemed to Michael wonderfully female and knowing as if she had seen and accepted all the quirks and weaknesses of men.

"I don't want you to be my mother," he told her.

"Good," Hannah said, looking straight into his eyes.

He felt an unfamiliar awareness of limitless possibilities, energy in his limbs, the luxury of the day, of this minute, and realized that it was happiness. He reached out for Hannah's hand.

"I'm sorry that I came in and made a clumsy pass at you," he said.

Her other hand held the strands of hair back from her cheek. He had never seen her look plain before, and he had never wanted so much to go on looking at her, holding her face in front of him, her hand linked in his.

"Isn't that what men do?" she asked.

Michael hesitated. He thought it had to be what men did to women who looked and acted like Hannah, and that that must be all she knew.

"Not necessarily."

Then, miraculously, she leaned closer to him and touched her hand to his mouth. "I didn't mind. I'm glad you did."

"I still want to take this thing off you," he said after a moment.

"Not now—I can't let you now. Mandy will be back soon with Laura."

"Then when?"

"I don't know. Does it matter?"

He smiled at her. "No. As long as it's when, not if."

"When," Hannah said, softly and seriously.

On election day the windows of the Frosts' house were papered with blue posters. Andrew and Janice had invited their friends to a late supper and to watch the election results. There was an air of uneasy but pleasurable expectancy.

"A hung parliament, I think," Michael said in answer to someone's question. "And another election within a year."

Andrew overheard him. He was jovially busy, pouring wine with a bottle in each hand, his round face radiating confidence and satisfaction.

"Don't you believe it. Share prices are up, and the word is that exit polls are promising. I wouldn't have bet on it a week ago, but the last couple of days have been crucial. My money's on a small majority for us."

Gordon was standing in the same group. He had looked quickly through the rooms in search of Nina even though he knew she had not been invited. Andrew had explained to him discreetly that he needn't worry. Janice and he had nothing particular against Nina Cort, he had said, because it took two people to have an affair, and in any case it was none of his business, but it was much easier on everyone not to invite her. Gordon had even thanked him. He looked around the crowded room now and remembered how she had looked in her chiffon dress on the night he met her.

To Andrew and all the other familiar, irrelevant faces gathered around him he said something like, "I wish I felt as confident. I think we may well have a Labour government tomorrow morning."

Jimmy Rose piped in, "The night will tell, but I hope to God you're wrong. Still, they can't make me pay tax on what I'm not making, can they?"

Star had left Jimmy's side as soon as they arrived. She was wearing a black-and-white striped jacket with a red rosebud in the buttonhole. It was a joke among the couples that Star was the only Labour voter allowed to cross Andrew Frost's threshold, and Star had been known to retort that Andrew was as guilty of tokenism as the BBC.

The noise level was rising. There was a deliberate gaiety while they all absorbed enough wine to fortify themselves for the results. An elaborate cold buffet was laid out in the dining room.

The Cleggs arrived late, complete with Barney and the twins. Barney was carrying a case of Bollinger, which Darcy presented to Andrew.

"Put the whole lot in the fridge. We'll crack it just as soon as we know we've won, and I'm not going home until it's all drunk."

There was a mottled flush across Darcy's cheeks and a new looseness about his throat that made him look unkempt, although his hair was sleekly brushed and he was wearing one of his loud chalk-striped suits. He declined wine and filled himself a tumbler of whisky. The three younger Cleggs and Hannah melted into the thick of the party.

"*Please* come and eat," Janice begged a few minutes after the Cleggs arrived.

They crowded into the dining room and dished her good food onto their plates, then settled down to eat and drink and talk before the television coverage began. Only Lucy Clegg ignored the food, but she filled and refilled her glass of wine. Marcelle found a corner of a sofa and picked at a salad until Jimmy came and sat beside her.

"Sad face," he said gently. "Why's that?"

Marcelle looked at the animation all around them. She could hear the ebb and flow of three different conversations, but couldn't think of anything to contribute to any of them.

"Do I look sad? I don't mean to."

"Talk to Uncle Jimmy," he cajoled her. He didn't look much like an uncle, with his bright eyes and demonic smile.

"I talk too much as it is."

Gordon and Vicky were across the room in a group that included Barney Clegg and the Kellys. Jimmy followed the direction of her glance.

"These things pass," he said smoothly. "See?"

At eleven o'clock the big television was turned on. Jon Snow's face filled the screen, and there were cries for quiet. The experts' view at the close of polling was that the results were too close to call. There were ironic cheers and whistles.

Andrew had photocopied the newspapers' lists of marginal and key seats and now he distributed them among the watchers. The political enthusiasts prepared themselves for the first results while the rest of the party congregated in noisy groups in the kitchen and elsewhere. Cathy Clegg proposed to Lucy that they slip away soon, but Lucy mutely shook her head. She hovered at the margin of the gathering, holding firmly onto her glass and keeping her face turned away from Jimmy. She looked paler and less pretty than usual.

Star was sitting on a tall stool by one of the kitchen counters with a half-full bottle of wine beside her. Gordon slid into the place next to her and filled his glass from her bottle.

"How long until Darcy's champagne, I wonder?" he murmured.

"Forever, I hope," Star said crisply.

He smiled at her. "I'm sorry, I forgot. And you're wearing your party badge, too."

There was a shout from the television room as the first results were declared.

"Don't you want to go and watch?" she asked.

"No. It won't make much difference, whoever gets in."

"Yes it will."

Gordon envied her conviction, but he didn't want to embark on a political argument with Star tonight. "How are you?" he asked instead.

"Nothing has changed. You know how I am."

It was an acknowledgment of some unfinished business between them that now never would be addressed. Star drank her wine; Gordon noticed, as he had before, that she wore her sadness like armor.

Vicky was watching the television in the other room; no one else in the kitchen was within earshot.

Star looked up and said, "I've been seeing Nina. I like her. We're becoming friends."

It gave him pleasure to hear Nina's name spoken with sincere affection.

"I'm glad. I know she needs a friend, and she couldn't find a better one than you."

There was a chorus of groans and some booing from the television room.

"Sounds like we won one," Star said.

Darcy looked at his watch. It was not yet one o'clock, and although all the signs were promising, there was no clear indication of victory yet. He glanced around for Hannah but couldn't find her. He didn't particularly want any champagne—his head felt fuzzy and there was a weight beneath his diaphragm that threatened to expand into pain—but the moment of victory and the uncorking of champagne to mark it gave him something to focus his attention on. He drank down some more of the whisky.

Lucy had been sitting in Janice's bathroom, a welcome refuge for a few minutes, but Jimmy hadn't noticed that she was missing or come to look for her. It made her angry that he was so easily able to ignore her in the midst of this braying party. As she stared at herself, the wine she had drunk produced a sudden acid knot in her stomach and she leaned experimentally over the basin to see if she would be sick. When nothing happened she straightened up and decided that if Jimmy wouldn't come find her, she'd look for him instead.

Hannah had grown tired of listening to Darcy and Jimmy shouting politics in front of the television. She wandered through the chintz-patterned drawing room where quieter groups were sitting and talking, and past the stairs where Barney was good-naturedly entertaining Janice's boys. Hannah patted his shoulder and wandered into the deserted dining room. She hesitated beside the wreckage of the supper table, and then realized that Michael was standing with his back to her, staring out through the French windows into the dark garden. She felt a distinct surge of happiness at the sight of him.

When she went across and put her hand on his arm, he shifted a little to one side as if he had been waiting for her.

"Don't you care about the results?" she whispered.

He shook his head, then he quietly opened the door. "Come out here with me," he said.

They stepped into the darkness. The mild air tasted damp and clean. Michael took her hand and they stumbled away from the lights of the party. Beyond an arch in a black hedge they came to the swimming pool, which was still closed up under its winter cover. Michael guided her around the perimeter until they came to the little cedarwood pool house. He tried the door and it creaked open. Inside they could just distinguish the black outlines of garden furniture. There was a scent of dried-out grass clippings and canvas and two-stroke motor oil.

Hannah shivered a little and Michael took off his jacket and covered her shoulders. They felt their way forward to the Frosts' canopied swing seat.

"Sit here with me," he whispered.

The swing rocked and groaned under their weight.

"It'll soon be summer," she murmured.

"And then autumn again, and Halloween, and Christmas," Michael answered, nuzzling her hair.

From the refuge of the seat they could look out through the half-open door down the length of the pool toward the house and the curtained windows of the Frosts' television room. They were both recalling summer afternoons when children dived and splashed with their wet, dark heads like seals and the couples basked in deck chairs with drinks in their hands, when everything smelled of charcoal smoke and grilled meat and sun-cream.

Hannah asked, "Does everything break up in the end?"

Michael tried to reassure her, without much conviction, "No, not everything." He kissed her because he didn't want to think of anything beyond here and now. They lay back against the flowered cushions, and his hands found her bare shoulders under his jacket and the tight band of the top of her green dress.

"Is it when now?" he asked, and she laughed softly into his ear.

"The beginning of when."

The seat rocked and emitted its mild summer creaking as he undid the zipper of the dress. His tongue moved slowly over her skin and he tasted the faint spirituous burn of her perfume.

Lucy stalked through the party feeling that no one could have paid her less attention had she been invisible. She saw her father in the middle of a larger crowd in front of the television, but to her relief Jimmy was no longer ensconced beside him. Star Rose was leaning in the doorway, looking in at the television watchers with her habitually superior expression. Lucy slid past her, eellike, her face averted. Barney was nowhere to be seen, so she figured he must already have gone off in his own car in search of livelier company. Even Cathy seemed to have deserted her.

The dining room smelled unpleasantly of congealed food and cigarette smoke. She breathed shallowly, fighting back her nausea, and then, in a group at the far end of the room, a group that included the Kellys and a quartet of dull golfing people, Lucy caught sight of Jimmy and darted to his side.

"I want to talk to you," she said. Her voice had risen in pitch.

"Lucy, my lovely girl, talk away," he said warmly.

"Somewhere else. Please."

Jimmy's benevolent expression didn't change, but when he took her arm he gripped it a little too tightly. He excused them both from the group jovially and steered Lucy away, but out in the empty hallway she saw that his mouth was a tight line and his eyes had gone flat. She had made him angry, and the thought suddenly caused her eyes to sting with tears.

Jimmy glanced around them, then opened the front door and hustled her through the cold until they reached the safety of his car. Once they were inside, in the dark, Lucy felt they were in their own territory, where she was the acknowledged queen.

"I needed to see you," she said with a touch of melodrama.

"Don't be an idiot. In front of your father and everyone else in there?"

Lucy saw that he was still angry and dissolved at once into helpless tears. "I love you. I can't bear to see you and not to be with you," she forced herself to say.

"I know that, but you must. How do you think it is for me?"

He was softer-voiced now. Lucy flung herself against him and sobbed. "I want you, I need you now."

"How much have you had to drink?"

"Quite a lot. I feel sick."

He put his hand on her shoulder. "Are you going to be sick?"

"It isn't that." She pushed her hair back from her puffy eyes and turned to look full at him. "I think I feel sick because I'm pregnant."

As she looked at him, all his features seemed to contract, sharpening and hardening while the reactions ticked through him.

"I thought you were on the pill."

"I am. Only I don't always remember it . . ." Lucy's voice trailed away and she bit her lip.

"How many days late are you?"

"Eight."

Jimmy relaxed a little. "Ah, that's not so much. It might not be what you think. A week's no time at all."

Lucy found her own determination in the softening of his. "And what if I am pregnant?"

"We'll fix it, don't worry."

She put her fingers on his arm. They felt clawlike as she dug into the layers of his clothes.

"I don't want it fixed. If it's your baby, our baby, I want to have it. I've thought of nothing else for a week, Jimmy."

He shook off her hand and then grabbed her by the shoulders. "You can't have it. I'm not your husband. I'm married already, and you're nineteen years old. Be sensible."

"Sensible? Is *that* sensible? Don't you want a child, your own baby? You haven't got any children. You *must* want to be a father."

Her teeth rattled in her head from the shake he gave her.

"No, I don't. Not like this. You don't want that either."

Lucy breathed in a gulp of air to stifle the wail of loss and fear rising up through her chest and into her throat.

"If you don't, I'll tell your wife," she said after a moment. "I'll tell Star; she'll know you intend to murder your own baby."

Jimmy grabbed at her, but she had already flung open the car door. She staggered for two steps and then tensed when she heard him spring after her. She fled up the Frosts' driveway and plunged in through their front door.

A burst of noise struck her in the face. People were in the hallway, cheering and jostling and chanting "Five more years."

Lucy slipped past them, searching for Star, desperate to find her before Jimmy caught up with her.

She saw her father in the middle of the room with a dozen people laughing around him. Darcy himself was not laughing. His face solemn, he lifted up a bottle of champagne like a trophy. Lucy could see his thumbs whitening as he pressed upward on the cork.

The room was full of sound, but he was in an eye of silence at its center. The effort of forcing the cork showed in his face. His mouth drew back from his teeth and his eyes began to close.

There in the silent eye, everything seemed to happen very slowly.

As Lucy watched, her father's face darkened and became a mask of pain. There was a sheen of sweat on him that glinted in the light. The champagne bottle fell out of his hands and rolled away, unopened. Then Darcy's body buckled him and he slipped sideways, toppling into the thicket of people.

A gasp pierced the silent bubble, and at the same time she could hear a jubilant voice crying out, "A majority of at least twenty. Break out the bubbly."

"*Darcy.*" Someone was calling out his name. A press of people surged around him, and he disappeared from her sight.

Andrew and Vicky were closest to him, and Andrew tried to fend off the would-be helpers, shouting, "Keep back. Give him some air."

Vicky knelt down beside Darcy. When she put her hands to his ashen face she found that it was clammy. Then she lowered herself over him, in the parody of a kiss, and felt the faint stirring of his breath. Her fingers clumsy with fear, she struggled to loosen his tie and unfasten the collar of his shirt. There was a violent movement in the silent circle above her head and Lucy leaped down beside him, crying, "Daddy? *Daddy?*"

Andrew put his arm around her and tried to lift her away, but she was clinging to her father's hand. Vicky looked down into Darcy's face. She had no idea what to do. She heard her own voice begging, "Find Michael. Somebody get Michael."

She bent over Darcy again. Her fingers pinched his nose and she dipped her head once more so that her mouth covered his. She blew air into his lungs, and when she listened she heard the sigh of his exhalation. His lips moved, forming a word she could not distinguish.

"For God's sake, where's Michael?" she shouted.

The question rippled outward. No one in the kitchen had seen him. Lucy and Vicky were kneeling on either side of Darcy. His face was gray but he was breathing; they could hear the painful indrawn gulp and the rasp in his throat. His mouth was open and a thread of saliva looped from it. Vicky wiped it away.

"Someone call an ambulance," Andrew ordered.

There were voices beyond the kitchen now, crying out for

Michael. Marcelle and Janice came in from the dining room, their faces in shock.

"He's here somewhere," Marcelle was saying. "Isn't he watching television?"

Barney and Cathy appeared together from the upstairs room, where they had been playing games on William Frost's computer. The kitchen doorway was jammed with murmuring people.

"Keep everyone else out, Jan," Andrew said.

"Where's Hannah?" Barney asked from his father's side.

The flesh of Hannah's inner thigh was as soft as butter. Michael rolled the tight nylon skin down to her knee and then knelt to slide his tongue upward. Hannah lay back against the cushions, a serene odalisque in the darkness. When he lifted his head he could just see the lazy glint of her smile.

He heard a voice, and then several voices calling out, but he did not listen. No one would come to the pool house, and his senses were all occupied with the taste and the scent and the softness of Hannah.

Then he heard his name—it was *his* name that was being called. The seat creaked and Hannah sat up, frozen into stillness.

Michael—where's Michael? the voices were saying.

"Someone is hurt," he whispered. "Shit."

He scrambled to his feet, brushing at his clothes and raking his hair with his fingers. Hannah held out his jacket and he took it from her, pushing his arms into the sleeves.

"Wait here for a few minutes," he told her.

He left the pool house and ran, slipping on the damp grass. There were little knots of anxious people peering into the garden. He stopped running when he saw them and tried to stroll with his hands in his pockets.

"He's out here, in the garden," someone called out.

"What's going on?" Michael asked as he stepped into the house.

Darcy was lying on the kitchen floor with his children and Vicky and Andrew kneeling around him like saints in a religious tableau. Darcy's eyes were open.

"Don't crowd him," Michael immediately snapped. "Has someone rung for an ambulance?" They moved back, silently and obediently, to let him through.

At his back, as he bent over Darcy, he could hear the murmuring voices, "Where's Hannah? Somebody must find Hannah."

"We'll have to get you to the hospital, Darcy," Michael told him. "Can you hear me?"

Darcy looked up at him, his eyes unnaturally dark in his ghastly face. Then, just perceptibly, he nodded.

"You have had some kind of cardiac seizure. I can't tell much more until you've been examined. Just lie still until the ambulance comes."

There was a flurry among the watchers, and then Hannah appeared in the midst of them. She stared wide-eyed at Darcy. Barney stood up and put his arm protectively around her. Hannah's bare arms and shoulders were goose-pimpled with cold, and there was a bracelet of earth and grass around the two black, satiny spikes of her stiletto shoes. It was obvious that she had been outside. Another small shock wave traveled outward from the center of the circle. Across from Darcy, and over the heads of the twins, Michael saw Marcelle look at Hannah and then turn her brown eyes on him.

"He's all right," Michael said to Hannah. "We'll get him to the hospital as soon as we can."

She put the back of her hand up to cover her mouth. He had kissed away her lipstick.

The ambulance came, and the attendants carried Darcy out on a stretcher. Michael and Hannah followed them; Marcelle stood to one side of the kitchen door to let them through.

"I'll come home when I've made sure how he is," Michael murmured to her as they passed, but Marcelle did not look at him now.

In the speeding ambulance, Michael watched attentively over Darcy while Hannah sat huddled in the opposite corner. They did not speak. Barney and the twins followed behind the flashing blue lights in Barney's Golf.

The party had abruptly ended, and almost everyone had gone quietly home. Marcelle sat at Janice's kitchen table with her hands folded around a mug of tea. This reminder of familiar domestic life made what she had seen appear all the more ugly. Michael had been making love to Hannah out in the garden. She kept seeing their faces when they had stumbled in, over and over, and had to accept that there was no explanation other than the obvious, humiliating one.

Janice came to sit beside her and put her arm around her shoulders.

"You okay?"

"Yes, I'm fine."

She would not let on that she was not, because that would be too much to give away. Currents of anger and bitterness, and fear and disbelief coursed through her like electric shocks.

"Andrew'll take you home," Janice said.

"No, I'm fine. I'll just finish my tea and then I'll go."

She kept her voice cheerful, warding off the sympathy she anticipated from Janice.

It was seven o'clock in the morning and fully light, but the day was dim and cold, promising no warmth.

Nina had been awake for more than an hour. She was lying on her back, looking up at the ceiling from her bed, when she heard someone knocking at her front door. She got up at once and wrapped herself in her dressing gown.

Barney stood on the doorstep. He was unshaven and looked utterly exhausted.

"What's happened?" Nina asked anxiously. Her first thought was of Gordon.

"Can I come in?"

"Yes. Yes, of course you can."

In the kitchen, where it was warm, Barney told her about Darcy. "It's all right," he went on. "Michael was very good, and then the cardiologist or whoever he was came and told us that Dad had a heart attack, but a minor one. He's in intensive care now under observation. There was nothing else for us to do there. I took Hannah and the girls home."

He lifted his shoulders and then dropped them again, helplessly. He looked very young.

Nina put her arms around him.

"Don't worry," she said soothingly.

"I saw Hannah and the twins to bed. But I knew I couldn't sleep. And I wanted to talk to you. Do you mind?" he asked.

Nina shook her head. "No. Do you want to try to sleep here?"

Barney's hand found hers and he held it. They looked at each other for a long, quiet moment.

"I'd like to lie down, if you'll be with me."

She should have smiled and gently extricated herself, but she suddenly knew how comfortable and natural it would be to lie down against the warmth of him. The subtraction sum, the difference in their ages, slipped out of her head.

"I'll come and hold you until you fall asleep."

Upstairs in her bed, the rumpled quilt still held the shape of her body.

14

Michael drove home from the hospital, having reassured himself that Darcy was out of danger for the moment. It was four o'clock in the morning, and the darkness seemed to enclose the car like a solid cube that traveled with him and closed off all the avenues of escape.

He was thinking about Marcelle and their children; he could see Marcelle's face as he had stepped in from the garden, but he was thinking mostly about Jonathan and Daisy.

He knew that he had never been a wholehearted, enthusiastic father, in the way that he had blithely imagined he would be before Jonathan was born. He loved his children, but quite often they seemed to be unpredictable obstacles to his pursuit of a civilized life. They consumed Marcelle's and his time, and although he was proud of them he knew that they didn't entirely repay this investment of energy. Sometimes they turned on him and stared with mute, accusing faces, and at those moments he felt his heart twist inside him with the knowledge of his own guilty inadequacy.

Now, as he drove along the over-familiar road, he felt he was looking at things from a different perspective. He knew that with Hannah he was trying to meet a need that Marcelle no longer filled, but he also knew that he was also risking the loss of Marcelle and his children. When he imagined life without them, he suddenly saw them much more clearly. He saw Jonathan's stubborn, interrogative stare and Daisy's upper lip buckling with the onset of her too-frequent tears. He felt the demands of his responsibility for them sharpening, and he was fearful for their safety.

He remembered how Darcy had looked in the emergency room, gray-faced and at the mercy of the cardiac team. Michael knew most of the nurses and doctors, at least by sight, and some of them much better than that, and it had been shocking to see Darcy in the midst of them, reduced to a body on a gurney. At the thought of Darcy, and of his fears for his children, Michael suddenly found his eyes so blurred with tears that he could barely see the road.

When he came into the house, carefully relocking the doors behind him, the silence and the darkness seemed even blanker and thicker.

He opened the bedroom door, and the floor creaked as he reached the end of the bed.

"I'm awake," Marcelle said in a clear voice edged with alarm.

"Are you? It's very late."

She reached up and clicked on her bedside light. "How is he?" she asked.

Michael was standing with his shoes in one hand and his jacket in the other, the very picture of stealth.

"Oh, probably all right, in the short term."

Marcelle listened while he told her about Darcy and the hospital. He undressed as he talked, putting his cuff links in the carved wooden dish that stood on the chest of drawers, dropping his shirt and underclothes into the wicker laundry basket. Marcelle thought of the thousands of other nights that had slipped by and now stretched behind them. Their joint history.

"And Hannah?"

Michael lay down on his side of the bed.

"Worried, of course. But coping with it well enough."

Marcelle wanted him to turn over and put his arms around her, some gesture of reassurance, but she knew that he would not.

"So what was going on tonight?" she asked.

There was a brief silence, and then he said, "I'm sorry, I know how it must have looked. We'd both had a few drinks, we'd agreed that we were sick of the election. So we went outside, that's all. There was a bit of fooling around. You know what Hannah's like."

"Not really, evidently," Marcelle said.

Within her head gnawed the conviction that Michael was lying to her. She turned his words over and over, trying to prise the truth out of them, but they remained defiantly flat, refusing to admit her.

"What does 'fooling around' mean?" she persisted. The expression was not quite right; she had never heard him use it before. Was that the false note?

"I kissed her, that's all. A friendly, flirtatious kiss. These things happen."

"Do they?"

Michael moved his arm awkwardly, and then found her hand and squeezed it.

"Yes, of course they do. I'm sorry that I hurt you."

She knew she would get no more out of him now. There was nothing for her to do but accept what he told her; in a sense it was easier because it allowed her to put aside her anxieties. *These things did happen*, she told herself. She knew as much from Jimmy.

Michael withdrew his hand and settled himself for sleep.

"I'm tired," he said. "And I've got a busy day tomorrow. How about you?"

"The same."

Marcelle closed her eyes, and they lay next to each other amid their separate thoughts.

Barney was sitting on the edge of Nina's bed, talking on the telephone with the hospital. She closed her eyes and then opened them again. There was still a narrow space of crumpled sheet between them and then his startling, solid shape. She looked at the lines of his neck and imagined the hard outline of his skull under the scrolls of hair. His face was hidden from her, but his questioning voice sounded like an anxious boy's, a contrast with his masculine presence in her bed.

Barney replaced the receiver and turned back to Nina. "He's stable, and his heart is being monitored. He's asleep at the moment."

"Good. That's good news."

"May I call Hannah now?"

"Of course. But don't tell her where you are, will you?"

"Not if you don't want me to."

He dialed again and almost at once began talking to Hannah. Nina knew that she must have been sitting at Wilton, waiting by the telephone. She turned over onto her back and thought about that morning to detach herself from Barney's conversation with his stepmother.

They had come upstairs together, and in the shuttered silence of her bedroom Barney had seemed neither a tired boy nor a predatory man, but simply himself. He had kissed her and undid her dressing gown, and she had stood there quietly while he looked at her. Then he had touched her arm.

"Don't catch cold," he had said.

He had lifted the quilt and she slid into the warmth beneath it. He had taken off the clothes he had put on for the Frosts' party, ages ago, and gratefully lain down beside her. She had held out her arms to him.

"May I?" he had asked, sounding so much like a polite boy at a birthday party that it made Nina laugh.

"Well, yes, since we've come this far."

Barney had laughed too, with relief, then leaned over her and kissed the corner of her mouth.

"Thank you. It would be quite difficult to go to sleep right now."

Nina had not wanted to compare him with Gordon, but she couldn't help it; Barney couldn't make her forget herself, as Gordon had been able to do, nor did she want that from him. She felt his eagerness, and his clumsiness, and she had wanted to reassure him.

"It's all right. I want you to be here. I'm glad you are."

Barney had closed his eyes, sighed, and then murmured, "I wanted to be. I have for ages. I thought you knew."

"I did."

They both laughed, temporarily lessening the gap between them.

It was easier after that. She had given him confidence, and he was as warm and natural as she had imagined he would be.

Afterward Barney had said, his mouth against her cheek, "Thank you. Did I tell you that you're beautiful?"

"I think you did, more or less."

"Less isn't enough. You are."

Nina had smiled. "Thank you," pleased that they had safely negotiated their way to this comfortable moment.

Barney had slept for an hour while she lay quietly beside him.

Then he had opened his eyes again, at once wide awake and seemingly completely rested. It made her realize again how young and healthy he was.

"I should telephone," he had said.

Now, after he had spoken to the hospital and to Hannah, his anxiety visibly lifted.

"I told her she should go to bed and try to sleep," he said. Then he added, "She thinks I'm at Tom's."

He lay down beside her again. They contemplated each other openly for a moment, squinting a little because of the closeness of their faces, each of them evaluating this new stage of their intimacy and trying to work out what should happen next. Nina put her fingers to his mouth, approving of its shape and all the other remembered details of earlier that morning. It came to her that she liked him being just where he was.

"This is between you and me, Barney. It was very nice, very surprising, but I don't want the rest of the world to know about it."

"I want to tell everyone. To climb up on the roof and shout about it. How could I not?"

When he propped himself on one elbow to look down at her, his wide smile disclosed his healthy teeth. His uncertainty had all evaporated now. He was pleased with himself and his conquest. *Cocksure is exactly the word*, Nina thought with a touch of weariness, feeling dry and jaded and ancient in comparison. She would have been relieved to dislike him, but recognized that the exact opposite was the truth.

"Just the same, I don't want anyone to know."

"Of course not, if that's what you prefer. Are you ashamed of me?"

"Not at all. Just ashamed of myself."

He looked surprised. "Why? Didn't you like what we did?"

"Yes, Barney. I did like it. There's just the matter of . . . suitability."

"Because we aren't quite exactly the same age? If you and I feel that this is suitable, then who else matters?"

His very reasonableness was appealing. Recognizing that he had gained a point, Barney persisted. "If no one knows about us, whatever it is we are, can I come and see you again? I'll steal in secretly, in the dead of night, if you insist."

She saw that he was laughing and his lightness lifted her, too. She had been thinking of Gordon and preparing herself instinctively for pain to accompany pleasure. But Barney's view of the world was so simple that she wanted to respond to it.

She reminded herself that they were both adults after all, free, and of corresponding inclination, however temporary that inclination might turn out to be.

"You'll have to visit under cover of darkness and wear a false beard and a long raincoat."

"Whatever turns you on," Barney said philosophically. "Can I, then?"

Nina nodded, and was rewarded by the flash of pleasure that crossed his face.

Two days after his heart attack, Cathy and Lucy went to the hospital to see Darcy. He was sitting up in bed in a general ward. His face was still an unhealthy color, but he seemed to have recovered some of his impatient energy.

"Diet and exercise," he complained to them. "These damn doctors come and stand around with their long faces, telling me what I can't eat and can't drink and how I must walk and swim and guard against stress. What kind of a life does that sound like?"

"You must do what they say," Cathy told him. She turned to her twin. "Mustn't he?"

Lucy sat with her chair turned a little to one side, winding new knots in the teased and plaited tails of her hair.

"Yeah. Give up cigars and start eating grapefruit."

Darcy flapped the covers around him. "I'll promise them whatever they want as long as they'll let me out of here. And if I don't get some answers soon, I'm just going to get up and walk out."

Cathy shook her head. "What's the hurry? Why not have a real rest?"

"I don't need a rest. There are things that I want to do. Need to do."

Startled by his vehemence, Cathy glanced uneasily at her sister, but Lucy appeared to be intent on the knots of hair that hung in front of her eyes.

"Just listen to what they tell you, Dad. We all love you, you know."

"Do you? All of you? Even you two and Barney?"

"You know we do," she reassured him.

"Barney said he'd be in to see you tonight," Lucy said by way of a contribution.

"Did he? Where is he? College, I hope."

"I dunno." Lucy pushed back her hair and shrugged, feeling how difficult it was to hide her exhaustion, especially confronted with the unpleasant sight of her vigorous father beached and help-less in a hospital bed. She was relieved when Cathy looked at her huge black watch and said, "We should go, Dad. Marcelle'll kill me if I miss any more of her demos."

"Off you go, then."

They kissed him, one on each cheek, as they used to do when they were tiny. Darcy sat up for them but allowed himself to sag back against his pillows once they were gone. He could feel all the muscles in his face and neck pulling in different directions, and his heart seemed too big, dull, and heavy for his chest.

Cathy was driving the Renault.

"Can you stop in town? I want to get something," Lucy said to her as they skidded out of the hospital parking lot.

"Where?"

"The pharmacy."

"Okay."

The following morning Lucy went through the pregnancy test with the kit she had bought. She left the glass tube in the holder provided and went downstairs.

Cathy had already left for her day at the Pond School, but Hannah was in the kitchen with Freddie and Laura and their au pair. The children were eating boiled eggs while Mandy cut but-tered toast into fingers for them. Lucy went to lean against the warmth of the stove and tried not to look at the mess of food.

"Coffee's fresh," Hannah offered.

"No thanks," Lucy said through dry lips.

Hannah looked at her. Lucy was supposed to be studying to retake the A-levels she had failed once already. She was also meant to be looking for a part-time job, but there was no sign she was undertaking either activity. She looked pale and heavy-eyed this morning, and sulky as well. Irritation with the girl broke through Hannah's own preoccupation.

"What is the matter?" she snapped at her. "Were you out late last night?"

"No, I wasn't. And nothing's the matter—why should there be? Everything's utterly wonderful."

Lucy turned sharply and ran out of the kitchen, leaving the children making round-eyed, mock-gloomy faces at each other.

Hannah poured herself another cup of coffee and stood at the window, staring at the gardener's rows of soldier-red tulips without deploring the color as she usually did. She had enough to worry about, she fretted, without having to take on Lucy's problems. Privately, she believed that all three of Darcy's older children were hopelessly spoiled, and that Lucy was the worst. It was a pity that the girl's own mother did not live closer, but she had remarried and was living in San Diego. The children had opted to stay in England with their father.

Responsibility weighed heavily on Hannah. With her eyes still fixed on the brash tulips, she prayed that Darcy would get better quickly. And then, like glittering fish escaping a net, her thoughts flicked to Michael again. What if Darcy didn't get better? What if she found herself married to an invalid?

Upstairs, Lucy stood and looked at the test tube. There, reflected in the mirror the manufacturer thoughtfully provided with the kit, was a ring exactly like the one in the leaflet illustration. It was a positive result, there was no doubt about it. There *was* a baby—her baby, and Jimmy's.

The telephone on Jimmy's desk rang. His secretary had taken the morning off, so he looked up from his sketching plans for a cosmetics sales conference and answered it himself.

"I need to see you," Lucy said at once.

Jimmy picked up his pen and twirled it in his fingers.

"How's Darcy?" he asked cautiously.

"Okay. It isn't about that."

"Do I know what it's about?" Twin images of her, the responsive woman and the uncontrollable girl, collided uncomfortably in his mind. What had he said to her? *We'll fix it, don't worry* . . . .

"I *need* to see you. Now."

"How about lunchtime?" It was a fine, bright day, and it had always been a pleasure for Jimmy to have a couple of drinks in the afternoon, to admire Lucy's long legs in one of the tiny skirts she wore. Jimmy named a country pub they had visited in the past.

"I haven't got the car. Cathy's taken it."

"Then borrow Hannah's. Or take Darcy's, or the bloody au pair's. How many cars have you got out there?"

"I'm not insured for the other cars," Lucy's voice wobbled. She was about to cry.

"I'm sure you'll think of something," Jimmy urged her, his voice warm and encouraging. But the afternoon seemed a less inviting prospect. "I'll be there at one. I have to go now."

Jimmy arrived early. He was already sitting at the bar with a drink in his hand when he saw the Range Rover swing into the parking lot. Lucy looked surprisingly small perched up behind the high steering wheel. When she came into the bar, in her little skirt with her blond hair tangled as if she had just gotten out of bed, Jimmy thought how young and fresh and entirely irresistible she was. The recognition warmed his smile of greeting.

"I'm not insured to drive that thing," Lucy repeated. "I just took Dad's keys. You'll have to say it was you, if anyone's seen it."

"You looked entirely the part of its owner," he said, grinning at her.

Lucy would not have a drink. He bought her a Coke and they went to sit on an oak settee with a high back that partly shielded them from the rest of the room.

"I did a test," she announced. "And I'm pregnant."

Jimmy glanced around them. "For sure?" he asked.

"For certain." Lucy's eyes were fixed on his face with an intensity that he did not like.

"Have you seen your doctor?"

"Dr. Robertson? The family physician? Oh, sure: 'Doctor, doctor, I'm expecting a baby.' 'I see. And is the young man pleased about it?' 'Actually, he's my father's best friend.' "

Her fingers clenched his, pinching him, reminding him uncomfortably of the scene outside the Frosts'.

"Lucy, Lucy, don't do this. I know it's difficult for you, and it's a bad thing to have happened, but we'll make it all right, don't worry." Jimmy looked round the bar again. Several conversations in the vicinity seemed to have faltered. He finished his beer and pushed the glass away. "I can't talk to you in here. Let's go for a walk, shall we?"

To his relief, she stood up to follow him.

Outside, the sun was shining. Across the road was a green signpost and beyond it a stile and a path leading over a ploughed field. Jimmy had noticed the path before, and the little wood on the far side of the field. He took the lead over the stile.

"Spring has sprung," Jimmy said in an attempt to be cheerful, but Lucy gave no sign of having heard him. She was walking quickly, her eyes on the ground, her clenched fists pulled up within the sleeves of her baggy sweater. He took her arm, making her slow her pace.

"What would you like to do?" he asked as gently as he could.

Lucy shrugged and shook her head so that the knotted hair bobbed over her forehead. "I don't know. It's a baby, isn't it? It's our baby, yours and mine."

"Not yet it isn't. It's a cluster of cells, that's all. We can arrange for you to have an abortion, you know. It will be quick, and safe, and when it's over you'll feel very relieved."

They had reached the second stile that led out of the field into the little wood. The sunlight slanted through the trees and made pale-green and silver vaults ahead of them. Lucy swung her legs over the stile. She looked back over her shoulder at him.

"I thought you were a Catholic," she said.

"I am."

"I thought you didn't believe in abortion, then."

It was quiet in the wood, Lucy had turned to face him and was now walking backward, in front of him.

Jimmy said, "I don't, in general. In this specific instance I do."

"That's nice and convenient, isn't it?"

He felt anger in the pit of his stomach and lunged forward for her before she could scramble out of his reach. He saw the mixture of sullenness and defiance and fear in her. Her skin looked pasty and her lips were chapped. Her appearance could change almost by the minute—it was one of the things about her that appealed to him—and now she looked positively plain. As she scowled at him he felt the flame of his anger perversely transmute itself into desire.

Without loosening his grip on her, Jimmy moved his head forward and touched her ragged lip with the tip of his tongue.

"You're like a snake," Lucy said.

"Is that so?"

He slid his hands down her back to her small, hard bottom and drew her hips against his. He moved his tongue between her teeth, forcing the kiss on her until at last her mouth opened to him. Then her arms came around his neck and it was Lucy who was kissing him. She clung to him, almost hanging from his neck.

"I love you," she groaned. "I really love you, you know."

Jimmy glanced left and right into the undergrowth over her shoulder. There was a little clearing to one side, under a canopy of trees.

This will have to be the last time, he told himself.

He half-lifted, half-drew her after him into the clearing. He pulled off his jacket and put it on the wet grass, and Lucy wriggled out of her sweater and threw it down, too. She unlaced her shoes and then peeled down her thick tights. Jimmy knelt in front of her, his eyes on the white skin of her thighs and the lick of fair hair exposed by the hiked-up elastic hem of her skirt.

He undid himself, thick-fingered with haste, and Lucy leaned forward, greedily taking him in her mouth.

He let her for a moment, then he forced her backward onto the crumpled bed of their clothes. He ran his fingers over the veins faintly visible under her white skin, then he slid his fingers inside her and watched her face as her eyes half-closed and her mouth opened, inviting him.

"*Jimmy*," she whispered.

He withdrew his fingers and he extricated himself from his own clothes, hurrying, and then pushed himself inside her.

"Jimmy." Her legs tightened around his waist and her fingers knotted in his hair as he thrust at her. They rolled over, locked together, blind to everything now, and brambles tore at Lucy's hair and her bare legs. Jimmy's anger melted into greed and became one and the same thing, and he bit at her mouth and her throat as they twisted over and under each other. He knew he was hurting her, but her fingers dug into the muscles of his shoulders, and her legs wound more tightly around him to hold him where he was, buried in her.

When she cried out there was a whirring of wings in the trees overhead and a few wood pigeons took wing. Jimmy didn't hear her or the birds; his eyes were closed and his lips were drawn back from his teeth as if he were snarling. At last, after he came, he collapsed on top of her, his ginger fox's head resting, exhausted, on her shoulder. Lucy lay back, staring up at the sky laced with twigs and new leaves. Her face was burning and her throat felt dry and sore.

After a little time Jimmy lifted himself so that he could look at her. There were leaves in her hair, and long bramble scratches, beaded in places with droplets of blood, on her calves and thighs. He sat up, pulled his clothes together, then found a handkerchief in the pocket of his trousers and gently dabbed at the blood. When he looked at her face he saw that she was crying. He touched the handkerchief to her cheek but she rolled onto her side, drawing her knees up to her chest.

"Don't cry," he said.

"I'm crying because I'm angry. It isn't fair. Why is it like this? We could be happy, if you weren't married. If you were mine . . ."

He interrupted her. "I don't want you saying anything to Star. Do you hear me? I don't want anything like the other evening. You are not to run after her and tell her any of this."

Something in his voice or the set of his mouth reminded Lucy of the different, frightening Jimmy she had tried to run away from that night. It came to her now that the other Jimmy had always been there, only she had not looked at him hard enough. Her voice when she answered him came out somewhere between a sob and a whine.

"I wish I was her. I wish I was your wife."

To her relief, his hard face softened. "No you don't," he said. The absence of logic in her reminded him of how young she was. "You don't really wish that at all." He stroked her hair and gently picked the leaves out of it. She was young, and mistaken in her feelings for him. The knowledge eased his guilt a little.

"What's going to happen?" Lucy whispered.

"What will happen is what you know must happen."

While he waited for her to assimilate this, Jimmy listened as patiently as he could to the repetitive calls of the wood pigeons.

Lucy shivered and then picked at the blades of grass a few inches from her eyes. "You don't want our baby. You don't want me." Her expression changed from disbelief to desolation. Jimmy summoned up his patience again, and then he whispered. "Lucy, darling, the truth is that I *can't* have you. I'm married already."

He helped her sit up, then shook out her sweater and pulled it over her head for her. When she was dressed he took her face between his hands and gazed into it for a moment, and then he kissed her on the lips.

"There," he said. "That tells you what I feel for you, and what you mean to me. But I thought you understood how things have to be between us. Hmm?"

He tilted her chin up with the tip of his finger. Even now her distraught look was half-irritating, half-enticing. Even more gently he murmured, "Don't worry. We'll see each other through this. I promise you. And in time you'll look back on it, and on me, and wonder why you ever thought you wanted me."

Lucy rubbed her face with the cuff of her sweater. "I do love you," she mumbled. "Only I'm so confused."

"I know you are. Of course you are. Now, do you want me to find out what you should do? Where you should go?"

"No," Lucy said. Her chin had lost its wobble now. "I'll do that, if I have to. If that's what I must do."

"If you need money . . ."

"Okay."

She picked up her black tights from the tangle of his jacket, and held the jacket out to him. Lucy got dressed and then stood up, towering over him until he scrambled to his feet. He tried to lean close and kiss her, but she turned away from him. They began to walk back along the path, the way they had come.

Jimmy was relieved, and also sad, for the end of their affair, but much more depressed about the baby. Only, of course, it wasn't a baby, not yet; he had assured Lucy of that. This much he told himself, too, but still he knew that he would have to make his own amends for the severance of its life. Only he wouldn't let Lucy know this, no more than he had ever shared with her any of his true thoughts. Nor would Lucy ever come close to guessing what was on his mind.

They reached the parking lot. Lucy was pale, remote, entirely occupied now with her perception of herself at the center of some broad, tragic canvas. Jimmy walked with her in silence to Darcy's Range Rover, and with the ritual glance around them to make sure that no one was watching, they let their lips just touch. Then Lucy stepped up into the driver's seat and checked her reflection in the driver's mirror before putting on her Ray-Bans. Jimmy stood back, lifting one arm in a salute as she drove away. Once she was out of sight he crossed to his own car and drove gratefully back to work.

When Lucy reached Wilton, Cathy was just parking the Renault in its place at the side of the house.

"Where on earth have you been in Dad's car?" she gasped.

"I had to go somewhere. To see someone." Lucy took off her dark glasses. All at once her face crumpled and she began to cry with abandon, without regard for how she looked or sounded.

Cathy ran to her and put her arms around her.

"You have to tell me right now what's been happening. Please, Lucy, what is it?"

"Oh, Cath. I need to tell you. I really do need to."

"You've looked so miserable for weeks on end. It has to do with Jimmy Rose, isn't it? Has he hurt you?"

With their arms around each other, both in tears now, they went into the house and upstairs to Lucy's bedroom.

After they held hands, sitting on Lucy's bed, and Lucy had poured out everything between sobs and half-smoked cigarettes, the twins sat back and looked at each other.

"Why didn't you tell me about him, about this, before now?" Cathy demanded.

"I don't know, I suppose I felt partly ashamed of myself, but I did love him. I *do* love him." Lucy blew her nose, ran her fingers through her knotted fringe, and reached for another cigarette.

"I think I'd guessed without knowing I'd guessed, you know?"

"I should have told you. Only I was afraid of what you would think of me."

"How could you have been afraid of that? You must have known what I would think. That if he made you happy that was fine, and if he hurt you or made you sad then I would want to kill him."

"He did make me happy."

"So I won't kill him. What do you want to happen?"

Lucy looked down at her hands, at her fingertips with their bitten nails and raw skin. She was thinking. Then at last she said, "I suppose I wanted to have the baby, for him to leave Star and marry me, for us all to be together, you know, a family?"

Cathy waited, but her expression betrayed her skepticism.

"And I suppose what I've just realized, in the wood today, is that it won't happen. He won't leave her for me. He never even thought about it. He won't stand by me now, isn't that what they say?" Then Lucy laughed, sniffling back her tears at the same time. "Dumb of me to think he would, really."

They heard a car coming too fast up the drive.

"Barney's back," Cathy remarked.

Lucy looked up. There were more tears in her eyes. "I'm so lucky I've got you, and Barney. Now Dad's ill, and Jimmy's not where I thought he was. *We* can still stick together, the three of us, can't we?"

"You know we can."

They sat together on the bed, cigarette smoke curling around their heads, knowing that they were allies.

"Luce, what do you want us to do about this?"

With the thought of Cathy and Barney to support her, Lucy's will reasserted itself. She said with new determination, "I don't want Dad or Hannah to know anything about it. I don't want Star to, either."

"That will suit Jimmy," Cathy said.

There was even defiance now. "That suits me, too. And I don't want his help. If it has to be done, we'll do it on our own."

And then, as the tide of her momentary courage ebbed again, Lucy curled on her bed, as she had done beside Jimmy in the clearing, and gave herself up to tears once more. Cathy sat beside her, patting her shoulder and rubbing the curve of her spine, waiting for the storm to blow over.

They heard running feet on the stairs, and Cathy leaned to look out of the window. She saw Barney jump into his car and drive away again.

"I wonder where Barney's going in such a hurry, all smartened up?" she mused.

At last Lucy sat up, swollen-eyed. Cathy lit yet another cigarette and gave it to her. "Thanks." Lucy blew out a long, meditative plume of smoke. Having recovered a bit, she was able to shift her focus away from herself. "Why are you home? I thought you had to be at the Pond today or get thrown out of the course."

"Yeah, I did. But Marcelle was ill, so the class was canceled. She came in, I saw her, but then she had to go home with a migraine. She looked pretty awful. Not like her, really. I've never known Marcelle to call in sick before."

Lucy was sitting and smoking, her chin resting on her drawn-up knees. She had no views on Marcelle to contribute.

Michael walked down Southgate. He had left his car in the multi-story parking garage, in a remote corner of the top level, although in these last few minutes of the shopping day there were plenty of spaces lower down. Most of the shops along the street were already closing, but he had already seen that La Couture was still open. Michael paused at its door. There was a little placard hanging against the glass that announced OPEN in the same curly script as the shopfront sign. Then he looked beyond the placard into the honey-colored interior. He saw Hannah sitting at a spindly desk toward the back. She was reading, her tortoise-shell glasses slipping down her nose. A little bell tinkled somewhere over Michael's head when he pushed the door open.

Hannah looked up. Her hair was piled up on top of her head

and she was dressed in a navy-blue suit with big gold buttons down the front. The clothes and her spectacles on their gilt chain gave her a businesslike appearance that was new to Michael, and completely enticing.

"I'm afraid I haven't come to buy a cocktail dress," he said.

Hannah took off her glasses and chewed meditatively on one of the arms while she looked at him.

"No? You don't want a little number for the golf-club dance? The parents' party? I'm sure I could find something to suit you."

"Ah, I don't think so. But do you mind my dropping by like this?"

Hannah folded her glasses and placed them on the desk in front of her. She put her stocklist aside and stood up. He thought she was coming to him and he clumsily lifted his arms, but she slipped past in the confined space and went to the door instead.

"Do I mind? No, I don't mind. I looked up and there you were like something in a fairy tale. I was just about to lock up. It's past six, isn't it?"

She flipped over the little placard and turned a key. They were left coccooned in the glowing interior.

Michael looked around him. He had never been inside La Couture before. It was like stepping into a box of elaborate, expensive candy. Everything was pale and soft and scented, every surface padded and buttoned and puffed. There were thick carpets and curtains and drapes in cream-and-honey beige and dull gold, and in the middle of the floor a plump satin-covered chaise longue was heaped with glossy magazines. The clothes hung around the walls, spotlit at intervals like pieces of modern art. They were all silks and chiffons and clouds of net; there was nothing here that acknowledged the world of work, of lives lived before six o'clock in the evening.

Michael felt the exotic scent and softness of the place rising around him like a tide. The remoteness from reality seemed female and mysterious and drowningly erotic, and he saw Hannah in the midst of it, pale-skinned and luscious, the very embodiment of all these sensations. He remembered the pool house, the creaking of the swing seat, and all the contrasting musty scents of canvas and creosote and dried grass.

"Are we safe here?" he whispered to her.

Hannah nodded, smiling, her mouth curving in and offering him dimples and tiny, cushiony recesses.

"Yes. No one will come in now."

"But they can see in from out there." He gestured to the wet, cobbled reality of Southgate, of Grafton, beyond the window.

"Not through here they can't."

Hannah took his hand to guide him. He followed her at right angles beneath an arch. There were more curtains here, striped cream and honey, and thick gold tassels to fasten them. Michael saw a wall of mirrors, and the fabric over their heads gathered like a Bedouin tent. Hannah turned off more lights, and then let a curtain fall behind them so they were enclosed in the secret space, with only their own reflections to observe them.

"Fitting rooms," she whispered. "Women need privacy to be pinned and tucked and stitched into their own fantasies."

Michael stood behind her while they faced the mirrors. For a long moment they just looked at each other.

Then he raised his hands to her breasts. There was a deep vee at the front of her dark jacket. Watching himself as he did it, and with Hannah's wide eyes reflected on him, too, Michael undid the gold buttons one by one. Underneath was black lace, and her white powdered skin, and the cleft between her breasts. When he looked at her he saw the little rims of flesh pushed up above the waistband of her tight skirt; they had been hidden from him by the peplum of her jacket. He loved her ampleness, the promise of softer folds and curves to be released from the constriction of her clothes. He found the zipper at her waist, and Hannah dreamily arched her back against him.

"Have you done this in here before?" he whispered into the curve of her neck. "In front of these mirrors?"

"No. But I've imagined what it would be like."

"Like this?"

"No," Hannah confessed. "Not nearly as good as this."

She turned to face him now, and over her bare shoulder he watched his hands slipping over her hips and her bottom, then greedily drawing her against him. He ducked his head to kiss her, closing out the images in the mirrors, so that there were only the two of them left in the world.

Hannah undid his buttons. "Striped shirt, gold cuff links," she murmured. "The very picture of a professional man."

"Half-dressed? In the changing room of a ladies' dress shop?"

They were laughing as they stripped off the last of each other's clothes. Michael let the shreds of her black lace drop to the floor behind him. And then, just as suddenly as it had begun, their laughter stopped.

He put his hands on her waist and Hannah raised herself on her tiptoes to bring her mouth level with his. He looked down at the roundness of her belly and the heavy swell of her hips, at her small hand clutched around him, at the red marks in her soft flesh left by her clothes, and he was filled with tenderness and longing for her.

"Lie down," he told her.

Obediently she knelt down and then lay back, and he knelt beside her and lifted her arms and then her legs so that she made a star for him against the pale carpet. He leaned over her and let his mouth travel slowly, exploring the map of her skin, until her head fell back and she lifted her hips and he found the soft center of her.

"Yes," he heard her whisper. "Yes, oh *please*, yes."

Their striped and mirrored tent became a miraculous kingdom.

As he entered her, Hannah's legs wound around his waist and they looked sideways to see their reflections, light and dark, locked together. Their faces appeared suffused, abstracted, unlike themselves and yet like each other, conspirators in pleasure. It was a long time since Michael had known pleasure like this. He felt that he was drowning in it, a death that he reached out for, welcoming as it came.

Afterward, when they still lay wrapped in each other, Michael whispered to her. "I don't want this moment ever to end. I don't ever want to have to leave you."

Her fingers touched his spine. He felt the caress of her fingers with their painted nails so intensely that he could see them, and he lost the distinction between felt and seen, mirrored and real.

Hannah's face had all the taut lines rubbed out of it. She lay looking at Michael, half-smiling, shrouded by her own hair.

"You make me happy," she said softly. "I didn't expect you to."

"I can't ever remember feeling so happy. I love you."

She touched his mouth, warning him. "Be careful."

"I can't be careful. It's too late to be careful. I love you, Hannah."

Warmth spread through her, under her skin, unpinning her. *It's too late to be careful.*

"I know," Hannah said simply.

15

"I should have done this. It's our tennis court that's being christened, after all," Janice said in her comfortable, insistent way.

She was standing with her hands on her hips, head to one side, contemplating the two garden tables and the unmatched chairs arranged on the Ransomes' terrace. Janice wore candy-striped Bermuda shorts, familiar from other summers, although this May Sunday evening was the first time she had put them on this year. Their reemergence seemed to mark the official opening of the season.

Vicky shook out a William Morris print tablecloth and smoothed it over the sun-warmed wooden slats of one of the tables.

"No, I wanted to do it. It's time I did; we haven't had anyone over for ages."

She couldn't even remember the last time she and Gordon had properly entertained the Grafton couples. It must have been back before Helen was born. Long ago.

"Will this be all right, do you think?" she asked. "If we sit at this one and put the children over there?"

"Of course it will," Janice said. She was laying out knives and forks on the flowered cloth. "There. Two, four, six, eight, and two more if the Cleggs make it. And six children, eight if the Cleggs ditto. Perfect."

Janice wished that she could bring everything else to order as easily as she marshaled the silverware. She was troubled by the suspicion that too many familiar features of their lives were changing, and by a more obscure and generalized fear that she couldn't place and found all the more alarming for that. She kept her anxiety under control by paying attention to the glasses and plates.

Star had been wandering in the garden. It had been a hot day for early May, and the first cool of the early evening was welcome. The Ransomes' garden was not as big as the Frosts', but she had always liked it better. There were damp, wild corners here under the shade of tall trees, and even the flower beds next to the house were tangled with an unkempt mass of foliage, the antithesis of Andrew's manicured borders.

She came back across the grass toward the house, her hands full of lilies of the valley. She was thinking, as she skirted the childrens' noisy game, that the three women on the terrace made a pleasing picture. Marcelle was sitting in a deck chair, one arm crooked behind her head. Janice and Vicky in their pale summery clothes moved calmly between the tables, and the sun slanted on the glasses they were laying out, making them look as if they had been poured full of light. The scents of grass and leaf-mold mingled with charcoal and smoke and warm earth.

Star held out her flowers to show Vicky. "I picked these for the table; is that all right?"

"Of course it is. Here put them in these." Vicky held out two of the glasses and Star arranged the flowers, admiring the freshness of the tiny white bells.

"I was saying that *I* should have given the dinner," Janice explained. "But really this is much better, thanks to Vicky. Otherwise it would have been tennis all evening as well as all afternoon."

"It's nice here," Star reassured them.

It had been a tradition among the five families to come together for a barbecue party in the first spell of fine weather of every summer. It was one of the cyclical parties and gatherings that were the landmarks of their year.

This year there was a new development. Andrew had recently installed an all-weather tennis court in his garden, and he had invited the men to play an inaugural afternoon match. And so the women had gathered in the Ransomes' garden with the children to prepare for the evening as they had done often enough before.

Only this evening, not everything was quite the same.

The absence of the Cleggs was part of the difference; Darcy was out of the hospital and installed at Wilton again, but the couples had not seen much of him. They agreed among themselves that he did not look fully recovered, although Hannah was determinedly cheerful. He needed rest, she insisted, that was all. She had promised that they would try to come to the barbecue, if Darcy wasn't too tired, but there was no question of his playing tennis. All of them felt the chill of that. A month earlier Darcy would have pitched himself into any match, energized by the competition and his own determination to win.

And yet it was not only Darcy's illness that had altered the pattern. Marcelle sat in her deck chair with her head turned slightly to one side, seemingly a part of the little group but also separate from it. Janice leaned over her once and asked. "Are you all right?"

Marcelle turned immediately and said, "Yes, of course. It's just so nice, sitting here watching the children. But there must be something I can do to help? Vicky, what can I do?"

"Nothing. Sit right where you are."

Marcelle did not know whether they exchanged concerned glances behind her head. She remembered how the women had expressed their anxiety for Vicky, and the concern that Janice and the others sometimes privately voiced for Star when Jimmy behaved badly, but she felt too withdrawn even to speculate about what they might be thinking of her. Marcelle let these reflections slip out of her head almost as soon as they had entered it. It was enough to do to hold herself quietly, only half-listening and half-watching.

Vicky was smiling, busy with her arrangements for the evening, and Star was intent on arranging her flowers, her dark face momentarily lightened by pleasure. Janice strolled across the lawn to the children, her hands in her shorts pockets.

The women had drawn closer. No one had mentioned the change in the air, but each of them was aware of it. There was a thin vibration of watchfulness and anxiety between them, but also the low, steady note of friendship.

Marcelle's eyes fixed on her children again. Jonathan was almost the same age as William Frost, but he was physically much smaller. There seemed to be an anxiety about him, a tentativeness that made him poke nervously at the ball instead of hitting out when it was pitched to him. When her turn came, Daisy was bolder. She swung out with the bat and the ball soared in a triumphant arc and dropped into the green waves of ivy and honeysuckle at the far end of the garden.

"Daisy, Daisy's lost the ball, we'll never find it in there . . ."

"It's not fair . . ."

The children's voices rose in complaint and then faded again once Janice found another ball and threw it to them.

"They should be here soon," Vicky said, meaning the men.

But it was another half-hour before they did arrive, in their tennis shoes and shorts, wet-haired from their swim in the Frosts' pool. They came out into the garden with beer cans in their hands, full of reports of their game, breaking the companionable net that the women had woven between them.

Jimmy and Gordon had beaten Andrew and Michael, but the match had been close enough for all of them to feel satisfied. Gordon put his hand on Vicky's shoulder. "Are we very late? I'm sorry. They took us to five sets, by some fluke, and it was eight-six in the last one. Do you want me to start barbecuing?"

"Well done, Daddy," Mary Ransome said. She wound her arm around his leg and he rested his other hand on the top of her head, feeling the fine hair warmed by the sun. The three of them stood for a moment, connected by his hands, until Vicky moved lightly away.

"Do the children's sausages first," she said.

"And what about me?" Jimmy asked Mary. "Don't I get a well done?"

He swung her up by her arms so that she shrieked with delighted fear, and then he settled her on his shoulders and cantered across the grass.

"You're a horse, well done, horse!" Mary shouted.

Marcelle sat still in her deck chair. She had watched Michael come out of the French doors, the last of the group, and saw how he glanced at her and lifted one hand in a wave, and then went straight to where Star and Andrew and Janice were standing, laughing at something one of them said, wiping the froth of beer from his top lip. Marcelle did not even know what she had been hoping for from him, but its denial cut her so that she had to blink, and the hard edges of the terrace in front of her grew threateningly blurred.

Jimmy lifted Mary over his head and set her on the ground

again. His shoulders and arms ached pleasurably from the hours of tennis, and the glow of the win was still with him. He stood in front of Marcelle's deck chair so that his shadow fell across her. He noticed that she was wearing big, bright earrings that looked too large for her face.

"Hey, Mar, you haven't got a drink."

"I haven't, have I? I'll have a glass of wine. Whatever there is."

He brought her one, and one for himself, and then sat down on the flagstones at her feet, resting his back against the chair.

There were wood pigeons in the tall trees. The thought of Lucy came into Jimmy's head, followed by a surge of relief that Darcy was not here. It was more than a week since he had heard from Lucy, and he was beginning to be afraid that she might tell her father. Jimmy had resolved on each successive morning that he would telephone her to determine when the abortion would take place, but each day he had found some reason for not making the call.

Marcelle felt the warmth of Jimmy's shoulder against her leg. It seemed to spread through her, and she realized that she was cold. She touched the collar of his tennis shirt with the tips of her fingers, intrigued in spite of her detachment by his solidity, the prickle of rufous hairs at the nape of his neck, and the scent of beer and swimming pool that emanated from him. By contrast Michael had become insubstantial, slipping away from her, so that on the rare occasions when they did touch it surprised them both and they drew back, unsure of themselves. Neither of them spoke of this new degree of separation between them.

Now Marcelle found that she wanted to press her face against Jimmy's neck. She wanted to cry and have him stroke her hair and comfort her. She was appalled by her own weakness.

"Your fingers are cold, Mar," Jimmy said, turning to face her. She withdrew her hand at once, but he seized it and began to rub it between his own.

"Talk to me," Marcelle said, to cover her distress.

"What shall I tell you?"

She saw that Jimmy was bright-eyed, pleased with himself and the evening.

Tell me you can see me, that I'm not invisible, that I still exist, Marcelle cried inside. Aloud she said. "Oh, whatever you like. Some gossip."

He pretended to think. He didn't like the idea of gossip now; it had become uncomfortable to him.

"Hmm. Gossip. Do you know, I don't think there is any? Dull bunch, aren't we?"

Michael sat astride one of the garden chairs, watching Gordon flipping sausages on the barbecue. As soon as he turned into the Ransomes' street Michael had been hoping for the sight of one of the Cleggs' cars, and he had carried his disappointment inside, along with the vain hope that Hannah might somehow have arrived with one of the other couples, or even have sent some innocent message via Janice for him to hear. But there was no sign of her, and no word either, and now the evening stretched pointlessly ahead of him. He fiddled with the tongs, getting in Gordon's way and not knowing what else to do.

At length the children were called to the table. The parents had another drink while Gordon turned steaks onto the flames. The sun moved behind the trees and the dimensions of the garden seemed to change, expanding beyond its indistinct margins of green and gray.

The four couples were already sitting down to eat when the doorbell rang. Gordon went to answer it while Vicky hastily relaid the two places she had removed.

A moment later Darcy and Hannah emerged into the garden, with Gordon at Darcy's elbow on the other side from Hannah. At first Michael could take in nothing but Hannah. She was wearing a vivid yellow linen shirt, and white trousers that stopped short of her bare ankles. The evening light seemed to brighten again, and settle around her head. With this focusing came sharpened recollections, how taut and silky her skin had felt, the scent and taste of her, the wonderful secrecy of the curtained Bedouin tent in her exotic shop, its infinity of mirrored reflections. He realized that he had half-risen from his place, and made himself sit down again, awkwardly bumping the table as he did so. Darcy was no more than a dark shape beside Hannah's luminous presence.

There was a confused babble of greetings, but the only voices were the women's. Jimmy sat unnaturally silent in his place, and Andrew was staring at Darcy.

Darcy detached himself from Hannah and Gordon and seemed to launch himself at the table. He loomed suddenly at one end, fists on the back of Gordon's chair, surveying them all. There was a moment's quiet—even the children fell silent—and then Darcy demanded. "What is this? Don't I get a drink?"

"Darcy . . . ," Hannah began.

He didn't even turn his head. "I can have a fucking glass of *wine*, can't I?"

Hannah lifted one buttercup-yellow shoulder, then sat down between Andrew and Jimmy without looking at Darcy again. It was Vicky who stood up, walked to the other end of table, and poured the drink for him. Everyone looked at the glass, as if the Californian cabernet had taken on some significance of its own. Darcy sat in Gordon's place, pushing away Gordon's plate with his forearm. He drank half the wine and then set his glass down with exaggerated care. It was obvious that it wasn't his first drink of the day.

"So who won the big match?" he asked loudly. "Jim?"

Jimmy had steeled himself for a different question. But now his certainty that Lucy had talked to her father was in doubt, permitting him different, much more hopeful interpretations of Darcy's mood. He grinned at Darcy.

"Ah, Gordon and me. Piece of cake."

Jimmy heard the little musical jingle of Marcelle's improbable earrings as he dropped one arm around her shoulders, and he absent-mindedly squeezed her as if she were the trophy.

Andrew protested that it had been no piece of cake. The conversation resumed in little relieved eddies. Darcy had been drinking, that was all.

Michael's eyes guardedly met Hannah's across the table. He saw now that she was carefully made up, but the artifice did not quite hide a shadow in her face. She looked less pretty than usual. He found this juxtaposition of public Hannah with the other he had discovered both touching and disconcerting. He made himself look away, to Darcy.

Darcy was talking loudly, tilting his glass, complaining that he had not been able to play tennis. Michael was shocked by what he saw.

There was a flush over Darcy's cheeks and nose, but the skin seemed loose on the bone. There was a bluish tinge to his lips that bled out into the lined flesh around his mouth. He was still handsome, even imposing, but it was as if all along the good looks had been only pasted onto some crumbling substructure.

Michael's mind began to tick. He recalled the name of the Cleggs' GP, and resolved to have a quiet word with his colleague, Darcy's cardiologist.

Then, fully-formed, the thought delivered itself to him. *What happens if he dies? What happens to Hannah? Hannah . . .*

Once it had come to him, it seemed absurd that he had not asked himself the question before. But Darcy had always been a solid, massive presence, among them and in Grafton itself. How invincible could he seem to Hannah? Yet he had suffered one heart attack in front of them all, and he was plainly ill.

A new set of reckonings took root and multiplied while Michael looked over at Hannah. He shivered a little, torn between apprehension and desire. Hannah was talking, making Andrew laugh.

The children dispersed indoors. Gordon brought candles in holders to the table and the flames gradually steadied inside their glass chimneys. At once the darkness concentrated beyond the margin of the circle. Tiny moths were drawn to the light, and spiraled upward in the treacherous heat of the lanterns.

The talk within the fragile dome of light fragmented, growing thin, as if they were each aware of other, unspoken, and much more significant conversations.

Darcy barely touched his food, but he drank steadily. He could not let the smallest talk begin at the other end of the table without leaning forward, scowling, and demanding, "What? What the hell are you talking about?"

It was as if he wished to demonstrate his supremacy at least, here among them. Everyone was kindly to him, allowing his interruptions and pronouncements. Darcy's words began to slur and he frowned, as if affronted to find his own tongue beyond his control.

"What do you know?" he said, pursuing some argument in

Andrew's direction. "What the . . . what the *fuck* do you know?" His face was contorted with anger and frustration, but the reason for the disagreement had already escaped him. His helplessness was suddenly apparent to them all.

Hannah would not look at him.

Gordon left everyone's glasses empty. But then, with a small, cunning smile that made him seem entirely sober for a second, Darcy bent down and reached out for an uncorked bottle that was left half-hidden in the shadow beside the barbecue. It clearly cost him a physical effort to bend and twist, and there was an instant, with the bottle in his grasp, when it seemed that he wouldn't be able to heave himself upright again. But Darcy did sit up, and placed the full bottle beside his glass with a hiss of triumph.

"Anyone join me?" he called.

His fist tightened around the neck of the bottle. He lifted it, brandished it over his glass, and then tilted. Misjudging the distance, he clipped the rim of the glass with the bottle. The wine gushed, but the glass was already falling. Darcy tried to catch it, but his hand fumbled and the bottle fell, too, a dark plume of wine making a twisted arc in the candlelight. A crimson jet sprayed across the cloth, and the wine glass rolled over the edge of the table to smash on the flagstones.

There was a confusion of movement. The bottle was caught and hands reached out to mop up the rivulets of wine.

Michael said, "Darcy? Are you all right?"

Darcy did not answer. His head was bowed; he seemed to be staring down at the shattered glass. Very slowly and painfully, he lifted one arm and then the other, so that his elbows rested on the table. Then he covered his face with his hands.

Very quietly he said, "Oh, God."

In the candlelight, every face except Hannah's was like a pale moon, reflecting its separate concerns, its diffidence and embarrassment.

Michael had begun to stand, but Vicky was quicker. She reached Darcy's side before he lifted his head from his hands.

"Yes, I'm all right," Darcy said.

He seemed suddenly completely sober, surprised to see them all staring at him.

Vicky touched his shoulder. "Come inside. I'll make you a cup of coffee. It's getting cold out here."

"Yes. Yes, all right." Darcy went with her, heavy-footed but as obedient as a child.

Gordon watched them go. He was impressed by the calm directness of Vicky's intervention, and he felt a quiver of renewed love for her as she led Darcy out of sight into the house. And at the same time, as a subconscious recognition swam toward the surface of his mind, a question formed in his head.

Janice began to collect the plates, and Gordon bent down to pick up the broken pieces of glass. The others pushed back their chairs, feeling the tension ease. A little buzz of concern centered on Hannah.

"I'm sorry," she said to Gordon. "We shouldn't have come. Only he wanted to, and you know he can't be stopped when he wants something." She spread her hands in a gesture of helplessness.

"How is he?" Michael asked. The others were quiet, deferring to his medical insights.

Hannah hesitated. "Well . . . perhaps if I could just talk to you about it, sometime . . ."

Their eyes met, signaling to each other, *I must see you, I need you.*

Gordon cut in promptly. "If you want to have a quick chat, if you think Mike can help, why don't you go in there, in my study?"

There were French windows open to the garden, on the other side of the house from the kitchen. Hannah nodded. "I'd be grateful. That's if you don't mind, Michael? I'm sorry the evening's ruined . . ."

Marcelle held herself still, listening to the rushing sound her blood made in her ears.

With the yellow linen shirt brushing against his sleeve, Michael walked into the house with Hannah.

It was dim inside Gordon's study. He closed one of the doors behind them, leaving the other ajar, wondering how closely Marcelle was watching. Hannah faced him, stepping backward a little in the thick blue dusk. He saw the cushiony oval of her half-open mouth. Without saying anything Michael held her. He had intended only to comfort her, but the seams in her tight clothes gathered the flesh beneath and made him think of the swollen hemispheres of summer fruit. He breathed in the scent of her hair and her skin and then he kissed her, his fingers at the neck of her yellow shirt. Michael's head began to spin with dizzy calculations about the open windows, and the compound scents of the Frosts' pool house came back to confuse him.

"Not now," Hannah whispered. "We can't now."

"Yes we can," he murmured against his own better judgment. "No one will come in."

She was already half-lying on Gordon's desk. Michael could just make out a neat pile of household bills and a dish of paper clips.

"No. Marcelle's outside. Darcy's somewhere, you saw how he was."

He knew that Hannah would not give way, and he wondered why he was trying to coerce her, at this inappropriate time.

"When, then?"

"Come to the shop on Tuesday. At closing time."

She had planned it already, and his desire for her intensified. There was no question about going or not, though he couldn't remember what he was supposed to be doing on Tuesday evening.

"Yes. I'll come. You know that I will."

Hannah slipped out of his arms. Outside, a bright light flicked on, illuminating the garden. They could see each other clearly, and the arrangement of Gordon's paperwork on his desk, and they both heard the clink of plates and the scrape of chairs as the tables were cleared. Michael walked slowly around the desk and sat down in the chair. He swiveled it through a little arc and pressed his fingers together at the point of his chin.

"What about Darcy?" he asked reluctantly.

Hannah sat down in another chair. Michael thought that anyone looking in from the garden now would see them sitting in just the innocent way they ought to have been.

"You can see how he is. I don't even know if he's afraid, or weak, and can't bear to show it even to me. There are all these . . ."—Hannah's hands chopped at the air—". . . issues, the booze, his aggressiveness, his determination to go on doing business as if nothing has happened, which make everything so opaque that I can't see through to the reality. But I think he's afraid. I can feel the life seeping out of him when he's asleep. He sleeps so badly, and his muscles quiver like a dog's."

"Do you think there's anything else he is worrying about? Beyond the fact that he suffered a heart attack a month ago?"

After a moment Hannah said, "No. What could there be?"

"I imagine that it would be difficult for an individual like Darcy to admit any physical vulnerability. His reaction might take a dozen different forms. There might well be other manifestations before he comes to terms with it. And Darcy is a complicated man."

Michael offered her some reassurance, although he thought that Darcy's brand of bullish confidence was in fact rather straightforward.

Hannah nodded. She added, as if it were important to make the point, "I still love him. And I think I hate him as well."

"I don't think that's particularly uncommon," Michael said softly. "Do you? Sitting where we are now?"

He felt as if his own ears were suddenly tuned to previously inaudible frequencies. He could just hear the high-pitched humming of sexual conspiracy minutely disturbing the air between the couples and radiating beyond them, through his own and Hannah's and other people's marriages, outward into infinity.

Darcy might die, he thought again. That sudden idea, the chaos of responsibilities that he might have to bear, gnawed at him. *I still love him*, Hannah had said. She had her own weakness, he understood, for all her apparent strength. He looked at her now, as if she were indeed a patient in the chair beside his desk, and felt caught between pity and desire.

"No," Hannah agreed at length. "I suppose it is quite ordinary."

Then she smiled at him, her face warming and lightening. "I'm glad you're here. I'm glad of this, between us."

"That's good," Michael said, feeling his own ambivalence.

Star and the Frosts had gone inside with Vicky and Gordon, and Marcelle and Jimmy were left alone in the garden. Jimmy had secured the half-spilled wine bottle, and he refilled their glasses now. Marcelle drank in the hope that alcohol might anesthetize her. She wished that she were not here, but couldn't think of anywhere else to be. The lights on the house wall shone too brightly overhead; she closed her eyes for a second and a painful red glare burned behind her eyelids. There was still no light showing in the window of Gordon's study.

"Let's walk down the garden," Jimmy proposed, breaking the silence. He offered her his arm in an old-fashioned gesture.

Beyond the glare of the terrace, the garden was dark and soothing. Released by their feet, the scent of the earth and crushed grass grew stronger. It made Jimmy think of the last time he had seen Lucy, and the brambled clearing in the wood. He swallowed his anxiety a little more easily now. If Darcy knew anything, it would have come out tonight.

Jimmy and Marcelle sat down together at the end of the garden, on a wooden seat hidden from the house by the rounded bulwark of a silver-frosted ilex. Marcelle wrapped her arms around herself. She felt as if she were slipping out of sight, down some treacherous slope into a mire of isolation. She wondered, as she identified the sensation, if this were a weakness that an act of self-discipline might correct and catapult her once again into the bright landscape of ordinary life.

"Do you think I'm a fool?" she asked abruptly.

He answered at once. "No. Not any kind of fool. What makes you ask?"

Marcelle's head fell back. Jimmy's arm was resting on the seat behind her; it was a luxury to lie against him. She had felt the same earlier, when she had touched his collar and noticed the prickle of reddish hair at the nape of his neck. *The confirmation of touch*, she thought absently. *The comfort*. There had been nothing with Michael, neither touch nor comfort, for a long time. Her loneliness came into sharp focus, burning like the pinpoint of sun through a magnifying glass. And then, with a sudden flare of anger, she thought, *Why should I be denied it, why only me? When everyone else takes what they want . . .*

Without any warning, she was overtaken by longing, a need for love that was stronger and more affirming than anything she had felt for a long time.

She had almost blurted out her fears about Michael and Hannah, but now her anxiety contracted, diminished by the urgency of the new feeling. She remembered clearly what had happened on Christmas Eve, the secret she had shared with Jimmy and then wished she could take back. If there really was anything to confide, Jimmy was not the right recipient. But still, Jimmy felt like her friend. More than a friend, as he had offered to be on dozens of occasions in the past. Jimmy was just what she needed.

"What makes you ask?" Jimmy repeated softly. She could see that he was smiling.

Marcelle was thinking that they were all like dominoes standing in a tidy row. Then Nina had been set down carelessly at the end of the line, had toppled over, and all the couples had begun falling on top of one another in obedient sequence all down the line, and now the momentum had reached her, and it was her turn to fall too. The thought made her want to laugh, and then a little to her surprise she realized that she *was* laughing, out loud, resting her head against Jimmy's arm and looking up at the stars in the dark sky.

"Nothing. Nothing at all," she managed to say.

"I'm glad it's funny, whatever it is," Jimmy replied.

Marcelle stretched her arms and legs, catlike, uncoiling the tension that had kept her hunched into herself for weeks.

The need for love and attention had not evaporated with her laughter. It had become a specific itch. Slowly she turned her head to look at him, at the outline of his small-nosed, tidy profile. *Like a pleased dog*, she thought. *Or some nocturnal animal, tilt-eared and poised.* When she lifted her hand to the nape of his neck the hairs felt very soft under her fingers. She stroked, tiny enouraging movements in the reddish fur. There was a thick, wet heat between her thighs.

Jimmy's top lip lifted a little, showing his teeth. He was looking at her full-on now. Marcelle was singingly glad of the darkness. She felt beautiful and queenly in the dark.

Then Jimmy leaned forward an inch and kissed her. It was a light, brotherly little kiss that fell at the corner of her dry mouth. Marcelle waited, imagining that she could trace the course of her own blood all through the cells and ventricles of her body. Then, in the flush of warmth, she tilted her head so that their lips touched again, and opened her mouth and kissed Jimmy in return. She had kissed him before, in the hazy glow of evenings when the couples drank and laughed and danced in one another's houses, but there had never been an invitation in it until now. Tonight she made the invitation explicit with her tongue, and her fingers knotting in his hair, drawing him toward her.

Jimmy sat still. His arm was awkwardly trapped behind Marcelle's shoulders. He noticed that her skin was hot; there was a faint, scorched scent coming off it, as if she had a fever.

Jimmy liked Marcelle because she was part of the spread of other men's wives for him to admire, but also because she was herself. He had imagined, quite pleasurably and not all that infrequently, what kind of lover she might be. Nor had he ever dismissed, in their amiable skirmishes, the interesting possibility that one day one of them might lead to his discovering whether or not his predictions were accurate. But now, with Marcelle's tongue in his mouth and the pulse in her cheek pounding wildly against his, his only feeling was of dismay. He shifted a little on the bench, resisting the need to clear his throat.

Marcelle's other hand came to rest, palm up, on his thigh. He grabbed hold of it and used the business of kissing her knuckles as an excuse to detach his mouth from hers.

He could only think of Lucy, Lucy white-limbed in the clearing in the wood and all the other times they had been together, but without any flicker of retrospective passion that might have come to his rescue now. He could only think of her as pregnant, a confusing double identification as both his innocent victim and the malevolent repository of a brood of accusations that might swarm out of her at any time. He was smitten simultaneously with longing for her and a desire to escape from Grafton as quickly as possible before Darcy came for him. The relief he had felt at dinner was subsumed again by the certainty that it was only a matter of time before he was found out. Darcy had acted freakishly enough tonight to make Jimmy afraid of what might lie ahead.

And now, there was the painful irrelevance of Marcelle. Jimmy wondered, with a twinge of curiosity, if he might have taken up Marcelle's offer were it not for Lucy. A brief image flashed through his head of the two of them on this bench, with Marcelle straddled bare-legged across him, her face tipped back in a spasm of pleasure. He dismissed the thought, but with the possibility of returning to it later, and kissed the knuckle of Marcelle's little finger again.

"You don't really want this, do you?" he chuckled.

Marcelle hesitated. Her wide, cloudy eyes focused on him and he saw the shiver of confusion in them.

"This? Oh, yes. I do."

Who was he to tell her what she might or might not want? Marcelle thought. There had been a moment when everything had seemed sweet and intense and also perfectly simple. She was desirable and desired and Jimmy would love her out here in the rustling garden and later, without knowing exactly how, she was sure she would bury this secret and carry it safely back, like an amulet, into the couples' evening and all the other evenings.

Only now, she understood too late, she had opened herself up, like some saleswoman opening a case, and Jimmy had turned her down.

"Mar." His voice was cajoling, cracked with their mutual embarrassment. "You know I love you, but . . ."

"But you don't want to fuck me, after all. Have I got that right?" Marcelle coldly interjected.

Anger welled up inside her. She would not laugh, and make it easy for him, so they could dismiss this as yet another episode in the saga of Jimmy's flirtations. He had propositioned her often enough. What had he said, with his foxy little grin? *When? When Mike's at the hospital?*

He had allowed her to, no, *made* her, think of him as her refuge when she needed him. But all along it had been only to flatter himself; it had nothing to do with her or her feelings, and least of all to do with the unsavory package of her needs and desires.

Marcelle had never felt such anger, and mercifully the anger burned up her humiliation. She drew away her hand and wondered whether she should slap him. Her fingers itched and she could already hear the way the sharp, satisfying crack would be amplified in the black air.

"Of course I do," he mumbled. "Only here, in the garden, with Star and Mike just in the house . . ."

"Don't lie about it," Marcelle said. "Don't you know how disgusting it makes you?"

Her desire to strike him passed. She stood up instead, then ran back over the grass to the house.

"Marcelle, wait a minute," Jimmy called after her.

Marcelle could see Michael now. He was standing in the kitchen, his back to the window, talking to Gordon and Andrew. She put her fingertips up to her face and pushed the folds of burning skin back, taut, to open her eyes and force her mouth into a smile. She stepped onto the terrace, into the glare of the lights. She was afraid of the feelings that would come later, but for now she was protected by the armor of her clean, bright anger. She opened the door and walked into the kitchen, where all of them could see her.

Jimmy sat on the bench. He took out a cigarette and lit it, but smoked only half before throwing it away with a quick gesture of distaste. Then he stood up and followed Marcelle back to the house, stepping in his turn into the lights.

Vicky's bedroom was the same, but Darcy's memories of it seemed to belong to a much more distant time than the few weeks that had actually passed. He sat tentatively on the end of the bed. He was thinking back to the other times when he had come up here, of Vicky standing in the thin, chilly sunshine of wintry mornings to unbutton the loose layers of her maternal clothes. He had entirely submerged himself, forgetting everything, in the blue-veined folds of her body. He could recall the precise choreography of their passion as clearly as he now saw the lace-bordered cushions, the intimate terrain of the white bedcover; it was like studying a series of photographs of their encounters now he was cut off from that sweet series of mornings by the recent chaos as effectively as if by a steel door.

He was possessed by the certainty that he could not go back, or obliterate what had intervened, or even hope to make a partial mending. An overwhelming sense of loss weighed him down, and a nostalgia for his life as it had been then, now unrecoverable. His heart contracted and expanded in his chest, forcing a muddy and sluggish current around his body.

Only when he was drunk did he see things in proper perspective. Sober, Darcy knew, it was still possible to feign a kind of busy blindness, to deceive himself and others. But now that the day's drinking had cleared his sight, he wondered if he should make a move before it was too late.

Still he went on sitting at the end of Vicky's bed. He was tired, and he had no idea where to run to.

Vicky put a cup of black coffee into his hand. "There you go."

He bent his head. As the warmth fogged his face, a recollection stirred: another cup held for him, the elusive warmth of his mother.

Vicky sat down beside him. "How do you feel?" she asked.

Darcy considered the possible responses. "Drunk," he offered. "Sorry about the evening."

"The evening doesn't matter in the least. But you shouldn't drink so much."

Simple, he thought. *Good, wholesome advice. Too late now.*

"Hannah . . ."

"No." Very gently. "It's Vicky."

"I know that. I'm not that far gone, Vicky. I was going to say, Hannah tells me the same thing. And the doctors. Ha. Bad for the heart. Only I keep thinking, it might have been easier to go the first time. Saved a . . . saved what? I don't know." Darcy shrugged. "Saved a lot of formalities."

Vicky took the empty cup away from him. He felt the mattress absorbing the shift of her weight, and he was reminded again, with the same detachment, of the mornings they had spent on this bed. Vicky put her arms around him. She was murmuring to him, cajoling.

"You mustn't say that. You mustn't even think it. You've been ill, but you're getting better. You have to let yourself get better, wait for it to happen naturally, not think it's something you can fix the way you're able to fix everything else."

Her broad hands rubbed his shoulders, her fingers cupped his jaw, holding the weight of his head. The associations stirred in him again.

"*Was* able to."

Slowly, Darcy let his head drop forward until it rested against her. Vicky still held him, her words becoming indecipherable croonings as she cradled him in her arms. "I'm tired," Darcy said. It was true. He could feel sleep thickening at the back of his eyes.

"I know."

Then he told her, "I'm also afraid."

To Vicky, he sounded like a child acknowledging his fears at the end of the day.

"I know," she said again. "It's all right."

"No. It isn't. It can't be."

"Don't go to sleep now. Hannah will want to take you home."

Later, after the couples had gone, Gordon came slowly upstairs. Vicky was already in bed, sitting up in her nightdress. He perched on the edge beside her so she had to put down what she was reading.

"What did you make of Darcy?" he asked.

"Beyond the obvious, you mean? He told me that he was afraid."

"Of what?"

"I don't know. The same things we're all afraid of, I suppose."

To Gordon her clear eyes seemed to deflect his questions. He could have asked her if she had had an affair with Darcy, but he didn't think that Vicky would divulge her secret. Perhaps he shouldn't try to make her; he probably didn't even want to know the truth.

He stood up, and he heard her calmly pick up the magazine she had laid aside. He was thinking of Nina as he undressed, Nina in her cool house. He wondered if it would be his fate to think of her with longing every night until he was an old man.

The next morning, Darcy was downstairs early, before anyone else. He hadn't been able to sleep, and so he came down to the kitchen and made tea. He sat at the table with his cup, staring out at the garden and the view beyond it.

He heard a car coming up the driveway. It was quiet enough in the house for Darcy to hear the driver leave the car and cross the expanse of gravel to the front door. A moment later the bell rang. Darcy pulled his bathrobe tighter around him and went to answer it.

There was a man standing under the wisteria overhanging the

front door. Darcy knew him quite well; he was an accountant called Geoffrey Lawson. The last time they had met was when both men had played in a charity golf tournament.

"Geoffrey? This is very early. We weren't scheduled to meet today, were we?"

"No. But may I come in?"

The man followed Darcy through the quiet house to the kitchen. He stood in the doorway holding his briefcase, stiff in his dark suit.

"What can I offer you? Coffee? Or breakfast, perhaps?" Darcy asked. He glanced pointedly at the kitchen clock. It was not yet 8:00 A.M.

"Nothing, thank you. Darcy, I'll come straight to the point. I had a call from my client Vincent Templeman yesterday evening."

Darcy stood without moving. He could only wait for what would come next.

The man said, "Could we go into your office?"

"Of course," Darcy said.

In his briefcase, Geoffrey Lawson had the books of Vincent Templeman's private company. Templeman was a property magnate, now retired to the Isle of Jersey. Darcy had managed his assets for almost five years. Lawson laid the books on Darcy's desk.

"When Vincent called me last night, he told me that there are one or two aspects of these figures"—he tapped the folders under his hand—"that are troubling him. I promised him I would drive down here first thing to see you."

There was a moment's silence. Upstairs Darcy heard one of the children, Laura or Freddie, running the length of the landing. The au pair girl was calling them to get dressed. Soon Hannah would be downstairs.

"May I see the company checkbooks?" Lawson asked.

Darcy went to the safe, took them out, and handed them to the accountant.

Lawson indicated Darcy's desk chair. "And may I sit here?"

"Of course." Now that it was happening, after the weeks of convincing himself that it could not, Darcy felt only a merciful detachment. He watched the man set out his papers, his neat silver pen and his calculator in a leather folder.

"I'll go put some clothes on," Darcy said. He left Lawson,

head bent over the accounts at his own desk like some threatening doppelgänger.

Hannah was out of bed. When he went back into their bedroom, Darcy heard her singing "Eleanor Rigby" in the shower. He went into his own bathroom and shaved, and then dressed in a dark suit better cut than the accountant's, and a silk tie, as if it were one of his days for going to London. Then he went slowly back downstairs. He could hear Mandy talking to Laura and Freddie over their breakfast in the kitchen. The man in his office looked up at Darcy when he came in, then returned to his work.

A little while later, Lawson replaced the cap on his silver pen. His fingers rested on the calculator keypad as he spoke. His voice was perfectly level.

"Darcy, it appears that five unaccounted checks have been drawn on the Templeman company account. Three are in your own name, the others are to Kleinwort Benson. The sum in question amounts to a little over nine hundred thousand pounds. Is there any explanation you would like me to relay to my client?"

"Not immediately," Darcy said. The explanations would come, of course. He would have to begin the counterplay, even though he was so tired that he wondered if he could even lift the telephone.

"I shall have to call Templeman. You do understand that, don't you?"

Darcy inclined his head. He watched Lawson gather his papers and the checkbooks and lock them in his briefcase. He escorted him to the front door and watched him climb into his car and drive away.

"Who was that?" Hannah asked when she came downstairs.

"Geoff Lawson. Came to pick up some papers."

Hannah clicked her tongue, then kissed his cheek. He could smell her perfume. It was one he liked, but he couldn't remember its name.

"How do you feel? I didn't know you were going to town today."

"I'm not," Darcy said vaguely, turning away. "I forgot, when I got dressed."

He went back into his office and sat down at the desk.

Hannah popped her head in the door to say good-bye before

she left for the shop. He heard Mandy leaving to drive the two children to nursery and school, and then Cathy scrambling downstairs and running out to the Renault. It was another sunny morning, he noticed, as the light warmed and brightened the silent room.

Darcy sat at his desk and waited. Somewhere in the house either Lucy or the housekeeper was playing loud music. The cheerful sound intensified his sense of isolation. He looked at the black file drawers ranged against the opposite wall but he did not move to look into them.

The fingers of sunlight moved slowly across the wall. Darcy drank the cup of coffee that the au pair brought him at lunchtime, but ate nothing. Just once, his hand reached out to the telephone, but he did not pick up the receiver. He thought of how Vicky had held him the night before, and her assurance that everything was all right. He would have liked to speak to her, but he remembered that she was at her clinic. His business line rang only two or three times and he sat motionless in his chair, letting the answering machine click and hum in response.

In the afternoon the house came back to life again. Laura and Freddie were at home; he saw Laura run past his window and across the striped breadth of lawn. The sun had moved around the house; his desk was in shadow now. Hannah came back, too, although she did not look in to see him.

Then, at almost five o'clock, when he was stiff and chilled from sitting for so long in the same position, he heard another car coming up from the lane. The front doorbell rang again. Darcy waited, all of his senses strained to anticipate what would come next.

He heard the sound of voices, and the swift click of Hannah's high heels. And then she knocked at his door. "Darcy? There are some people here to see you."

There were three of them. They wore dark blazers, unemphatic striped ties, and cheap watches. When the door had closed again on Hannah's faintly flushed face, one of the men introduced himself and his colleagues. They were from the Fraud Squad.

The senior policeman explained that they had come with a search warrant under the special-procedure provisions of Section 9, Police and Criminal Evidence Act. Darcy didn't move; he had been waiting for this all day. He turned his head and saw Laura running back over the mown grass to Mandy.

And then, because there was nothing else he could do, he gave the three policemen access to his safe and filing cabinets. They stayed in his study for three quarters of an hour. When they left, they took with them most of the books and ledgers and files relating to Darcy's business.

When they had gone, with their evidence in the gray Ford Scorpio that they had arrived in, Darcy walked stiffly into the sunlit drawing room. There were bowls of fat, blood-red peonies on the tables on either side of the fireplace. Hannah and the twins were standing in the middle of the room, watching.

"Who were they?" Hannah asked. She came to him and put her hands on his arms, but the twins stood together, comforting each other. "Darcy, what's happening?"

"They were policemen," he replied.

He saw the identical stiffening of shock and fear in his daughters' beautiful faces, and the way that the color changed in his wife's, leaving two dull blotches of crimson high on her cheekbones.

Darcy said, "Don't worry, it's all right. There's nothing to worry about." His voice sounded brittle, with all the bass resonance gone. He turned away from all three of them.

"I have to go and ring my lawyer," he said in his altered voice.

16

"Mrs. Clegg for you," the medical secretary's nasal voice announced to Michael in his poky hospital office on Tuesday morning.

"Put her through," Michael said. The long day ahead, with its line of patients, was like some sentence he had to serve before Hannah could be delivered to him.

"Michael?"

He smiled into the receiver. "You just caught me. I'm about to do rounds."

"Something's happened. To Darcy." Her voice sounded urgent and thin, stripped of its usual warmth.

"His heart?"

The complex of possibilities that he had already imagined delivered themselves to him again. Even as he envisaged them, Michael realized that his own heart leaped with a wild, momentary hope.

"No. He's all right. Nothing like that."

"Then what?"

"Michael, it's very weird. The police came yesterday evening. They had a special warrant. They took away all Darcy's files and books, everything to do with the business."

"What does Darcy say? Is he there?"

"Yes. He says it's all a mistake. He was on the phone to his lawyer for an hour last night after the police left, and the man has just arrived here now. They're shut up in Darcy's office. It means I can't see you tonight, although I want to so much. I have to be here if Darcy needs me, don't I?"

"Of course you do. Don't worry. It must be some mistake, if Darcy says it is."

But even as he reassured her, Michael was already sifting the possibilities in his mind, weighing the chances that Darcy might in truth be guilty of something. There had often seemed to be just too much money at Wilton, an overheated largesse spilling out of Darcy in a way that Michael suddenly and perfectly clearly recognized as ominous.

"I hope you're right," Hannah whispered.

The vibration of doubt and anxiety in her voice was plainly to be heard now. Michael understood that she was not convinced by Darcy's protestations.

"Listen," he said urgently. He had to grasp at a thread of hope because the promise of their evening had been snatched away.

"I had planned to go to a medical conference next week. Two nights away, Wednesday and Thursday. Marcelle knows I'm going. I'm supposed to be presenting a paper, but David Keene, one of my colleagues and the paper's co-author, came to ask me this morning if he could read it instead. There isn't the funding for both of us to go. If you could manage to be away, too, we could go somewhere together instead. Could we?"

Now that Darcy had further hemmed them in with uncertainties, it seemed vital to have this much to hold on to.

"I don't know." Hannah sounded distracted. He couldn't blame her, but it was suddenly imperative that she should agree to what a minute ago had only been the vaguest possibility.

"Please," Michael said.

"I . . . I could do it, if I said I was going on a buying trip for the shop. If all this is resolved by then . . ."

"It will be. That's what we'll do." Michael could see a posse of white coats in the corridor outside. He was already late for rounds. "I have to go. Listen, Hannah. I love you."

He had said it before, in the cushiony sanctuary of her shop. He wasn't even certain that he meant it now, but in the shabby and pressured reality of the hospital morning it seemed better, even nobler, to feel this threatening and disorientating love rather than to feel nothing at all.

"Do you?" Hannah doubted him, too, but he could not stay to tell her any more.

"I'll call you tomorrow," Michael promised.

* * *

On the evening of the same day, Cathy and Lucy Clegg sat in the upstairs room at Wilton that Hannah had designated as the older childrens' sitting room. It had a pretty view of the garden and the fields that dipped toward Grafton, but it was underdecorated compared with the rest of the house. The curtains were no more than striped ticking hung on plain wooden poles, and the walls were bare except for a series of tired Guns'n'Roses posters that were beginning to peel away from their Blu-Tak anchors. There was a sofa on either side of the empty fireplace, each heaped with magazines and broken-spined paperbacks. In the past, the room had been a place of refuge from Hannah and the upholstered extravagance of the rest of the house.

Lucy was sitting on one of the sofas with her hands folded behind her head. Cathy was leafing through a book. They had been sitting in silence for what seemed a very long time.

Lucy suddenly said, "I hate all this waiting. It's horrible being suspended, not knowing how to go forward or back. I don't know what to do, and now there's this with Daddy, too. What's going to happen?"

Cathy watched her as she stood up and went to the window. They were waiting for Barney to arrive, because Darcy had said that he wanted to speak to the three of them together. The house was full of a queasy silence that barely contained the confusion of the day.

"I don't know," Cathy answered. "I don't understand what's going on. But I do know one thing—*you* can't wait much longer. You have to decide what to do."

Lucy did not turn from the window. "He's not going to do anything, is he?" she whispered. "I thought he might. I thought he might come after all, when he had had time to realize what it meant. Me and his baby. And then how would it have been, if I had already had an abortion?"

"Jimmy isn't going to come for you," Cathy said. "How could he? Think of the damage it would cause."

They had trodden this ground before.

"He hasn't even called me."

"I know that. Lucy, do you want to go ahead and have the baby by yourself?"

Lucy crossed her hands over her chest and massaged her own arms. Up until today, although she understood the reality perfectly well, she had let herself hope that Jimmy might contradict everything she had learned about him and come to her rescue. That he had not wasn't surprising, but it was the tiny hope itself that had become precious. She longed to hold on to it. But now there were other reckonings to be made.

Darcy had always been the secure and generous rock in his children's lives. Yet suddenly he was not only ill, betraying a frailty that she had never even imagined before, but there were also other more disturbing intimations of his fallibility. Lucy could only dimly conceive what the visits from policemen and lawyers and the urgent telephonings and Hannah's half-concealed tears might really mean, but she felt that the structure of security and insulation, never so much as questioned before, was being knocked out from underneath her. Lucy began to be afraid that not only might her father not be able to look after her forever, however terribly the world might assault her, but that without warning he might have ceased to be her protector and be instead in need of *her* protection.

The thought made her feel exposed and precarious, but also suddenly and surprisingly older. She pressed her fist into her stomach as if she wanted to reach inside.

"No," Lucy said. "I don't want to go ahead and have the baby by myself."

"Then there's only one alternative, isn't there?" Cathy lifted her blond head. "Listen—I think Barney's here."

They heard Barney's voice and the rumble of their father's. Then the door opened and Barney appeared, with Darcy behind him. Darcy had changed out of his business suit into an old sweater. His shoulders were hunched forward.

He's old, Lucy realized with a surge of panic stronger than what she had felt when she witnessed his heart attack. *He's an old man.*

Darcy waited while his children sat down. Barney glanced at his sisters, his face telling them that he didn't understand this mysterious summons or the air of foreboding in the room any more than they did.

Darcy himself wouldn't sit down. He began pacing the floor, his big head half-turned away from them. As he walked, he told them that they had better hear what would soon be public knowledge.

"I am accused of theft," he said. "My client Vincent Templeman and his accountant claim that I have by means of forgery and false accounting misappropiated for my own use certain funds belonging to Templeman's private company."

Darcy turned, completing one negotiation of the room and beginning another. It seemed that he was intent on fitting his words to the number of paces. His children sat still, waiting, their eyes fixed on him. Lucy had opened her mouth in protest, but Barney took her hand and held it, silencing her.

"The police were informed, which is why they came here last night. They have taken away various sets of books without which I can't continue to do business. My lawyer advises me that there will be some charges to answer. I don't know yet exactly what will happen. But I think there will be . . . publicity, difficulties, before everything is set right again. Because the business is based in this house, it won't only be difficult for me, but for you and Hannah, too. I wanted to tell you."

Darcy reached the window yet again. This time he stopped and stood, as Lucy had done, with his back to them. "I wanted to tell you myself, and to say I am sorry."

There was a silence while his words fitted together in his children's minds and began to make threatening sense out of random impressions.

Lucy sat upright. "They can't accuse you," she shouted. "They can't just say you've done something you haven't. This is a free country, not . . . not some police state."

Barney was still holding her hand. She realized that he was hurting her by trying to hold her down and she snatched it away.

"Dad?"

Darcy turned again, and each of them could tell the weight that he was carrying from the sluggishness of the movement.

"I know you didn't do it," Barney said, "but what's the basis of the accusation?"

Darcy smiled, the upward lift of the muscles not quite aligning, and his upper teeth showing so that he looked momentarily, grotesquely, as if he had suffered a stroke.

He's being brave, Lucy thought. *He's being brave because he has to be.*

"I haven't done anything dishonest. But you know who I am. I'm not always conventional. I have been a maverick. I wouldn't be where I am now, would I, if I had never broken a rule?"

He shrugged with a gesture of dismissal. Out of bravado he was trying to be the father they had always known, and the threadbare attempt made the change in him all the more disturbing. For a few seconds none of them could think of anything to say without dislodging the fragile construction of Darcy's assurances. The three children sat still, looking nowhere, trying to assimilate what he had told them, to piece together their own interpretation out of the windy spaces between his words.

"Then it's all right," Cathy said at last. She stood up and went to Darcy, and he put his arms gratefully around her, stroking her hair as she leaned her head against him.

"That's my girl," he said.

Lucy and Barney followed her lead. They wrapped their arms around their father, and their combined strength made his frailty more apparent to all of them.

"Don't worry," Lucy told him.

"I'm not worried. Not at all. Only for what it might mean for the three of you, and Hannah, and Laura and Freddie. If I hadn't been ill, you know, I could have put everything back in order. No trouble. A matter of days, that was all it was."

They didn't want to ask him any more. Their conjectures were enough.

"There we are, then," Darcy said, with his terrible, hollow, confident bluster. "Now you know all there is to know. Thanks for being such good kids. I'd better go back downstairs to your mother."

This vagueness was telling to them all. "To Hannah, that is," Darcy corrected himself.

* * *

Hannah was in the drawing room. The space filled with warm, diffuse light and the planes and angles of polished surfaces and billows of soft fabrics seemed newly precious to him but, because of his fear, troubling as well.

"Did you tell them? Did they understand?" Hannah asked.

"Yes, of course they did. Wouldn't they?" Darcy responded in the cheerful, positive manner that was important for him to adopt. He went to the silver tray and picked up a bottle from their shining ranks. Alcohol would blunt the sharp edge of his anxiety, he knew that, although it would not dispel the dark mass itself. "Let's have a drink, shall we? Celebrate getting to the end of today?"

Upstairs, Lucy had begun to cry in heavy sobs. Barney looked at her, his good-humored face creased with concern.

"He'll put it right. It doesn't sound too healthy now, but I'm sure he will."

"It isn't only that." She took a ragged breath, staring at him with streaming eyes. Lucy looked ugly when she cried. She shouted at him, "I'm pregnant! I don't know what to do! I want to tell Dad about it!"

Barney turned to Cathy, who nodded somberly.

"Who?" Barney asked.

Lucy told him outright. "Jimmy Rose."

While his sisters watched him, Barney assimilated this.

"Then you can't tell him." Barney was rarely angry, but they saw his anger kindling now. "You can't bloody well dump that on him as well. You can see how he is, can't you?"

Lucy's cheeks wobbled with her sobbing. All her outrage at the turn her life was taking was expressed in her cry, "What about *me*?"

"I'm sorry about you."

"You sound it."

"Barney," Cathy warned him. "Look at her."

Barney sighed. His big hands floundered in the air around his sisters' shoulders.

"I am sorry, Luce. I am. Only you can't run down to Dad now, at this of all times, and tell him his best friend's got you pregnant.

What were you doing with Jimmy Rose anyway? He's old enough
to be your father. How can you have let it happen?"

"The pill. I forget it sometimes. And I thought I loved him."

"*Jimmy Rose?*" Barney let out a long, derisive breath. And then
he nodded, understanding her even if unwillingly.

"Yeah. Okay. I can imagine how. Poor Lucy, but you can't tell
Dad about it. You've told me instead. And what I ought to do right
now is go around to see Jimmy Rose and kick his ass up his windpipe."

"Put his balls in the Cuisinart?" Cathy murmured.

"Yeah. And his dick on a skewer. The little rat."

A small sound came out of Lucy that wasn't a sob or a sniff.
She had let out an unexpected peal of laughter.

"That's better," Barney said. He sat down next to her, holding
her and cradling her head against him. He whispered with his
mouth close to her ear, persuading her now that there was a chink
in her misery. "So we can sort this out ourselves?"

Lucy nodded slowly. "I want to have an abortion. And get away
from Grafton."

"Sure thing," Barney promised her.

Nina heard the knock and saw Barney standing on the step.

"Are you working?" he asked her.

"Yes."

"Can I come in anyway?"

She held open the door. Nina was not surprised to see him;
Barney had taken to dropping in on her without calling first, as if
he felt that it might be too easy for her to turn him down on the
telephone. What was surprising to her was that she was not at all
displeased by his arrival in the middle of her workday.

Barney followed her down to the kitchen. He gestured for her
permission, then went to the refrigerator and took out a can of the
beer she had begun to keep there for him. Nina also liked the
familiarity and freedom he took with her tidy arrangements. It
made her empty house seem populated. Barney pulled at the metal
tag, and over the little hiss of gas he asked her the question. "How's
it going?"

Instead of irritating her, this made her feel much younger, as if she were still part of some conspiracy in which work and responsibility were inconveniences to be negotiated before the real business of life, pleasure, could continue. Nina laughed as she told him. "Well, thank you. I've done lots of work. Been to London about a new commission. And you?"

Barney drank some beer.

"Not so good."

Nina recomposed her face, ready for a recital of catastrophes that might have befallen Barney's car or this week's studies.

"Tell me?"

He moved away from the corner of the table where he had been leaning and came across the kitchen to her. His surplus energy made him look awkward but also graceful, and she knew before he reached her that she wanted to touch him. When he took hold of her she let herself fit neatly against him.

"Come upstairs?" he asked when he had kissed her.

"We can't always go up to bed."

"Why not?"

"Um. I can't think of any specific reason, now you ask me. Just that one shouldn't always give way to one's urges. As a matter of principle. Self-discipline."

"Crap," Barney said.

In the end, she led him upstairs to her room.

In bed, he was awkward and graceful in just the same way as when he sloped across her kitchen or worked in her small garden. He acknowledged his over-eagerness and occasional clumsiness, and when he smiled at himself, with their faces so close together, his eyes seemed to flatten and slide apart so that she imagined that she was looking into the mask of some friendly, healthy, silent animal. Then, if she tried to guide him with a small movement of her thighs or wrists, his face would sharpen with the intensity of his concentration, like an animal again, and she would be quick to reassure him with another movement, lest he should misunderstand her intention and be hurt.

The second or third time he came into her bed Nina had asked him, "How many girls have you made love to?"

"Half a dozen. Six," he corrected himself in case this should sound dismissive, "including you."

"The same as me. Lovers, that is," Nina told him.

This limited history of hers diminished the distance between them. But unlike Gordon, Barney did not ask her to talk about Richard, or any of the other features of her unknown and therefore irrelevant past. Barney's appetites were all for the present. After the rawness that Gordon's departure left under her skin, Barney's puppyish immediacy seemed natural, and inevitable, and welcome to her.

With the palms of her hands Nina traced the solid muscles of his back while Barney made love to her. She began by dreamily staring up at the ceiling, beyond him, but his insistence drew her in and made her an equal participant, as it had done each of the times before. This, as well as other things about him, surprised and pleased her.

Afterward, when they lay with their arms around each other, Nina reminded him,

"You said before that something was wrong. Was that why you came to see me?"

"Nope." He moved his finger along the prominent ridge of her collarbone and grinned at her, flat-eyed like a satisfied animal. "But there is something. Can I tell you?"

"Of course you can."

He told her first about Lucy and Jimmy Rose. Nina listened, and although Barney's account of Lucy's difficulty was brief and bloodless, it propelled her back fifteen years into her own late teens.

In her first year away from home, Nina had fallen in love, for the first time, with a painter of difficult and non-commercial abstracts who taught at her art school. Within three months she was pregnant, and within as many weeks the painter had faded out of her orbit and resubmerged himself in his life with a wife and two small children.

After she had listened to what Barney had to tell her, Nina offered her own story in response.

"His name was Dennis O'Malley," she confessed. "He was not so unlike Jimmy. I haven't thought about him in years."

"What did you do?"

"Had an abortion."

The thought of Lucy Clegg sharpened her memories; Nina

found that she could recall exactly the metal-framed furniture in the office where an unsympathetic doctor had interviewed her, the street in a London suburb where she had walked up and down under the plane trees for hours before deciding finally to enter the clinic, and the nauseating complex of feelings—fear and loneliness and anger, with the alarming longing for the baby itself—that was all the more disturbing for having to be stifled and denied. Afterward she had felt empty and stricken.

Those brief weeks carrying the flutter of fear had been the only pregnancy Nina had achieved. When Gordon Ransome had admired her flat and unmarked belly, she hadn't told him the whole truth. Nor had she kept the promise to herself, made when she reemerged into the suburban street, that she would never again entangle herself with a married man.

She thought of Star now, and the cool and dignified way she moved through the Grafton parties, her face turned away from Jimmy's antics, and the offer of friendship she had extended to Nina. Nina wondered how many other Lucys there were, and whether Star knew about them, and, with a kind of internal shrinking, as if to deflect a blow, she also thought of Vicky Ransome. Nina shifted a little, turning away from Barney and onto her back so that she could look up again at the impassive ceiling.

"Lucy's going to have an abortion, too," Barney said.

"As long as that is what she wants. And Jimmy?"

"Jimmy nothing."

"Yes, I see."

Barney came closer to her. She could feel the tiny currents of displaced air between them in the places where their naked skin did not quite touch.

Barney said, "There's an added complication. To do with Darcy. Maybe I shouldn't tell you this, but I can't ask for your help without letting you know why. Can I?"

Nina sighed. "I don't know. I think you imagine I'm much wiser than I really am. The truth is that I'm full of confusion and misgivings."

"Please. I need to tell you."

"Then do."

She listened again, this time to Barney's much longer account of the police arriving at Wilton, and the suppressed concern in the house, and Darcy's blustering, clay-footed explanation of the events to his children. Nina was filled with sympathy for Hannah, and for Darcy, because she liked him, although she did not believe that he was entirely incapable of a criminal act.

And then an image came into Nina's head, as pin-sharp as if it were projected on to the blank plaster above her. She saw the Grafton couples dancing, two-by-two, as she had first seen them at the Frosts' Halloween, only the smiles that they wore were the Halloween masks, and behind the masks there were the hollowed faces made unfamiliar by the shadows of secrets and fallibility. She saw herself among them, first with Gordon and then, in response to some unseen dance-master, changing her partner to Barney. Around her the couples changed their partners, too, and danced on in their broken gavotte, their faces hidden behind the grinning masks.

"Are you asleep?" Barney whispered.

She had turned away from him a little and had kept very still, but she had heard every word he said. He hadn't asked her what she thought, nor even suggested that his father was anything but innocent. Nina liked him the more for it. She thought that Darcy would be generously supported by his family.

Nina turned her back to him again. "No, I'm not asleep. Poor Darcy. I'm sorry."

She kissed the corners of the boy's mouth and held him. Now she did feel the span of the years separating them.

"Do you see what it means?" Barney was intent on his explanation. "Lucy wants to tell Darcy what's happened to her so that he can make it better. That's what he does, always has done for her. Only she mustn't now. He shouldn't have to worry about anything else."

"I think your instinct is right," Nina said.

"It's just that Lucy isn't particularly . . . stable, or reliable. She needs someone who knows what to do, to help her get through it. So I'm asking you. Is that trespassing too much?"

The small movement he made took in their proximity, and the tiny world they made together between the curled ends of Nina's bed.

"No, it isn't trespassing at all. I could give Lucy the number of my gynecologist. He's on Harley Street, although there are plenty of other places and different agencies that Lucy could go to. But I know that Doctor Walsh will understand what she needs and how it should be handled. I should think that with his help Lucy could be in and out of a clinic within a couple of days."

"How much will it cost?"

The memories of that distant, suburban clinic and the doctors behind their metal desks and her own long-ago desolation gathered around Nina again. She was not sure whether to interfere at all in Lucy Clegg's life would be damaging, but now that she had come this far she resolved that she might as well go on. She said very carefully, "You can tell Lucy that I can easily afford to help with that, too. Perhaps she can pay me back one day."

Barney touched her cheek, and then her mouth, with the tips of his fingers. She could see the relief in his eyes. Nina was pleased to be able to offer him what he and Lucy needed, but she knew that she was also doing it for Star's sake. If Star could be shielded from at least this much, then it would be something.

"And if Lucy would like somewhere in London to stay, before or afterward, just for a day or so, we could always ask Patrick."

"Thank you," Barney said humbly.

"Not at all," Nina murmured. He answered by kissing her, and she felt the neat contraction of her own pleasure in response to him.

It was raining. Thick ropes of water twisted out of the gray layers of sky overhead, bouncing up again and breaking into steely threads as they hit the streaming pavements. Hannah and Michael ran, hand-in-hand, with the wetness plastering their hair to their skulls and cheeks and soaking in black patches across their shoulders, gluing their clothes to their skin. They ran, ducking through the rain-stalled London traffic, until Hannah was gasping for breath and stumbling in her ruined shoes.

"I can't run anymore."

"It's not far," Michael called to her.

There were lines of taxis in the streets, but not one of them offered the comfort of a yellow light. He pulled her on behind him, across the murky rivers swirling in the gutters, until they turned a corner and saw the windows of their hotel. A minute later, with the doorman offering them the pointless protection of his umbrella, they reached the revolving door and were delivered into the mirrored warmth of the hotel lobby.

"Safe," Michael proclaimed. He was exhilarated by the dash through the rain. He took Hannah's soaking arm and steered her into the lift, and they were swept upward in the company of their own dripping but still flatteringly tinted reflections. They left a trail of watery steps down the corridor to the door of their room.

"Let me dry you," Michael said. He came out of the bathroom with an armful of towels, and he unbuttoned Hannah's clothes and bundled them away from her and knelt down to unstrap her shoes from her cold feet. He swathed the towels around her and patted her face dry, seeing how the black stuff with which she made up her eyes had touchingly blotted over the soft, pouchy skin beneath the lashes. The rain clattered against the windows, isolating them in the hotel bedroom with its glazed chintzes and empty cupboards. Michael thought the moment was both sexy and melancholy, but when he turned his mind to try to pin down either his excitement or sadness, they both slid away from him, leaving him standing awkwardly in his wet clothes, with Hannah in her towels held against him.

"I'm cold," she said.

"Have a hot bath and get into bed. I'll order us some tea."

It was five in the afternoon. They had already spent one night together, under the gray eye of the television perched at the foot of the bed. Michael had tried to submerge himself in Hannah until his insistence had made her ask him, only half-jokingly, "What are you trying to prove, Doctor Wickham? This isn't a competition."

"I just want you," he had answered. "I can't help it. Do you want it to be different?"

Only he had not been able quite to submerge himself, however intimately he connected himself to the folds and fissures of Hannah's body, and so he was troubled by a sense of separation from her. She was still herself, and desirable to him, but they were not quite easy with each other. Michael found that he was thinking about Marcelle and his children, that their faces and voices inserted themselves between Hannah and himself, when he had wanted to dismiss them just for these few hours.

Today Michael had followed Hannah to some designers' showrooms. He had sat a little apart, uncomfortable in a visitor's chair, while house models paraded clothes in front of Hannah. He had liked to see this other, businesslike side of her, but she shrugged at his questions.

"It's just a matter of picking what I like, what I think I can sell. I don't even need to go to the showrooms, really. I just made the appointments to give myself an alibi for being here with you."

He had felt flattered by that, but the sense of distance between them had not been dispelled. They ate an indifferent lunch in a restaurant he had chosen from the *Good Food Guide*, and afterward, without admitting that they felt at a loss, they went into the National Gallery. They had wandered through the Sainsbury Wing with the tourists, exiled from their proper setting among the Japanese tour groups and elderly American couples, and afterward they had emerged into the downpour.

Michael felt energized by the plunge through the streets, and the stinging rain, as if the woolly insulation between Hannah and himself had been washed away. When she emerged from her hot bath, pink and glowing, his desire for her recharged itself without any tinge of guilty melancholy. The tray of tea with silver teapot and thin china was brought by a white-coated waiter, but when he had withdrawn they let it go cold on the side table. Michael knelt over Hannah's rosy body so that she could close her warm mouth around him.

He felt as he had done the first time, within the curtains of her shop and afterward, clean, hollowed out, reconciled. He lay there for a little while, drifting in the trivial backwaters of his own imagination.

Then, when he looked at Hannah's face on the pillow beside him, he was amazed to see that she was crying.

"What is it? Hannah, what have I done?"

At first she wouldn't say anything. She shook her head, and more tears squeezed out from beneath her eyelids.

"You must tell me. I can't put it right unless you tell me." A flicker of irritation came with the sense of his own powerlessness.

"It's all right," she muttered, contradicting everything he could see. "It's nothing to do with you. Or not really. I felt lonely, suddenly."

"Lonely, when we're this close?" He smiled and pressed his lips against her cheek to comfort her. But his awareness of the distance between them returned, intensified by Hannah's recognition of it, too. Looking at the close tangle of her hair, robbed by the rain of its springy distance from her skull, he saw that the roots were darker than the honey-colored strands. Her vulnerability oppressed him.

Hannah cried for a minute, snuffling damply against his shoulder. Then she lifted her head and stretched her round arm to the brocade-boxed bedside tissues.

"Sorry."

"Don't be silly. But I don't like to see you cry." That was true. It was the courageous, chairlift Hannah he valued, the foil to his own cowardice, and her erotic mutation into the woman he had discovered within the Bedouin tent of her shop. He did not care so much for this weepy, sniffing version.

"I'm worried about Darcy. I'm afraid of what's going to happen next, and he won't tell me anything except that it's all going to be all right."

Michael stroked her hair. "Of course you're worried."

"Most of all I'm worried that I won't be able to cope with whatever it is that's coming. Arrest, trial, I don't know. I want to be able to withstand whatever he has to face up to, and I'm afraid of letting him down."

The tears had started to gather again at the corners of her eyes. She dabbed at them with a tissue.

"I'm completely certain you'll be able to cope," Michael assured her. "I know you well enough for that."

"Do you think?"

"I know."

Hannah blew her nose. "I think I just needed a good cry." Then she laughed, with the corners of her mouth moving as if she were a film actress who had just been told to go for a close-up. "That's better. Stupid, isn't it? If this isn't letting him down, I wonder what is?"

"Do you wish we hadn't come?"

"No," Hannah said after she had thought about it. "I don't wish that at all." She snuggled closer to him, and he put his arm around her, settling his chin against her matted hair.

"What would you like to do this evening?" he asked her.

"Nothing at all. Stay here like this and watch television. Have room service later, with those silver domes on a heated trolley disguised as a table."

He picked up the television remote control and clicked it.

They lay back amidst the tangle of sheets and pillows and watched the end of Channel 4 News. Michael felt that the fragile shell of their intimacy had been tossed like a tiny boat through some sudden storm and had pitched through it, waterlogged but still afloat, into a calmer sea.

It was this pleasure at the survival of some delicate organism that Michael took back with him to Grafton. Hannah had caught an early train, and Michael drove home alone. He realized that their brief, awkward time together had left him with a residue of happiness, and the happiness colored the dull drive and softened his apprehension at returning. He turned on the radio and whistled as he drove. He felt a generalized affection and tolerance for all the world, and a new tenderness for his wife and children.

When he reached his house he first saw the front garden, the neat oval of raked gravel under the cherry tree and the peony bush heavy with red, taut buds, and then Marcelle's car parked in front of the garage doors. He had expected that Marcelle would be at the school at this time of day, but there was still the ghost of a whistle in his head as he lifted his briefcase out of the car. He put his key in the front door and let himself in. The house was quiet, but emanated a comforting note that it took him a second to identify as the smell of cooking.

Michael walked through to the kitchen. Marcelle was there, standing at one of the countertops amid a muddle of bowls and utensils. When she looked, her face was like a cold blade.

"How was the conference?" she asked.

He hesitated, apprehension prickling him. "Fine. Like all the others. Interesting in parts. Why aren't you at school?"

"Was your paper well received?"

"Yes. Very well. Rather gratifying."

Michael picked up the handful of letters waiting for him and flipped through them, registering nothing. The tension in the air was like a smell, poisonous, the opposite of the wholesome scent of food.

"What are you cooking?" he asked.

When Marcelle didn't answer he looked across at her. Her hands were jerking around in a mound of flour. A little puff of it rose and drifted up like incense.

"I don't know," Marcelle murmured. "Isn't that funny? I've no idea what I'm doing."

Her head fell forward, and the cords in her neck tightened as her mouth gaped and she began to cry. Michael stared at her, appalled.

"You haven't been to the conference," Marcelle said suddenly.

Michael thought of the volleys of accusations and lies that would follow if he attempted a denial.

"No," he agreed.

"Where have you been?"

"In London."

"Why did you lie to me?" The knifelike accusation was gone from her face now, which was contorted in pain instead. Michael hunched his shoulders to protect himself against it.

"Because I didn't want you to be hurt."

"Who were you with?"

"Marcelle, do you have to know that? Does it make any difference?" He took two steps across the enormity of space that separated them and tried to touch her arm.

Marcelle tilted her head on one side, as if giving the question due consideration.

"I suppose not. Not to the fact that everything has ended." She lifted her hands and the flour puffed up again, as if she were trying to whiten the blackness around them. "This is how marriages end, isn't it? Ever since I met Caroline Keene on Wednesday and she told me how generous she and David thought you were to let him go in your place and present the paper, I've been thinking, so *this* is how it happens. Even to us. It just finishes."

Michael tried to think back to a time when he and Marcelle had been happy in this house. He knew that there had been such a time, but he could not locate it now by a date, a particular year. Had it been when the children were smaller? Before they were born? It seemed now that his feelings of tenderness as he drove down from London had been no more than post-coital sentimentality.

"If you say so," he answered tonelessly.

"I telephoned Wilton," Marcelle went on. "Cathy told me that Hannah was in London for a couple of days."

Caroline Keene, Michael thought. It must be a year since she and Marcelle had last met. Why should they have encountered each other on that particular, critical day? Then he was surprised by his own resentment. It was inevitable that they should have, wasn't it?

"This hasn't anything to do with Hannah. It has to do with you and me first, Marcelle, do you understand that? Hannah is only what happened next."

Marcelle was crying. These were not pretty, photogenic tears that asked to be brushed away, like Hannah's.

"What do you want to do?" Michael asked.

"I want you to leave. You can't just come back here, strolling in with your bag and your fully-fucked smile, expecting to be fed and fueled and serviced ready for the next adventure. What happens is that you lose me and your children and your home. But you're half-gone already. Why not go the whole way?" Michael made no response. She continued, after a pause, "You can find out how it is without us. See if you like it better out there. Perhaps Hannah will be able to do everything for you. If it doesn't mean she might break a red bloody fingernail."

"You're angry," Michael said at last. "Don't be angry with Hannah. She has enough difficulties of her own, whatever you think of her at this minute."

"Yes. I'm *angry*."

There were white flecks at the corners of Marcelle's mouth, and she ran her powdered fingers through her wild hair. He was afraid of her.

"I'm so angry that I want to kill you. I want to hurt you. I want it so that . . ." The words escaped her, and she licked her smirched lips and then clenched her fists, staring at the knuckles as if they belonged to someone else. "I want it so that you know what it feels like."

Then she turned her back on him. She stumbled away to the window and stood there, her face hidden and her whole body stricken with her crying.

"I'm sorry it's such a shock. I'm sorry for what I did," Michael said helplessly.

Marcelle turned once more. "I want you to *go!*" she screamed at him. "Get out of here!"

"What have you told the children? What do you think it's going to mean to them, if their father suddenly isn't here any longer?"

"Why didn't *you* think about that?" She ran at him, with her arms swinging, and struck at his face and head with her floury hands. He had to struggle to hold her, to keep her at bay.

"Stop it. Marcelle, *fuck* you."

They were both still shouting when the front doorbell rang.

"It's the children. Janice brings them home on Fridays."

Marcelle stepped back from him, panting. She wiped her mouth with the back of her hand and pulled at the whitish horn of hair that sprang from her forehead.

Michael walked down the hall to the front door. Through the frosted glass panels he could see the dark, round heads of his children and the comfortable bulk of Janice behind them.

"Hello," she called. "All well?"

Jonathan and Daisy sidled past him, pale-faced.

"Yes, thanks, Janice. Have a good weekend."

He closed the door against the bright outdoors.

"Hi, kids. Had a good day?" His voice sounded as false as a clown's red nose.

"Where's Mum?" Jonathan asked.

"In the kitchen," Michael said.

Going in, the two children moved to either side of Marcelle. Trembling, she put her arms around their shoulders.

"What is this?" Michael asked, watching them range themselves against him. He was rebuffed by the accusing stares of his children.

"Your father wants to tell you something," Marcelle said.

"Marcelle," he warned her. "Don't do this in front of them."

"Why not? *Why not?* Are you ashamed now? Don't you think they have a right to know what their father has done?"

The children's rounded eyes looked from one parent to the other.

"It's okay," Jonathan said. His mouth was drawn tight with his efforts not to cry.

"Why do you always have to be like this?" Daisy burst out. Jonathan kept his anxiety within a shell of control, but his sister couldn't.

Michael wondered. *Are we always like this?* He didn't even know how much of the discord between himself and Marcelle had seeped into the children's lives. He felt vanquished, defeated by the impossibility of trying to reassure them.

"Come here."

He opened his arms to encourage them, but they stayed at Marcelle's side. Michael hated her for forcing this division on them, but then he thought that she would claim he had created the divide himself, long ago. Yet it seemed that Jonathan and Daisy had always belonged first to Marcelle, and only then to him. That was the way Marcelle had ordained it.

Michael let his arms fall to his side. He said quickly, to get it over with, "Your mother is very angry with me, and she's right to be. I told her a lie about where I've been the last two days. But that isn't the only trouble between us. We haven't been making each other very happy. I'm sure you know that, in a way."

"So what's going to happen?" Jonathan asked, out of his clenched mouth.

"I think I'm going to have to leave. To live somewhere else for now."

Jonathan nodded, very quickly two or three times, as if he were merely satisfied to get the facts.

"Daddy, I love you," Daisy burst out. She ran to him and threw her arms around his waist, crying noisily. Over her head Michael looked at Marcelle. *This is indeed how it ends*, he thought. *With a strip of kitchen floor between us like a crevasse.*

"See? Do you see what you have done?" he shouted at Marcelle.

"I didn't do it. You did," she spat at him.

Michael knelt down so that he could look at Daisy. "I love you, too. I always will, and we'll always be your parents, whatever happens."

Daisy began to wail, "No. Nooo! Don't!"

He stood up again. As firmly as he could, he steered her back to her mother. Then he left the kitchen and went upstairs, noting the scratches in the wallpaper and the chips like little eyes gouged out of the paint, the honorable scars of family life. He packed another suitcase and came downstairs again. The house had fallen silent once more. He could not think of how to say good-bye, and so he didn't try. He closed the front door softly behind him.

17

The doorbell began to ring. Once it had started it seemed that it would never stop; whoever was doing it must be holding his thumb pressed to the buzzer.

Darcy was already awake, lying in bed beside Hannah in the room flooded with yellow early-morning light, but still the sound pierced his skull like a dart. He had not heard any car.

Hannah stirred and mumbled. "What is it?"

Darcy left the bed and put on his dressing gown over his pyjamas.

"I'll go see," he said.

He met the au pair at the top of the stairs. She too was in her dressing gown.

"I'll get it," Darcy said to her. The bell stopped shrilling and was replaced by a barrage of knocking. The stairway dipped in front of him, and the wide mouth of the hallway, and the slivers and lozenges of reflected sunlight lay like broken glass on the floor. He could hear the sounds of his children waking up, disturbed by the thunderous noise.

Darcy descended the stairs, flat-footed in his slippers.

He opened the door, but he already knew who he would find there. There were five of them this time, not the same, but enough like the men who had come before. They wore shirts and ties and short casual jackets, aggressive clothes, and in his nightwear Darcy felt vulnerable and exposed.

"Why are there so many of you?" he asked. It was half past six in the morning, nearly the end of May.

"Darcy Clegg?" one of the policemen said.

"You know who I am. Yes, I'm Darcy Clegg."

"My name is Detective Inspector Hely, Serious Fraud Office."

The other four men had come into the house and gathered in a phalanx around Darcy, as if they were afraid that in defiance of them and his faltering heart he might still break out and try to run away across the lawns and into the dewy countryside.

"I have a warrant for your arrest."

The policeman recited the charges and advised him of his rights. To Darcy the scene had a cardboard quality, like the cheapest of cheap police dramas. In his cold and rational moments he had understood that they would come in just this way, and had feared and dreaded it, yet now that it was happening it seemed insignificant, almost comical. He might even have laughed, until he turned and looked behind him and saw the ring of faces at the top of the stairs.

Freddie and Laura stood behind the banisters, gripping the oak spindles with their hands, staring down in bewilderment. Cathy hovered beside them, with her suntanned legs bare underneath her short robe. Lucy had gone to London for some reason, Darcy recalled. He knew that the policemen were staring up at his daughter, too. Her beauty struck him anew, and he felt a spasm of despair that he should have exposed her to this. He saw Barney with her, rubbing his face in disbelief, and then Hannah pushing past them and running downstairs.

Hannah's robe was silk, like her nightdress, and the sheeny double skin seemed to slide over the loose curves underneath it as she ran. The policemen looked at her, and Darcy knew that they would talk about this afterward, and laugh about it. He clenched his fists, and in a welter of hot images wondered if he tried to hit them whether they would pinion his arms behind him and tell him to come quietly. He felt an inappropriate urge to laugh again, and his heart squeezed, a needle of pain in his chest before inflating again, to remind him that he was old. And guilty.

Hannah grabbed his arm. "What do they want?" She asked him.

She was holding her hair back with one hand, and down the calyx of her sleeve Darcy saw the way the soft flesh of her underarm sagged away from the bone. This evidence of her aging reminded him that he loved her, and of the life that he had seemingly destroyed by trying to preserve it. That was all he had tried to do, wasn't it? The mechanism of denial quivered wearily within him again, and the detachment of being a spectator at a bad drama faded and left him.

"We shall have to ask you to come with us," Hely said.

Darcy wanted to lay his head on his wife's shoulder. He felt tired enough to close his eyes.

"They have come to arrest me," he said.

At the top of the stairs, Mandy was trying to lead Laura and Freddie away. Laura began to howl. Hannah spun around to the policeman. She looked ready to fight him herself and shouted at him, "You can't come to an innocent man's house and drag him away in front of his children."

"Don't, Hannah," Darcy said. "It's all right. There's nothing to worry about." It was the litany he had repeated to her a hundred times already, but the look of disbelief that he saw broadening across her face made it seem a pointless reiteration.

"I may get dressed first, I suppose?" he asked the policemen.

Barney and Cathy were beside him.

"Can they do this?" Barney demanded of Darcy.

"Yes, we can," one of the younger men said with relish. "Even to your dad."

Two of the policemen accompanied Darcy upstairs. They let him dress in a dark suit, but they did not give him time to shave. When they came down again Darcy looked shrunken inside the dark envelope of his clothes.

"When will you let him out?" Hannah demanded.

"I couldn't say," the senior policeman told her. "The charges are serious, and bail depends on a number of factors."

"It shouldn't take long, perhaps only a few hours," Darcy said. "Call McIntyre and tell him what's happened. Tell him to get there as soon as he can."

The men took Darcy outside, the two of them who walked on either side of him, holding his upper arms. They ducked into one of the waiting cars with him. Hannah and Barney and Cathy went out after them, but Darcy did not turn around as he was being driven away.

Barney muttered, "Oh, Christ, I can't believe it. Why didn't he say it meant *this*? What has he done?"

Hannah turned to him, hard-eyed, as angry as when she had confronted the policemen.

"He's done nothing." Her forefinger with its red nail jabbed at Barney, as if she were going to gouge it into him. "Nothing at all. Remember that when they ask you."

Then she broke away from them and ran back into the house.

The news traveled quickly enough. By the evening of the same day all the Grafton couples and seemingly most of the rest of the world had heard about Darcy's arrest. Hannah grimly answered the telephone every time it rang. To the newspapers and their reporters with their insinuating or openly insulting questions she responded with a terse refusal to comment. To the friends who telephoned in shock or sympathy she said something like, "It has to do with an alleged misappropriation of funds, but he's not guilty of anything. His lawyer is with him; he's very confident that he'll be out in a matter of hours. I'll tell him you rang. Yes, yes, of course I'm okay. It's only Darcy I'm worried about."

Almost as soon as she replaced the receiver after each of these calls, the ringing would start again.

Barney and Cathy telephoned Lucy at Patrick's Spitalfields house.

"Should I come home?" Lucy asked them.

"I don't think you need to right now, if you don't want to," Cathy advised her. "How do you feel?"

"Worried about Dad."

"Yeah. But I meant you."

After a moment Lucy answered, "Strange. Sad, and small. But I feel relieved to be just myself again. Just me; no one else to be afraid for. As if I can deal with anything, as long as it only has to do with me."

"Good. That's good, isn't it? Look, stay where you are for now. It's probably better. I'll let you know as soon anything else happens here. There are reporters hanging about outside, trying to see in."

After she hung up, Lucy remained sitting in her leggings and tattered gray sweater, cross-legged among the needlework cushions

on Patrick's sofa. She pushed her thicket of beaded plaits and miniature pigtails away from her white face.

"My dad's been arrested on a fraud charge. The police came
this morning."

Patrick had heard about Darcy Clegg from Nina.

"Poor Lucy."

"Poor him, more. Don't sympathize too much with me, or I'll
start crying."

He patted her shoulder. "Fine. Not another sympathetic syllable."

Lucy looked up at him. "Why are you and Nina being so nice
to me? You don't even know me."

Patrick shrugged. "Nina has her own reasons, so I can't answer
for her. As for me, you can see I've got plenty of space."

Lucy loved the spare grandeur of Patrick's house. Even though
she was a stranger, even though she felt weak and dismayed, she had
been comfortable in it as soon as Patrick had brought her there from
the clinic, the day before. The rooms were half-empty and wholly
soothing compared with those at Wilton. The covers and cushions
here, all made of dark heavy material that seemed to have been mended
and made from something else, looked even better after they had been
sat on and lived with. Unlike Hannah's.

Lucy had slept surprisingly well, without needing the pills she
had been given at the clinic, between darned linen sheets in a huge
oak bed with an embroidered canopy.

"It's not really just because you have that spare bedroom, is it?"

"It is *very* spare, I admit."

"Are you lonely?"

Patrick frowned at her. He liked this girl, with her alternately
disaffected and inquisitive manner, as Nina had assured him he
would. He also thought that she was probably quite brave. There
had been no sign of tears, despite Nina's warnings, but that did not
make him think that the ordeal she had undergone had left her
unscathed.

"Yes. But no more so than plenty of other people."

Lucy reached for his hand and wound her fingers between his.

"Is this all right? I felt lonely in that clinic. They were quite
kind—I wouldn't want Nina to think it wasn't anything but fine in
that sense—only it was just me who was doing that thing. No one

else could help me, and it was right that I should have to do it on my own. I felt very solitary. No baby, no nothing. Perhaps it was good for me. Being a twin, I've never had to be singular before. But this time I didn't even want Cathy to come."

Very softly, almost to herself, Lucy added. "It was right to do it that way. My responsibility. No one else to blame or judge. Anyway, you don't have to be lonely now, with me here, do you?"

"Thank you."

Patrick settled beside her on the sofa, not trying to disengage his hand, although the connection felt strange. He didn't hold hands much.

Understanding that she did not want to talk any more now about her abortion, he said, "Tell me about your father."

She tilted her head downward so that the teased hair hid her face.

"All my life he has seemed so—huge. When we were tiny he seemed to fill the sky, and my sister and I thought he could do anything. Like fly, or stop the rain. He wasn't around all that much, but when he was, everything seemed to flow out of him, fun and excitement and money and reassurance and confidence. He never said no to things the way our mother did."

When she saw Patrick's expression, Lucy grinned through her fringes. "Yeah. Spoiled kids, eh? He was always telling us that himself."

The smile vanished. "Oh, God. Why am I talking about him in the past? When he fell ill it was, it was like the first time I'd understood that he really isn't immortal. Now there's this, whatever's happening. When I first heard about it I felt like I should be looking after *him*."

After a moment, she said, "I really love him. I don't care what he has or hasn't done."

Patrick felt suddenly envious of Darcy Clegg, in prison or not. "I'm sure he would like to hear you say that."

She nodded. "Yeah. I'll have to try to tell him when we both get home again."

Jimmy Rose put through a call to Wilton as soon as he heard the news. Hannah had gone upstairs with Laura, and it was Cathy who answered the telephone.

"Lucy? Is that you?"

"Who's calling?" Cathy said coolly.

"Ah, don't be that way. I've been thinking and worrying about you. Have you decided what you want to do?"

"Lucy isn't here. She's gone to London."

In the silence that followed, in spite of everything else, Cathy allowed herself a little smile.

Anger edged the brogue out of Jimmy's voice. "Why didn't you tell me it was you?"

"You didn't give me the chance."

"All right. How is she?"

"Why do you want to know?"

"Jesus. Why wouldn't I? Do you think I don't care for her?"

Cathy sighed. "She's all right. She's staying with a friend."

"Did she . . . ?"

"Yes. Yes, she did. By herself, because that was what she wanted. Are you happy now?"

"Of course not." Jimmy twisted in the armchair to peer over his shoulder. He realized that Star had come home earlier than usual with her bag of exercise books. She put her stuff down without looking at him and left the room again. Jimmy changed his tone.

"I just called to talk to Hannah. Will you tell her that if there's anything I can do, she's only got to ask?"

"I'm sure she'll be grateful."

Cheeky little bitch, Jimmy thought. *Both of them*.

"But I don't think there's anything now. Daddy's lawyer just telephoned. He's been released on bail, and they're on their way home."

"That's grand news. Who put up bail for him?"

"My uncle. And Andrew Frost."

Jimmy was shocked by this. He protested. "He could have asked me. Why didn't he ask me?"

"I don't know. Because he asked Andrew. I suppose."

"Yes. Well, if there's anything else he needs, tell him I'm here."

He hung up. Staring out of the window into the garden, he saw the unpruned branches of shrubs whipped by the cold wind, and the first threads of rain scribbling the glass. He was angry with

Cathy Clegg and felt snubbed by Darcy. The sour view from his living room, the wedge of garden and the hedges and back windows and ornamental conifers of the backwater of Grafton—his failure and disappointment—fed his anger. Jimmy sat still, with his fists clenched between his knees, until Star came in again. She sat down in a chair at a distance from him and opened a book.

Watching her, Jimmy thought that her supercilious detachment was calculated to enrage him. A quarrelsome dialogue rehearsed itself in his head until, as if the preamble had already been uttered, he murmured. "Why are you such a bitch?"

Star lifted her head. Her face was cold, her top lip lifting slightly as if she were suddenly aware of a nasty smell.

"If I am, it's because you make me one."

Her cool voice recalled Cathy Clegg. Darcy's failure to ask for his help took on the status of a deliberate insult. Had the destructive little Lucy said something to him after all? Even as he thought of her, a wave of longing for her and the little baby and what might have been weakly washed over him. His resentment fastened on Star, crackling, ready to ignite.

"It has nothing to do with me, except that I have to live with you. Why is it me who has to be married to a frigid dyke?"

Star closed her book and it slid to the floor. She stood up and stepped deliberately toward him. Then she swung her hand and slapped him in the face. His head jerked backward and a thread of spittle whipped from the corner of his mouth.

"Don't ever call me a dyke," she said through clenched teeth.

Jimmy licked his lips, then smeared them with the ball of his thumb, looking down at it for blood.

"I'll call you whatever I bloody like."

She was already backing away from him, but too late. His hand shot out and grabbed her wrist, and he dragged her back within his reach.

"*No . . .*" she started to say.

He hit her, a quick double blow, his knuckles smashing against her cheekbone and then the palm of his hand cracking against the other cheek.

"Fuck you," he said.

Then he let go of her, the taste of disgust thick in his mouth. For an instant, until he looked away from it, he watched the white print on Star's cheek fill with a quick tide of color.

Star slowly turned, moving cautiously as if she were afraid that her legs would give way. She stooped, holding her back straight, to pick up her book and place it tidily on the coffee table. Then she went out, leaving the house and walking away down the suburban avenue.

Jimmy poured himself a whisky. When he had drunk it he pulled the telephone toward him again.

"Andrew? Jimmy. Yes, I heard." He listened to the snap and rumble of Andrew's voice.

"How much did you have to put up?"

His mouth puckered in a soundless whistle. "It'll be in the papers anyway. Two hundred and fifty grand *each*? Bit of a nuisance if he skips the country."

Andrew spoke again and Jimmy nodded, looking at the empty room while he listened. "Do you feel like a drink, later on? I thought I'd go down to the golf club. No? All right. Saturday, then."

After Andrew had hung up, Jimmy poured himself a second and drank it down straight.

Star found herself walking along the path beside the river. The start of the summer had brought out the first tourists, and even in the intermittent rain there were pairs of them strolling under the snaky fronds of the willow trees. They were mostly elderly couples, filling in the interval between exploring the cathedral and the hotel dinner. She passed them with her head averted, eyes on the water, conscious of the bruise beginning to discolor her face. The wind was licking the surface of the river into glittering silver menisci.

The vista of old stone and water meadow on the opposite bank and the low hills in the distance had always pleased her, just as numerous other corners and recesses of the city, rubbed and rounded by the passage of time like stones on a beach, pleased her, too. It gave Star satisfaction and a sense of peace to have her small daily itinerary defined and contained by the medieval boundaries. She was thinking as she walked that it was such simple things that had kept her in

Grafton, and her preference for order and routine over the risk of the unknown that had prevented her from leaving it behind.

But now, threading her way among the tourists and the flags of the willow branches, she resolved that it was time to leave. She did not love her husband anymore, if she had ever loved him. It was not even the acceptance of that truth that convinced her, but the recognition that this evening had marked an end point, a definitive break in the slow decline of her marriage. There could be no reversal or cosmetic redefinition.

Star began to make her plans. She walked for a long way, following the wide sweep of the river, until Grafton dropped out of sight behind her.

In the evening, twelve hours after his arrest, Darcy was driven home by his lawyer. Hannah and Cathy and Barney had been waiting in a tense huddle in the drawing room, but when they heard the car they stood up in unison and hurried into the hallway, not knowing what to expect. When the car drew up on the gravel sweep in front of the house, two of the reporters who had watched the day's traffic to and from the front door jumped up from the garden seat where they had been smoking and talking and ran toward it.

Darcy emerged from the passenger seat, and Hannah and his children heard him from within the safety of the house. "I have no comment to make. This is private property, and you will remove yourselves from it immediately. Either that or I will have you removed."

Tim McIntyre, the lawyer, hurried in Darcy's wake. "Mr. Clegg told you. He has no comment to make."

Darcy swept him into the house, slamming the door behind them.

"Have those little rodents been out there all day?" he shouted. He seemed to have swelled again to fill the confines of his dark suit. It was as if leaking air had been pumped into him again, smoothing out the creases in his flesh and puffing away the dark patches in his face. Hannah and the two children glanced at one another, startled and hopeful.

"Of course I'm all right," Darcy said when he looked at them. "Were you afraid I wouldn't be?"

His lawyer nodded in confirmation while Darcy shepherded them back into the drawing room. "Bail was granted without too much difficulty. It took a little time to arrange the formalities, as it often does in these cases."

Darcy stood with his arm around Cathy's shoulders, surveying the room, once again the host and master.

"Hannah, we need a drink. Two or three drinks, after the day we've had. Tim's done a good job. Everything is going to be fine."

In the furnished apartment he was renting from the hospital, Michael waited for Hannah.

The apartment was in an annex to the main building that also housed the nurses' residence, and it was usually occupied by medical families new to the area while they searched for a permanent home. When he had heard that it was temporarily available, it had seemed the answer to his problems, but now that he had moved into it Michael felt less sure. The apartment occupied an uncomfortable middle ground, neither part of the hospital nor completely separate from it. The kitchen windows looked out on the parking lot and a set of blue-and-white signs pointing the way to the X-ray and obstetric departments. The bedroom and living room windows faced the other way, over a grassy area where groups of student nurses sat on summer evenings with their coffee mugs and ring binders filled with notes.

After turning away from these reminders of the hospital into the leaky silence of the apartment itself, Michael would wander uncertainly through the small rooms. They were furnished with an accumulation of unrelated pieces, tables with brown Formica veneer and white particle-board shelves whose emptiness betrayed their lopsidedness, armchairs and a sofa upholstered in nubbly orange tweed, and a standard lamp with a burn on the shade that showed when the light was on like a tumor revealed on an X-ray plate. All of this reminded Michael of rooms he had occupied as a medical student, places he had passed through with the easy certainty that they were only temporary, only worthy of his attention insofar as they were convenient, or cheap enough, or not uncomfortable enough to be irritating.

Now it was as if in middle age he had acquired a forlorn clarity of vision. He saw the irregular stains of spilled wine and coffee on the carpets as the ghostly imprints of previous occupants' lives, of their riotous parties or seismic quarrels, and the longer he lived in the apartment the more shadowy and insubstantial he felt himself to be. It was as if his removal from his proper home had reduced him to living an existence no more corporeal than that of these other vanished occupants.

Michael found it odd that he was waiting for Hannah, so emphatically flesh and blood herself, in this whispery no-man's-land.

He *was* waiting for her, he realized. He had no idea whether she would come in the end, exchanging Darcy and the splendors of Wilton for whatever it was he would be able to offer her instead. Nor did he know whether he even wanted her to come, or whether what he really longed for was to be free of any obligation, either to Hannah or to Marcelle or his children.

He was simply waiting out the days between the familiar routine of the hospital and the vacuum of the rented rooms, passively suspended in his solitude.

Now, on a June evening, Michael looked out his kitchen window and saw Hannah walking across the parking lot away from her BMW. She walked quickly, in high-heeled sandals, with a little handbag swinging from a shoulder strap. It was more than a week since they had last met.

He picked up a smeared glass and some dirty plates from the table and hastily put them in the sink. He ran the cold tap on them and the water sprayed up over his shirt-front, making him jump backward.

Hannah knocked. He crossed the hallway and opened the door, taking in the sight and scent of her and the realization that he was happy she had come. He smiled and tried to reach for her.

"I can't stay very long," Hannah said. "I just told Darcy I was picking some things up for the shop."

"Come in, anyway."

He followed her into the living room and poured her a glass of wine from the bottle he had bought expressly for the occasion. Hannah drank some, then sighed and let her head fall back against the sofa cushions. Michael looked at the white line of her throat and the rounded outline of her chin.

"I'm sorry I'm late," she said.

"Tough week?"

"You could say."

"What's happening?"

"Oh, more or less what I expected. Darcy is going full-tilt into preparing his defense. He seems energized by it all, in a manic way. Endless meetings and telephone calls. His lawyer has briefed George Carman. Nothing but the best, of course. I hardly dare think what it will cost. I'm told that it could be a year or more before the case even goes to court."

"What happens in the meantime?"

"I don't know. I don't know what we'll live on."

"Darcy must have assets," Michael said gently.

"I suppose so." Hannah lit a cigarette and drew on it. "I don't know much about any of that. If I needed money in the past, it was there. Real bimbo behavior, eh?"

"I don't think so. Wasn't it just how Darcy encouraged you to live?"

Hannah looked sharply at him, wondering about the logic of defending her husband to her lover.

"What does it mean to you and me?" Michael persisted. It was not the first time he had asked the question.

After a pause Hannah said, "I don't know that, either."

He put his hands on her shoulders, and their faces slowly drew together. When their foreheads touched they held still, not kissing.

"Poor Hannah."

Hannah was thinking that she didn't want his sympathy. She was too busy with her anxiety about Darcy and her own fears for the future. She was afraid of having to sell Wilton, of being cut adrift in a sea of insecurity when she had grown used to luxury and certainty. She didn't doubt that they would survive being poor if they had to, but the threat of it still repelled her.

When all had been well, even after Darcy's heart attack, a love affair with Michael had offered itself as a pleasurable indulgence.

Now it was incongruous, even unwelcome. She didn't want Michael to feel sorry for her, nor did she want to have to feel guilty for what he had lost, or feel sorry for him in return. It was not what had been intended in the beginning. It was not an escape, but another responsibility.

She couldn't tell Michael how much she hated to see him in this sordid apartment. It reduced his status in her eyes, and it was like a warning of what might be in store for her and Darcy. Perhaps they would be reduced to living with Freddie and Laura in rented rooms like these, with burn-marks in the nylon rugs and the outlines of other people's pictures left on the bare walls.

"What about you?" she asked.

Michael made a gesture of indifference, a new habit of his. He poured her more wine, slopping a little over the rim of the glass. Hannah knew that it would make a sticky ring on the Formica-topped coffee table that he wouldn't bother to wipe away.

"Just what you see."

"And Marcelle?"

"I can't fathom Marcelle. I took Jon and Daisy out for the day on Sunday. She seemed rather pleased to see us all go."

"Poor Michael."

He laughed, but without much humor, and then took her hand.

"We shall have to take care of each other," he said.

They sat side-by-side on the orange sofa, watching the light filtering through the leaves of the chestnut trees outside.

"I'm glad you're here," Michael said finally, leaning across to kiss her. His hand traveled to the buttons of her silk shirt.

As she submitted to this, Hannah wondered if it would be better to get up now and drive straight back to Wilton. Michael's hand slid inside her shirt. She closed her eyes, and knew that she had no serious intention of doing so. It was pleasurable to be the focus of this much attention. It was satisfying to be about to take what she wanted from someone else, just for an hour. The strain of giving endless, cheerful credence to Darcy was beginning to take its toll on her.

The sofa was cramped, and the tweed felt tacky against her shoulders.

"Let's go to bed," Hannah whispered.

The bedroom was small, with a pink-and-burgundy striped

roller blind drawn against the sun and a beige sculpted carpet. The modular dressing table stood cornerwise, the mirror reflecting their midriffs. The top of the dressing table was bare except for the limited, mundane contents of Michael's pockets, keys and loose change and his wallet. The depositing of this handful of belongings had scratched a rough hieroglyph in the faint film of dust on the wood.

Hannah felt a sudden contraction of sympathy for him. She closed her eyes and let him kiss her, concentrating on the warmth and the glow of light behind her eyelids until the disabling sympathy receded.

They undressed each other and lay down on the bed. Michael had straightened it out in readiness.

Hannah liked what he did, and liked his good, muscular body. Michael's lovemaking was pleasurable, even if he sometimes did it too vehemently, as if he had forgotten that there could be subtler rhythms. She closed her eyes again. Her back arched as her hips reached upward for him. It was good to forget her outside self in favor of the internal landscape that Michael slavishly created between them.

Afterward, when they drew apart, Hannah lay on her side, her face toward him, but Michael rolled onto his back. She drew a playful finger down his chest and over his belly to his flaccid penis.

"That was good," she said, smiling, ready to be affectionate now.

Instead of responding, Michael asked stiffly, "Are you going to say anything to Darcy?"

Hannah sighed. She hadn't planned to talk about this now. She would have liked another glass of wine and then a bath before driving safely home again. "Do you want me to?"

His shoulders twitched. "I don't know what this means, otherwise."

"What should it mean?"

He turned on her then. She had made him angry.

"It means that I've moved out of my home. Left my wife and children and come here because of you. I need to know what, if anything, you're planning to tell your husband about it. What I want it to mean is that I love you. Does Darcy know anything?"

"No," Hannah said carefully. "Or only that you and Marcelle have separated for the time being. He's sorry, of course. We haven't talked a lot about it, mostly because he's preoccupied with other things." There was no point in trying to explain the disconcerting, obsessive energy that had reflated Darcy.

"Would you rather he heard about this from someone else?"

"Will Marcelle tell him?"

"No, I don't think so." Michael thought that he knew her as well as he knew himself; he didn't believe Marcelle would want even Janice to know the real reason for their split. She was too proud, too much of a perfectionist to betray it.

Hannah said softly. "So let me get this straight. You're warning me that if I don't speak to Darcy, you will?"

"That isn't what I said, or what I want."

Michael felt that he had been maneuvered into a confrontation that was threatening to become a quarrel. They would not look at each other now, and a lengthening silence and six inches of cooling sheet separated them. Michael made an effort and said as reasonably as he could, "Both of us know Grafton. How long is it likely to be before someone sees us and gossips?"

"Both of us know this place, yes."

"Hannah, that's all I meant."

Hannah bit her lip. The skin felt bruised. Her instincts were all to protect Darcy; the urgency of her intention surprised her. *We do deserve each other*, she thought. And then: *I'm tired of him but I can't let go of him. Like a mother with a toddler.*

She tried to focus her wits on what to say to Michael.

"I can't talk to Darcy now. How could I? 'I know you've lost your livelihood. And are likely to go to prison. And are accused in the filthy tabloids of being the biggest thief and fraudster since Maxwell. And, oh, yes, I'm leaving you, too.' I don't know what you expect from me, Michael. I didn't ask you to love me, and that's the truth."

The light in the room was fading. The rays that struck through the paler stripes of the blind seemed heavy, as if they might drift downward under their own weight through the still air. There was the sound of girls' voices outside, and the distant trill of an ice cream van. Sadness crept through their bones like radiation.

"I know," Michael said.

Their hands moved and found each other again. They lay quietly, a little apart, listening to the outside sounds.

At last Hannah lifted her other wrist to peer at her little gold wristwatch. "I have to go," she murmured.

Michael released her at once. She slipped from under the covers and then knelt upright, shielding her breasts with her forearm.

"I'll call you," she promised. Her expression was sweet and serious in the dim light.

"I'm here," he answered.

He lay back and watched her put her clothes on again, thinking that they had saved each other's dignity with these promises. He was glad that they hadn't quarrelled.

After she had kissed him and closed the door quietly behind her, he wrapped a towel around himself and walked through to the kitchen. He saw her crossing the parking lot to her car, walking briskly on her high heels. He stood at the window until she had driven away. Then, without bothering to dress himself, he began to wander through the empty rooms again, stepping between the marks of other people's lives as if they reared up like so many obstacles.

Sunday came again. Michael drove home, as he had agreed with Marcelle, to pick up his children for the day. Jonathan was kicking a ball in the front garden when Michael's car turned in at the gate.

"Hi, Daddy."

"Hi, Jon." He hugged the boy and rubbed his hair. "How was the week?"

"Okay. Daisy's waiting inside."

Marcelle opened the door. Michael noticed that she was wearing a new shirt, made of some soft material in a cinnamon color that suited her. She stood back to let him in.

"Daisy's just in the bathroom."

They were like strangers to each other.

"How have they been?" Michael asked.

Marcelle shrugged. "How would you expect?"

Daisy ran downstairs. Michael shepherded the two children

into the back of the car and drove them away from the house, noticing that the front door closed immediately.

As they turned toward the ring road, Daisy asked from the back seat, "What are the plans for today?"

"I don't know," he answered. "I haven't made any. What would you like to do?"

"Oh, Daddy."

It was Daisy's protest, but neither child said anything else. In the silence that followed, looking in the rearview mirror, Michael saw their pale faces turned in opposite directions, and their eyes fixed on a view that could not have interested them. He didn't know what to say or what to do with them; they would rather, he understood, have spent the day at home with Marcelle.

Marcelle went upstairs with the Sunday papers. She found Jonathan's cassette player in his room, took a tape of Beethoven late quartets from the rack that Michael had left in his study, slotted the tape into the player, and brought it into the bathroom with her. She turned the music up so she could hear it over the bathwater. Then she undressed and looked at herself in the mirror, giving her body a long, shrewd appraisal. She even turned her back and looked at herself over her shoulder. She could see her ribs and the knobs of her spine. Her buttocks did not sag, nor were her thighs pocked with cellulite.

"Not bad," she said aloud. "Considering."

Then she stepped into the hot water and lay down, shivering with pleasure as the warmth engulfed her. The music and the steam cleared her head. She closed her eyes and let herself drift.

Marcelle could not remember the last time she had done exactly what she wanted to, the way she was doing now. Sunday mornings had always meant a family breakfast, after which Michael liked to go off to play golf. After that he had liked to come home to a proper Sunday lunch. Today, Marcelle knew, she would not have to cook anything for anybody. Nor would she have to drive either of the children anywhere, or arbitrate between them, or go swimming or play tennis or attend to a late-homework crisis. She did not have to do anything.

With that realization, she felt her shoulders tighten again under the skin of water; she was waiting for the fear to descend.

But then, even as she waited, she knew that she did not feel afraid. This would be the second Sunday she had spent entirely alone, and the solitude was welcome, even blessed. Last Sunday, while the children were with Michael, she had filled up the hours with ironing and housework. She had crawled into bed tired, and then had lain in the dark and asked herself if she had worked all day because she wanted to prove that she was a good mother or because she couldn't think of anything else to do with the time.

The answer had come to her eventually. She hadn't allowed herself a day of freedom because she didn't think she deserved it.

Why not? Marcelle asked herself lying rigid under the freshly-changed sheets. *Because your husband is having an affair with one of your friends? Because you are just a wife and mother and teacher, and that means you are invisible and unworthy of consideration? Why not you? If everyone else deserves a day off?*

She had felt angry with herself, and weak, but the hot anger had cauterized a wound that had been seeping for a long time. And without the disability of a wound to carry around, she had felt her strength returning.

All through the week, Marcelle had noticed it and hoarded it for herself. She did not miss Michael, although she felt the cold space that his going had left. She did not worry too much for her children. They were anxious, she saw, and needful of her, but their needs and their demands might easily grow and grow until they overpowered her. Coldly she resolved that the best thing for her to do was *not* to be overpowered. And the best thing for her would also be better, in the long run, for the children. Marcelle liked thinking in this clear, new way.

All week she had thought about herself. She did it awkwardly at first, with many false starts and mistaken directions, because she had grown rusty at it. But then, as her concentration improved, she began to feel small darts of gladness, even exhilaration. Once, after the children had gone to bed, she made herself a meal. Ordinarily she would have finished their leftovers or gone without. But on this evening she spent an hour chopping and sautéeing and arranging a salad for herself alone. She laid a proper place setting at the table, opened some wine, and sat down to explore her own company. It had felt odd. There had been a quiver of sadness that so many years of marriage should have brought her to this, but there had also been a strong, surprising beat of assurance. She had eaten her own food, with critical attention, and relished the wine, and afterward—made pleasurably careless by the amount she had drunk—she had abandoned the washing up and had gone straight to bed.

She lay spreadeagled in the luxurious cool space left by Michael's absence and let herself sink, thoughtless, into sleep.

Janice and Vicky telephoned and called on her so regularly and with such perfect alternate timing that Marcelle knew they had been talking about her. She was grateful for their concern, and sometimes glad of their company, but it was satisfying to discover that she did not depend on it.

Vicky, in particular, was eager to talk. She would sit in Marcelle's kitchen, with a cup of coffee or a glass of wine while Helen rocked in her baby seat, and recall how she had felt when Gordon confessed to his love affair. She described her ways of dealing with the weeks when they had lived apart, and Marcelle listened and nodded.

"I found out things about myself that I never knew before," Vicky confided. "About my level of dependence on Gordon. About the way I used the children as a defense against the rest of the world. About my own sexuality as well."

Marcelle noted the flicker in her eyes when she mentioned this, but she didn't press her for more details.

"In the end, it was a good thing that it all happened. We're stronger and happier together now," Vicky said tranquilly. "Don't overlook the possibility that it might be the same for you and Michael."

"I won't," Marcelle promised.

She didn't tell anyone about Hannah and Michael. It was only partly, as Michael had guessed, out of pride; more important, it was that what concerned her was herself and what was happening within her own head. She allowed herself not to think about Michael, and by extension Hannah, and was interested to find that to do so was even quite comfortable.

Janice's concern for her expressed itself as solicitude.

"Are you lonely?" Janice worried. "You can always come over to us, you know. Or just call, anytime. What about the weekends? Perhaps we could all go somewhere with the kids next weekend, for a break? Andrew and I would both like that."

This was almost precisely what Marcelle did not want. She murmured something about the children seeing Michael on weekends. The mention of the children distracted Janice, as always.

"Are they all right?"

"They seem to be. Clinging and anxious, but also stoical, in a way."

"That's the most painful part, isn't it, what it does to the children?"

Knowing how Janice idolized her two boys, Marcelle thought that for her that probably *would* be the worst part. But with her new insight, her own view was that children elsewhere in the world, in Sarajevo or the horn of Africa, were suffering far greater pains. Jonathan and Daisy would probably survive the separation of parents who loved them but could not, for the moment, be sure that they loved each other. She did not tell Janice that she felt this.

On this Sunday morning, Marcelle lay in her hot bath for a long time, letting these thoughts and their offshoots revolve in her head. The water cooled, and the Beethoven tape reached its end. She did not bother to stretch out her hand to change it over. The silence of the house settled around her, an unmatched luxury. The thought of kindly Janice and Andrew, and a noisy weekend with all their children in some borrowed or rented house, made her smile once, briefly.

When the coolness of the water became uncomfortable, Marcelle stood up and briskly toweled herself off. She noted the prickle of stubble on her shins with a passing frown. In the bathroom cupboard she found a forgotten bottle of body lotion, tipped glistening pools of it into her cupped hand, and rubbed it into her legs and knees and elbows. Then she left the bath unscoured and wandered back into her bedroom. She had spread the Sunday papers out on top of the crumpled covers. The pillows still held the dent of her head. Instead of reprimanding her with its dishevelment, the bed openly invited her. Marcelle slipped under the covers again.

As she lay there, with the newspapers crackling faintly beneath her shoulder, a memory stirred.

Marcelle found herself thinking of a particular weekend, years ago, when she was still a girl. A weekend she had spent in bed with a boy, a student, whom she had not known particularly well but had been fiercely attracted to. It was not that her tidy room recalled his grimy one-room apartment or his stiff and becrumbed sheets in any way; it was rather, perhaps, the angle of the light, and the newspaper beneath her, and some sensation within herself. That weekend had been Marcelle's proper introduction to sex. On Monday morning she had got up and gone home. She had seen the boy around after that, but she had not felt any particular interest in repeating the experience, nor had he asked her to. Perhaps they had both felt that it had been enough, and complete, in itself.

It was a long time since she had thought of it, Marcelle realized.

Now, in response to the memory, she slid her fingers over the lotioned skin of her thigh and dipped them between her legs. She began to stroke herself.

The thought of Jimmy in the mossy shadows of the Ransomes' garden came back to her. Jimmy's rejection had added another layer to the sediment of misery within her, but now the sediment was draining away. It ran out, faster and faster, and the clear water of anger swirled in in its place. She was angry with Jimmy and his silky tongue and devious ways, a good, hot, centered anger, but she was also indifferent to him. She forgot about him and the garden.

Marcelle knew that she was good. Very good and right and strong, and happy *now*. She came quickly and pleasurably. She lay for a little while in the silence, enjoying the weight of her limbs and the slow, sidling trickle of her thoughts, and then she did the same thing again, this time laughing as she came.

Afterward, flagrantly at twelve-thirty on a Sunday morning, Marcelle fell asleep.

18

The little silk and satin dresses still hung in their spotlit niches at La Couture, but it was as if the light that shone on them had changed in some way, losing its rosy glow. When the women gathered in the shop one afternoon in July, it seemed to Star that the pretty, frivolous clothes belonged to another era, that they had become almost historical. She wandered along a rail, touching the lace bodices and silky tiers of cloth with the tips of her fingers.

"Try the gold one," Hannah suggested from behind her little desk. "It would suit you."

"I haven't got the money," Star said, and smiled. Or at least she didn't want to spend the money she did have on buying clothes like these. She had different intentions.

"Nobody has the money. Unfortunately," Hannah said.

Vicky and Janice were sitting on one of the overstuffed sofas, drinking the coffee Hannah had poured for them. It was the last afternoon before the school holidays began. There were no customers in the shop to disturb their talk.

Janice looked around. "Business will pick up again in the autumn. Andrew says it's just the same in the construction trade. As soon as interest rates come down, everything will start to move again."

"Maybe."

Beyond the shop windows, the tourists were passing up and down Southgate under the municipal hanging baskets filled with geraniums and lobelia. The weather was windy and changeable, and most of the visitors were wearing pastel-colored anoraks over their summer clothes.

In past seasons Hannah might have sold an occasional item to a tourist, but the majority of her customers had always been local women, established Grafton and county wives whom she knew well and bought for individually because she understood what they wanted. But now, this summer, they had not come in for their Ascot clothes or their holiday evening wear. The taut little suits and the tan-enhancing loose white draperies still hung in their places on the overcrowded rails.

Hannah understood the circumstances perfectly well.

Some of the women were practicing small economies, buying a new hat instead of a complete outfit, for the same reasons that their husbands' expensive cars were now two or three years old instead of brand-new.

But other customers, many more of them, stayed away because of Darcy. When the news first appeared in the papers there had been a little flurry of inquisitive visitors who commiserated with her and whispered about her afterward, but none of them had bought, and none of them had come back. There was no particular reason why women should prefer not to buy their party dresses from the wife of a man accused of theft, forgery, and false accounting, but Hannah imagined that she would probably have made the same choice herself.

Perhaps La Couture could have survived either the recession or Darcy, but not both. Her takings in the last weeks had dropped almost to nothing.

"But I don't think I'll be here to see the upturn when it comes. If it ever does," Hannah said.

She walked away from her desk to a niche where a red-and-white polka-dotted afternoon dress postured coquettishly against the wall, waiting for its saucer hat and net veil and its afternoon of champagne and speeches in some flower-scented wedding marquee. Only it was quite clear that none of these would now be forthcoming. Hannah deftly unpinned the dress, and the empty folds collapsed in her arms. The hidden pins and tucks that had upheld it in tidy outline were all revealed. The dress seemed to leave a dusty silhouette on the wall.

"Is it as bad as that?" Janice asked.

Hannah held up the limp frock, then let it drop in a heap. "Yes."

"Oh, Hannah." Janice's face flushed with her distress.

Star had been looking out at the passersby. The view was entirely familiar to her, but she was often aware now that she was looking at Grafton simply to preserve it in her mind's eye.

"What will you do?" she asked Hannah.

"Do?"

The women drew closer to Hannah. Looking at one another, they felt as if they were under siege, embattled within the labyrinths of their uncertain friendships while the walls of established rituals crumbled away.

Janice felt afraid, as she had on the evening of the Ransomes' barbecue. She could not pinpoint the fear; it evaporated when she tried to confront it, only to coalesce again at the periphery of her inner landscape, a thick, dark cloud of anxiety. It made her want to hurry home to secure her children and her husband in case the erosion she could see all around her had begun to nibble there, too. But she knew that if she voiced her fears Andrew would robustly dismiss them.

"I shall close it," Hannah said decisively. "It's only a shop."

"No, it's much more than that," Vicky said. "It's what you do. You made it."

They acknowledged this among themselves.

"Even so, I can't keep it going at a loss. We can't afford it."

It was strange for all of them to hear Hannah, the rich man's wife, admitting as much.

"What are you going to do?"

It was Vicky who asked this time.

Hannah understood that the women wanted to know more than just what she planned to do with the shop. She thought of Darcy at home, alternately animated by the preparation of his case or, more often now, sunk into uncommunicative silence. She thought of Michael, too, remembering the morning they had spent together at the fashion-house showroom looking at the autumn collection. All the hemlines had been calf-length, and Hannah loved short skirts. She had felt her interest detach itself from the clothes paraded in front of her, and curiously that detachment now seemed to extend to Michael himself.

"Oh, I'll stick by Darcy, of course. Wait it out, whatever it is."

She meant the trial and afterward, if Darcy had to go to prison.

Janice nodded. Vicky was thinking that Darcy would need all of Hannah's support. She remembered the childishness that their own intimacy had uncovered in him, and how disconcerting and finally unappealing she had found it. Her eyes met Hannah's, and she saw the glimmer of a challenge in the other woman's stare. Hannah looked vulnerable for all the armor of her chic dark suit, but she was also steely in her determination.

"I admire you," Vicky said softly. "Darcy is very lucky."

They looked at each for a moment longer. Vicky's eyes were the first to drop. She would have liked to reach out to Hannah and hug her, but something in the armor held her away.

Star had abruptly turned around again, toward the window and the view of the shoppers on Southgate.

"Yes," Hannah agreed. "Isn't he? Do you think the role of stalwart little woman becomes me?"

It was not a question that seemed to require an answer; none of the others tried to supply one. Hannah said in the same even voice, "I suppose I'd better do something about all these clothes."

She went to another niche and unpinned a second dress. This one was buttercup-yellow with big black buttons, like shining eyes. On impulse, she held it out to Vicky.

"Come on. Put it on. Let's see what it looks like."

Vicky looked from the dress to Hannah.

"Put it on? With *my* hips?"

"Don't be such a killjoy. Try it, the color's right."

Hannah's face had lightened. She went to the racks and lifted an armful of clothes. "Let's dress up. We might as well have some fun. Look, Janice, this number's made for you."

"Darling Hannah, it's orange."

"Marigold. Doesn't Madam care for marigold?"

Star turned back from the window. She was smiling now.

"Give me the gold one, then," she said. "And the harlequin suit as well. I've had my eye on that for weeks."

Vicky disappeared into the tented changing room and came out in the yellow dress. Hannah examined her head held to one side.

"Mm. Needs jewelry. Big earrings. Hang on." She unlocked a glass-topped display case and held out a fistful of glitter. "Try that. Next?"

Janice swayed forward, half-tripping in the orange sheath.

"Long gloves," Hannah pronounced. "Black suede ones. Over there. Star? There, didn't I tell you the gold one was perfect?"

The women were laughing now. Vicky hitched a taffeta ball dress off one of the rails and held it up, cinching the waist with her forearm and posing for the others.

"I've always fancied myself in one of these."

"Now's your chance."

"Vicky, those earrings are a masterpiece."

"Can you zip me up?"

"Try this on top of that dress."

They dived in and out of the changing room, and the sofas began to disappear under a pile of discarded clothes. More and more outlandish outfits were put together. They giggled like children raiding their mother's closet, Hannah egging them on all the while, pulling open cupboards and drawers and producing accessories like a magician.

"I've always wanted to do this," Star sighed happily. "It's like being let loose in a grown-up toyshop."

They came together in their borrowed magnificence and posed in front of the full-length mirrors. Their dazzle reflected back at them. They had forgotten the windy, mundane afternoon outside.

"My God, we look like the Supremes," Vicky said.

"My Supremes," Hannah agreed.

Suddenly this had become the right way to let go of her shop, by making a voluptuous game of it. She felt a surge of affection for the women and the bright, fragile reflections of their different identities in her unsold clothes.

Star pirouetted slowly in her column of gold.

"I want you to buy that dress," Hannah told her. "I'll let you have it at cost. And look." She unpinned a heap of gold and crystal from a velvet cushion. "I'll throw in the earrings for nothing."

Star wound her long bare arm around Hannah's shoulder and held her.

"You are a consummate saleswoman. I give in. I'll take the dress and the earrings, and I'll have to find a whole new way of life to go with them."

"Why not?"

"Why not, after all," Star agreed quietly.

But Hannah wasn't listening. "Wait a minute." She found another velvet cushion. "These are for Janice and Vicky. A present, one each—look, to wear on your summer holidays." There were more earrings, a pair of gold seashells, and a pair of silver starfish.

The Ransomes and the Frosts were taking neighboring houses by the sea for part of the summer. The Cleggs would be staying at Wilton instead of making their usual trip to Greece. Darcy had had to surrender his passport to the police.

They smiled at one another in the mirror. Vicky did reach out to Hannah now, putting one hand on her arm. Without trying to arrange the form of the words, she hurried out, "I wish you and Darcy were coming on holiday, too. I wish it could all be the same as it used to be."

"I know," Hannah said, acknowledging the apology and the truth at the same time.

Suddenly, for all of them, the years of their friendships and the parties and celebrations seemed precious and fleeting. They had thought that all these things were as immutable as the couples themselves, and they had not properly appreciated them until the disintegration was under way.

The women became serious again when the incongruity of their exotic clothes sunk in. Janice slowly unpeeled her long suede gloves.

"Oh, Hannah. I'm sorry about it all. If only there was something . . ."

She made a little gesture of helplessness with the glove, the empty fingers flapping loose.

"It's all right. Andrew put up half of the bail, didn't he? What more could we ask?"

Hannah didn't want to cry, but found herself close to it. She was reminded of a day, a lunch at Janice's a long time ago, when she had said something clumsy but now forgotten to Nina, and Nina had sat at the table and cried. Hadn't that also been about loss, and the necessity of concealing it?

The shop bell tinkled behind them, and the door opened. Hannah and the women looked around and saw Darcy. He seemed large in this feminine enclave, and faintly unkempt. His hair was longer than it usually was, and his clothes looked as if he might have put them on without considering whether the various items matched.

"Am I interrupting?" he called out.

"Not at all. Come and see," Hannah answered. She recomposed her face. Darcy should not see any threat of tears. "What do you think?"

Darcy whistled. He slid between the women, big hands touching a bare shoulder, the curve of a hip. He carefully gave exactly the same due to Vicky as to the others.

Star was reminded of how Darcy had once been, proprietorial among them all, the couples and not just the wives. He was going through the same motions now, determined not to surrender his mastery.

"All for me? How did you know I was coming?" he joked, a shade too loudly.

"Women's intuition."

Obediently they joked back, adopting a kind of awkward flirtatiousness, not for the first time since his arrest revealing that they didn't know quite how to treat him.

When the three women had retreated into the changing cubicles in search of their own clothes, Darcy said to Hannah, "I wondered where you were."

"You knew I was here," she said quietly, replacing the discarded dresses on their hangers.

"I wanted to see you."

It was the truth. The polished, reproachful silence of Wilton had become intolerable, and he had found himself sitting in the pointless expanse of his study and wishing for his wife. He had gone straight out to his car and driven into Grafton.

"It's all right," Hannah said, as she did to Laura and Freddie.

She put down the coat hangers and held out her arms to him. Darcy went to her, shuffling a little, his confusion momentarily evident to both of them. Hannah patted his shoulder, looking beyond him as if she could see what might be coming.

Her thoughts slid to Michael, and then surprisingly away again to Marcelle. She wished that Marcelle could have been here this afternoon, with Vicky, in the same unspoken forgiving way. The recognition made her wonder sadly what it was she had been doing or hoping to find with Michael Wickham. The evening they had spent here in the shop seemed a long, long time ago; the reflection in these mirrors might have belonged to someone else.

When she considered it, Hannah was not quite sure that she even liked Michael. Not, in any case, half as much as she liked Marcelle.

Hannah rested her hands on Darcy's shoulders, then briskly shook them as if to force him upright again.

"Come on," she whispered.

Darcy felt a tired admiration for her strength, and at the same time he did what she told him, jerking his head up before the women could see his weakness.

Star emerged from her curtained tent with the gold dress shimmering in her hands.

"You're taking it, aren't you?" Hannah insisted.

"I'd better pay for it before I change my mind."

Hannah led the way to her little desk.

"She's done it again, has she?" Darcy joked. "What a saleswoman. I should put her to work on my reputation, don't you think?"

Hannah said nothing. Her blond head was bent to reveal, unthinkably, a darker shadow at the roots. She wrote out the bill for Star.

When the dress was in its dark-blue bag, Vicky and Janice and Star hovered with the Cleggs in the shop doorway. It was time to pick the children up from school. The term was over; in a day or so the Frosts and the Ransomes would be on their way to Cornwall.

Darcy made an elaborate round of kisses and good-byes. He was like some overbearing master of ceremonies, dismissing them at the end of a performance.

"It's only three weeks," Janice protested. She felt the cobweb of fear shiver over her skin again.

"Jimmy will still be here," Star said. "We haven't planned anything."

"Jimmy, my boy." Darcy nodded heartily but vaguely, leaving them almost wondering if he remembered who Jimmy was.

The women kissed one another, murmuring their assurances, then left Darcy and Hannah and walked away down Southgate, between the slow surges of shoppers and visitors. At the corner, where Star would turn in a different direction, they stopped to look at the oblique view across the cathedral green to the west façade. The contractors were removing a section of scaffolding, which permitted a glimpse of pale, bare stone.

"Aren't you and Jimmy going away?" Vicky asked Star.

A scaffolding pole was thrown down, the crash minutely delayed by the distance.

Star was still looking across the green while she answered slowly, "I don't know. I don't know at all. I've resigned, you see. I'm not going back to school next term. And I haven't any idea what I'm going to do instead, so don't ask me that."

Janice and Vicky glanced at each other. Everything was changing, sliding out of the old alignments.

"Is it a good thing?" Janice ventured.

Star's sudden smile flashed at them like a beacon. She stood up straight, and the blue bag swung from her shoulder.

"Who can tell? It feels like a good thing now. I feel . . ."—she pointed across the green—". . . cleaned up, like the old saints and martyrs. All peeled of the old layers, porous and ready for the new rain to fall on me. It might sting a bit, of course. And the nights might feel colder without the coat of grime. But I've done it anyway. I just have to decide what to do next. Wish me luck?"

When they did so, she thanked them with a touch of her old irony. Then she hoisted the dress bag again and strode away.

Nina liked Grafton at the height of summer. She liked the way it seemed to belong to her, with everyone she knew away on holiday, and she was happy to share the city with the tide of tourists that washed across the green beneath her windows. She worked in her studio, the pinnacles of the cathedral floating in the sky over her head, and in the afternoons she went for long walks in the green lanes and fields surrounding the town, as she had done in the first weeks, before she knew Gordon.

Her only regular visitor now was Barney Clegg.

One afternoon at the beginning of August, Nina drove Barney out of town in her red Mercedes. It was a warm day, with a faint haze of cloud, and the air was heavy and still. Nina followed the road that led up into the low hills until they found a picnic spot overlooking the valley, and Grafton, in the distance. Barney lifted the picnic basket out of the car. It was a wicker hamper fitted inside with plates and recesses for cutlery and bottles, that had been given to Nina by Patrick. Barney watched in admiration as she unpacked champagne and brioches and raspberries.

"I always thought picnics meant banana sandwiches and warm Pepsi and sand."

"That doesn't sound much like Darcy."

"No, but Dad never took us on picnics. I went with other people's parents."

Nina handed him a champagne flute and they clinked the glasses together.

"Now you know different. I'm glad it was me who showed you."

"Are you?"

Nina was wearing her hair tied back at the nape. Her face was bare, her skin transparent in the clear light. She looked her age today. Barney leaned forward and kissed her, tasting the specks of moisture on her upper lip. When he drew back again, uncertainly, he saw her eyes sharpen. But she only said, "Yes, I'm glad of everything that has happened between us. Are you hungry? Stupid question?"

Barney was always hungry. The quantities of food he consumed had become one of their shared jokes. They ate their picnic sitting together companionably, knees drawn up, looking out over the valley. Nina always liked to think that this view of Grafton, shrouded in the haze of distance and heat, had not changed much since medieval times. She half-closed her eyes, eliminating the sprawl of industry and housing that skirted the edge of the city, and the cathedral shimmered for her in the midst of its protective huddle of buildings.

The light grew bruised and purplish while she watched; there was a threat of thunder in the air now. Nina felt hot and languid, drowsy from the champagne. She let her head drop gently to one side, to rest on Barney's shoulder. Only he didn't move closer or away from her.

"What is it?" she asked, breaking a silence.

"I need to talk to you."

"Talk."

"What do you want to happen?"

She could feel that he felt awkward, holding a little artificial space between them, and the awkwardness was uncomfortable.

She answered, "Oh, I want everyone to have enough to eat, some dignity, the opportunity for happiness."

"Don't try to make a joke out of it."

"That wasn't a joke, Barney."

"All right. Thanks for your world view. What do you want to happen between you and me?"

While she thought, Nina took his hand. Barney's was big and dirt-ingrained from his summer gardening jobs. There were coarse blond hairs on its back and the thumb crooked inward.

"I want what we have had. No more than that. Is that a fair answer?"

"Only partly. You say what we have had, but does that mean you want it to go on? Or not?"

Gently, Nina said, "I see. Shall we say that I don't want it to end, but I know that it can't go on for very long?"

She felt a small but distinct pinch of sadness that was amplified beyond its proper significance by her loneliness, and yet also a murmur of relief, and an affection for Barney that kindled a secondary, distinctly physical reaction.

"Is this important now, today?" she asked carefully, sorry that the afternoon's languor should be disturbed.

"I failed my exams," Barney said flatly. "Not a great surprise, of course. I'm not going back to college next term. There isn't much point, and I don't want to, now that this thing is happening to Dad. I feel I ought to be here, around the place, like some kind of support for the twins and Hannah and the kids as well, if I'm needed."

"But?"

"Yeah, but." Barney disengaged his hand, resting his chin on his fist. "I want to be somewhere else as well. I've been offered a job by the father of a guy I know, just some landscape work, laboring really, in Australia. Perth. I want to go for a year, travel to some other places on the way back. The kind of thing everyone does."

"Yes, I see."

He was very young, Nina thought. She felt ancient in comparison, but she could still just remember how the smooth surface of youthful self-preoccupation could be ruffled by notions of duty and responsibility. Poor Barney.

"I should go, if I were you. There isn't much you can really do here, is there? Your father's case might not even go to court for another eighteen months."

"I still feel as though I have these responsibilities. Even though I had to shuffle Lucy off onto you and Patrick."

Lucy was still in London, staying with Patrick. They had struck up a friendship, genuine for all its improbability. Patrick had promised Lucy that he would help her to find a job.

Nina stroked Barney's bent head. His hair was thick and floppy, and she combed her fingers through it, as she had done before when she held him in her arms. The memory came back to her now, regret and a sense of reprieve neatly twisting together with her growing awareness that what she wanted now, this minute, was for them both to take off their clothes and lie down on the grass. The afternoon had grown very heavy and still.

"Do you feel responsible for me?"

"Kind of."

She sat up a little, moving away from him. "Please don't. I don't want you to."

"Is that the truth?" He was looking at her now. This was what he had hoped to negotiate, evidently.

"What else?"

Barney stood up. He stuck his fists in the pockets of his jeans and walked slowly around the car. When he came back to his starting point he drew Nina to her feet and settled his big hands on her hips.

"You're great, you know?"

Nina betrayed no sign of her amusement. He was so large and good-natured and transparent. "Thank you," she said solemnly. "I think the same of you."

"You really think I should go to Oz?"

"I do."

Barney grinned, at last. "Yeah. Perhaps I will. But not yet."

He edged a step or two backward, still holding her, until he felt the hood of the Mercedes behind him.

"This car," he murmured.

"Don't you like it?" She didn't care what Barney thought of it. The car belonged to Gordon, the windy day at the car showroom, the motel off the freeway.

"What about the environment?" he asked in the faintly prissy way of his generation.

"Oh, I know. I tell you what—I'll sell it."

"But not yet," Barney said. He leaned back, sitting on the sweep of the hood, his feet hooked on the bumper, conscious of the attractiveness of this posture. He drew Nina closer, catching her between his knees. Smiling back at him, willing to enter into this game, Nina unfastened his belt-buckle. As she undid the jeans buttons one by one, she saw the first fat drops of rain splinter into scarlet starbursts on the shining paint.

"Are you afraid of getting wet?" Barney asked, nuzzling her throat.

"Try me."

She didn't want him to talk anymore. The differences between the spoken and unspoken Barney were becoming too apparent.

The rain grew heavier as they kissed, but the drops that slid over the car and over their upturned faces were warm and oily. Nina licked a trickle of water from the corner of her mouth. She unbuttoned her shirt, which was beginning to stick to her skin in the downpour, and bared her shoulders. Barney knelt down in the wet grass to take off her shoes. The rain drummed a jungle rhythm on the roof of the car.

Barney gathered up their discarded clothes and bundled them inside. Then they stood up, pressed together, with the wetness of their skin making a slick seal between them. When they kissed again, greedily now, they felt that they were enclosed within a gray, vertically-washed world that contained no one but themselves.

Nina had begun to remind herself that she was too old and too sober to be cavorting naked in a thunderstorm with a blond boy, and had started to formulate laughing, tactful evasions in her head. But then she thought, *Why should I be too old for this, or for anything else, if that isn't what I feel?*

Suddenly she was struck by a view down the long tunnel of the past that made her feel dizzy.

The years of her marriage shrank back, peeling away before her eyes and diminishing to a mute, one-sided tribute that she had made to Richard, and to Richard's work and needs and opinions, while her own cares and concerns had been sidelined. Even her brief affair with Gordon might only have been what Gordon chose to take and then to reject, while her own part had been to offer herself for the taking and then to accept his withdrawal as if it had been no more than her due.

She had made a life of this meekness, Nina thought, and had assumed that she was happy.

But now, with this extraordinary and disorientating shift of perspective, she wondered if after all it hadn't been happiness at all, but the colorless security of acquiescence.

If it had been, and she could not tell now for sure because of the distorting glass of distance, and the blurring rain, and the absurdity of finding herself here like this with Barney; but if it had been so, then she didn't want it to be so any longer.

Nina felt something shrivel and crack. It was as if her old, thickened skin had split and fallen away in harmless shreds to reveal a new one. Like the cathedral statues, except it was the rain and her nakedness that had regenerated her. She felt suddenly free, neither lonely nor apologetic, and intoxicated by her freedom.

Nina lay back on the hood of the car. Its curved length was warm and smooth under her back, and the rain coldly plastered her hair to her cheeks and pattered on her belly and her eyelids. She spread her arms and then her legs like a starfish on the sand.

Barney mumbled. "That's quite a turn-on."

Nina briefly opened her eyes. "Good," she said simply. Only she knew that she was making this offering not to Barney, but to herself.

He was heavy on top of her, and warm, sheltering her from the rain that had grown cold and sharp. Their bodies slithered together and Nina heard the tiny resonances of the complaining metal as it buckled under their weight.

Briefly they found a rhythm that connected with the rain. Once, the sky split with a livid wire of lightning. Then Nina's fingers dug into the smooth muscle of the boy's back and she moved beyond him, without him, to an illuminated compact sphere of her own devising. He felt her mouth curving in a smile and he glanced down at her, puzzled, ready to be reassured but unable to see into her closed eyes.

Nina's fingers curled into fists and her hips lifted as she came, quickly, with a protesting echo of steel.

Then she lay still, entranced by the taste of rain and the rub of smooth paintwork and skin and the rumble of distant thunder and the sound of the boy's panting breath against her ear, all of these knitting together to produce a shell, a private sphere within which she was perfectly contained as neatly as a baby folded inside the womb.

Afterward, Barney lay still, his heavy head resting on her shoulder, while she moved the tips of her fingers gently down the groove of his spine the way she had done on the first morning. He still felt very firm and young, as if he were modeled from fresh clay.

"Are you cold?" he asked her.

"No. Very warm, and pleased with us."

"Yeah. Not bad, eh?"

Not bad, Nina echoed to herself. *Much better than not bad.*

Barney slid away from her, brought his shirt from the car, and tried ineffectually to rub them both dry with it. It was still raining, but the air was lighter and there was a wash of clear light in the sky beyond Grafton.

The inside of the car was a warm, leather-scented bubble that misted over with their breath as they struggled into their clothes. When they were more or less dressed again, Barney grinned at her.

"That was a bit of a first for me."

"The rain, or the car hood?"

"The two together, actually."

"Ah. Me too, as it happens."

The admission did not betray anything more, Nina thought. Nothing more was necessary.

As they were driving home again, the sun came out. Barney glanced sideways at her. "Why are you smiling so beautifully?" he asked.

She told him the truth. "Because I'm happy."

Michael took the children to Cornwall for ten days. They were staying near the Frosts and the Ransomes because Marcelle and he had agreed that it would be good for Jonathan and Daisy to spend this time with their father, and it was hoped that the company of the other children might help make their mother's absence less apparent.

Marcelle stayed on alone in Grafton. The Pond School was closed for August; there wasn't even the distraction of a holiday course for executive wives. She moved carefully through a succession of solitary days. Without Janice and Vicky and their tactful visits she felt unfounded, as if she had become less than flesh and blood, but the same isolation also made her much more clearly aware of herself instead of some extension of her husband and children and their friends.

She read the occasional newspaper reports about Darcy. She had heard that Darcy and Hannah were immured at Wilton, and once or twice she imagined herself driving the familiar route to call on them. It did not now seem such an improbability, because she no longer felt any particular animosity toward Hannah. All of the knot of anger and grief and bitterness that weighed inside her was twisted around Michael.

For exactly a week after the children's departure with Michael, she saw nobody and hardly emerged from the alarming, fascinating stillness of the house. The weather stayed cool and cloudy; even the garden seemed threateningly open to neighboring windows, although she knew that most of the houses were empty, the occupants away in Corfu or Tuscany. She thought of the labyrinthine longings and subterfuges of all these family holidays, couples and children confronting one another without the buffers of routine, and felt no particular awareness of her own loss. She felt, rather, a sense of the confused buzz of domesticity that had always surrounded her, and the sharp, clear silence that she now inhabited in its absence.

She was not unhappy during this time, although she could never quite recapture the pleasure and release of that second solitary Sunday.

On the evening of the seventh day, Marcelle was sitting in a wicker chair in the garden, in a corner that was made secluded by a projecting wall of the house. There was a row of earthenware pots beside her, planted with a colony of alpines and saxifrages that she had weeded and tidied earlier in the day. The neat little whorls and rosettes of leaves were unassertively pleasing against their collars of gravel. When the bell rang, Marcelle realized that she had been sitting staring at the pots for a long time, with a book lying unopened on her lap.

She thought at first, confusedly, that it was the telephone ringing. The children, perhaps, with the day's news, or Michael with some message. Then she realized that it was the door. She stood up a little stiffly, glancing down at the clothes she had given no thought to for a week, and then went obediently to answer the summons.

Jimmy Rose stood on the step.

"Is this entirely unwelcome? Only say if it is, and I will beat a retreat. Not hasty, but quite orderly."

She knew from the yellowish creases at the side of his mouth as much as his ornate phrases that Jimmy had been drinking. He was not drunk yet, but on the way. She looked at him dispassionately, as if he were a stranger to her.

"It isn't unwelcome." Her voice felt rusty from disuse. "Come in."

From behind the jug of white nicotiana that she had left on the countertop in the tidy kitchen, Marcelle asked, "Would you like a drink?"

Jimmy had been out to lunch with his bank manager. This was a regular enough arrangement; in the past, after a nominal reference to Jimmy's company account, they had always moved on to more congenial discussions about local politics and business and their golf games and, over a last drink, whatever tidbit of gossip they had heard about their mutual acquaintances. Although the man had been no less cordial than usual, today, however, he had reminded Jimmy that his business account was overdrawn substantially. No one understood better than he, of course, that in the present climate things were not easy, but he believed that it would not be in Jimmy's own best interest for the bank to extend any further credit.

Jimmy had nodded, his fork cutting through the flaky pastry of some dish he did not want. Every mouthful he took tasted like chalk, and he needed a long swallow of wine to wash the paste out of his mouth. Business showed signs of revival, he said. He was confident that by the autumn the picture would be different.

The manager pursed his small mouth. He did not press the subject, but neither did he agree to stay for the brandy that Jimmy suggested and definitely wanted.

After they had shaken hands and the man left, Jimmy sat on his own and ordered one anyway. He drank it too quickly, then had to go back to the office. The afternoon yawned around him, and at five o'clock he abruptly left and walked the skein of Grafton's medieval streets until he reached an unfashionable pub at the edge of the old cattle market. The bar was empty, but in his depressed state it seemed to be haunted by hollow-eyed cattle-drovers in greasy jerkins, and rank with the smell of animals. He sat at a smeared table and drank two and a half pints of beer with the television blinking over his head. When he could not face any more beer he stood up, with no idea where to go except that he did not want it to be home. He thought of Marcelle.

In her kitchen, he said, "Scotch, thanks. Aren't you having one?"

"Just some wine, I think."

Marcelle produced glasses and bottles. Jimmy kept his eye on the whisky, and folded his fingers around his tumbler as soon as it was offered. The spirit cleared a fiery space in his heavy stomach, making him think that all would be well.

"Are you hungry?"

"Not really. Lunch with the bank manager. The usual crap."

He felt angry now, properly angry with the man. Through the

swirls of his indignation he understood that Marcelle was suggesting something, and without bothering to decipher what it was he followed her. Then, a moment later, he found himself sitting in the garden, in a sheltered corner with a surprising pool of westerly sun spilling onto some fussy little plants in flowerpots at his feet. It was quiet except for birds singing in the trees.

Marcelle was gazing at him. She looked calm and neat, with her brown hair shiny, not unlike some glossy little bird herself. She was better off without Michael, probably. Much better. Anyone could have predicted that.

Jimmy let his head fall back against the cushion. There was a comfortable creak of wicker. It had been a long day, and he was too tired to be angry any longer. The sun felt pleasantly warm on his face, like a woman's soothing fingers

"You look nice," he said to Marcelle. "You look much better."

"I am better. Funny, isn't it?"

He did not much want to talk about Marcelle's problems; he had enough of his own. But it was good to be sitting here with her. When had that other time been, in someone else's garden, when he had had to discourage her? That had been because of Lucy, of course. He felt a swell of regret for the loss of her, and then with a determined jerk he sat upright. There was no point in thinking any more about that.

He leaned forward and put his hand on Marcelle's bare leg, stroking with the tips of his fingers. Her skin was soft. He was deciding that he might just salvage something from the dismal day. A pleasant prospect began softly to unravel in his mind.

Marcelle leaned forward, too. He could smell her clean hair, and see her un-madeup eyelashes and the tiny shreds of dryish skin on her lower lip. Recollections of her body in a bikini from beaches and picnics were superimposed with his imaginings while he undressed her in his mind. Jimmy thought that he would kiss her now. He swallowed a belch and shuffled himself into position.

Her fingers snapped around his wrist and dropped his hand back in his own lap. He didn't understand what she was doing, so he wheedled, "Mar, come on. Just a kiss. We know each other, don't we?"

"Yes, we do."

"Why not, then? I thought you wanted to."

The whisky on top of the beer had tipped him over the edge into drunkenness. He had an erection now and wondered how long he could keep it if Marcelle was going to insist on persuasion. Renewed irritation fretted at the margins of his consciousness.

"No, that's where you're wrong. I don't want to, Jimmy, not with you. Not a bit."

He looked down at his feet, at the empty glass he had carefully put down beside his chair, at the flowerpots, while the soft, rosy moments he had anticipated flaked away and vanished to expose a tinny and monotonous substratum, the reality of his life. His shoes were dusty, he noticed, and there were cracks in the leather across the toes.

"Why?" he managed to ask. Not that he wanted to hear the answer. "We're both lonely tonight, aren't we?" It was obvious, and mawkish, but it was some of the truth that he suddenly wanted to confess. He did feel lonely.

Marcelle appeared to mull it over. She was remembering how she had felt beautiful, for an instant, in the Ransomes' dark garden, before Jimmy had rebuffed her and anger had finally burned up her humiliation.

She let herself taste the satisfaction of the moment before she told him, "I've been here on my own, you know, for a whole week. Just me, in the house. But I'm not that lonely. You can do a lot of thinking in a week, and one of the things I've thought about is doing what I want. Or not nearly so much of what I don't want. And I've just realized, only just, that you fall into the category of what I don't want. Do you think you can just turn up here, because Michael's gone, and I'll lie down for you without a word? I don't want to kiss you, and I don't want to go to bed with you, although I might once have."

She was smiling, Jimmy noticed, a beatific smile that stirred the irritation in his blood into sluggish, nauseating waves.

"I don't want you to touch me, not the way you do to all of us in corners at parties. It's a bit too indiscriminate to be flattering. I don't like the way you treat Star, or the way you whisper everyone's secrets. I don't like the way you smell of the pub tonight."

She hesitated, then put her hand up, half-covering her mouth,

as if the old Marcelle was alarmed by the discovery of this new one
and was afraid that she might go on spilling out more.

Jimmy stood up, unsteady against the wicker chair. Whisky
fumed in his head.

"Silly bitch," he whispered.

He raised his hand and examined the opened palm, then
clenched his fist and swiped out with it, needing to hit something
to vent his rage. His fist struck the wall of the house, and pain shot
up his arm to his elbow. When he looked down at the curled fingers
he saw blood springing in the creases. Marcelle was fixed in her
seat. At least she wasn't smiling any longer.

Jimmy kicked his glass aside and heard it ring and then smash
on the flagstones. He made his way uncertainly back through the
house, slamming the front door behind him. He found his car, after
searching among the cars parked along the road, and drove home
with his throbbing fist curled in his lap.

Marcelle sat where he had left her. Even the birds seemed to
have stopped singing. After a while the silence began to be oppres-
sive. She went inside and wandered through the quiet rooms, and
saw how over-neat and unoccupied they seemed.

The scene with Jimmy had broken a kind of spell. She wanted
to see the children, and to talk to Michael, and hold all of them
because they belonged to her. As soon as the realization came to
her, it intensified. The house was only a shell, but she was not so
empty herself. She almost ran to the telephone. There were still
three days of the holiday left. If she set out now, she could be in
Cornwall long before bedtime.

Michael answered the telephone.

"You sound different," he said.

"Michael, I want to come down there. I don't know why I'm
here on my own without you all. Can I come?"

There was only a second's silence. "Yes," he said. "Yes, come
now."

Star watched through the window as Jimmy parked the car.
When he slammed the door, a loop of seatbelt caught in it so that
it wouldn't lock, but he flung himself away from it without trying

to put it right. As she looked at him, Star felt a thread break inside her.

The front door juddered open and then shut, and Jimmy came into the house. She stood where she was, waiting, until he stalked into the room. He walked past her to sit down on the worn sofa. He looked up at her then, with his shoulders hunched and his hands hanging down between his knees. A scent of aggression was emanating from him, and his anger shone in the red points in his eyes. Star thought she knew what was coming.

"Why are you looking at me like that?" he demanded.

"Like what?"

"You know how. Like a saint smelling a bad smell."

"You said it, not me. How much have you had to drink?"

He took his wrist in one hand. His face contorted. "Not fucking enough, not nearly. Christ, stop looking at me, will you?"

Star didn't move. Jimmy got to his feet and came across the room.

"Don't touch me again," she warned him. She saw the blood on his hand now. "What have you done? *Don't touch me!*"

There was a little series of pictures in her head, like a slide show, only they were not happy images. Jimmy had not hit her very many times, but she could see each occasion as clearly as if it had just happened. She had collaborated with him, she knew that, in keeping these pictures hidden. Although the scenes were shameful, they were not dark in her head; rather they were illuminated by the harsh white light of anger. The light hurt her now, in anticipation of the violence.

Jimmy hesitated. They stood in the middle of their living room, with the evidence of their shared life crowding around them. Star knew every detail too intimately, and felt herself float free from all of it.

"I wasn't going to touch you," Jimmy mumbled. He looked down at his own fist. "I hit a wall. At Marcelle's." The aggression leaked out of him. His eyes were dull now.

Star was watching him. She began to nod. There was nothing that connected her to this room, for all its familiarity, nor to the man in the pictures in her head. She had known this for a long time, and understood that she had been waiting for the minute that had just arrived.

This, then, was how it ended.

She was still nodding, slowly, confirming it for herself. The end came neither banging nor whimpering, but in silence, as they looked at each other, with their furniture and books and photographs as mute witnesses.

"I'm going," Star said at last.

Jimmy held out the good hand, but he was standing too far away.

"Going where?"

She saw his confusion, but dispassionately, because it didn't belong to her any longer.

"Nowhere in particular. Just not to be here. I'll take a few things from upstairs. I'll call you, when . . . when we have to arrange the rest."

Star left him and went upstairs. She packed a few clothes in a bag, taking shirts and underclothes out of drawers without examining them. She felt no more for the room than she would have done for a hotel suite.

When she came downstairs again, Jimmy was sitting in his usual chair in the living room, with his face turned toward the window.

"I'll call," she said again, but he did not look round. Star went out the front door carrying her bag. She walked across town to the cathedral green, to Nina's house on Dean's Row.

The two women sat facing each other in the upstairs living room. Star had drunk two glasses of wine, but she had refused Nina's offers of something to eat.

"You're lucky to live with this view," Star murmured. The unveiled statues floated ethereally in the dusk. The bare room and Nina's company were like a quiet full stop at the end of the day's sentence.

"Was she pregnant?" Star asked. "The Clegg girl?"

"Yes."

"That must have been hard for her. Is she all right?"

"I think so. My friend Patrick has adopted her."

"I knew about her and Jimmy. And the others, of course. Going back over the years."

Nina said what she could, which was not much, and prepared to listen.

"I'm not going home again," Star told her.

"What do you want to do?"

Star looked into her glass and then smiled. "This isn't a bad start. Thank you for taking me in."

"I'm glad to have you here. It's been lonely, lately."

That was the truth. There had been no disagreement with Barney, but since the picnic he had stopped turning up in his gardener's overalls on the way home from a day's work. Nina poured more wine.

"Do you remember in February, when we first got to know each other, when everyone seemed to be away skiing? We walked across the bridge to the school. It felt as though we were the only people in Grafton."

"Yes," Star said softly. "I rather liked that. It's the same this evening, don't you think?"

They sat and looked out at the glimmering stonework as the light faded and softened it. New layers of understanding seemed to shift and settle between them.

"What will Jimmy do tonight?"

"He'll sit where I left him, with a glass and a bottle. In the end he'll fall asleep. Lying sideways on the sofa, with his knees drawn up and his hands folded between them."

The intimacy that this betrayed touched Nina with a sudden sadness. Husbands and wives knew each other so well, she thought, through all the unbeautiful accretions of habit and routine.

"Don't you want to go back?"

"No. I won't go back." Star did not betray a tremor of doubt. "He wouldn't notice if I was there or not."

There was a flicker, and a wash of light filled the room. Star and Nina blinked at each other, momentarily dazzled by the brightness. Then they turned again toward the windows. The cathedral façade was blazing with golden light that turned the greenish summer twilight into darkness. The pale and naked stone reflected in their eyes.

"I didn't know," Nina murmured. "Gordon said it would be a whole year before they lit it up again."

The mention of Gordon was like a further acknowledgment of intimacy between them. Nina never spoke of him to anyone now.

They left their chairs and went to stand side-by-side at the window. Dark attendants were busy with the buttresses of lights at the edge of the green. The women watched, and then looked up once more at the miraculous ranks of reborn saints and angels. The hands and faces and folds of fabric were sharp again, as if centuries had been struck away.

Star put her arm around Nina's shoulder, and they stood there, silenced by the glory of it.

Then, with another blink, the lights were doused again. The darkness seemed impenetrable while the brilliance lingered in their eyes.

"They must have been just testing them," Nina said.

"For our benefit, then," Star asserted. "I'm glad we saw it like this."

Nina wanted to celebrate the moment.

"I think we need some more wine. I'll go get it just as soon as I can see again."

They drank the wine and talked, but neither of them wanted to eat. It was late when they went upstairs to the room above Nina's, which had the same view of the dim green, although from a different angle and through smaller windows. There were bare oak boards here, and a wrought-iron bed with a white cover. Nina turned the cover down, then went to release the shutters from their cases.

"Leave the windows so I can see out in the night," Star said. She was sitting on the edge of the bed, looking suddenly unsure of herself in the unfamiliar room. Nina remembered that Gordon had liked the shutters downstairs left open, too. The links seemed to shiver and catch her again. She sat down beside Star and took her hand.

"Will you be comfortable?" she asked.

There was only one light in the room, a small shaded bulb on the night table. There were strong shadows across each woman's face, revealing unfamiliar planes and hollows that were startlingly bleached of gender.

Star did not answer. Instead she leaned forward and put her mouth against Nina's, and with the tip of her tongue she made a tiny question mark against her lip.

Nina sat still, with the beginning of the kiss in her bones.

Then, not knowing whether the shiver she felt was relief or regret, she felt herself draw back. There was a hair's breadth of space between them, then a handspan.

"I'm sorry," Nina said humbly.

"It's all right. It helps to know, don't you think?"

"I don't think I know anything."

"Barney Clegg, is it?"

There was something so droll in this that they began to laugh. Their laughter broke up around them, filling the room and dispelling the confusion.

"Yes. But no, not in the way you think."

Or not even in the way I think, Nina realized, admitting a bizarre possibility to herself for the very first time.

"I see," Star said mockingly. And then, "Go on, go to bed now."

From the doorway, Nina said, "You can stay for as long as you want, you know. Whatever you need, whatever you like."

"Thank you," Star answered, the shadows momentarily and mysteriously bleaching her face again.

19

*I*t was past midnight when Marcelle reached the rented house on the Cornish coast. She had lost her way twice in the lanes leading to the cove, and she was tired as well as hesitant while she negotiated the last mile of sandy track.

Her headlights picked out a low hedge and the windblown humps of trees, and then the little group of houses at the end of the track. The keel of an upended dinghy made a pale blur in the lee of one of the houses. There was only one light showing, a yellowish square that thickened the darkness around it. Marcelle located Michael's car and eased her own into the space next to it. Before her headlights flicked off, she saw sailboards propped against a low wall, and a wetsuit like a peeled skin left out to dry. She stepped out of the car, stretching to ease her cramped muscles, with her nervous breathing making an irregular flutter in her throat.

The sea air filled her lungs, and she heard invisible surf washing on the beach. At once there came confused memories of a dozen seaside holidays, with her children and from her own childhood, all of them dissolving into one solution of salt and waves and sunlight.

Now that she was here, she did not think of family holidays in the way she had done back in Grafton, when she had been excluded from their conspiracy. Rather the associations gave her a powerful sense of continuity, of the importance of such memories for Michael and herself, to be handed on to the children, and to their children in turn. She was a mother, the truth could not be obliterated even if she wished it, and her family dues could not be as simply denied or withheld as she had imagined in her solitude in Grafton.

Another rectangle of yellow sliced through the salt darkness when a door opened in the house with the light. Marcelle made out

Michael's silhouette within it. She walked through a sandy rut to a gate, and then up a concrete path toward the door. Michael stood aside to let her in.

There was a living room with standard holiday-rental pine furniture, and red-and-russet rough-weave curtains left open in the window. The room reminded Marcelle of the chalet at Méribel, and thus of Michael elated in the snow, and Hannah in her silvery suit.

She blinked in the brightness, uncertain of how she should act now that she had gained her objective and reached the place.

"How was the drive?" Michael asked.

"Long. Uneventful, except at the end, when I got lost."

"Jon and Daisy will be glad you're here."

"Where are they sleeping?"

Michael pointed to the ceiling.

"I'll just go up and see them, shall I?"

There was a small room with the door left ajar so that light from the landing cast a narrow bar across the floor. Daisy would still not settle down in the dark. Marcelle crossed softly to the bunk beds and inhaled the warmth of sleeping children. Jonathan slept as he always did, with the covers pulled defensively over his head. Daisy lay on her back with her arms and legs flung out. Marcelle drew the blanket up to cover her shoulders and the child turned in her sleep, mumbling some lost words. Then she opened her eyes, and immediately her face lit into a smile. She lifted her arm and crooked it around Marcelle's neck as her mother bent over her in the confined space.

"Good," Daisy said distinctly. Then she retreated into sleep again.

Marcelle felt a lurch of unmitigated love for her children tangle her innards.

Michael was sitting at a drop-leaf table against the drawn curtains when she came back downstairs. There was food on the table, bread and fruit and cold ham, and a bottle of wine.

"Have you eaten?"

"No. I'm not very hungry. But thank you for this."

He poured the wine and Marcelle gratefully took the glass he handed her. After her week of solitude, these little attentions seemed exotic. She was surprised by the nervous uncertainty that made her breath taut in her throat, because his presence was entirely natural and familiar to her. They were on holiday, in a rented cottage beside the sea, as they had been many times before. It was hard to remember that they had separated, unless she concentrated on the recollection.

They talked a little about the children, and the other families, and Marcelle listened to the small pieces of news that Michael had to relate. She drank her wine, watching his face and trying to see behind it.

"Why did you decide to come now, tonight?" he asked her at last.

Marcelle told him about Jimmy's visit. She described it exactly, but in dry, colorless language, as if it had happened a long time ago. Even so, she could hear that her words fitted into circles, closing links that had gaped open before. Hannah and me, she could hear Michael thinking, Jimmy and you, Nina and Gordon. This is what happens at our age. These needs are admitted. We are shamed by them, but we cannot deny that they exist.

The easiness of his assumption pricked her, but she let it go, understanding that they had inched closer for it.

Michael said, "I still don't understand. Why did what happened with Jimmy make you want to come down here, to us?"

"I went inside after he had gone and walked through the rooms. Everything was very tidy, just how I wanted it, nothing like the house is when Jon and Daisy are at home. I had spent a week, you know, putting it all in order."

"I can imagine." He laughed then, and for a second she saw the man she had married. She laughed with him, in surprised harmony.

"I realized that I didn't like it. It was empty, and it made me think of you all here without me."

Michael heard her take a sharp breath, filling her lungs for some effort of expression. It made her seem birdlike, a fragile but determined creature. He thought then that he did love her, but that somewhere on their complicated journey together he had forgotten how to acknowledge as much.

"I could hear the silence, and I missed the comfort of being a family. I had thought that being on my own made me feel clear, and defined, and I liked the feeling. But at the same time I was so solitary that by the end I was wondering if I really existed. Jimmy didn't exactly confirm anything for me."

She spread out her fingers, as if checking her own corporeality.

"In the end, I came just because I wanted to."

It was important, she understood, to admit to her own wishes.

"I'm glad it was what you wanted."

Michael left his place and walked around the table behind her. He put his hands on her shoulders. The ridges of scapulae and clavicles felt prominent, barely covered by her thin skin. Different from the silky layers of Hannah; different but also the same, womanly. Michael bowed his head, so that his cheek just rested against his wife's head.

"What about me?" he asked.

Marcelle felt a ripple of amusement, but she concealed her smile. Some of the bitterness that she had knotted around Michael was unraveling.

"I wanted to see you."

"Good," he said quietly.

Marcelle slipped from under the weight of his hands and stood up to face him. She leaned her head forward so that it touched his shoulder.

It was not a resolution, she knew that. It was a long way from that, even. But it was something, a small exchange of faith.

The next day the weather turned warm and clear, as if to welcome Marcelle. There were delighted greetings from the Frosts and the Ransomes when they arrived and found her having breakfast.

"We missed you," Andrew said for all of them.

The three families went to the beach and made their encampment of windbreaks and folding chairs and watersports equipment among all the other families. Marcelle contentedly sat in a deck chair and looked at the children in the sea. Helen Ransome slept in her stroller with a little white frilled sunshade tilted over her head. Small additions were made to the geological strata of Marcelle's memories. *That was the year such-and-such happened. I remember so-and-so that year.* She realized with relief that this moment right now was not an ending but a continuation.

"Are you all right?" Vicky and Janice found opportunities to murmur to her. "Is everything all right again?"

"I don't know," Marcelle told them truthfully, "Maybe." She watched Michael wading into the surf with Toby Frost's boogie board. He looked like a stork, with his elongated legs striking arrows through the foam. Some of her anger at him had gone, partly replaced by a kind of tolerance that seemed to be forming like new skin under an old scab. In the night they had lain side-by-side, just touching, comfortable with that without attempting anything more. Marcelle had listened as Michael's breathing slowed and deepened. She was tired, too, and it had seemed natural, even luxurious to lie and listen to her husband sleeping, with the rustle of the waves in the distance.

It was a happy day on the beach, and the adult happiness affected the children, too. They played generously and uncombatively together, although Jonathan and Daisy kept referring back to Marcelle as if they were afraid that she might disappear. At the end of the afternoon, when it grew cooler and it was time to leave, they clamored for more.

"Let's all have supper together," Jonathan begged. "Can't we, now that Mum's here?"

"Why not?" Janice looked pleased and plump in her candy-striped shorts. "We can scrape something together at our place. Everyone come to us."

The Frosts' holiday house was further along the headland, set a little back from the coastal cliffs in a sheltered hollow. The families congregated in the garden, where wooden pub benches were drawn up against a rough slatted table amid a jumble of sandy towels and discarded flip-flops. For the adults it felt pleasantly relaxing to leave the day's lumber and sit in the late-afternoon sun, drinking beer and talking. The children swept into the house in search of potato chips and Coca-Cola and then out again onto the headland. Andrew fussed over the barbecue until the smell of charcoal smoke drifted into the air. Everyone had pink patches on their bare arms and cheeks flushed from the sun. Michael and Marcelle sat together on one of the wooden benches.

"It's like long ago," Vicky said. "Being here like this, just us."

The couples agreed, knowing she meant that it only seemed so long since they had been together in this uncomplicated way.

Janice brought out more bottles and they changed from beer to wine, glad because there were only beach paths to be negotiated on the way back to their own beds. The sky faded from blue to pearl gray and then, for an instant, to glimmering eau-de-nil.

The children were rounded up from their games and everyone crowded around the table. The smaller ones were tired now and the first quarrels broke out, but the parents were loosened with wine and officiated good-humoredly until the food was eaten. Marcelle propped her chin on her hand. She felt comfortable with the evening's gossip and drink and with the undemanding reverberations of friendship. She found herself smiling. All her joints seemed unpinned; it would be a big effort to stand up when the time came.

The sky darkened until they couldn't see beyond the unkempt summer garden. Andrew brought out some candles from the house and stood them in empty jam jars so that the flames burned upright. The visible world contracted to a golden circle around the table, the children running in and out of it, their voices coming back from beyond the margins.

"Bed for my lot," Gordon called out. "Mary? Alice? I'll take them, Vicky. You stay if you like."

"I would quite like," Vicky admitted. "Only I seem to have had a lot to drink already."

"We're on holiday," Andrew insisted, pouring more wine.

Gordon went away down the track that led to the other house. He was carrying Helen asleep in his arms, and the other two little girls held on to his legs while they negotiated the steep path.

The group around the table heard Mary protesting, "It's not fair, Daisy's staying up," and the beginning of Gordon's answer, until the receding voices were absorbed by the still air.

"Shall we go, too?" Michael asked Marcelle. His arm was around her shoulder, and she dropped her head to rest against it.

"Not yet."

"Not yet," Daisy repeated. "We want to play." She was elated to be allowed to stay up with the Frost boys and Jonathan.

"Just half an hour," Michael called out. It was completely dark now. Toby Frost, the leader, was announcing the rules of some game from beyond the garden wall.

"Wait for me," Daisy shouted to the boys. There was a sugary thud as someone jumped off a low wall into the sand, then the sound of running footsteps. They heard William counting, and then singing something, his choirboy's voice very clear and high in the silence. After that there was only the sound of the waves and the talk around the cluttered table. Andrew leaned over one of the jam jars to stick a fresh candle into the melted ruins of the old one, and for a moment his face was grotesquely lit from below, like a Halloween mask.

Vicky lifted her drink and tilted it toward her nose.

"Here's to all of us," she said.

They drank, echoing the toast after clinking their glasses.

They were reminded of the dozens of other evenings they had spent together, the Christmases and the summer barbecues and all the other landmarks of the year, and separately they felt the absence of the Cleggs and the Roses with an unspoken shiver that made them draw closer together and begin to talk of the plans for another season. They were laughing, with their heads close together in the candlelight, slightly drunk with wine and good humor and sea air.

There was a small, bitten crescent of moon hanging low in the sky.

"It's a beautiful night," Marcelle whispered. "Just listen to the waves."

The surf was clearly audible now, as if some volume control had been sharply turned up. Its sound seemed suddenly to emphasize the silence that overlaid it. There were no voices, no running feet.

"How long have the kids been gone?" someone asked.

They listened again, but there was nothing except the sound of the waves.

"Did they say where they were going?"

"I didn't see which way they went."

Andrew stood up abruptly, jogging the table so that the candle flames wavered. "They won't be far away. But I'll wander down to the beach to find them. It's time they were heading for bed."

They listened to his footsteps swishing along the beach path.

"I'll make some coffee," Janice said into the silence.

She was carrying out the loaded tray when they heard Andrew come back again.

"Any sign of them?"

"They're not on the beach."

"How long have they been gone?"

"It must be half an hour. Perhaps a bit longer."

"You said half an hour, Michael."

"I know what I said."

"We'd better go find them. Mike, you go over the headland that way. I'll do the opposite direction."

"What about us? What do you want us to do?" Janice asked. There was a panicky note in her voice. "What have we been *doing*, sitting here while they were getting lost?"

"All right, Jan. Just stay here. Michael and I will find them."

After the two men had gone, the women sat at the table with the debris of the evening still around them. Marcelle began to pile the dirty plates. She had lost coordination, and the rattle and clink of the cutlery sounded unnaturally loud and domestic in the thick silence. They were straining their ears for different sounds. Vicky put her arm around Janice's shoulders and found that she was shaking.

"You're cold. Have you got a sweater?"

"In there somewhere."

Marcelle went to look for it. The light in the kitchen was over-bright and harsh, and as she hunted clumsily for Janice's sweater she realized just how much she had had to drink. Her mouth was dry and there were queasy flutters of fear buckling her diaphragm. She found the sweater over the back of a chair and carried it out into the garden. She was remembering how she had gone upstairs to look at the children last night, and the way that Daisy's face had broken into a smile of delight even though she was fast asleep. *Please*, she found herself whispering.

Janice was standing at the end of the garden, gazing over the wall into the dark. She took the sweater from Marcelle but didn't put it on.

"Something has happened," she whispered. "I know it has."

They waited, and the minutes slid past in silence.

"How long since Andrew and Michael left?"

"Ten minutes. Perhaps a quarter of an hour."

"Where *are* they?"

After another moment, Vicky turned her head sharply. "Listen—what's that?"

It was the sound of running feet now. They heard them thudding and slithering on sand, and then two small figures appeared. It was Jonathan and Daisy. *Thank God*, Marcelle thought. Their faces were little white patches emerging from the blackness directly in front of the house. Neither Andrew nor Michael had gone the right way.

Marcelle began to run, with Vicky and Janice at her heels. The children came at them full tilt. Marcelle's relief evaporated as they came closer. Both of the children were choking for breath and Daisy was stumbling with exhaustion.

"William's fallen," Jonathan cried.

There was a long, terrible second while he gasped for air, and the children clung to Marcelle. *Just a minute ago*, she thought wildly, *everything was all right. Just that little while ago we were all sitting here, drinking wine and laughing, and now all that easiness has gone . . .*

Janice's eyes and mouth rounded into dark holes of shock and fear. Her hands went up to her cheeks.

"Where, Jon?" Vicky insisted. "Where has he fallen?"

"The cliffs. He was climbing up and he fell on the rocks. Toby's trying to get down to him. He told us to run for Andrew and Dad."

Janice's head was spinning. Her face had gone greenish-white, but she was already heading in the direction Jon had pointed out.

It was Vicky who took charge. "Marcelle, phone for help. Stay here with Daisy, tell the men what's happened when they come back. Jon, you'll have to show us where he is."

She turned and ran after Janice, with Jonathan scrambling off beside her.

Daisy was weeping. "William's hurt," she blurted out. "He wasn't moving. Where's Daddy?"

"Looking for you."

Marcelle seized her hand and propelled her back to the house. She wasted seconds because she had no idea where the telephone was, and when she found it she cursed her unfamiliarity with the area while she struggled to describe where the accident had happened. When she hung up at last, she turned to look at Daisy's blotchy, terrified face.

"Help's coming. What happened?"

The child began to cry again. "We went to the beach, and we came back the other way. There's a path up the side, the side of the cliffs, it's steep but it's much quicker because we knew we were going to be late and you'd be angry, and then William said he could climb straight up the rocks anyway, and we watched him and he got more than halfway, only we could see it was harder than he thought, and then he grabbed a piece of rock that stuck out and it came away and he fell."

"Oh, Daisy."

Marcelle sank down onto a kitchen chair and held the child against her, hands cupping her head, as if she would at least keep this one safe.

"We shouldn't have let you go off like that in the dark." There was no sound except the sea. "I wish Daddy would come."

Toby was waiting at the foot of the cliff, crouched on the rocks beside his brother. He was trembling. It did not look so steep or so high from down here. He thought that William should have been able to do the climb easily. If only the piece of rock had not been dislodged. The waves were very loud. William was lying so still, with his eyes closed. He had rolled rather than fallen straight down. If only the rock had not broken away.

Toby could hear the phrases in his head, broken pieces of explanation, mixed with incoherent, begging prayers. He was afraid to touch. Afraid to do anything. There was black blood on William's forehead, and his hair was wet with it.

If only they would come, Jon's a good runner, isn't he? They must have found their way back by now . . .

Toby even couldn't tell if William was breathing. He was afraid of the stillness.

There, was that voices? He looked up. Above him, thirty or forty feet up, he saw the glimmer of faces. It was his mother, at last, with Vicky and Jon.

"Please come," he called up to them. He was giving way, now that they were here.

Then he heard his father's voice, shouting, away to the left. *"Andrew!"*

That was his mother. The sound of her panic increased his own.

"Help us," Toby screamed. William still did not move.

Marcelle and Daisy sat in the kitchen, waiting. There was a clock on the wall, with red numerals and thin red hands, and each sweep of the second hand seemed to last forever.

When the garden gate creaked they leaped up and ran to the window. It was Vicky, with Jonathan. Jonathan was crying, too, and the two children met and huddled together.

"Michael and Andrew are there now. Is the ambulance coming?"

"Yes. Yes, it's coming. It must be ten or twelve minutes since I called."

"I'll call again. Mike says they'll need a rescue crew."

When she came back from the telephone, the two women looked helplessly at each other over the heads of the children.

"What happened?" Marcelle whispered.

Vicky shook her head, warningly, the corners of her mouth turned down. Marcelle closed her eyes, but when she opened them again the kitchen and the clock and the fierce brightness were all unchanged. The electric hum of kitchen appliances was hostile, trapping them in some mine field of fear and paralysis. The barbecue seemed a long time ago, part of some other life to which they had now forfeited all rights.

"Will William be all right?" Daisy asked.

"I hope so," Marcelle said.

"Look." Jonathan pointed to the window that faced away from the sea. There were revolving blue lights bumping down the lane.

William was carried up from the rocks in a rescue stretcher, with Michael stooped beside him. The stretcher was loaded into the ambulance at the clifftop. Michael and Janice went with it, and then the journey over the headland began in reverse. A police car brought Toby and Andrew back to the house. The women and

Daisy and Jonathan were still waiting in the kitchen, the clock hands sweeping impervious circles above them.

"How is he?"

Andrew shook his head.

"I don't know. He has head injuries. I'm going to follow on to the hospital."

"I want to come," Toby said. His set mouth and jaw made him look mulish, the expression at odds with the fearful pallor of his face.

"No. Stay here with Marcelle and Vicky."

Andrew drove away in the wake of the ambulance. The police and the rescue team had gone, and to those who were left the darkness and drumming of the surf seemed to possess the house.

The women made hot drinks for the children and persuaded them to go to bed, Jonathan in William's bunk above Toby, and Daisy in Janice and Andrew's double bed. Toby was shivering and all three of them protested dully that they couldn't sleep, but they did anyway, collapsing quickly into oblivion as if escaping from the night. Marcelle sat downstairs at the kitchen table, trying not to listen to Vicky in the next room murmuring to Gordon on the telephone.

She thought of the election party, when Michael had gone to the hospital with Darcy after his heart attack and she had sat just like this at Janice's table, waiting to find the strength to go home alone. Why had all of that seemed to cost so much? The memory of Michael and Hannah, of Hannah with the tiny ruff of mud and grass around the tips of her stiletto heels, her own shock and disbelief, was diminished now, pressed into near-insignificance by the hideous events of this evening.

If only William is all right, she thought desperately, *if only he's all right, how different then will we all be, knowing what we know now?*

Marcelle fitted her cold hands together, palm to palm, feeling a guilty gratitude that her own children were safe. She also thought of Michael, as she had not done for a long time, as a doctor. Michael could do something other than sit. Her admiration for him came awkwardly, because she was not practiced with it, but still it came, refilling an empty space inside her.

Vicky came and sat down opposite her. She stretched out one hand and put it over hers.

"What can we do?" Marcelle whispered.

"Pray, I suppose. Just pray."

Michael came back again in the small hours of the morning. They saw at once that there was no good news. Marcelle stood up and went to him, aware that she didn't really know how to comfort him.

Michael said, without preamble, "A blood clot has formed under the site of the skull fracture. They'll have to operate to remove it. The plan at the moment, unless his condition deteriorates, is to do it sometime tomorrow."

"How bad is he?" Vicky asked.

"Fifty-fifty."

"Poor little William," Vicky whispered.

"What about Andrew and Janice?"

"They're sitting in a waiting room. Those red hospital chairs, plastic beakers of tea. I've seen it so often, the parents there looking up at you when you come in with the notes as if you're God instead of some surgeon, with . . ." Michael shrugged, his face hidden from them.

With his own pain, Marcelle silently completed the sentence for him, *and no better answers than anyone else.*

"It was terrible to see them sitting like that," Michael said, without lifting his face from his hands.

Marcelle got up, stood behind him, and put her hands on his shoulders, then leaned forward so that her cheek rested against his head. His hands reached up to her wrists, holding her there.

"I should go back to Gordon," Vicky said at last.

Michael saw Vicky home down the path that Gordon had taken, seemingly ages ago. When he came back, Marcelle was already in bed. He undressed quickly, dropping his clothes haphazardly, and slid under the covers on the opposite side. Daisy lay between them, her mouth slightly open and her breath thick with sleep. They both turned inward, knowing and loving the shape of her and fearing the fragility of the smooth limbs and the skull under the floss of fine hair, as they feared for Andrew and Janice's child in his hospital bed.

Outside it was already growing light again.

* * *

The operation to remove the blood clot from William's brain took place the next morning. Janice came back in the late afternoon with the news that he was stable, although he had not regained consciousness. Bruised pouches of tiredness had swollen out of the soft skin beneath her eyes. Toby clung to her, she tried to reassure him that it had been an accident, that it was no one's fault.

The children were given their supper at the same table in the garden. By their own unspoken agreement they left the place that William had occupied the night before empty for him, as if he might suddenly materialize in the midst of the meal.

For all the difference in their ages, the children seemed to draw together, finding a common ground in their anxiety and in their sober awareness at discovering themselves to be a part of this emergency. They ate quietly, passing each other the ketchup.

While Janice tried to sleep for an hour, the four remaining adults looked over the diminishing row of heads, from Toby to Alice, through the kitchen window. The parents felt the tension dividing them as well as linking them, invisible fine threads tangled in the air. They were all heavy with the thought that they had been drinking wine and laughing in the garden when William fell, and the knowledge isolated them but drew them together, too.

Marcelle was drying plates, polishing them over and over with a tea cloth.

"When he does regain consciousness, is he likely to be permanently damaged?"

Michael said, "I don't know. I don't suppose they do, either. But it must be a possibility, even if no more than that."

She did not stop her slow circling with the cloth, nor looking out from time to time through the checked curtains at the children around the table.

"Is it our fault?"

Michael knew it would be Marcelle who articulated the question. She was the quickest to draw blame to herself. But he thought of this as a matter of fact now, not as a judgment.

"It can't be undone, whether it is a matter of fault or not."

It was Gordon who answered her. He made a gesture that drew them all into a net that they swam in together.

Vicky looked up from feeding Helen, who was perched in a high-chair affixed to the edge of the Formica-topped table. The baby's face was joyfully smeared with apricot pudding. Gordon hadn't been there, hadn't been in the garden when the older children vanished, but still he included himself in the net. She smiled at him, knowing that she loved him.

"Gordon's right," she said to Marcelle.

They heard the floor creak overhead. Janice was getting up again. This time nobody needed to articulate what they all felt, the steady reverberation of friendship.

Janice went back to the hospital to wait with Andrew.

Two more nights and days passed, and when the end of the holiday came William's condition was unchanged.

The families reloaded their station wagons and headed back to Grafton in the late-August traffic. Andrew and Janice had agreed that they would take it in turns to stay near the hospital, so that one of them would be with William when he regained consciousness.

September came, and the leaves on the great chestnut trees in Bishop's Garden began to reveal mottled veins and margins of brown. In the colder early mornings the river meadows were overlaid with a faint breath of mist, and the cathedral bells rang flatter in the damp air. The city streets emptied a little with the receding tide of visitors, and ordinary business revived again after the summer's hiatus.

The couples waited somberly for news from the Frosts. When they saw one another it was in quiet pairs, as if they were chastened by the year's happenings. William was still in a coma.

Star lived with Nina in the Dean's Row house, although she was making preparations to go abroad. Her negotiations with Jimmy were oddly formal and polite, as if they had never known each other well.

Nina herself was restless. She finished a project for her publisher and couldn't settle on a new one. She went for long walks, asking herself, as she trudged over the fields, questions about her future that appeared to have no logical answers. It was only partly enjoyable, now, to have Star's company. She also longed for solitude, as if that would enable her to think more clearly.

One late afternoon she was crossing the green under a whitish, autumnal sky when she found herself slowing and then stopping to look up at the cathedral's west façade. Then she turned slowly, for no particular reason, and went into the cathedral through the west porch. She had not been inside it for a long time, but the ecclesiastical smell, and the echoes of footsteps and murmuring voices, seemed as familiar as the inside of her own home. She walked a little way down the nave and then slipped into a seat.

It hadn't been her intention to come to Evensong, but she had only been in her place for a few moments when she noticed that the front two or three rows were occupied by a handful of people.

It was only then, with her mind busy with other things, that Nina noticed the man kneeling diagonally across the aisle from her. When he lifted his head after a moment and sat up to listen to the singing, she saw that it was Gordon. He was in his business suit, and there was a briefcase on the seat beside him.

In her distant seat Nina sat and stood and knelt with the rest of the tiny congregation. Enclosed in the great, dim space she felt a touch of happiness, as she had done here once before, with Gordon.

When the service ended the organist began a voluntary, and with the peal of music Gordon left his place and came to sit beside her. It was a very long time, Nina realized, since they had been alone together, and yet no time at all.

"I saw you come in," Gordon said. "You looked sad."

He didn't tell her that the brightness of her hair had seemed to bleed into the air around her pale face, and that he had wanted to leave his seat at once to come to her.

Nina smiled. "I'm not sad. I was thinking, I suppose I didn't know you liked to come to Evensong."

"I was at a conservation meeting." His fingers were resting on his briefcase "And then I realized that it was the right time. I came because I wanted to offer up some thanks."

"For?"

"You haven't heard? William Frost has regained consciousness. He had been showing some signs of improvement, and this morning he opened his eyes. Janice was sitting with him. He said hello and asked where Andrew was."

The organ voluntary and the choir voices still rang in Nina's head. Impulsively she reached for Gordon's hand, and he took hers and held it between his own.

"How wonderful. How very, very good. Does that mean he'll be all right?"

"Andrew didn't stay long enough to tell me very much. He drove off down there almost at once. But I should think the chances must be good, wouldn't you?"

Nina nodded. Her head was light and her hand felt warm in Gordon's.

"Yes. I'm so pleased for them. It's the best thing I've heard in a long time."

Gordon had been praying, she remembered. She would have liked to kneel down to offer her own confused and inarticulate thanks for William and also for an answer to her own riddle, which now, suddenly and without any warning, revealed its clear and happy solution to her as if it had never been a riddle at all.

"Do you have to go anywhere right now?" Gordon's face was so close to hers that she could see the little flecks of color in his eyes.

"No."

"Should we go have a drink?"

Nina thought of her own house and Star, and the unacknowledged association between Star and Gordon and herself, and then of the bar at the Eagle.

"Not a drink. A walk, if you'd like."

"All right. Shall we go?"

They stood up, and when they stepped out into the aisle he tucked her hand under his arm. They walked slowly, looking up and ahead of themselves like newlyweds.

Gordon drove them out of Grafton through the lanes that led toward Wilton. He parked his car in a gateway, and they took a footpath that climbed away across a sloping field to a low ridge crowned with trees. They walked comfortably together up the shallow gradient through bramble clumps weighted with unripe blackberries. Gordon answered Nina's questions about the summer holiday, and about Vicky and his children, and the next phase of the conservation work.

When they came into the belt of ancient oak and beech trees that ran along the top of the ridge, their conversation faltered. The layers of leaves underfoot muffled their steps, and the canopy overhead was filled with the crackle of blackbirds. They walked on through the dim space in silence, among huge tree trunks that reminded them of the cathedral and the first evening they had spent together.

They reached the other side of the tree belt, but they hesitated in its margins, as if reluctant to leave its shelter. The little wood seemed noisy with the wind and birds and the movements of the branches. They stood together looking out in the direction of Wilton Manor, although the house itself was hidden from view.

"Have you seen Darcy or Hannah?" Gordon asked.

"No, not recently. I don't see much of anyone, except for Star, of course."

"I'm sorry," Gordon said at last.

"For my not seeing anyone?"

"You know I didn't mean that."

"Yes, all right," Nina agreed. She stood a little in front of him and to one side, with her face turned away. She wished now that she hadn't suggested this walk, although similar scenes had sometimes presented themselves in her imagination. She didn't know what to say, and she felt that they had suddenly become uncomfortable together.

"I'm sorry for the way it ended, although not for what happened," Gordon said at last. "Why won't you look at me?"

She did turn her head then. They looked straight-on at each other for a moment, and then Gordon took a step through the leaves toward her and held her. They stood still, with their faces close together, listening to the sound of each other's breathing. Their mouths didn't touch, and Nina looked past him now, down the sloping ground toward Wilton.

"I can't think of a way that anything could have happened differently between us. But I've wished that it might, over and over again, as if wishing enough could change anything."

This was not attempt at justification or an apology, but a statement of simple truth. Nina understood that he had wanted to tell her as much, and she felt her discomfort fall away again.

"I wished so, too," she said softly. "Although it doesn't make any difference, as you say."

He held her tighter, with his fingers knotting in her hair. Nina closed her eyes for an instant and then opened them to see the bars of cloud low on the horizon and the shadows between the trees.

"What about you?" Gordon asked.

"I don't know. Not for sure, anyway. But I've begun to think that I should leave Grafton and go back to live in London. I've been here for nearly a year. I have a feeling that the cycle should be completed, and then abandoned."

"Is that what it was, a cycle?" Gordon wondered aloud. "All the things that have happened this year, beginning with when you came?"

"Does that mean you think my coming here caused them?"

His arms were still around her.

"No. Only that you were the catalyst. I think that when people like us have been married for a number of years, when our children have begun to grow and our circle of friends is set, we let ourselves imagine that these things are immutable. Time passes, and if there's no particularly piercing joy, well, there's no sharp pain, either. Then something happens, or someone like you appears, and the balance shifts. Everything that had once seemed clear and secure is revealed to be something else. To be blurred and precarious."

"Perhaps that's true," Nina said. "Perhaps. And now what happens?"

"Some of the balance will be regained, some won't. And there will be different perspectives for all of us."

"Including you and me."

"Yes. Perhaps for us most of all, because of what might have been."

Nina nodded, a little sadly.

Gordon let his hands drop and she stepped away from him, lifting her hair back from her face and knotting it behind her head. He felt that the gesture fixed her back within herself, cutting him off from her.

They listened to the birds for a minute longer, and then they began to walk again, retracing their steps through the band of trees toward the open hillside.

"When do you suppose you'll leave?" he asked her, unwilling to hear the answer.

401

Nina walked more briskly now, with her hands pushed into the pockets of her jacket.

"I don't know. Once Star has gone off to America, once I've found somewhere to live. In a month or so, perhaps." She shrugged, and her dismissiveness hurt him.

"We'll miss you."

"Only a bit. And then the equilibrium will be restored."

She saw his face then, and put her arm through his, so that once more they walked as they had done down the cathedral aisle.

"Now you're looking sad."

"And you are happy," Gordon realized.

"I'm all right," Nina answered at length. She might have said more as they drove back through the lanes to Grafton, but didn't.

After Gordon had dropped her off, Nina sat at her kitchen table with a cup of tea growing cold in front of her. She was thinking that she might easily have told Gordon her secret, but she was glad now that she had resisted the impulse. It gave her pleasure to keep it to herself for a little while longer.

Nina was certain that she was pregnant, and an added certainty had come to her in the cathedral. She wanted the baby more than she wanted anything else, and she wanted it to be hers alone. She wouldn't tell Barney.

It had not been Nina's intention to become pregnant. She had not, she now realized, even considered that it might happen. There had been so many married years when she had hoped for it, and been disappointed, and borne the disappointment alone. Richard had not been much interested in the prospect of a family. He had enjoyed his life as it was, and Nina had supported his satisfaction and lamented her infertility in secret. Only now did she understand that the infertility must have been his and not hers at all.

Happiness and excitement and apprehension made a queasy knot within her. She wanted a baby, this baby, and she would have it. She was rich and independent and newly strong. She would make a life for her child. She was certain that she could do it, and that she should.

Nina stood up and carried her full cup to the sink. She poured the cold tea down the drain and rinsed away the cloudy residue so that the stainless steel shone blamelessly back at her.

20

Star was wearing the gold dress from La Couture and the earrings that Hannah had given her. She checked her reflection in the small mirror in Nina's upstairs bedroom, trying to look at her own face as if it were a stranger's. But the features remained obstinately familiar. Star shrugged and stood back again, and then acknowledged with a flicker of amusement that it was absurd to be dressed up like this just for a dinner *à trois* in Nina's kitchen.

It was the involuntary amusement that did make her look different, just for a second.

Star turned away from the mirror. Her suitcases lay on the bed, almost ready to close. There was a plane ticket to Portland, Oregon, in a folder beside them. Tonight was her last evening in Grafton; tomorrow she was flying off to visit her sister in the States. She didn't know exactly how long she would stay, or where she would go once she had exhausted her sister's hospitality. The uncertainty was exhilarating rather than alarming.

Nina had insisted that there be a celebration of her last night in England, and they had asked each other who to invite. They rejected the Grafton couples, although they both knew without saying as much that they would have welcomed Gordon alone for the proper evening they would now never share. In the end they had settled on just themselves and, laughing a little at the idea, Barney Clegg.

Star went slowly downstairs to the kitchen. She had enjoyed her stay in Nina's tall, bare house and the freedom it had given her. The separation from Jimmy had convinced her that she would never go back to him.

Nina was cooking. She had dressed up for the evening, too, in black lace and velvet. She whistled at the sight of Star.

"You look wonderful."

Star had not seen it herself, but it was the truth. The old, inimical look had gone and a faint flush of excitement warmed her cheeks. She twirled a little to show off the dress.

"I'm glad Hannah made me buy it. But aren't we rather all dressed up with nowhere to go?"

"Not at all. We have everywhere to go, and tonight is only the start. Drink this."

Nina gave her a glass of champagne. Star came to peer over Nina's shoulder at the contents of the saucepans. The gold dress swished behind her.

"Looks good. Barney will be happy."

"Barney's always happy," Nina said with a laugh.

The black velvet dress left her back bare. Star looked at the freckles on Nina's shoulders, at the tender points where they ran together and coalesced into faint blotches. She reached out and stroked the discolorations with the tip of a finger.

Nina turned her head. She was used to these odd, oblique caresses now. She had grown to like the intimacy they implied, the way that intimacy was partly undefined, and she knew that the house would seem cold and predictable when Star was gone.

"I shall miss you," she said.

"I'll miss you, too," Star answered.

She leaned forward and kissed Nina, her lips just touching the corner of her mouth. Then, with the same grave attention, she rubbed away the tiny lipstick mark that she had left.

The doorbell rang.

"It's the boy," Star said, grinning, and went to let him in.

"Oh, God," Barney wailed when he saw them. He was wearing jeans and a sweater, and he was carrying two more bottles of champagne in the crook of his arm. "Why didn't you tell me?"

"Tell you what?" Nina asked innocently, relieving him of the bottles.

"That I should be looking different. Wearing Dad's cowboy DJ, perhaps."

The women laughed. There was a hint of conspiracy between them that made Barney see them for an instant as two halves of a whole from which he was excluded.

"If we had wanted Darcy, and his dinner jacket, we would have asked him," Star said.

"I'm flattered that it was me who was invited."

"So you should be. Shouldn't he, Star?" Nina smiled. She filled three glasses and lifted her own.

"Bon voyage," she wished each of them simply. In another week, Barney would be on his way to Australia.

They toasted one another.

"You look beautiful," Barney said, truthfully, when he had downed his drink. "Both of you."

He felt a little in awe of them, and of their faintly distant, distinctly female collusion. It was as if he had been taken up for an interval and was now being returned, gently but firmly, to his own generation. This might have been disconcerting had the champagne and the smell of good food not lifted his spirits. Barney reminded himself that he was looking forward to his own adventures as well as to an honorable release from the anxiety at Wilton. He was also relieved that his affair with Nina had so gently come to an end. He did not want to hurt anyone, nor had he any intention of being hurt.

Nina serenely filled his glass again. They would enjoy their evening, as they had enjoyed their summer together. It had been a lucky affair.

"Shall we eat?" she asked, nodding toward the table. It was laid with her best linen and glasses, and the candles were lit. Barney drew back chairs for each of them.

It became a good evening when the champagne took hold and blurred the differences among them. That they were each on the point of separate voyages created a general bond, and they each determined that this good-bye should be a benign one. Nina and Star gently drew Barney into their conspiracy, alternately teasing him and flattering him and then suddenly offering some revelation about themselves, so that he could relax and accept his role of diligent squire to their glittering black-and-gold partnership.

He also drank a good deal, thawing in this feminine warmth.

By midnight, Barney couldn't do much more than sit at his end of the table, smiling and blinking and offering his benevolent assent to the women's talk.

At length Nina said, "Barney, you can't drive home, you know. Leave your car here, and I'll call you a cab."

"Can't I stay with you?"

He flung out his arm and caught her as she passed his chair. He held her and pressed his face against the smooth velvet folds of her dress, sighing with pleasure.

"I'm a happy drunk, aren't I? Don't cause aaaa-any trouble?"

Nina stroked his hair. "None. But still, you'd better go home tonight. I'll telephone a taxi for you."

But she was barely back in her seat before there was a heavy knock at the front door.

"Da-daah!" Barney shouted. He stood up, not very steadily.

The women glanced at each other. "I'll go," Nina murmured.

It was Jimmy.

"I'd like to see Star," he said in a reasonable tone of voice. "To say good-bye, or whatever else needs to be said."

"Is she expecting you?"

Jimmy looked much as he always did. If he had been drinking it was difficult to detect, as it always was with Jimmy. But Star had told Nina enough to make her wary.

"Is she *expecting* me? What are you, the maid or something? No, she's not expecting me to turn up at this moment, we don't have an *appointment*, but I'd like to see her just the same. She's here, isn't she?"

His voice grew perceptibly louder. Nina stood back a little. "You'd better come in, then."

Jimmy followed her downstairs to the kitchen.

Barney was on his feet now, leaning one shoulder against a cupboard, his huge hands knitted around a cup of coffee. Star was standing up, too. The candles burning on the table behind her outlined her dress with a secondary rim of gold. Jimmy looked at her, and at Barney, and the empty wine glasses and the comfortable detritus of the evening.

"I didn't know it was a party. I'm sorry."

No one spoke for a long moment, although Star looked directly at him, with her head held up.

And then Jimmy lunged toward Star. It was a movement that was so uncontrolled and so undecipherable that Nina called out

"No, Jimmy!" and Barney collected himself sufficiently to threaten some counterattack, spilling a good deal of his coffee on the way. Jimmy shook him off without a glance.

Star held her hand out to Jimmy. She caught him by the wrist so that he wouldn't lurch into her. But there was as much support in her holding as there was self-defense.

"What's happening?" Barney mumbled.

"It's all right," Star said coolly. "Everything is all right."

"Is it? Would you say that?" Jimmy's face was twisted to one side, as if from the beginning of some paralysis.

To the surprise of the other two, who were still waiting ready to defend her, Star put her arm around his shoulder, stooping a little to reach down to him. She guided Jimmy to Barney's chair and helped him sit down.

There was another knock at the front door.

"That'll be your cab," Nina told Barney.

"I'm not leaving you with *him*, him here, if he . . ."

Jimmy ignored him. He was sitting at the table with his head in his hands, with Star at his side.

"Say good night, Barney," Nina warned.

To her relief he did as he was told. Upstairs, with the taxi waiting, he mumbled to Nina. "I'll call you. Before I go, you know? Perhaps come by, if that's . . . I'm pissed, now, that's the trouble. I'm going to miss you, and this . . ." He pointed upward at the house.

"I know," she said gently.

"Will you be all right? With Jimmy?"

"We shall be quite all right," she promised him.

He kissed her clumsily. "Well then. Thanks for . . . you know. All of it. And for being you. Most of all that."

"Thank you, too. For more than you realize," Nina added. She had drunk champagne too, although just a single glass, but now it seemed to go straight to her head.

Barney climbed into the cab. He turned back, sentimentally, for a last glimpse of her through the rear window, but the house had already swallowed her up.

Nina waited in the hallway, listening. She could hear low

voices, nothing more. She hesitated for a minute longer, and then went thoughtfully upstairs to her bedroom.

"I've never seen that dress before," Jimmy was saying.

Its skirt fell around his feet in rich folds. He thought it made his wife look beautiful, medieval, but he could also only see this metamorphosis of Star's as a sign of her freedom. She had escaped from their narrow chrysalis, wriggled away from it, and unfolded a pair of miraculous wings. He was left behind, flightless. He felt his own weight pulling him down into solitude.

"What time is your flight?"

She told him, and they talked a little about the mechanics of her journey, and the routine plans she had made for the first days of her stay. The neutral exchanges maneuvered them toward the thickets of what remained to be said.

"Have you put the house on the market?"

Jimmy nodded. "The agents weren't very encouraging. There isn't a lot of demand for three-bedroom tract houses in a poor state of repair, would you believe."

"But we need to try, don't we?"

Half of the unloved house was hers, and it was now her chance for independence. Its walls and windows had once represented the exact opposite.

"Do we?"

His face had grown sharper and lost its healthy animal cunning. The lopsided twist was partly an uncertain smile, partly a sneer that denied it. His mouth slackened now, so that both the smile and the sneer faded. He looked dull and confused, almost frightened

"Don't go," Jimmy begged.

When Star said nothing he began to talk faster, mumbling at her, "I don't want you to leave, you know. I'd give anything for you to come back home. It could be made different, if we both wanted it to be. I know I haven't been all that great to you, but if I promised something . . . Christ, I don't even know what, but to try what you wanted, whatever that is, then we might be better, mightn't we? Could we not at least try that much, instead of letting our lives fade out into nothing? Like this, this defeated whisper we are now?"

He ran his fingers through his gingery hair so that it stood up in a barnyard crest, such a familiar gesture.

Star touched his arm. "Stop," she said.

"Stop what?"

"This. The speech. I can't come back, Jim. I don't want to. I want to do what I'm doing."

He looked full-on at her, surprised, and she saw that even this last moment had been a performance for an audience of one. He had still expected her to come back; the idea that she could truly abandon him must have been unthinkable. She was touched with pity.

Jimmy said slowly, "Jesus. You're brutal, aren't you?"

She considered the accusation. "I suppose. If I have to be."

His mouth hung a little open. Then he rubbed it roughly with the back of his hand and looked down at the faint glisten of spittle on the sandy skin.

"That's it, then? Is it?"

She said nothing, wanting to spare him that much. In the warm, rustling and ticking space of Nina's kitchen they sat side-by-side, listening to the seconds running out between them.

At last Jimmy stood up.

"I'll be in touch with you at Jane's if there is any news about the house."

"Thank you." Jane was Star's sister in Oregon.

He waited for a moment more, but there was nothing else to say. Star sat with her head bent and heard him go upstairs to the front door and let himself out. She was wondering, fearing, if even now she might have capitulated.

She sat still for what seemed a long time after that, until the cold wrapped around her bare shoulders and made her shiver. Then she went upstairs and knocked on Nina's bedroom door.

"Come in," Nina said at once. She had been lying in the dark.

"Don't turn the light on," Star begged. When she found her way to the edge of the bed and sat down, Nina's warm hand touched her arm.

"You're so cold. Get in under here."

There was a rustle as Star unzipped her gold dress and laid it over a chair. Her heel tips clicked on the oak boards as she discarded her shoes. Then she folded her stiff legs and arms carefully into the warmth of Nina's bed.

"Have you been crying?"

"A bit."

"What did he say?"

Star looked up into the darkness. "Oh. The usual things."

"And what did you say?"

There was a brief silence. And then Star laughed, a little spurt of laughter that was still on the edge of tears. "None of the usual things. Not much at all."

"And now he's gone?"

"Yes."

They lay quietly. Star felt her limbs warming again. Nina's hand moved, then found hers and held it.

"And is that all right?"

Star answered, "I wasn't sure for a minute. There seems so much in a marriage to dismantle, and then the time comes and it suddenly looks small, in retrospect, almost insignificant for all the effort and pain that have been spent on it. There is a kind of pity and sadness that comes, and you think, perhaps, that it should be rescued. But I don't believe there can be or should be a salvage operation for us. So it is all right, in its way. I suppose Jimmy'll see that too, in the end."

She was thinking of him sitting at the table downstairs, with his hair rubbed up into spikes, and she was grateful for Nina's affection and the warmth of her hand. Star added, "Thank you for the celebration this evening. I'm glad it happened here."

Nina smiled. "Me too."

"Barney Clegg," Star mused. It was both a summing-up and a dismissal, although a kindly enough one.

"Yeah. Star, may I tell you something I haven't told anyone else?"

"Ah. You're going to marry him?"

It was Nina's turn to laugh now, a low, amused chuckle with an edge of triumph.

"No. But I am pregnant."

"Barney's?"

"Yes, but no. Mine."

Star took a moment to absorb this. Then she said, generously, "I'm very pleased. I think that's wonderful."

"So do I," Nina whispered.

Star turned on her side to face her in the darkness. Then she slid her hand over the ridge of Nina's hip to splay her fingers across the soft pocket of flesh on the other side.

"It's only eleven weeks, you know."

"But still. I think I can just feel something."

"Only just, perhaps."

"What are you going to do?"

"I've been thinking, planning it. Move back to London, probably. I can't stay in Grafton, can I? I'll sell this house, buy another close to the park or the Heath, near schools, where other people with children live."

The possibilities multiplied ahead of her, daunting and inviting.

"You're lucky," Star told her. "A baby. Think what it will be like."

They drew a little closer, so that their faces were almost touching.

"I am thinking," Nina said drowsily.

They were both tired. Soon, they fell asleep.

At the end of October, the Frosts telephoned the other couples and Jimmy to invite them for Halloween.

"It's not a big do," Janice insisted. "Not like last year. It will be just us, for a drink and some supper. But I think we should do it. You will come, won't you?"

The couples and Jimmy agreed that they would. No one suggested to anyone else that they should feel like survivors.

When the night came, the Wickham children and Mary and Alice Ransome wanted to go trick-or-treating with the Frost boys. The ghost costumes and skeleton masks were found, and the luminous gel and plastic talons, and the children dressed up. They streamed out into the smoky night, with Andrew and Michael in discreet attendance. While they were gone, Janice put on her best black dress, noting that it hung a little looser on her than it had done the year before, and turned her attention to preparing the dinner. Marcelle sat in the kitchen with her.

"Can't I do anything?" she asked.

"Nothing," Janice said firmly. "Not this time."

They knew that they were comfortable with each other again.

Michael was at home once more and Janice no longer asked if Marcelle was all right, and Marcelle could see that Janice had softened, grateful for William's recovery. They had fallen back into the pattern of making wry, humorous acknowledgments to each other that they were wives and mothers, and that these conditions were eternally imperfect. But there were also other pieces now, made clearer within this unspectacular domestic mosaic, that were concerned with relief, and near-satisfaction, and the small triumph of having preserved this much of the picture of their lives, this far, at least.

The meat was put into the oven to roast, and the table was laid ready for another evening.

"Let's hope they'll be back soon," Janice sighed, looking at her watch.

"Shouldn't bank on it," Marcelle said cheerfully.

The Ransome girls were to spend the night at Wilton with Freddie and Laura. The Cleggs' new au pair, Zoe, who had replaced Mandy at the beginning of another year, had already arrived to collect them before the front door banged open again. The children poured back into the kitchen, bringing the cold air with them. Their ghoul makeup was smeared with sugar and they brandished the bags of candy that their threats had extracted.

"We dropped an egg and a pile of flour on the Watkins' step," Toby shouted. The kitchen surged with children and noise.

Zoe was already rounding up the little Ransome girls with antipodean authority. "Mrs. Clegg says they'll be on their way as soon as we get back," she told Janice.

"Good. Andrew, did you let them dump stuff on the Watkins' front step?"

Andrew was taking beers out of the refrigerator. He gave one to Michael, and opened one for himself.

"Nothing to do with me."

"Ma, it's *Halloween*."

Daisy and Jonathan were spending the night with the Frost boys, and the tide of children began to ebb upstairs. Watching them go, Janice thought, *It's the same, and I was afraid that it would never be*. The sameness, shaded with the past year's differences, seemed entirely blessed.

Only William hovered in the wake of the others. His face was hidden behind a luminous fright mask, and his head was covered with a black hood.

"Take them off, Will."

He did as he was told, and when he did his face was revealed as moon-pale; there was a big, livid patch at the side of his skull where the hair had not yet regrown to hide his scar. Janice went to him and touched his shoulder. She wanted to lock him in her arms and cradle his head, although she would not permit herself this demonstration. In any case, William ducked away out of her reach.

"I'm all right, Mum."

"I know, I know."

He was only partly all right, she understood that, because the specter of his own mortality had left William with a legacy of fear. A tentative child who watched from the sidelines had emerged from the hospital bed in place of the younger William. And yet, as if in temporary compensation for the loss of his confidence, Janice's own nameless fear had disappeared. All the summer's weight of anxiety had lifted, replaced by a sense of deliverance and renewed strength. To her relief she felt that the currents between the couples, even the superficial patterns of all their lives, were no longer awry, and the fact made her want to sweep up the friends and absorb them into her own happiness. She had been determined that this evening take place as a counterweight to the year, to close off the long months that were now over.

William went away to join the other children. Janice took off her apron and reached for the glass of wine that Andrew had set down for her.

Jimmy was the next to arrive. He gave both Janice and Marcelle identical greetings, a kiss on the cheek and an arm appreciatively snaking around their hips. They let him feel, Marcelle as gracefully as Janice, but the frisson that Jimmy once induced was no longer there. Without Star Jimmy seemed deflated, smaller, touched with sadness. The women humored him with their responses; it occurred to Janice that the men had always humored Jimmy in their own way. He had never been a real threat, she thought, except to Star.

The Ransomes brought champagne, once Darcy's prerogative. Vicky submitted to Jimmy in her turn. She had lost weight and showed it off in a narrow calf-length dress and high-heeled suede ankle boots, and Jimmy's hands smoothed greedily over her behind as he kissed her.

Gordon was thinking of Vicky a year ago, flushed and mountainous in her white maternity dress, and then of the colored lights that had revolved over Nina's hair. He had crossed the cathedral green earlier in the evening, not because he needed to but because the house on Dean's Row still drew him. There had been no lights showing in any of the windows, and he had loitered like a boy, among the trick-or-treaters, wondering where Nina was.

The couples hovered in the kitchen, drinking champagne, waiting for the Cleggs. Jimmy was boisterous, his voice rising and chopping through the surges of talk. The Cleggs were three quarters of an hour late but appeared at last, with Darcy in Hannah's wake. He was thinner too, much thinner than he had been before but he still looked unhealthy, and there were loose folds of skin under his jaw.

"What are we celebrating?" Darcy asked, seeing the champagne. "Birth or marriage? Or some other life event?"

There was a small silence before Gordon said, "We could celebrate the cathedral, perhaps. The work on the west façade is complete. And we heard today that there is the possibility of more funds from English Heritage, which means we could renew . . ."

Darcy interrupted him. "Is anyone as tired of the bloody cathedral as I am? As if there were nothing else in Grafton worthy of love or money?"

Vicky stood beside Darcy. She wanted to protect him from his own impatience, to deflect attention from it. Hannah was talking to Janice at the other side of the room. "I'm tired of it, too. Gordon's *always* there . . ."

Andrew passed among them, pouring champagne.

"We could spend a few grand restoring my place instead," Jimmy joked. "Then some poor sod might think of buying it and Star can get to Mexico. Or wherever it is she wants to go."

"Is that what she's planning?" Marcelle asked gently.

"Yeah. Good luck to her," Jimmy pronounced.

Marcelle would have asked about how he was without Star, and tried to discern what their separation meant for him, but his barefaced flippancy rebuffed her.

Janice summoned them to the table.

Once they would have taken their places without thinking about it, well practiced at neatly alternating themselves, but now that their number was uneven they found themselves hesitating. In the end Jimmy sat between Hannah and Vicky, leaving Gordon and Andrew together at the end of the table.

Janice said, "I should have asked an extra woman, shouldn't I?"

"Nina, perhaps?" Jimmy goaded.

The invisible and silent threads of anxiety shivered around the table, but Vicky gave no sign of having heard anything. Her even flow of talk never faltered, and her smooth face was bright with animation as she leaned across to make some point to Hannah. Gordon's dark head involuntarily lifted, just for an instant, at the sound of Nina's name.

"Perhaps not," Janice murmured.

"Don't worry on my account. I am as happy as could be right where I am," Jimmy told her, putting his arm around Hannah's shoulders.

Hannah had faded a little. She seemed less voluptuous now than simply plump, and her hair and her makeup and clothes were dimmer and more perfunctory in their design. The other couples had seen little of the Cleggs over the summer, although Hannah had been generous in offering whatever help she could to Janice while William was in the hospital.

Hannah sat still, with the unwelcome weight of Jimmy's arm pressing on her. She was thinking with a touch of weariness that this evening was the same as a score of others, for all the complicated dances of the last year. She glanced over at Michael, who was at a diagonal from her, as far away as he could be. The confusion over the seating had placed him next to Marcelle, and Hannah noted that that was appropriate. Michael was Marcelle's husband; she felt nothing more for him than that. The nimbus of desirability that had surrounded him had entirely faded; it was surprising even to recall their meetings in the tented secrecy of the shop, to remember that he had left his home and staked himself out in the particle-board confines of the hospital apartment.

Had he done that for her, or against Marcelle? Hannah's thoughts skidded away from the riddle. She was tired, and the speculation seemed not worth the effort. There were other concerns now, concerns that were no more welcome than thoughts of the dead business between herself and Michael, but simply more pressing.

La Couture was closed, and Hannah was trying to sell her lease. The money would help, although the mysterious wellsprings of Darcy's income seemed not to have dried up entirely. But although the Southgate location was prime, there had been no serious interest in it. There were not many new enterprises budding in Grafton now.

Without the shop, Hannah knew, all she had was Darcy. She looked at him now, and he raised his eyes to hers at once. The wine in his glass was almost untouched. She was strict with him about what he ate and drank, and he had begun to be obedient to please her. He suffered from outbursts of pointless anger or bitterness, but mostly he was docile, like Freddie. Hannah had determined that Darcy would stand trial, and that she would help him and support him as far as it was possible to go. It was the only way, she believed, to salvage something of their lives. That was how she regarded it now, as salvage, but she was determined to preserve what she could. There was not much energy left over from that for anything else.

It was an evening like scores of others, Hannah thought.

She had a feeling that similar occasions were waiting ahead of her. In time, Jimmy would introduce someone new—or a series of new women, bimbos, Hannah reflected maliciously, smiling at Jimmy as he withdrew his arm at last, and in the end one of them would become permanent—but she did not believe that any newcomer would have the impact that Nina had. Not that it had been Nina's arrival alone; the time, and the unvoiced and unan-swered needs ticking away within all of them, had also been to blame. And then it had all shaken down again, all the disorder except for Darcy's and her own, and returned to the end point of this evening.

Hannah looked at Darcy again. Was this what she wanted to salvage? If not this, what else was there? She bent her head, and with the tines of her fork traced parallel lines on the white linen of Janice's tablecloth.

Jimmy patted the back of her hand, but Hannah ignored him.

After her chocolate soufflé had been praised, and eaten and praised again, Janice leaned forward. "I have got something to say," she announced.

Her expression declared that it was serious, and they fell silent one by one in amusement or uneasy expectation.

"I know you all think I'm sentimental," Janice began, bright-eyed.

The murmurs around the table were teasing but affectionate.

"And that I've had a couple of glasses of wine, as usual."

There were more murmurings and some gentle laughter.

"But I want to say this because I know it's important. I want to thank you all for being here this summer. You made Andrew and me feel that we were surrounded with love and care when William had his accident, and it helped us both, and it made me feel grateful even when I was most afraid. When I thought he might die. Even then, do you know?

"I'm not as good at expressing myself as Darcy, or Vicky, or any of you, really, I know that. I only seem able to talk like this when I've had a couple of drinks. Only I feel so happy tonight, and so lucky, and I want you all to be part of it with me. I wanted us to be here together. It's not just because of William, although what happened to him made me see things I hadn't looked at properly before.

"We're lucky, you know, even though it has been such a year. We're friends, all of us, and we love each other, and that friendship is what is truly valuable. I want to hold it and keep it."

At the beginning they had sat still, not meeting one another's eyes. But this naive speech of Janice's, its happy honesty, touched something in all of them.

Andrew looked across at her, separated from him as she was by the length of the table. He had been relieved, up until now, that the evening had been civilized and that all the awkward undercurrents had remained tidily submerged. He would have advised Janice to keep quiet at all costs, but still, even though she had done the opposite, he knew that he was pleased.

Marcelle was watching Hannah, who had been staring, unseeing, at her own hands folded on the tablecloth. Then, without warning, Hannah looked up, too. They glanced at each other, expressionlessly at first, and then with the ghost of a mutual smile.

"I only wanted to say that, you know," Janice said, beaming at them. There were tears in her eyes.

"There's no use expecting eloquence from me, is there? I love you all, and I said once before that our friendship is what we all work for, as much as we work for our children, and that's what we should keep in our minds." She sniffed and then rubbed her cheek. "Oh, look at me. I'm going to have to stop, aren't I? Before I really start."

She took the clean handkerchief that Michael held out to her and buried her face in it.

There was a second's silence while embarrassment and the temptation to laugh quivered among them.

But then Darcy began to clap. It was a big, hollow sound, unidentifiable as either irony or assent. After two or three ringing claps that fractured the silence, the others joined in, and a patter of hands applauded Janice. It was real applause. Awkwardly, they smiled at one another.

"Bravo," Michael murmured to her behind the handkerchief.

"We love you, too, Jan," Jimmy cried out.

Nina was in London, at a party.

Patrick had brought her. The host was the architect she had met at the Hampstead lunch almost a year earlier, when she had run away from Grafton and the threat of Gordon. They had walked across Hampstead Heath; the architect had asked her to have lunch with him, and she had declined the invitation. This evening he looked pleased to see her when she threaded her way in Patrick's wake through the crowded room.

The architect's house was in north London, a red-brick semi-

detached villa on a hill that looked across a dipping vista of windows
and rooftops toward Alexandra Palace perched on its higher hill.
There were blond wood floors and minimalist furniture and large
modern paintings. It was a city evening, familiar to Nina in a dozen
respects; she could never have mistaken this setting for Grafton.

"Now, who do you know, apart from Patrick? Or who would
you like to meet?" the architect asked her, with the tips of his fingers
resting on her arm.

Nina looked at the room, at the heads and shoulders and décolle-
tages and the moving, lipsticked mouths and gesticulating hands,
and smiled. She didn't have any qualms about coming back to this.
Not much had changed in a year; not much, and everything.

"We seem to know quite a lot of people in common already."

It was true—there were at least a dozen acquaintances of hers
in the thick of the crowd, even Lucy and Cathy Clegg, who also
had been invited by Patrick. The twins were now out of their Lycra
miniskirts and into Seventies revival crochet and flares. Patrick had
helped Lucy find a job in a gallery, and Cathy was cooking in a
natural-food café in Covent Garden. The girls waved at Nina from
across the room. They were wearing their long hair dead straight,
and parted in the middle.

"You know those two? Aren't they great?"

"I do know them, as a matter of fact," Nina murmured.

The architect steered her into a group made up of a pair of
psychotherapists, a journalist, and a painter.

"I'll be back," he promised her.

Nina guessed that he would. He was not unattractive, and it
occurred to her that one or two brief love affairs might usefully
blur the truth of her baby's paternity. She smiled again as the
conversation drew her in. She rather liked this new, determined
self.

The groups of party guests milled and coalesced and split apart
again. Food appeared and was eaten, and the noise level rose. The
Clegg girls confided to Nina that living in London was a thousand
times better than Grafton, and that Patrick had been totally, amazingly kind to them. Nina passed from group to group, listening to
news and gossip. Late in the evening, as the crowd began to thin a
little, Nina found that she was tired from standing, and slipped

into an empty corner of the architect's long black sofa. The rest of it was occupied by a man in jeans and a woman who was partly hidden from Nina's view by the man.

"Shall I get some coffee?" she heard the man ask. Then he stood up and Nina was left on the sofa with the woman. Nina became aware that she was being stared at, and she turned her head.

The woman said, "I'm Miranda French."

She was younger than Nina, perhaps thirty or so. She had dark red hair pulled back into a short plait with a puff of frizzed fringe over her forehead, dark red lipstick that made her mouth look almost black, and thin, straight eyebrows with pronounced wings that bracketed her dark eyes. Her stare made Nina feel uncomfortable. There was something else about her too, an air of faintly threatening intensity that might only have been the result of too much to drink.

"Nina Cort," Nina offered.

"I know. You're a friend of Darcy Clegg's, aren't you? And those are his daughters?"

"Yes. How do you know Darcy?"

The woman gestured dismissively. "Oh, I worked with him, years ago. Bad news all this, isn't it?"

They talked stiltedly for a moment about Darcy and the press coverage and the trial, for which a date was still to be set. Miranda French kept her eyes fixed on Nina's face, and Nina felt a sudden discomfort that made her want to get up and leave the woman to be anywhere as long as it was out of her sight. She was rehearsing the move in her head when she saw with dismay that Miranda's eyes were full of tears.

"You don't know who I am, do you?" Miranda whispered.

"No, I don't know."

"Why should you?" She leaned forward and Nina resisted the longing to move away. "But I loved him. I was his lover."

Nina shook her head in confusion. "His lover? Darcy's?"

The woman said, forming the syllables carefully with her dark lips, "Richard's."

The party noise did not abate; Nina heard it like waves crashing around her.

Miranda's shoulders were shaking. She had begun to sob, pressing the palms of her hands against her cheeks. Nina became aware that people were turning to look at them. When she said nothing, Miranda continued, "Richard took care that you shouldn't find out about us; he was always careful of you. You were to be protected, always. But I was his lover. I was there with him, you know."

"Where were you with him?" Nina asked, her face stiff.

"In Norfolk, at the cottage that week. I only left him that morning. I was the last person to see him. He came out into the lane to wave to me when I drove away."

Nina could see the apple tree, and the path beneath it, and the cottage behind. When she had arrived that day, with Patrick, Richard's body had already been carried inside.

"How long?" She didn't want to ask, to hear any more, but she couldn't help herself.

"Two years." The other woman's mouth was stretched and her lipstick bled into the creases at the corners of it, and her eyes were streaming with tears.

More people were looking at them with curiosity now. For Nina the important thing became the need to limit the damage. She had to get away at once from the party, from the woman.

"Here we are," she heard someone say. It was the man in jeans, carrying a cup in each hand.

"Excuse me," Nina said slowly. She managed to stand up and make her legs move her toward the knots of people cutting her off from the door. She didn't see Patrick or the architect. There were people on the stairs, but she climbed past them, her fingers floating over the banister. Her coat was in the heap on a bed in one of the rooms. She put it on, turning up the collar as if to protect herself. Then she retraced her steps, hurrying, her head bent, praying that she might get away without even Patrick seeing.

Outside in the safety of the darkness she stood gasping for breath as if she had been running. The sky was clear above the orange varnish of the streetlights, and the air was cold.

It took her a moment to remember where she was, and longer to recall where her car was parked. When she found the Mercedes she sat huddled inside it, staring unseeingly along the hood at the lines of tidy houses spreading down the hill.

The image that kept recurring to her was of the red-haired woman, Miranda, driving away from the cottage, and Richard standing in the lane, waving. He had always done that for Nina, too. Come out to wave her off.

Nina's hands were locked on the steering wheel. A couple walked past along the pavement with their arms around each other's waists and glanced back to look at her in the car. The intrusion made her turn the key in the ignition; she drove away without any idea of where she was going.

Two years. She thought of the times with Richard, holidays and birthdays, and tried to remember if there had been any change, any one moment when he had become less her husband than another woman's lover. She couldn't think of any. Richard had always been the same, and that made her feel even more duped and disoriented.

She kept on driving through a maze of unfamiliar streets. She saw the lurid light of an all-night service station and stopped for gas. From the pay phone beside the attendant's booth she dialed Patrick's number and was surprised to hear his answering machine. The party seemed to belong to some remote time; it was bizarre to think that Patrick was probably still there. She left a noncommittal message saying she was fine but wouldn't be back that night.

She drove on, thinking about Richard and the long thread of their marriage, not just the last two years.

The familiarity of the Mercedes, the mechanical dependability of it, was oddly comforting. After a time she saw signs for the highway and followed them toward its orange-lit ribbon in the distance. It was a relief, once she swept into the fast traffic, not to have to stop at lights and make arbitrary decisions about whether to turn left or right. The rhythm of driving soothed her, and the shock of what she had heard began to subside. She felt sad and heavy, all her senses dulled.

The road carried her on in an arc around London; then, without thinking about it, she took the westbound link that led away from the city toward Grafton. Once out into the country, the blaze of oncoming headlights out of the darkness grew hypnotic. Nina realized that she was tired, that she wanted to close her eyes. She knew that it would be easy to let herself do so, to take her hands off the wheel and allow them fall into her lap. She would let go altogether, let everything go. Her head nodded once, and her eyelids drooped.

She jerked herself upright. Fear and self-disgust trickled icily down her back.

She opened the window and let the cold air rush into her face. She groped for the radio knobs and filled the car with loud music. She was shivering, partly from cold and partly with the horror of what she had almost willed to happen.

There was the baby. Not Richard's, but her own. And there were the other cars, in front of her and behind her, with their invisible occupants behind the eyes of oncoming light.

Nina remembered how, in the time after Richard's death, she had begun to long for her friends to stop doling out loving sympathy, to tell her that he was gone and she was still alive, and that she must get on with living her life. *Anyway, that's what I have done,* she thought now.

She had gone on living, some of the time competently, at other times handicapped by loss and resentful of it. There had been Gordon and Barney and her friendship with Star and the Grafton couples, and her work, and now there was her child. She would go on living, whatever truths sprang out of the past to ambush her.

The realization that she was glad of the fact came to her in a wash of relief, a relief that was also tinged with pride at having survived this much.

She thought back to her love affair with Gordon. Its pain and delight remained with her, even tonight, as she probed through the first numbness of shock and began to assimilate what Miranda French had told her.

Nina had not condemned Gordon then or now for what he had made Vicky suffer. So how, she wondered, could she judge Richard, whose life was over, and who would never be able to tell her the truth?

The sands of memory shifted treacherously behind her. The past that had seemed smooth and innocent was now riven with crevasses of deceit. She was angry with the woman for having opened these chasms, and the first waves of jealousy left her breathless. She gasped and curled her fingers on the steering wheel, whose rim was sticky with the sweat of her palms. Anger would come in the wake of jealousy, Nina knew, and then grief.

She drove on through the darkness, trying to make sense of her turbulent feelings. Her eyes were burning, and pain was stabbing in her head.

Richard was dead, and she missed him more than ever. The truth was in the past, as irretrievable as their shared happiness.

All she could know, Nina thought through a blur of exhaustion, was that her husband had been no more guilty than Gordon. And Miranda French had done no worse than she herself had done.

As she headed westward, her thoughts turned to secrets and betrayal, and the Grafton couples, and the delicate private equilibrium of marriage.

After another hour, she was growing drowsy again. The clock in the glowing instrument panel told her that it was 3:00 A.M. At the next exit Nina turned off the highway and chose a road at random, following it through a village and on into a patch of open country. When her headlights picked out a wide grass border, she swung the car off the road and switched off the engine. In the darkness she tilted back her seat and wrapped her coat tightly around her. Her thoughts quieted and faded, and she fell asleep.

When she woke up it was daylight. The rising sun was shining straight into her eyes, and she felt stiff and very cold. The grass in front of the car was touched with a glitter of frost.

Nina drove slowly back to the village she had passed through in the middle of the night. When she saw the name, she realized that she was only twenty miles from Grafton. There was a country road that she could take, and the road would lead her directly past Wilton Manor.

It was half past nine when Nina turned into the driveway of the Cleggs' house. The sun was melting the frost on the grass and Darcy was out in his Sunday morning gardening clothes, raking up leaves from the gravel.

Nina climbed out of the car, chilled and looking bedraggled in her party clothes, her whole body aching from the cold and the long night.

"Nina? Nina, are you all right?"

There were holes in the elbows of Darcy's jersey; Nina had never seen him look less than immaculate.

"Yes. More or less, I think. I was at a Halloween party in London, and I slept in the car on the way down."

Darcy took her hand in his, and Nina was surprised to see the concern in his face. She had not thought of Darcy as a man much given to sympathy for other people. He said,

"You're so cold. Come on, come into the house. Hannah's taken Freddie for a riding lesson, but I can manage to make you coffee and some breakfast."

The big kitchen was warm and seemed infinitely welcoming. Nina sat at the table, drinking the hot coffee that Darcy gave her. Laura ran through the room in her nightdress, and Darcy caught her and sat her at the table.

"Eat your breakfast," he ordered his daughter, smiling sidelong at Nina. "The house seems very quiet, with Barney and the twins gone."

"Yes, it must," Nina said.

"We were at a Halloween party last night, too, at Andrew and Janice's."

"How was everyone?"

He glanced at her. "The same, more or less, except for Jimmy. Janice had a few drinks and made a speech about friendship. It almost made me cry, as a matter of fact. I must be getting sentimental."

"I don't think it's sentimental to value friendship, is it?"

Again he looked at her sharply. "Perhaps not. Are you hungry?"

Nina realized that she was ravenous.

Darcy made her scrambled eggs, and she ate them gratefully. When she had finished eating, and Laura had run away to look for Zoe, Darcy asked her, "What is it, Nina?"

"I wanted to ask you something. May I?"

He gestured. "Why not? I have plenty of time."

She began without hesitating. "I met a woman at the party last night, a woman called Miranda French. She told me that she knew you. And she also told me that she was my husband's lover. Did you know about it?"

There was a small silence. Nina saw from Darcy's face that he was sorry for her, but instead of being embarrassed and ashamed by his pity, as she might once have been, she felt warmed, and even somewhat comforted. *Darcy has had to accept shame, to suffer a bigger blow to his pride than I am suffering now, and it has made him see things more clearly*, she thought. She liked him, she realized.

Nina almost smiled. That was just as well. Although he would never know it, Darcy would be her baby's grandfather.

"Yes, I knew about it," Darcy said at last.

He opened a drawer and took out a packet of small cigars. He lit one and drew on it. "These are utterly forbidden. Yes, I knew Miranda well before I married Hannah. I heard about her, and about Richard's death, but then I forgot about it. I only remembered again after I met you, when I realized you were his wife."

"You never told me."

Darcy said gently, "Why would I want to hurt you?"

No, Nina thought, he wouldn't want that any more than she had wanted to hurt Vicky, or unwittingly to set off the reverberations through the quiet world of the Grafton couples.

Richard had not wanted to hurt her, either; her security with him up until the day of his death was proof of that. Richard and Miranda French had done no worse than she and Gordon had done. *How little we know about one another*, Nina thought. *And how imperfectly we understand ourselves.*

"We're all guilty, aren't we?" Nina said aloud, unthinkingly.

Darcy laughed and for a moment he became the big, confident man she had met a year ago.

"No doubt of that," he answered, pulling on his cigar. "Guilty as hell."

They looked at each other. Nina understood that he was admitting a truth he otherwise might not have allowed himself to.

She nodded her head, slowly, then reached out and with the tips of her fingers touched the unraveling cuff of his jersey.

"It'll be all right," she promised him, without knowing whether it would or not.

"Certainly," Darcy assured her.

Nina looked at her watch. She didn't want to trespass any further, and she wanted to be gone before Hannah came back.

"Thank you for breakfast," she said with a smile.

"Don't go sleeping in your car beside the road anymore. It's dangerous."

"I won't."

He walked her out to the Mercedes. Before she stepped into it Darcy took her arm.

"Were you careful with my Barney?" he asked.

It was the first intimation Darcy had given of knowing anything about it. Nina looked at him evenly.

"I was. I promise I was."

He nodded, and then kissed her cheek before standing back to let her go. As she drove away, Nina saw him watching, his arm raised, waving her off.

Nina decided to collect a few more of her possessions and then drive back to London. She found the Dean's Row house silent and cold, with the ashes of the last fire she had lit still lying in the hearth. She went to the window and stood for a long time looking at the west façade of the cathedral, at the golden tiers of restored saints and martyrs and archangels. The vision of regeneration and renewal was deeply pleasing.

Then Nina folded the old shutters across the window again. She fitted the catches into their sockets, closing the November sunlight out of the cold room.